THE FAR REACH OF *Yesterday*

CHRISTINE ECHEVERRIA BENDER

Caxton Press

The Far Reach of Yesterday ISBN# 978-087004-660-5

First Edition

Library of Congress Control Number: 2025938516

Cover and book design by Jocelyn Robertson

Printed in the United States of America
CAXTON PRESS
Caldwell, Idaho

*This story is dedicated with gratitude and love to my grandmother,
the late Florence Louise Peterson Whitsell,
for her strength, kindheartedness, and wonder at the world's beauty,
and for her patiently guiding and always loving hand.*

1

Chicago's unpredictability strengthened with the darkness, and on that thundering, rain-sodden night two of its residents failed to foresee how their next steps would prove the deadliness of good intentions.

On the sixteenth floor of a high-rise in the heart of the Loop, Rachel Winston stood in her office before a massive mahogany desk and stared down at a funeral card bearing the name of Simon L. Winston. Dressed in a somber black dress with her hair pulled back in a bun, her face bore an expression markedly grave for its thirty-two years. With deliberate movements she skirted her desk, took a key from her purse, and unlocked a lower drawer.

"Hello, old friend," she said softly, and lifted a diamond-weave nine-foot bullwhip. She ran a thumb over the frayed edges of a small cross engraved near the knot of the handle, her thoughts distant. From this musing absorption her features began to shift, revealing a building grief and anger. With a step to the side and a practiced snap of her arm, she lashed the air, the whip's stinging crack mingling with her own cry. Again she swung the leather high and forward, drawing its explosion and fracturing the stillness. Over and over she flayed the emptiness until she stumbled and sank to the floor with a stifled sob. After a moment she forced herself to stand, and her eyes fell once more on the funeral card. She steadied her breath, and said, "Your secret's finally safe, Grandpa. The hell of it is, your death took you out of my reach as well as theirs."

There was a quick knock at the door before a deeply concerned middle-aged woman hurried in, but Rachel raised her hands to keep her at a distance. "Ellen, I'm okay. I thought you went home after the funeral. I thought everyone had."

"No, I've been waiting."

"I'll be fine in a minute."

"That whip only comes out when you're far from fine, Rachel. Your 'demon slayer,' you called it once."

"I should have beaten these demons long ago. Grandpa's death has just stirred them up."

Ellen studied the red eyes and tight brow before her. Though Rachel was officially her boss, and half her age, their years together had diminished the significance of such things. "I wish you'd let me try to help. Wouldn't some time away do you good?"

"Being somewhere else would only give me more time to think, too much time. I'm better now, truly, and you should head home." Returning the bullwhip to its drawer, Rachel moved to a wall of windows and gazed out at the shadowy skyline.

Ellen continued, "All I have waiting for me at home are two cats. Say, you've talked for weeks about wanting to finish researching your genealogy. That might be just the thing to keep you connected to your Grandpa Simon."

"I don't think the past is the best thing for me to focus on right now."

"Alright then, I'll let it be, but—"

The cell phone on the desk rang and Rachel glanced at the caller's name before answering. "Hi, Jason."

"Hello, counselor. It was a beautiful service today. It must have been tough on you, though."

"Yeah, it was both beautiful and tough."

"Am I wrong to guess that you're back at work?"

"No, you're not wrong. I hear your detective's tone of voice, and that's generally not a good sign."

"Yeah, well, I'm sorry to ask this of you today, but something's come up and I'd like to keep it unofficial at the moment. Listen, can you meet me at the Super 8 in Evanston tonight? Now, in fact?"

"Now? What's happening in Evanston?"

"A few young thugs worked over a mutual friend of ours, and he wants to see you."

"Just who got worked over, and how bad is he?"

That brought Ellen's eyebrows up, her stare demanding, *What are you getting yourself into now?*

"It's nothing life threatening," said Jason, "and he begged me not to call anyone but you."

"Jason, *who* are we talking about? And why me?"

"It'll be better if I explain things in person. Let's just say he's looking at a touchy legal situation. Can you come?"

When there was no elaboration, Rachel sighed and said, "I don't want your sweet wife to stop inviting me over for lasagna, so yes. You know I'll come."

"Thanks, Rachel. Hey, it just started raining here, so cover up and wear something...bulky. The less attention you draw, the better."

A pause stretched out while she absorbed this.

"Rachel?"

"All right, Jason, I'll be there in an hour."

"That's my girl. Park near the west entrance and call me when you get here."

"Will do. See you soon."

Avoiding Ellen's questioning gaze, Rachel hung up, wondering which of her clients might cause Jason to act so strangely.

With uneasiness betraying her attempt to maintain a calm voice, Ellen asked, "Care to fill me in?"

"Jason wants me to meet him and a client in Evanston."

"And you're going? At this hour?"

"You know Jason, and I've known him since high school. He wouldn't ask if it weren't important. And if I get moving maybe you'll vacate the building, too." Rachel gathered up her laptop and files, and flashed Ellen a reassuring smile. "Have a good night, and don't come in early tomorrow." She walked out, hoping to leave before further protests could be raised, but Ellen's worried voice followed her out the door, threatening, "I just may sleep 'til noon."

Fifty-seven minutes later Rachel turned off the ignition of her Lexus and scooted low enough to be nearly invisible to passersby. Rain drummed on the roof and spattered the windshield as she surveyed the hotel parking lot for several moments, then dialed Jason's number. "I'm here."

"I saw you pull in. Rachel, things have gotten complicated, maybe dangerous."

"For me?"

"It's possible. This may be a bad idea."

"Well, let me in and we can talk about it."

"I just don't—. Shit. Okay. Wait a minute... " Rachel waited, listening to Jason's breathing as he walked. "Almost there. Alright, I'm at the door."

She spotted his large body and dark head at a side door, glanced around once more, and hurried across the pavement dodging puddles. As he ushered her in, Rachel was surprised to see his revolver discreetly pointed at the floor, but they walked to room 114 without exchanging a word. Once inside, Jason eyed her costume with raised brows and a smirk, then nodded his approval. As she took off the floppy hat, a braid of her honey-colored hair fell from beneath, and the ankle-length raincoat dripping onto the floor could have covered two people her size.

"Quite the outfit," he said. "I'm glad you took my advice. There's more cause to be careful than I'd thought."

He took her coat and draped it over a chair as she turned toward the rumpled bed and caught sight of a smear of blood on the bedspread. "Jason, what—." She stilled as the bathroom door opened and a young man limped into the room, and it took an instant longer for recognition to come. "Carlo!" Stepping quickly forward, she reached out to steady him, and Carlo sucked back a cry of pain as she and Jason eased him onto the bed. Rachel's gaze swept his body, her face working hard to mask the force of her reaction. Other than his unruly brown hair, height, and slim build, there were few features that had not been altered.

A few drops of blood had leaked from the bandage above his left eye, leaving a trail that circled the outside of his eye socket. A larger bandage covered the right side of his jaw. His face was severely swollen and much of his tan skin was beginning to darken to red or purple. He wore a pair of torn jeans with the top two buttons undone, and a shirt with the left sleeve torn open to expose his thickly bandaged arm.

Rachel's disquiet quickly flared to anger. "Jason, *why* haven't you taken him to a hospital?"

Carlo answered before Jason had a chance, the words somewhat garbled as his lips and tongue maneuvered around at least one broken tooth. "Please, Miss Winston... you helped my mother. That's why—".

"Shh, Carlo, shh," she said, drawing closer. "Lie still and rest now." When the youth tried to speak again, Rachel sat down next to him and took his hand. "Hush, Carlo, please. I'll be right here." She looked down at the hand grasping hers and noticed little sign of injury. Forcefully keeping her outrage in check, she stared up at Jason, her expression demanding answers.

"Look, Rachel, he called a couple of hours ago and asked me to meet him here. Said to come alone, that he was in trouble. He'd managed to slip in through a side-door and was hiding in a bathroom stall. When I found him there he wouldn't let me take him out of the building, so I got this room and patched him up the best I could. I think he has a broken left arm, and maybe a couple of ribs. Probably a concussion too. I gave him a heavy dose of ibuprofen." In answer to Rachel's unrelenting stare, he added with reluctance, "He just admitted that some of the Valentis did this with a baseball bat."

"His *family*? Why, Jason? And why the *hell* is he still in this hotel room?"

Jason sighed and pulled up a chair. "They did it to keep him quiet, and he refused to move until he talked to you. If the Valentis knew his location they might well have acted by now, but they haven't."

Carlo spoke up again. "Don't worry, Miss Winston. I made sure they couldn't track me. Before I came here, I threw my phone into a pick-up, heading west."

Jason looked at him with approval. "That quick thinking might give us some time." He watched Carlo close his eyes at last, his breathing deepening as the pills finally began to kick in, and turned to Rachel. "This isn't the first time I've seen his family's methods. Rachel, when you were working on his parents' divorce, did you hear anything about the Valenti activities?"

"Nothing definite." Carlo didn't stir, so she went on. "Carlo's mother gave me a few vague warnings, said her husband could be ruthless. I wondered if he was involved in something criminal."

"Did he, Andrew Valenti, threaten you while you were on that case?"

"He called me once and *suggested* I take his first settlement offer. But I suggested he look at our counter offer again and settle out of court to avoid the publicity of a trial. In the end, he did just that."

Jason shook his head. "You were damn lucky he didn't try to scare you with more than words. Carlo just told me that when he was sixteen he was forced to witness the murder of an informant, under his father's orders. And he's seen a lot more than that over the past two years."

As Carlo began to snore softly, Rachel's troubled eyes watched him through several deep breaths before easing her hand from his. In a voice that betrayed her own fatigue, she said, "Go on, Jason."

"You probably know that Carlo's old man died a few months ago; natural causes, or so I heard. Carlo says he'd never wanted any part of this, and he'd hoped, with his father gone, to drift out of the business without much trouble. Well, tonight some Valenti henchmen made it clear they mean to keep him in."

Jason leaned closer, elbows on his knees, hands clasped. "Rachel, he says he'll tell everything he knows, everything, if we protect him. But tonight he won't talk to anyone but you."

"He'll give me evidence against his family?"

Jason nodded solemnly.

Her forehead furrowed. "Just how deeply has he been involved?"

"I can only guess. He probably did whatever he had to."

With mounting frustration, Rachel blurted, "Jason, you know I've never handled anything like this, anything related to organized crime. The closest I've ever come was that fatal domestic violence case."

"If it were anyone but Carlo... Rachel, I've known this kid since he played t-ball with my sons, but I haven't seen him for years so he's even leery of me. Now he sees me as a cop more than a friend. What he's looking for is someone to keep him safe, from both sides, and he's picked you."

"But I don't have the power to keep him safe. For *his* sake we've got to convince him to put his faith in someone who does."

"I tried. He's dug in his heels, says he'll get amnesia if we cross him. So... here we are." They stared at each other in a silent tug-of-war until Rachel's gaze faltered and drifted back to Carlo. Jason finally asked, "Got any other suggestions, counselor?"

"Look at him, Jason," she said very quietly. "He's hardly more than a boy."

"Yeah."

"If he talks, just what kind of shelter can you, I mean the police, or the Justice Department, actually provide? How good a chance does he have?"

"That depends a lot on him. So far he refuses to budge from this room and he won't let me call in more men. Not the safest of circumstances. I can't haul him in against his will unless he's committed a crime, which he hasn't confessed to, and he'll clam up if I try. But, Rachel, if he really can provide evidence, especially if it's related to a number of homicides, protection is exactly what he needs. It's incredible he made it here in the first place, but when he doesn't turn up where he's expected to be next, you can bet they'll be looking for him."

With deep regret, Jason went on, "If I'd had any idea how dangerous the situation might become, I swear I never would have called you. At first the kid convinced me he'd been mugged by some punks from school, said he wanted to sue the lot of them, so he needed you. I must be losing my instincts because I swallowed it all. I didn't even suspect the Valentis. The real story started spilling out only after I told him I'd spotted you at that corner stoplight. I tried to call, to warn you, but you didn't pick up. Then you were here."

The self-reproach declared itself so clearly on Jason's dark features and slumped shoulders that Rachel reached over and patted his arm. "Jason, it's all right. You did warn me, remember? Besides, if they don't know he's here, we've got some breathing room, right?" Careful not to disturb Carlo, she eased away from his side and began slowly prowling around the room. After some moments she faced Jason and crossed her arms. "Okay, I'll stay close until we get him to accept medical care, and a lawyer with more expertise. Does anyone at the station know what's happening here?"

"Not yet." He motioned for her to join him at a small corner table, and went on, "I could only persuade him to let me call my wife. If I hadn't, she'd have sent the whole force out looking for me."

"Oh, Jason," Rachel said guiltily, "I forgot all about Sylvia."

"I just told her you and I were going over a case. She knows how some of your divorce cases start with assault. I can tell her something closer to the truth after we figure out our next step."

Rachel nodded. "When will you be calling in to the station? And what about a doctor?"

Carlo spoke up from the bed, "No." He turned his head and tried to focus his good eye on them. "No cops. My family has at least three on their payroll. And no doctor until I talk to Miss Winston."

It took a minute for Jason to accept Carlo's revelation. "Can you tell me the names of the cops?"

"I don't know any names, or what they look like."

"Sons of bitches. Listen, Carlo, I believe what you're saying, but I know some guys I'd trust with my life. Will you let me call them while you and Rachel talk, so they can come guard you? And a good doctor who I'm sure will keep quiet? You need their help."

After considering for painful moments, Carlo said with uncertain resignation, "You'd better be sure of your friends, detective." Then, peering at Rachel, he added, "Miss Winston, maybe I should tell you what I know right now, in case...."

Jason looked down and studied his own fingers. "Rachel... it's not such a bad idea. Let's record my giving him his Miranda rights, then I'll leave you two alone. I want to make those calls and look around."

"But he's not under arrest," she said.

"I don't want to take a chance that some Valenti lawyer will cry 'custodial interrogation'".

"Yes, of course," she agreed. "It's been a long day. My laptop's in my car."

"I'll get it," Jason said, rising. "And I'm going to rent the rooms on both sides and across the hall. A little more privacy can't hurt."

"Good idea. The laptop is under the blanket in my back seat."

Jason leaned down and laid a light hand on Carlo's shoulder. But his young charge, who was in no mood to be so easily comforted, said, "Jason, if you don't know your people, I'm a dead man. Remember that."

Jason nodded and checked the hallway before sliding his large frame out the door. He was back in fifteen very long minutes, and handed her the laptop. "We're all set. The doctor should be here in about an hour."

Rachel set up both her phone and the laptop to record their interview. "Are you ready?"

"Yeah, let's get it over with."

Jason spoke into the screen, saying, "I'm Detective Jason Dorely and I'm with Carlo Valenti and attorney Rachel Winston at the Super 8 hotel in Evanston. It's March 19, 2024. Carlo, you're not currently under arrest, but I want you to know that you have the right to remain silent..."

When Jason had finished laying out Carlo's rights, and they'd been acknowledged, he left the room. Rachel kept the laptop and phone screens directed at Carlo, introduced him and herself again, and gently encouraged him to begin. He started slowly, but despite his injured mouth and sore jaw he left little out of the first telling. Then they went over it all again. He attempted to fully answer each of Rachel's questions, giving up every haunting detail. Midnight was approaching by the time they finished tying up the threads binding this intricate quilt of intrigue and violence.

She phoned Jason at last, and moments later he was at the door, accompanied by a doctor at least seventy years old.

"This is Dr. Jesko."

Rachel gave him a smile of appreciation and nodded her welcome.

The short, wiry, soft-spoken doctor said, "Well, young man, let me take a look at you. I'll have you more comfortable in no time."

While the doctor was unpacking his medical bag, Jason drew Rachel to the far corner of the room and asked in an undertone, "You get it all?"

Rachel's response was even softer. "It's ugly, Jason. He gave me everything he knows about six murders, and a long list of lesser crimes."

"Holy shit." Jason considered aloud, "If the kid testifies, he may actually get some very lethal scum off the streets." He held her gaze. "And I strongly doubt he'd have talked without you here."

"Maybe not," she admitted, her voice heavy.

With a rueful smile, he asked "You feel like using that whip of yours on me right about now?"

She could only manage a half-smile with her reply. "Funny you should mention my whip. I used it tonight on some old ghosts."

"Really? Care to elaborate? I've always thought you kept those ghosts too well protected."

Slowly shaking her head, she said, "You can't solve this one, Jason. Even you can't get rid of my past." Before he could respond she left his side and returned to Carlo, watching as the doctor injected a newly cleansed wound to numb it before stitching it closed.

All the while Dr. Jesko had examined, cleaned, and offered medication, Carlo had maintained a cooperative fortitude, and Rachel's admiration for his bravery continued to grow.

The doctor put away the last of his instruments and supplies, then passed Jason a bottle of pills and said, "Give him two more of these in four hours. He needs his chest and left arm x-rayed, and should see a dentist as soon as possible. Would you like me to make a few calls?"

"No, thanks," said Jason. "I'll take it from here, but I appreciate your help."

Carlo turned his head toward Jason and asked, "Are your men coming?"

"They're in the next room. I'll call them over now." Moments later he ushered in two plain-clothed officers. Jack Frasier, a rugged veteran of the force whom Rachel had met several times before, greeted her with a friendly nod. Jason forestalled any discussion by saying, "We'll make our introductions in a moment." Then, directing his request at Jack, he asked, "Can you accompany the doctor to his car?"

"Sure thing. Let's go, Doc." Both men quietly left the room.

"Carlo, Rachel," said Jason, "this is Lenny White." The youthful, broad, good-looking officer greeted Carlo and then shook Rachel's hand as if it were made of Murano glass.

Almost immediately Jason saw the familiar shadow of aloofness come over Rachel's expression. He noticed how casually she took a chair by the table and avoided eye-contact with the rest of them, especially Lenny, and it was like watching the lowering of a veil. As she answered Lenny's few direct questions she was almost too polite, and the warmth she'd shown Carlo and the doctor earlier were absent from both her words and body language. Jason might have told himself he was imagining this, but he'd seen the pattern too many times before. When unknown men close to her own age entered Rachel's sphere, she slid into this distancing pattern, evidently meant to build an emotional barricade. But from what? In this case Lenny was a cop and his friend, and too dedicated to his duty to hit on her under these circumstances. He'd heard others describe Rachel as "guarded," and maybe all beautiful women grew up learning some version of these tactics, but right now he couldn't help thinking that Fort Knox might learn a few lessons from her.

If there was a dark episode in her past, she'd never hinted at it as strongly as tonight. Still perusing her from across the room, he recalled the comment she'd made tonight about ghosts, and wished she'd trust him enough to help her exorcise them. Rachel never tried to hide the fact that Ellen and he were her only close friends. She seemed to prefer it that way. From what Jason had heard, her parents weren't especially devoted to either Rachel or her brother in Rome. Although she seldom brought up the subject of her family, he'd gathered that her parents had brought their children into the world and then more or less forgotten about them. And men? With Rachel's package of looks and smarts, she could easily have her pick, but as far as he knew she'd avoided dating anyone for long. The only exception was someone she'd met a year or two ago who lived out of state somewhere. She'd traveled to see him more than once, he remembered. She hadn't shared much about him, but she'd seemed pretty broken up when it ended. Even so, she hadn't mentioned the guy's name again, just added him to the list of things she didn't want to divulge. Due to his own wariness of the tight-lipped, hard-eyed attitude that flared in her if he pushed too hard for openness, Jason usually left that well-tended list alone.

And yet, considering how caring Rachel had been with Carlo, how she proved to be with anyone who truly needed her help, and then seeing her now, Jason could only shake his head and admit how little he knew about women. He turned his attention to the question Lenny was directing Carlo's way as Jack came back and joined them.

After some discussion, it was decided that Carlo would be taken to a small, discreet emergency care unit tomorrow, and that Jack,

Lenny, and just one other pair of cops would be assigned to protect him around the clock. Jason already had the other two men in mind and could easily get approval from his captain. As for the dentist, Jack would line one up who needn't know Carlo's real name or situation.

"Now that things are more settled," Jason said, turning to Rachel, "I'll follow you home and leave you in peace until tomorrow." She agreed, and they wished the others good night.

He remained watchful as they walked down the hushed hallway, and said quietly, "Just to make sure Carlo behaves, I told him he'll only be allowed to see you after he accepts his full share of medical care."

She pursed her lips. "Threatening to withhold counsel? Sounds like police misconduct to me."

More than a little relieved to hear the banter in her tone, Jason grinned. "You wouldn't deprive a man of his specialty, would you?"

2

Rachel was just about to turn on the shower when her ringing phone brought her scurrying back to her bedroom, wearing nothing but a towel.

"Good morning, Jason."

"Lord, you sound as bad as I feel."

"Thanks a lot."

"How long have you been awake?"

"About thirty seconds, after getting about an hour of sleep. I was almost in the shower."

Jason's soft chuckle was less than sympathetic. "Okay, so neither of us got the beauty rest we deserved, but I need to update you."

As she took a robe from her closet, she said, "Okay, tell me about it while I make some coffee."

His voice grew serious. "We have no reason to fear the worst, but we've moved our friend."

"I see," Rachel said, hovering in front of her coffee pot. "Do you think they knew where he was? Is he safe?"

"No, I don't think they knew where he was, but we got word that a couple of men were asking around about someone that fit his description, so my captain wanted him farther away. For now, he's as safe as the circumstances allow."

"If they don't know yet, they're probably still looking, right?" she asked, her tone still steady. "If, somehow, they learn that we're involved, what are the chances they'll try to contact me?"

"We are going to make that very difficult for them. I've just sent someone up to get you, by the name of Tim Granger. He's been guarding your building since around three this morning, and he'll bring you to me so I can go over everything. And, Rachel, follow his direction exactly, okay?"

Rachel let out a long breath. "Tell me you're just being overprotective."

"I certainly hope so, but I won't gamble at this point. You'd better plan on spending some time with us boys in blue for a while. Pack what you'll need but don't bring out a case that's conspicuously large."

Exasperation broke through. "Jason, I've got clients, appointments. How am I supposed to do my job?"

"Your priorities have just been changed for you, I'm afraid.

Sorry about the inconvenience, really, but I mean to keep you safe. We'll watch over you until we've found your replacement. When you're out of the picture, I'll ease up."

"It doesn't sound like I have many choices. Are you this much of a dictator with Sylvia and the kids?"

Another chuckle. "She'd beat the hell out of me."

Picturing Jason's tiny, easy-going wife, Rachel couldn't help smiling. "All right. I'll just make some calls to see who might be able to take this case, and try to arrange a meeting. I'd better call Ellen too. You know what a worrier she is. By the way, Jason, I really don't like having you as my boss."

"Yeah, well, we'll argue about that when I can stare you in the eye."

"Something to look forward to. What does this person you're sending up look like?"

"Tim's tall as an ostrich and about that handsome. Hazel eyes, brown hair, and ask him to show you his birthmark for identification. It's really unusual."

"But what about-?" She couldn't decide which of her many questions to ask first.

"Not to worry, dear," he said in a voice mellowing with understanding. "I'll see you soon."

"Give me long enough to get dressed and throw some things together."

"You've got ten minutes. And today a disguise is mandatory."

"Oh, shit. Bye."

Before her allotted minutes were up, she was standing in the kitchen, showered and dressed in loose jeans, a huge sweatshirt, and hiking boots. She'd coiled her wet hair into a loose knot and stuffed it under a knitted beret. Her impatient foot repeatedly tapped the hardwood floor as she waited for the coffeemaker to finish dripping. Glancing out her window for the third time, she wondered where Jason's officer could be. *He's on his way*, she told herself, trying not to dwell on possible reasons for this delay. To keep from pacing, she went to the backpack she'd substituted for her briefcase, drew out her laptop, and opened it.

She'd only glanced at the Tribune headlines when her head jerked up at the gentle knock on her front door. Walking almost on tiptoe, she made it to within three feet before she hesitated, unconsciously holding her breath, and leaned forward to peer out the peephole.

In the hallway stood a man at least six and a half feet tall, with an exaggerated Adam's apple and receding chin. Dressed in a beige overcoat and carrying a small case, he casually glanced up and down the corridor. Remembering Jason's reference to an ostrich, Rachel exhaled, asked to see his identification, and, opened the door.

"Hello," she said as he stepped inside.

"Hello, Miss Winston. I'm Tim Granger."

"Thanks for coming." She was more reassured by his presence than she cared to admit. "I was told to ask to see a birthmark of some sort."

Surprised and coloring slightly, Officer Granger said, "Jason's got quite the sense of humor. I'm afraid you'll have to take my word that I've got one."

Rachel surrendered a small smile. "Of course."

"Jason said to give you a new phone, at least temporarily. I'd be happy to transfer anything you'll be needing right away."

"Why a new one?"

"On the chance they've found out you saw Carlo last night, and may try to track you, Jason wants to leave it in a place we can watch. Chances are slim, but we might be able to trap one of them."

"I hope this is just an extreme precaution," she said, handing over her phone. "Please copy my contacts and emails, and as many Word files as you can."

"It'll only take a few minutes. Jason told me you wanted to make some calls, so you can use my phone 'til the transfer's finished."

Accepting his phone, Rachel walked into the kitchen and dialed Ellen's number, intending to leave a message. When Ellen answered after the first ring, Rachel kept her voice casual. "Morning, Ellen. This is early even for you."

"My boss keeps me chained to my desk."

Rachel let herself laugh. "Well, today I'll be coming in late. I can't go into details, but I need you to juggle my appointments, at least through lunch. If I can't make it in by one, I'll call you back."

"Does this have anything to do with your late-night meeting?"

"It does, and I'll tell you more later. I'll be with Jason and his men until I find my replacement for this case."

"With Jason's men? Are you okay?"

"I'm fine. Jason is just playing papa bear."

"By that, do you mean he's protecting you? From what? I knew nothing good would come from your going out last night."

"Now, Ellen, I'm already looking for another attorney, and I'm being *guarded*, for heaven's sake."

"If I know you, you're half enjoying all of this... whatever it is. It's that wild streak in you: skydiving, scuba diving, motorcycles, and now police protection. Rachel, you be careful."

"Yes, yes, I promise. Thanks for keeping the fires burning. Bye." Rachel hung up and had to smile at the lecturing. Ellen was a treasure who never hid what she thought or whom she loved.

Next, Rachel telephoned Jerry Guthridge, an attorney experienced with organized crime cases. Jerry was as cagey and meticulous as they came, and his immediate interest in meeting with Carlo gave her tremendous relief. Explaining that she would have to provide the full particulars later, she thanked him and hung up.

While Rachel was making her calls in the kitchen, Tim finished the transfer and phoned Jason to report that everything looked fine at this end.

"Good," said Jason. "I'm heading out now. Keep your eyes open, Timmy."

"I will," Tim said, and then added in an undertone, "Did you *have* to tell her about my birthmark?" Getting the expected chortle, Tim grinned. "I'll see you in half an hour."

"All set?" Rachel called from the dining room.

"I'll just need a few minutes to look around, then we'll go." Tim left her to scrutinize the elevator, the lobby, the parking lot and the street, then pulled his unmarked car up to the stone entrance, telling the security guard at the front desk that he'd be right back.

Returning to the apartment, Tim found that Rachel had pulled on her bulky overcoat, picked up her purse, and shouldered a backpack holding as many personal possessions as she could squeeze into it. They rode the elevator down in silence, and when it opened, Tim stood just in front of Rachel to scan the area. He glanced at the security guard, who looked up and smiled, and gave a quick wave as they crossed the lobby.

Smoothly keeping her a pace behind him as they advanced, Tim said, "That silver Honda right out front is mine." He scanned the exterior through rain-streaked glass, opened the lobby door, and they stepped into the drizzling shower. Only a few yards from the car, Tim sensed sudden movement to his left.

Spinning, he caught sight of a man in dark gray racing toward them with a pistol drawn. Tim shoved Rachel toward the Honda, crouched and pulled up his gun. "Get in the car!"

The man in gray shifted his angle of approach to gain a clearer shot at Rachel. He slowed just enough to steady his aim, and fired. As the bullet pierced the backpack dangling from her arm and penetrated her thigh, she let out a sharp cry and pitched sideways, still clinging to the pack. Tim fired three shots, striking his target in the chest each time. The security guard appeared at the door, fumbling to free his gun from its holster as he yelled, "On your right!" Starting to turn, Tim's body was jarred as a bullet ripped through his right arm and into his side. He heard Rachel scream his name as he dropped to his knees. His left hand grabbed for the gun in his right, but he teetered and fell to his side, striking his left elbow on the pavement. Jerking his gaze up, he saw the attacker's gun swing toward Rachel. With fingers desperately struggling to gain control of his own gun, Tim's peripheral vision caught sight of Rachel turning to help him. "No! Get back!" he yelled an instant before a bullet pelted the concrete between them. She leaped backward, scrambled to the car, and rose from her crouch to reach for the door handle.

Tim heard the hiss of another shot and saw Rachel's body pivot sharply, slam sideways against the car, and slip to the ground. Her eyelids closed as crimson flowed through her hair.

Tim cried out and yanked his gun up, pointing at the man who'd shot them both. He and the guard fired at the same time. Both shots hit the gunman squarely, throwing him backward onto the sidewalk where he lay unmoving.

With his gun wavering in his unsteady hand, the security guard hurried toward them, but Tim stilled his steps by ordering, "Call an ambulance!"

The guard managed to holster his gun, grab the phone from his belt, and punch in 911. "I'll get the first aid kit from my desk!" he called back as he ran back into the building.

Tim's blood was seeping quickly, darkening his shirt and pants. The gun dropped from his grasp and he shut his eyes against the growing pain, but he soon forced his eyelids open again and dragged himself the few feet that separated him from Rachel. Reaching for her wrist, he tried to find a pulse, but he was too shaky. He couldn't tell. With great effort, he pulled his cell phone from his pocket and found Jason's number. "Jason. They... they hit us, in front of her apartment."

"Oh, God. How bad, Tim? How bad?"

He tried to strengthen his voice and failed. "Don't know. Help's coming."

"On my way. Is someone with you right now?"

"Yeah. Is the kid okay?"

There was a terrible pause. "No, Timmy... they got him." Jason's voice cracked. "And Jack and Lenny. I just found them. Tim, you've *got* to be all right! You hear me? You and Rachel both!"

Tim's eyelids began to close again and his voice drifted farther away with each word. "I didn't keep her safe, Jason. I'm sorry. So... so... sorry..." As his hand slid from his mouth, the phone clattered to the cement. The last thing he heard was Jason yelling, "I'm coming, Tim! I'm coming!

As Rachel's body rolled over in her sleep the first thing to penetrate her leaden mind was a raspy creaking of metal. The sound was so foreign that it managed to nudge her to the edge of wakefulness, and she dimly recognized the more familiar sound of rain pelting the roof, but even this held the strange quality of drops pinging sharply against iron as they fell. Slowly, she pried open her eyes. Although the room was nearly dark, she could make out just enough to realize the place was completely unknown to her. With mounting confusion and a spark of fear, Rachel blinked into better focus and started to sit up when the bed frame announced her movement with a harshly punitive squeal that brought her head back down, stiffened her body, and thrust her intellect into a complete state of alertness.

Memories surged into place with ferocious intensity and clarification until she saw it all again; her building behind and the car just ahead, then guns firing, bullets hitting Tim, more bullets wounding her. Yes, she'd been wounded too, so...? The air left her lungs, her heart hammering and the color abandoning her cheeks as dread gripped her with such force that she couldn't move. The word *kidnapped* echoed through her consciousness. Had the Valentis kidnapped her and brought her here after they'd shot her? Were their men outside her door right now, waiting, listening? Fighting panic, she swallowed hard, and even that small inner sound seemed much too loud. She must be very, very quiet.

And Tim, where was he? He had pushed her toward the car, saved her life. She grasped the hope that he too was alive. Then, distinctly, she recalled the bite of the bullets as they'd struck her leg and her head, but where was the pain now? She slid her hand to the lower left side of her skull and ran her fingers over a raised scar. Completely healed. Stunned by this discovery and its obvious reflection of the passage of time, yet unwilling to risk the bed's squeaking again, she put off checking her thigh.

I must have been drugged, but for how long, and why? Have they been waiting weeks to question me? Or, have they questioned me already, and I just don't remember? She shrank from this explanation. *No, if they had found out all they wanted to know, I wouldn't be breathing.*

Raising her head and turning it enough to observe that the room was quite narrow and windowless, its only light filtering up through the two-inch gap at the base of the door, she then noticed the lumpiness of the mattress beneath her and the feel of her clothing. Carefully lifting her arm again, she stared at the long, white sleeve and ruffled cuff, and knew without looking that her bra was gone and her silk underwear had been replaced by something much bulkier. Realizing that her apparel must have been changed several times since her capture, anger rose so fiercely that it replaced a good share of her remaining fear. *Damn them! The bastards may think their fun has just begun, but I intend to disappoint them.*

She had to get *out* of here, but how? Studying her dim surroundings, she searched for any weapon or method of escape. The light was strengthening somewhat, perhaps with a dawning day, and she was surprised to see that the wallpaper around her bore the pattern of large pink-tipped yellow roses. An old-fashioned dresser stood in one corner. Along the far wall a row of six wooden pegs protruded from a narrow board nailed to the wall at shoulder height, from which hung a heavy gray coat, a full-length plain brown dress, and another long dress of finer light pink fabric, ornamented with white ribbons and lace.

After considering a moment, she decided she must take action before anyone discovered she was awake, which meant she must risk getting out of this damned bed at once. With a strengthening inhale she held both arms straight out and slowly rolled upward, gently, gently easing her shoulders off the pillow and eventually straightening to a sitting position. *So far, so good,* she thought as her ears strained to pick up the slightest sound of movement outside her door. Nothing.

With great caution she lifted the covers aside and swung her legs over the edge of the bed, letting her feet dangle eight inches above the floor while she again paused to listen. The rain had lessened, slowing to a pattering drip until it was barely discernible.

From her new position Rachel could make out the entire room. The only covering on the plank floor was a round braided rug next to the bed. On the dresser stood a pitcher and bowl, a small folded towel, a bar of soap in a dish, and a brush, comb, and mirror set. How strange that the Valentis left such items in her room. She contemplated the large pitcher, weighing its potential as a means of defense, and then decided that the hand-mirror would serve her better. But first she had to silently lift herself off the bed. She began to lower her body, touching one foot to the floor, and then the other, all the while thinking, *Shhhhh,* until she'd almost cleared the mattress, and if she could just hoist herself a few more inches without— but it was then that the bed frame let loose a long, traitorous "Scre-e-e-e-ch."

Leaping forward, she rushed to the dresser and grabbed the mirror, darted across the room, and flattened her body against the wall behind the door. With her chest heaving, she raised her right hand that clasped the mirror's handle, and kept the rest of her body motionless. Agonizing seconds elapsed into a minute, and then two. Surely they'd heard her. Where were they? But when the first sound from outside the bedroom finally reached her, she jumped in spite of herself. It shrilled so clearly that there could be no mistaking the neighing of a horse.

Her arm lowered. Where the *hell* was she? A horse? She tried to think lucidly. A policeman's mount, perhaps? Highly unlikely. Somewhere outside Chicago, near a riding stable?

She glanced again at her nightgown. Were the kidnappers playing some sort of mind game, resorting to these old-fashioned clothes, the nineteenth-century furniture, a horse? Other animal sounds began to reach her ears: two roosters crowed almost in unison and, from farther off, a cow mooed long and low. Yet there was a complete absence of more conventional noises, such as sirens or car horns.

Well, of course they'd bring me to a remote place, Rachel reasoned. Surrounded by four solid walls, she wished desperately for a window that would allow her to look outside.

Now, exterior sounds from the human inhabitants of this stable, or farm, or whatever it was, gradually increased in volume. A man called out a greeting and received a cordial response. Someone launched into an irregular pounding of metal against heavier metal, and Rachel's hopes of escaping dropped lower with each clang. If there were as many people here as these noises implied, her chances of getting away were next to none. Even after conceding this bitter fact, she pushed herself from the wall and faced the door. With determination she reached for the large black doorknob, turned it until she heard a soft click, then inched the door open and peered out. Seeing no one and hearing no sound, she opened it a bit farther until she'd gained a limited view of the adjoining room.

About twice the size of her bedroom, this area was furnished with a vintage brown couch against the wall to her right. In the far corner, a rocking chair stood near a small square table that rested beneath a curtained window, and just inches from the front door. There was an identical window on the other side of the door, but the green-checkered curtains were drawn tightly across both. To her left, a small dining table and four chairs had been placed before a cast iron stove, with four long, crowded shelves on the adjacent wall making up the rest of this crude kitchen. Again her gaze moved across each window, and then jerked back to the front door. Near the knob, a bolt had been shoved to a locked position, securing the house from the *inside*. Yet, she seemed to be the only one in the house. There must be another room leading off to the left, past the stove and beyond her line of vision.

Perceiving no movement from that direction, Rachel inched the door fully open and tiptoed across the plank floor until she could peek into the unexplored room. It was only another small bedroom, unoccupied. Frowning with incredulity, she retraced a few steps to take in the whole house again, and allowed herself a moment of measured relief as she surveyed the tiny kitchen more closely. The wood-burning cook stove, a half-filled kindling box at its feet, shared a wall with a large storage cabinet that faced the wooden table. A metal washtub the size of a semi's tire, a washboard, and a wooden ironing board hung on the opposite wall. Spanning the far corners of these two walls, the shelves bore cooking pots, a kettle, an antique butter churn, old clothes-pressing irons, baskets, a lidded wooden box, and several covered crocks of various sizes.

Unwilling to take time to scrutinize the oddities of her surroundings further, Rachel headed back to her bedroom. Returning the hand-mirror to the dresser, she yanked open one of the drawers and found more antique clothing, all of it made for a large man. In the bottom drawer, however, she came across two camisoles, a long full slip, what she assumed were bloomers, and what could be nothing else but a corset.

How in the world could she sneak out of here dressed in these? Well, she certainly couldn't go out in what she was wearing.

Settling on the pink dress from her limited choices, she pulled off the nightgown and stepped into it. As she buttoned up the front she was surprised by how well it fit, but pushed the thought aside to lift the hand-mirror, glance at her reflection, and brush her hair smooth. After a quick search that revealed nothing better to cover her feet than a pair of high-topped pointed shoes with buttons up the sides, she tugged them on and made a fumbling attempt to fasten a few of the buttons before wobbling toward the front room. Here she made another fruitless attempt to secure the loose shoes before giving up entirely and edging to a window. Easing the side of the curtain back, she peered out.

Wide-eyed, she gaped at the scene before her. Only a porch and railing, part of a wooden boardwalk that stretched out of sight, separated the house from the muddy road, across which stood several board-and-batten storefronts still dripping from the earlier rain, and each bearing a sign high above its doorway proclaiming the premises of Dr. L. Willis—Surgeon and Dentist; Major Sweetser-Miner's Broker; H.C. Anderson—Notary Public; Quong Hing-Laundry, and so on. No more than twelve feet from the window, a horse-drawn wagon rumbled past.

"*What* the...?" Her startled breathing lessened as she continued to gawk out the window, noticing that every person wore old-fashioned clothing and hairstyles, and every other visible detail from buildings to equipment to animals, every sound and movement, seemed authentic to this setting. And all of these people seemed far too busy working or socializing to show any interest whatsoever in this house.

Drawing away and letting the curtain fall, she stood in utter bewilderment, her mind scrambling to construct any explanation for all of this. Could the Valentis have created a deception this elaborate? No, there was no reason for such ridiculous extremes. But if it wasn't fabricated by them, then by whom...and for what objective? Could this be a movie set? But then why would *she* be here? And there were no cameras, no production crews. She continued to reject one far-flung rationalization after another until her thoughts were spinning. *Wherever the hell I am*, she concluded, *I can't just stand here doing nothing. I have to get out of this place before someone shows up*. She moved unsteadily to the front door where she straightened and, after a pause to gather her courage, opened it and stepped warily onto the railed boardwalk.

She had no more than cleared the doorsill when a woman crossing the muddy road spotted her and hollered out, "Why, Rachel, what's the special occasion?" Startled in mid-stride, Rachel tried to turn in the opposite direction, caught the heel of one shoe between the floorboards, and pitched forward. With her arms flailing but catching nothing to slow her fall, her head forcefully struck the wooden railing.

Before she could regain her senses and rise, someone was gently turning her by the shoulders onto her back. A small man wearing a curled mustache, clipped beard, and vintage business suit supported her while eyeing her head with apparent concern. Rachel opened her mouth to say that she was fine but was cut off by the alarmed exclamation of the woman who had called her name from the street and who was soon leaning over her, saying, "Oh, Rachel, honey, are you all right?" The man holding her barked over his shoulder to a freckled boy standing uneasily nearby, "Michael, go fetch Doc Willis. Quick-like!" Rachel lifted herself slightly, intending to stand, but he ordered, "No, Rachel, you best not try your legs until the doctor comes. You hit your head right fierce."

Overwhelmed and outnumbered, Rachel obeyed without protest.

Members of a quickly forming small crowd were shouting or whispering, "What happened, Mrs. Riley? Is she all right? Is it Rachel Milford that got hurt? How bad is she?" Someone muttered in reply to this last query, "She ain't said a word yet. Not a word."

The woman kneeling next to Rachel, evidently Mrs. Riley, asked softly, "Can you see me clearly, dear? Can you talk?"

Loosening herself from the man with the mustache, Rachel slowly sat up and stared at the woman. "Yes, I can see you."

A sigh of relief rose from the group. Rachel could feel drops of blood trickling off the side of her jaw and reached up to wipe it away, but Mrs. Riley intercepted her wrist, pulled a handkerchief from her pocket, and dabbed Rachel's cheek until she neared the two-inch cut below the scalp line.

A half-grown girl standing just off the porch exclaimed, "She's bleeding bad, and a bump's already started."

"Hush, Bertha," said the man who'd held Rachel. "How are you feeling, Miss Milford?"

"Miss *Milford*?" Rachel ventured.

Several voices murmured in worried tones and the man glanced at Mrs. Riley, who seemed to lose some of the color in her cheeks.

Leaning nearer and searching Rachel's eyes, the woman said, "Why, of course you're Miss Milford, honey. Don't you remember your name?"

Unwilling to venture any other response, Rachel muttered, "I guess I'm a little confused."

"Maybe we'd best get you inside," Mrs. Riley said kindly.

Rachel got out only, "No, really, I'm..." before a young man from the crowd stepped forward, saying, "I'll take her, Mrs. Riley", and scooped her up as if she were no heavier than a pillow. He carried her into the room where she'd awakened, set her down on the bed and, at a nod of thanks from Mrs. Riley, gave Rachel a shy but encouraging smile as he left.

Feeling ridiculously like a pawn in a chess game, Rachel heard the voices near the open front door quieting as Mrs. Riley came into the bedroom and shut the door. She sat down beside Rachel and asked uncertainly, "Rachel, dear, do you know who I am?"

Taking a moment as she struggled to choose just how to play this bizarre charade, she offered, "Mrs. Riley."

But the older woman had noticed Rachel's hesitation and, seeming to keep her expression calm only with great effort, tried again. "Yes, honey, I'm Mrs. Riley, but do you know my first name?"

After an uneasy pause, she said, "I'm not quite..."

At this, Mrs. Riley groped for soothing words. "Well now, you just never mind about that. You've had a hard fall, and that cut on your head must smart something dreadful. It's only natural you'd feel a little muddled for a spell. You just lie down and I'll find a cloth."

She returned momentarily with a small folded towel and a sizeable bowl of water, and finding that Rachel had ignored her instruction to lie down, seated herself on the bed and began washing the blood off her reluctant cheek. From the porch a sudden rough demand of, "Where is she?" stilled both women, and was answered by the voice of the man with the curled mustache, saying, "Now, hold on, Stan, she's being looked after."

The Irish accent became more pronounced with, "I will see for myself whether she's doing fairly or no."

"Not yet, Stan. You haven't the right to insist like that. You know how her pa feels."

"No right, is it? Stand aside, you men."

"We won't, but we want no trouble. Just wait 'til the doc's seen to her, for her sake, Stan."

After a brief silence, they heard boots clomping away from the front door.

"Don't worry about Stan, Rachel," said Mrs. Riley. "Before I came inside, I sent someone to fetch your folks.

"My *folks*. That's it. What kind of a set-up is this? Where *am* I?"

Now Mrs. Riley's control seemed to slip as her eyes filled with tears and she turned away to busy herself by rinsing the blood-soaked cloth. "Oh, honey, everything is going to be all right. We'll take real good care of you, and you'll feel fine in no time at all."

Too dumbfounded to form any response whatsoever, Rachel simply frowned at the woman.

With a light hand, Mrs. Riley placed the rinsed cloth over Rachel's cut, saying, "You hold this and I'm going to see what's keeping Doc Wills."

Rachel kept quiet and obeyed, convinced that she had no choice but to await the next move.

4

It wasn't long before the doctor, or whatever he was, arrived, storming past the remaining onlookers with a blustering, "Clear a path," and entering Rachel's bedroom with the subtlety of a tempest. Mrs. Riley stood and welcomed him respectfully as Doc Willis, but he resembled nothing so much as a walrus: large, round, grandly mustached, and erupting with a voice that seemed to rattle the walls of the tiny room. "Glory be, what have you done to yourself, Rachel?" He dropped his medical bag atop the bedcovers next to Rachel, lifted the cloth from her cut and scrutinized both it and her face.

"Well, Faith," he bellowed at Mrs. Riley, "you look downright troubled, and this niece of yours is suffering from no more than a ripe bump and a cut barely worth stitching, as cuts go."

Niece. Rachel managed to keep from voicing her annoyance at the claim.

Before Faith could express relief at Doc Willis' assertion, he turned and loomed over Rachel. "No need to worry, young lady, I'll have you mended quick and proper." Wordlessly, yet more gently than Rachel could have predicted, he lifted her hair away from the wound to get a better look. "Hmm, now. Hmm." Rachel remained still, determined to appear calm. At last, loud enough for the people down the road to hear and evidently proud of his abilities to estimate such things, he proclaimed, "I guess you'll need, oh, say, twelve stitches. I've never believed in scrimping on thread."

Tightly, Rachel said, "I don't think so."

Faith came close and asked with concern, "What is it, honey? You don't think what?"

The doctor snorted, "Come now, Rachel, I wouldn't have guessed *you'd* be one to flinch at a few stitches. You know I'll be careful."

"What I know," she said, enunciating each word with the sharpness of a blade, "is that I need some answers."

"Answers?" the doctor asked in surprise.

Their puzzled gawking suddenly dried up most of Rachel's remaining tolerance, and she demanded, "Look, *Doctor*, exactly where am I?"

Doc Willis' baffled stare moved from Rachel, to Faith, and then back again. "Why, you're in the Pinney house, Rachel. You've been staying here while Jim's gone to meet his goods coming down from Umatilla. Don't you remember?"

Mrs. Riley addressed the doctor with reluctance. "It's not just that she doesn't recall things, Doc. The way she's talking, her words are different like."

"Why I believe you're right," he mused gravely. "She almost sounds like a Yankee. Now, Rachel, don't you remember this house at all?"

Something in his and Mrs. Riley's expressions cautioned Rachel to consider, *If they think I'm really hurt, maybe they'll postpone any more questioning.* "I... I can't remember much about Mr. Pinney."

"Doc," said Faith, "she seems a little confused about who I am too."

"What?" Doc Willis bawled. "Is that true, Rachel?" Receiving a slow nod in response, he lumbered backward a couple of steps and paused, smoothing down his mustache thoughtfully. "Wait now, wait. I've read about folks growing inclined to forgetfulness after a bump on the head. Yes, it does happen now and again." He speculated in silence for a moment more before returning to tower above Rachel. "Tell me, just what *do* you remember?"

"I know my name is Rachel... but you're going to have to help me with the rest; like the name of this town."

"Astounding," he declared with eyebrows elevated. "Can you recall your ma and pa?"

"I have a ma and a pa too?"

Doc Willis looked at Mrs. Riley as he said, "I'll be... Appears to be a profound case." When the woman gasped softly and raised a hand to her mouth, Doc hurried on, "But let's not go assuming the worst. It's quite possible that her symptoms will prove to be temporary in nature."

"You hear that, honey?" said Mrs. Riley. "What you're feeling now won't last long at all, not at all. You'll let the doc tend to you now, won't you, Rachel?"

Doc Willis removed his suit coat and began rummaging inside his medical bag. Pulling out a huge needle at last, he started to thread it.

"Hold it." Rachel ordered. "You plan to treat me *here*?"

Bestowing a tolerant smile, Doc Willis asked, "Where else would I treat you? I have everything I need."

Rachel realized that these people wouldn't risk taking her to a public clinic or hospital. Where else would he treat her indeed? "Never mind," she said, unwillingly accepting that she must endure this man's needle.

"Please lie down, Rachel."

She did, but her determination to remain stoic crumbled little by little as Doc Willis proceeded to bring a chair in from the kitchen, scoot it against the bed, pick up a half-filled bottle in one hand and a cloth in the other, and lean over her. She couldn't remain silent. "I...

I'd greatly appreciate it if you'd disinfect your needle and thread, as well as your hands."

Slightly affronted, his hands poised in midair, he said, "I wash that needle after every use and the thread is right off the spool. And, young lady, I washed my hands before coming here. As for the wound," he said, lifting the bottle a little higher, "this is the best whiskey money can buy and I intend to use it liberally."

"Will you please boil the needle and thread in whiskey, and wash your hands in it just before you begin stitching."

"Rachel Milford," he said in the voice of a man not used to being trifled with. She eyed him piercingly, lips pursed, undaunted by the aggravated tapping of his foot on the floorboards. Seconds passed. Surrendering at last, he said, "Faith, it seems that my instruments must be bathed in something stronger than water. I use this particular whiskey for cleansing wounds only, but I'm sure Mr. Pinney keeps a bottle in a cupboard or drawer somewhere. Will you go and see if you can find it? And would you please boil my needle and thread for a minute or two in a small dose of that whiskey... while I go outside to wash my hands in the stuff?"

Of course," she said, and they both left the room.

It wasn't until her caregivers had returned and Doc Willis was reaching for the cloth and bottle again that Rachel said, "Doctor?"

"*Yes*, Rachel."

"Where's the anesthetic?"

"Anesthetic?" Surprised anew, Doc Willis shook his head. "I can give you a small dose of the whiskey. Will *that* do?"

"You mean whiskey is the only—?" Rachel stopped herself. It was apparent that Doc Willis was losing all initial cheerfulness. And, she reminded herself, this was their show. "I'll pass for now."

Before any further protest could be mounted the doctor bent to his task, his lighter nature gradually resurrecting itself. "If you were a man," he speculated as he re-examined the wound, "I'd shave the scalp around this cut. But I just can't bring myself to do such a thing to hair as pretty as yours. Well, Faith, if you'll keep her hair out of my way I'll get started."

When the whiskey-soaked cloth touched the open cut, Rachel's body jerked once, then succeeded in remaining still while the wound was thoroughly cleansed. Doc Willis then poured the liquor directly into the wound, and a muffled, "Mmmph!" escaped her tightened lips.

"I'm ready to start now, Rachel. Are you sure you wouldn't like a drop of comfort?"

"I've reconsidered, so yes, and make it a triple, Doc." This request produced fresh expressions of amazement, but Doc signaled for Faith to fetch it.

The woman soon brought back a generously filled glass and

handed it to the doctor, who observed the liquid abundance and raised a questioning eye to Faith. Looking uncertain, she said, "I didn't know how much to bring so I thought..."

"It's fine, Faith. It's not likely that she'll drink it all. Here you are, Rachel. I've never heard of you taking a drink in your life. This'll hit you like a mule kick, and it won't take long."

Sitting up, holding a cloth to her cut with one hand, Rachel reached out for the whiskey with the other. But as she took hold of the tumbler and smelled its pungent contents, suspicion gathered like an oncoming storm. Had ingredients been added, and what effects might they produce? Then again, they'd previously been able to administer whatever drugs they chose, and could do so again using less pleasant means. She put the glass to her lips and raised its bottom higher and higher.

While she drank, Rachel watched Faith and Doc Willis over the rim of the glass. Their eyes widened as the contents of the glass diminished, and they seemed even more astonished when Rachel passed it, empty, back to Faith without so much as a cough or gasp. A quiet, "Oh, my," escaped Faith's lips while Doc Willis loudly cleared his throat.

As Doc set his tools in order atop the quilt, the whiskey reached Rachel's empty stomach and began demonstrating the better side of its nature, spreading warmth and easing both muscle and thought. Unfortunately, the whiskey also increased an already unwelcome pressure in her bladder, a pressure that couldn't be forestalled any longer. "Doc, I have to go to the bathroom."

"The bathroom?" asked Faith.

"Yes, the *bathroom*," Rachel snapped, striving to hold onto the feeble patience she still possessed. What was wrong with these people? "I need to relieve my bladder, *now*."

"All right, honey, all right, I'll take you to the outhouse," Faith said, hurrying to help her out of bed as Doc Willis crossed his arms in defeat.

Outhouse! Good Lord. Rachel's mind was whirling as she tried to button the dreaded shoes again, but she made little headway before Faith found a button hook in a dresser drawer, lightly nudged her fumbling hands aside, and assisted her.

At the door Doc Willis furnished her with a clean cloth. "Take this, Rachel, and keep that cut covered until I get a bandage over it. Blood is already seeping through the other one." Rachel traded cloths without a word.

With her head lowered Faith made a path between the lingering body of onlookers and mumbled something unintelligible in answer to the questions cast at them. Rachel mindfully held the cloth to her forehead and did her best to appear unconcerned as she and Faith moved through the small throng without slowing. She, too, kept her gaze low, and allowed Faith to steer her around the corner of the house.

Leaving the crowd behind as they made their way over the muddy ground, Rachel forced herself to glance around. The town, overhung by diminishing gray clouds, seemed to be little more than two parallel dirt roads intersected by several smaller lanes. The shops were not merely false-fronts, as Rachel had half-heartedly hoped, but fully enclosed wooden structures. Rows of tiny cabins and off-white canvas tents clustered near the larger buildings. Encircling the entire settlement, a wide treeless area had been swathed through a pine forest. As she gazed farther to the east, her eyes moving skyward, her jaw sagged at the sight of rugged cloud-capped mountains. She was nowhere near Chicago. A wave of panic hit her stomach, and with great effort she subdued it by giving herself a mental shake. One thing at a time. First, the outhouse.

Faith gently nudged her into motion, but Rachel's legs now felt as if shackles weighed them down. Several feet before the outhouse, she stopped and swung her gaze to the right and left. A line of miniscule outbuildings extended behind every structure from one end of town to the other. Focusing on the one directly ahead and opening the door, Rachel's nose and eyes immediately revolted. If the need hadn't been so pressing she might have waited, hoping that less crude accommodations might somehow be found. But things being as they were, she took a sustaining breath and entered the small confines with not much less reluctance than a prisoner facing a firing squad.

Faith stood away from the door until Rachel had finished, then protectively accompanied her back to the house. Although she intensely wanted to wash her hands, she decided not to ask. She didn't want to try Doc Willis' nature any further; not when he was about to practice his craft on her forehead with a metal sliver and a bit of string.

Yet as they walked back she scanned the sky, seeing not a single power line or airplane. And there were no signs of any cars, only horses and mules. She hadn't been on a horse since she was ten, and even if she managed to stay in a saddle she had no idea how far away or in which direction the next town might lie. So, she went mutely back to the room where the doctor waited and where Faith helped her settle into the bed once more.

Closing her eyes, Rachel said, "I hope you have a damned steady hand, Doc."

With her lids down, she missed the latest expressions of shock and deepening concern. But the doctor hesitated only a moment before saying, "Of course I do."

"Well, that whiskey's already working. Go ahead."

She felt the stab of the needle and the drawing of the thread with every stitch. Thankfully, the liquor was dulling her senses enough to help her remain steady, and after what seemed like a fortnight, Doc

Willis declared, "There now, I've finished with the stitching. All that remains is a little bandaging." He sloshed a little more whiskey over the injured area and began wrapping a thin strip of white cloth around her head.

Standing back at last, he said, "Well, your ma won't be quite so upset when she sees you now, properly doctored and cleaned up, though the blood may never come out of that dress."

"Thank you, Doc," said Faith with feeling.

From the looks on the two faces that turned her way, Rachel gathered that she was expected to express some sort of gratitude to Doc Willis, but she couldn't form the words.

"You just lie quiet, Rachel, and I'll come check on you a little later."

Rachel closed her eyes.

"I'll see you out, Doc," said Faith, and they both left her.

The sound of the front door shutting came as a relief to Rachel, but it was soon followed by voices rising outside, and a woman asking worriedly, "Faith, Doc, is she all right?"

"Hold on, Juliet," Rachel heard Faith say. "We need to talk first. Maybe we should go over to your office, Doc, if you don't mind." Then Faith's tone grew firm, "Stan, please stay at this door and don't let anyone, not anyone, disturb her. If she calls out or gets up, send someone to fetch us right away."

"I'll do that, ma'am," the deep Irish burr replied.

The voices receded from the porch as the clomp and tap of footsteps trailed away. Rachel lay tensely on the bed, her ears straining to catch the slightest sound as someone set a chair firmly against the door.

5

The hinges creaked softly as the door eased open, and Rachel watched with growing wonderment as a woman entered the bedroom and sat beside her. This new face surprised her to such an extent that she could only contain it by blaming the doctor's whiskey for magnifying her perceptions. Yet there was no denying that the woman's features bore a slightly older yet striking resemblance. Apparently in her early forties, her pulled-back hair revealed the same variegation of golds to browns, her face bore an identical structure, her mouth smiled with the same shape and fullness, and those worried brown eyes might have been Rachel's own.

The woman said earnestly, "Doc tells me you've had a bad spill, honey. How are you feeling?"

"Well, I feel very strange."

"Your Aunt Faith says you don't remember anything but your name. Is that so?"

"I'm afraid it is," answered Rachel. "And... who are you?"

This question produced a struggle within the woman to keep her expression calm. "I'm your mama, Rachel. I'm Juliet Milford."

"My mother. Of course," Rachel said, hiding her distrust.

"That's right, dear." The woman smiled. "Folks always say you and me came out of the same mold."

"And how old are you?"

"I'll be forty-one this December."

"Forty-one. I see. And how old am I?"

"Why, you turned twenty-two last November, Rachel."

"*Twenty*-two?" Rachel blurted. How could the Valentis, or whoever they'd hired to set this up, have made such a blatant mistake? They were short by a decade.

"It must be frightening, not remembering folks," Juliet continued in a soothing voice, "but Doc says you might start recalling things real soon. We'll take good care of you 'til you get to feeling better. Your pa is just outside. We talked it out and we believe it would be best if you came home with us. Wouldn't you like that, honey?"

Just what kind of a home had they cooked up? "Where *is* home?"

As if she'd been withholding her touch for fear of upsetting Rachel but could no longer do so, Juliet lovingly took Rachel's hand, and said, "Why, it's four miles northwest of town. Your pa drove the wagon in, so we can tuck you up all warm and snug for the ride."

Rachel had to admit that this woman might be the best actress she'd ever seen, but years as a trial lawyer had taught her quite a bit about performing, and she would try to play her own part for as long as it might give her an advantage.

Juliet prattled on, "Your sisters and brothers were fit to be tied when they heard you were hurt, especially when we told them they couldn't come into town. They'll mollycoddle you something terrible."

Sisters and brothers? Well, sure, why not throw them in too? "Please, can you tell me the name of this town?"

"Of course, honey. You most likely have lots of questions about such things. This is Idaho City."

"Idaho City?" That explained the mountains. "In the state of Idaho, I presume."

"Well, folks say it won't be long before we earn our statehood, but it's only the Idaho Territory for now."

"*Territory.*" Rachel's repetition of the word, the faltering of her fortified assumptions, cut her breathing short and twisted her gut deep inside. She swallowed and forced out, "What... what *year* is this?"

Seeing the color ebb from Rachel's face, Juliet's tone grew fearful. "Maybe I'm telling you too much all at once. Maybe I should get Doc Willis."

"No, please," Rachel insisted, unconsciously squeezing the woman's hand, "just tell me what year this is."

"It's 1864, dear."

Rachel's gaze scrutinized Juliet's face for the slightest change in expression, anything that would expose her as something other than the earnest, caring woman she appeared to be. Seeing nothing to unmask her, Rachel shifted her eyes to the wall.

Juliet murmured something and left the room, returning moments later with Doc Willis and a man she introduced as Bert Milford, Rachel's "father." Giving Bert no more than a furtive glance, in that moment she took in his medium height and square shoulders, straw-colored hair, strong weathered face, and uncertain gray eyes. When he took an awkward few steps forward, Rachel turned her head away, so he merely patted her shoulder lightly and mutely moved to a corner of the room.

Their gestures and touches were evidently meant to comfort, and even Doc Willis now spoke in low murmurs, but Rachel was no longer focused on them. Withholding the numerous questions jostling her thoughts, she answered their queries only when necessary. Even when they packed the brown dress and female articles from the dresser into a satchel, helped her from bed, into her shoes and coat, and out the front door, she said nothing at all.

Rachel kept her face directed at the floorboards until she

reached the porch and spotted two boots blocking her way. She looked up into an unsettling combination of sky blue eyes and wavy black hair, the handsome face wearing an anxious expression that was becoming all too familiar. But no, this expression was more intense, more intimate, more demanding. When the man took hold of Rachel's upper arms, she could feel his restrained tension.

"Rachel, darlin,'" he said with his Irish accent conspicuous and his examination shifting from her bandage to her eyes.

"I..." Rachel said lamely.

"Lord, but you're white as a ghost. Are you badly hurt, Rachel?"

Bert stepped close and said brusquely, "Stan, she's coming home now and she needs rest. We'd appreciate it if she had no visitors but Doc Willis."

Stan's attention had never left Rachel's face, his eyes searching, but he found only blankness. "All right, Bert. She looks as though she can use a bit of rest. I'll not interfere, on the condition that you'll be sending me word if she turns poorly." With great disinclination, Bert nodded, but before releasing his hold on Rachel's arms, Stan moved his thumbs in a caress that revealed an established familiarity, even tenderness. Then he stepped aside. The touch, as unexplainable as everything else, sent a slight shudder through Rachel's shoulders, and she couldn't help staring after him as he eased away.

She was helped into a muddy horse-drawn wagon and nearly buried under a pile of quilts. When they suggested she lie down, however, she shook her head. Facing backward just behind the driver's seat, with her "mother" sitting protectively on one side and her "aunt" on the other, the wagon pulled away from the few people still milling near the Pinney house. Before they'd driven more than a few yards, Doc Willis yelled to them from the porch, "I'll be out this evening to see you, young lady. You let your family dote on you today."

As they rolled slowly through town, more than a few townspeople, the vast majority male, stared back at her. Some called out wishes for her recovery, and she fleetingly wondered how so many of them could know about her fall so quickly. She forced aside a measure of the overwhelming ache to resolve the mystery of this place, and studied the landscape, buildings, conveyances, animals, and the humans around her.

Not a thing differed from what she imagined existing in 1864. The general mercantile and the livery, the blacksmith, barber, and butcher shops, the cigar and tobacco store, the breweries, saloons, hotels, and physicians' offices appeared to be roughly but newly constructed. Other than the merchants, professional men, and a few respectably-dressed women, the rest of the population was digging, sluicing, or panning, evidently for gold. Undaunted by the earlier rain, men were spread out and toiling in the muck with the aid of strange equipment along every creek bed and ditch bank, even to the very edge of some of the houses.

Rachel looked again for transmission towers or power lines, watching anxiously for any suggestion of concealed poles, meters, or transformers, but saw none. If power and transmission reception really *were* absent from this community, that fact alone eliminated the existence of so many conveniences that it was almost impossible to envision. She had no understanding of what was happening, and she couldn't guess how long it might continue, but she dismally comprehended that she'd have to do without every one of those amenities for now.

The dirt road was in such appalling condition, with deep ruts and holes made unavoidable by their abundance, the wagon jostled them about like rag dolls. They swayed and bobbed out of town and headed north for less than a quarter mile before turning westerly. Although she was in no state to appreciate it, Rachel couldn't help inhaling the scent of pine that surrounded her with a crisp sweetness as it drifted on the slight breeze. The clouds were thinning as they fled eastward and the sun blazed through the ever-widening gaps between them. Tiny finch-like birds flitted and chirped among the limbs of massive trees that stood so close together, they blocked much of her view from anything beyond.

After a great deal of winding, the road reached the base of a significant incline and the wagon halted. The other two women told Rachel to stay put and climbed down to walk until the horses had reached the top of the rise, where Bert paused to rest the team. Here a clearer view lay open, and Rachel, still facing backward, lifted her eyes to the peaks that rose before her. In spite of everything, Rachel was captivated by their beauty, sensing that she was being welcomed somehow, as if the mountains were embracing her with their magnificence. They towered extremely close, cloaked in shadowy green that darkened to midnight blue beneath mantles of snow and, higher still, crowned with clouds. The trees marched in clustering diagonal files up to the very peaks, highlighting massive faces of deeply scored gray granite. *So you are the Rockies.* How ironic that she'd visited the Alps several times but had never traveled far enough westward to discover these peaks.

Unexpectedly, Rachel's conscience was overtaken by the image of Ellen, and she realized that her assistant must be beside herself with worry by now. When Rachel had failed to show up or even phone in to the office, Ellen must have called Jason. And what had Jason told her, that her boss, her friend had been shot and then disappeared? That she was dead? *Was* she dead? Her racing thoughts shifted again. *What about my mother and father*? Would they, a couple who'd never shown much interest in their two children, care a great deal that their daughter was missing? Yes, in spite of their troubled history, Rachel sensed that they would care. Facing this uncomfortable conclusion, perceiving times when at least her mother had tried to love her in her own way, Rachel lowered her gaze from the mountains to stare at the quilt covering her legs.

Once the horses were breathing easier and the two women had climbed back into the wagon, Bert clicked his tongue and drove on, heading slowly down a long, easy slope. The three adults riding with Rachel seemed to be remaining silent in the hope that she would say something. She could feel their frequent glances but kept her tongue still and her thoughts to herself. This mental distancing proved difficult, however, when Juliet bowed her head as if in prayer and Faith followed suit. After a mumbled "Amen," these two took turns adjusting the quilts around Rachel's shoulders and gently moving her wind-tossed hair away from her face to check her bandage. Rachel began to anticipate that if they touched her once more with such familiar solicitude, she'd scream. Thankfully, they settled back into their places before she lost whatever control she'd fought to retain.

On the occasions when she glanced over her shoulder, she saw Bert sitting heavily on the wagon seat, his frame hunched comfortably forward, and his tranquil attention focused on the team. As the silence stretched on, however, he proved her wrong about his composure by starting to fidget and at last addressing Juliet with, "Remember that day when Rachel was twelve and I came in from the fields and told you what she said about the Indian school?"

Juliet nodded. "I do."

He flitted a glance at Rachel to see if she was listening. "I was just finishing the edge on my two-sided axe when she came up to watch. She said nothing at first, then she smiled dreamy like and said, 'Pa, I want to start a school where the Indians live. I could teach them about letters and numbers and they could teach me how to ride better and how to hunt with a bow.'"

Juliet smiled. "Yes, I remember you telling me."

"I told her she already rode as well as any Indian, but she said we ought to learn the ways of other folks so we get on better." He shook his head, saying as if he and Juliet were alone, "Rachel thought deeper and farther than any child I ever heard of, and I told her so at the time."

When no one else spoke, he tried again. "Who would have guessed back then that in a few years we'd be leaving Iowa and heading west?"

The two women beside Rachel seemed as reluctant to speak as she was, and Bert gave up his attempt at conversation, so Rachel listened to the plop of the horse's feet and the groaning of the wagon and hoped that everyone would keep silent. She had enough to contemplate without having to pretend to listen.

Just before noon, Juliet turned to Rachel and said, "We're almost home, honey."

And so they were. Not a furlong ahead, Bert drove the horses off the main road and over a short, plank-covered bridge scarcely wider than the span of the wagon. As they rattled across the fragile expanse, Rachel got to her knees and turned to catch a glimpse of what lay ahead. Her gaze found the stream flowing beneath them, splashing and rolling over rounded rocks of every size, spilling downward for eighty yards before bending to the south and disappearing from view.

She felt the wheels touch solid ground, looked ahead of the wagon and stretched taller. As she caught her first sight of the dwelling, Bert said, "Now that you're here, Rachel, you'll be feeling better in no time."

6

As the wagon bumped along past the split-rail fence of a corral on the left and a partially-cleared field on the right, Rachel took in every natural and man-made feature of the place. Sunshine glinted off the stream into a web of ditches and rows of unsprouted crops. Several dark brown cattle with heavy bodies and massive heads watched the wagon lumber by, and as one cow let out a low bawl, Rachel caught the scents of manure and wood smoke. Just ahead, a log barn stood within the shade of towering Ponderosas. These and two pines of similar stature that stood behind the house evidently had been spared the bite of a voracious axe.

The house bore little resemblance to the structures Rachel had seen in town. More rustic than the business buildings and framed homes of the wealthier residents, it was still a vast improvement over the tiny miners' shacks. Under other circumstances, its sturdy, two-story log exterior and overhanging front porch might have struck Rachel as charming. She took it in, from its rock foundation to its wood-shingled roof and stone chimney from which a thin stream of smoke rose. Another sweeping glance encompassed the entire homestead and surrounding hills, the ground cleared for the house, barn, pasture, and field constituting the only level portion of the acreage. Where the stream followed the base of a knoll behind their property, a young black man was digging and emptying his shovel into a large wooden box atop half-moon supports. A much older white companion rocked the box back and forth, and then paused to examine its contents. At the sound of the wagon drawing to a halt, they both abandoned their tools and walked to meet it.

In front of the barn, two enormous dogs bounded up barking their greetings, and from the house a small herd of golden-headed children stampeded in their direction. Two girls and two boys of varying sizes clamored to the wagon, crying, "She's here! Rachel! Rachel!" The children jostled noisily around as Bert helped Rachel down. She turned to face them and, staring at each in turn, felt her throat tighten. Their multi-shaded blonde hair, the heart shape of their faces, the leanness of their bodies all brought to mind the photos of her childhood. *They look like me, more so than my own brother.* Glancing from Juliet, to Bert, to Faith, Rachel was met with painfully hopeful expressions, as if they were waiting for a sign that she recognized these supposed brothers and sisters.

The older of the two girls, perhaps eleven or twelve, asked, "Oh, Mama, how is she?"

"She needs some rest, Kate, and lots of quiet."

A boy, not much Kate's senior, muttered, "Look at all the blood on her dress!"

"Hush, Phillip. Kate, go turn down her bed and set some water on to boil." Watching Rachel closely, the girl hesitated, unwilling to miss any new development, then spun around and ran light-footed into the house.

Phillip, still fascinated, said, "She looks fearful!"

"No, she don't!" cried the littlest boy, no more than four years old. "No, she don't neither!" He suddenly threw his arms around Rachel's knee and hugged it hard.

Rachel looked to Juliet for help. Bending down to the child, Juliet said, "Now, Charlie, let go and move back a little so Rachel can get by."

Charlie only clung tighter, so Bert scooped up the boy, saying, "Come on, little man. You can help me unhitch the team." Despite the boy's shrill protests, Bert kept moving.

The old man who'd been by the stream working the rocker box watched Rachel pass without a word, but when she reached the porch without so much as a glance in his direction, he bent his head low and shook it slowly. "Come on, Lewis, let's get back to work. They'll come tell us what they know after she's settled."

Standing at the foot of the stairs, Rachel gazed around while Juliet and Faith hung the shawls and coats on wooden pegs by the door. It was a good-sized room with bare log walls, except in the far corner where someone had hung the oval portrait of a young man in a blue Civil War uniform. Animal skins partially covered the plank flooring, and upon these rested a pair of rocking chairs and two high-backed benches. The furniture was arranged in a semi-circle facing a river rock fireplace, and above the half-log mantle rested a long rifle on two pegs. A second pair of pegs stood empty. Two unlit oil lamps, one made of metal on the mantle and one of cut glass atop a side table, appeared to be the only sources of artificial light. In front of her climbed a flight of narrow stairs framed on the open left side by a log spindled railing. To her immediate right, a door stood ajar to reveal a small bedroom. Between the stairway and the fireplace, a doorway led into the kitchen, of which Rachel could see little more than a long table covered with a blue-checkered cloth.

It all felt warm, simple, mellow, solid, and totally foreign.

Juliet took her arm. "Let's get you up to your room." She led Rachel up the stairs and into one of three rooms on the second floor. The bedroom's furnishings consisted of a bed draped with a quilt of yellow, brown, and pale green squares, a washstand holding a white porcelain pitcher and bowl, and a dresser. Yellow curtains swayed in the half-open window that overlooked the front of the house.

Kate had obediently turned down the covers, and she had placed a purple and white wild iris on the pillow.

"I'll help you into your nightgown, honey," said Juliet.

Rachel offered no resistance and was soon tucked into the soft embrace of the feather bed. Juliet examined the stained pink dress in her hands, hesitated a moment, then asked, "Rachel, do you recall where you were headed this morning? It must have been somewhere special since you were wearing your best dress."

"No, I don't remember," Rachel replied in a tone meant to discourage further questioning. She wanted to be alone, to think, to try to make some sense of things. Actually, what she really wanted was to be home rather than in this place speaking to a stranger, perhaps even a dangerous one.

Undaunted, Juliet sat down on the edge of the bed and said, "It's odd, you being in this dress, because you were supposed to be at work."

"Work?" Dammit! Questions would keep this woman talking. Rachel tightened her lips, determined to keep her mouth shut.

"You've been working for nearly a month at the mercantile for Mr. and Mrs. Mack."

The voice of the little boy, who had apparently finished helping Bert with the team, rose up the stairs like a strengthening wind. "Why can't I see Rachel? I want to see my Rachel! She bumpeded her head and I want to make her all better!" Small feet pattered swiftly toward Rachel's bedroom, closely followed by the pounding of much a larger pair.

"Charlie. Charlie!" Bert bellowed after him. Charlie burst into the room and ran to Rachel.

"Oh, no you don't," Juliet declared, grabbing him before he could leap onto the bed.

Charlie broke into tears as Bert, tight-lipped with exasperation, lifted him from Juliet, tucked him under his arm with his small head and arms still beseeching Rachel, and gave him a slight whack on the butt. In his distress, the little boy didn't even notice the swat. "But she's *my* Rachel! *My* Rachel!" he bawled all the way down the stairs. "She *wants* to see me, Pa! She does!"

Stunned anew, Rachel gawped at Juliet.

"Now, honey, don't fret about Charlie. He's always been your little shadow, is all. He'll simmer down soon." They could hear him wailing louder than ever downstairs. "Does your head hurt much, Rachel?"

It certainly did. "No," she said distractedly, trying to erase the image of Charlie weeping as if his heart were breaking, his arms stretching out to her.

"I'll go down and see how your sister's coming along with the tea." Juliet patted her arm and left the room.

Rachel sat benumbed with her eyes on the door, which had been left ajar. Her thoughts seemed to be on a merry-go-round, repeatedly circling the words: *What the hell is going on here*? That little boy *knew* her, or at least thought he knew her. A child so small couldn't pretend that well. She wondered wildly why she'd allowed herself to be brought to this house and put to bed by strangers. At least *she* didn't know *them*. Their behavior insisted that Rachel was sister, daughter, granddaughter, and niece to the whole clan. This family was more familiar and intrusive than her *real* family had ever been.

Just as it had in town, her mind seized on one thought: She needed to get out of here. Sliding her legs over the side of the bed—at least this one was quiet—Rachel held very still and listened. The commotion downstairs told her that she'd be exceedingly lucky to clothe herself and sneak out without being spotted. She had just decided to take her chances, nonetheless, when the door opened and the eight-year-old girl entered, carefully and proudly carrying a china cup and saucer.

Rachel's legs slipped back under the covers. As the girl approached, their physical similarities struck Rachel once more: long legs, thick, gold-brown hair, dark eyes and brows, the same oval-heart faces, smallish noses, and broad lips, even the high carriage of her head.

Placing the teacup on the low dresser, she sat down on the bed and observed Rachel thoughtfully. "Mama says you went and forgot all of us," she said, her expression showing a touch of reproach. "She says if we tell you stories you might start to recall things. I'm even to tell you my name, which seems mighty silly. I'm Maggie. I brought you some tea," she inclined her head toward it, "and I'll sit with you as long as you like. You can ask me about things or I can just talk."

"You're right," said Rachel, "I do need someone to explain things I don't...remember. For instance, can you tell me what towns are nearby?"

"Towns? But, don't you want to know about our family?"

Score one for Maggie. "Yes, of course, please tell me about the family."

"Why, sure," said Maggie, now smiling grandly. "But you best get comfortable and drink your tea, 'cause it will take some time to hear about so many folks."

Rachel took a sip from her cup and tasted sugar and cream enriching the tea. Only after the first swallow did she momentarily wonder if it might be drugged. But the whiskey Doc Willis had given her hadn't been modified, she acknowledged, and allowed herself to suppose that the tea was just as safe.

Maggie adjusted herself into a cross-legged position. "Would you like to hear about me first?"

"That would be fine."

"I'm just eight years old but Mama says I make stew like I was twelve. You should see how True eats it up. True is sixteen so he's pretty near grow'd."

"*True* is, uh, our brother?"

"Yep. You are the oldest of us kids, and Pa liked you from the start, and then Esther came along, but he wanted a boy next to help him with chores. Just after True got born, Grandpa Ezra found Pa and told him he had a son. Pa ran into the house yelling, 'Is it true?' and Mama said, 'Yes, it's true.' Grandpa says the name just stuck around after that."

"I see," said Rachel.

"True's a good miner and even better with a rifle. He's out hunting right now in fact. When Pa can't take us into town, he lets True."

"True needs to be good with a gun to take us into town?"

Maggie peered at Rachel as if she'd lost her good sense right along with her memory. "It's a *mining town*. Kate says half the men in town are in love with you or Esther. But since Esther went and got married, it's likely not so many."

"Then tell me about Esther."

"She's eighteen and Richard Lete got her to marry him over a year ago, maybe because he's the best barber in town. He's also real good at cooking Basque food. His grandma, his *Amuma*, back in Spain taught him how to make the best beans we ever tasted. Esther is powerful partial to him and his cooking." Cupping a hand to the side of her mouth, she whispered with a grin, "Now there's a baby coming."

Rachel placed her teacup on the dresser. "And Kate was who turned down my bed?"

Maggie nodded.

"And she's, what, ten years old?"

"She's eleven, but Pa won't let her go hunting too often even though she begs and begs. When she *does* go, she brings something home nearly every time. Kate's wild as a coyote, at least that's what True says."

"What about the older boy downstairs?"

"It's a funny thing about Phillip. He most likely *behaves* better than any of us kids, other than Charlie, 'cause he's only four, but Phillip still gets into trouble right regular on account of what comes out of his mouth."

"So, there are Esther, True, Phillip, Kate, you, Charlie, and me. Seven, right?" *Seven!* "Is that everybody?"

"Well, there's Mama and Pa, and Grandpa, of course. Grandpa's awful old but he still works real hard. He, and Pa, and True learned the mining business together, and they've dug up a good share of gold since we came here."

"Uh-huh, and is *that* everyone?"

"Yep. Oh my, I nearly forgot Lewis. He's not truly part of the family, but mostly he is."

"And who is Lewis?"

"He helps the men with their work. He's powerful strong and black as ink. He's pretty quiet most times, but he sings sweet as molasses when he thinks no one's close by." Her brows knitted together then lifted as she offered, "I can name you our dogs, and horses, and cows, and chicks, too."

Saving Rachel from a response, the sound of footsteps climbed the stairs and Juliet entered the room with a questioning glance. "Do you want to be alone now, Rachel?"

"I am feeling a bit tired," she admitted, but seeing Maggie's mouth droop, she added, "but Maggie has been very helpful."

The girl brightened. "Do you recall things any better now?"

"I think so, a little."

"Come along, Maggie," Juliet said, holding out her hand.

Maggie gave Rachel an apologetic shrug and leaped off the bed, an innocent action that nevertheless jarred Rachel's strained nerves and aching head.

Juliet asked, "Is there anything I can bring you?"

Exhaustion was beginning to encumber Rachel's thinking but she forced it aside, pondering, and then asked, "Do you have a newspaper?"

"Say now, that's an idea. Reading about things that have happened, things you've read about before might bring them back to mind. We have a newspaper or two tucked away. I'll go and see how many I can find."

After Juliet and Maggie left, Rachel reflected on the girl's words as well as the manner and behavior of the whole household, struggling with the germinating perception that these people truly knew her, or rather, knew someone they believed her to be. But how could such a thing happen? And if this was a case of mistaken identity, where had the *other* Rachel gone?

Juliet carried a few papers and a chair into the bedroom, handed the slim stack to Rachel, and sat down to watch her eyebrows lift, then fall, as a skim of the first few lines pulled her into a story. "Honey, can you read what it says?"

"I can read every word," Rachel said, staring at the page. The date leaping from the top of the *Boise News* was Saturday, May 14, 1864.

Juliet waited, but when Rachel neither looked up nor spoke, she stood and slowly walked out, pulling the door almost shut behind her.

Rachel had closed her mind to everything but the large sheets she held. The first article, entitled "Indian Matters," described how Colonel Maury was leading a company of cavalry from Fort Boise to force Snake Indians from their present location and "drive them to the wall." This was deemed necessary in order to protect the miners between the Payette River and Fort Hall. It went on, "...to rid the country of these pests is the highest service the military could render."

Indians, and the cavalry. Allowing herself only a moment to absorb this before hungrily scanning for more, she paused at an article titled, "The Negro's 'Status.'" A schoolmarm from Syracuse claimed that Negroes seemed to be able to learn the rudiments of reading, writing, and spelling as readily as whites. But when it came to abstract reasoning needed for mathematics, most of them failed. Any exceptions to this last observation, the woman avowed, were due to the presence of white blood in the individual's lineage. She concluded that the Negro status was naturally and appropriately below that of the Caucasian race so there was no use in them "crying equality."

Swearing under her breath in disgust, Rachel skipped descriptions of the unhealthy level of gambling in San Francisco and turned the page. Here was a piece about Indians murdering a family along the Burnt River, and another on the shooting death of a Mr. Partin by the proprietor of a Payette River ferry. Further down, she read that at Booneville in Owyhee County, a drunken man named Robert Lytle shot and killed John Walker rather than Mr. Miller, the intended target.

"One killing after another," Rachel murmured in appalled fascination. Greedily devouring each line, she read about a proposed mail route from Salt Lake City to Walla Walla that might lead to a mail run into the Boise Basin, as well as the possibility of a new tri-weekly stage line from Idaho City to Boise City.

The third page announced that Mrs. Kingsley would be opening a school for boys and girls at her home in the rear of the new church on Commercial Street. *Did the Milford kids go to this school?*

Flipping quickly to the last page, Rachel skimmed the paragraph about Congress proposing a five percent tax on gold and silver, then her absorption locked onto a news release from Albany, New York. It read, "It is understood that all the artillery regiments and detachments now in the government forts have been ordered to the front. The militia will be called out to take their places." 1864. The *Civil War*. Very slowly, she lowered the paper. After remaining motionless for a time she lifted it again, reading and rereading about the thousands of prisoners taken by each side, the intentions and movements of the Union and Confederate generals, and the seizures or losses of various strategic positions.

At last she squeezed her eyes tightly closed and tried to remember everything she'd ever learned about this war. She knew that Lee had surrendered in the mid-1860s, but exactly *when* had victory for the

North been decided? She also recalled that President Lincoln would be assassinated not long after the war ended, but not the date.

"President Lincoln, Abraham Lincoln, alive," she muttered.

No, none of this is possible! With a sudden jerk of her arm she flung the paper to the floor. Yet even as she placed her face in her hands and silently screamed, the determination to reject all that she'd sensed and experienced since this morning weakened. Would she be edging near insanity to consider that somehow she'd truly been thrust into this world? Several seconds later she lifted her head and opened her eyes, and without perceiving that she was disminishing her previous musings by forming the next question, she wondered, *Why am I here?*

Her head began to pound and her wound to burn, and she slid deeper under the covers. She again closed her stinging eyes as she tried to concentrate on nothing but breathing deeply and relaxing. It took many long inhales and exhales along with the lingering effects of the whiskey before her body and mind slipped into an uneasy sleep.

Around one o'clock that afternoon the sound of the opening door brought one of Rachel's eyelids up. Juliet stood there quietly watching until Rachel focused on her. Maggie was being held behind Juliet's skirt, where she remained until Rachel cleared her throat and slowly sat up.

"Are you hungry, Rachel?" Juliet asked.

There was a hollow rumbling from her stomach in response, and as the last tendrils of sleep loosened, she realized that she had eaten nothing today. All numbing effects of the whiskey were gone, leaving her to suffer the strangeness of her situation more acutely. Even so, she clung to the hope of finding a way back to her own life, and she would need to face the occupants of this house sooner or later. "I'm famished," she answered, adding with resolve, "and I feel perfectly capable of coming downstairs to eat lunch with the rest of you, if that's acceptable."

Juliet looked at her as if she'd just spoken Italian.

Even more puzzled, Maggie demanded, "What's 'lunch'?"

Juliet regained her composure quickly. "Now, honey, you'd best stay in bed 'til Doc Willis says you can be up and around." Her words were kind but firm. "I'll send one of the kids up with something to eat. You just try to lie quiet. Maggie, come with me."

"Can I stay with Rachel? There's so much yet to tell her."

"Not right now. You know what your Pa thinks about not being at the table when you're able. If Rachel's not too tired, maybe you can come talk to her after dinner." Juliet had been looking at Rachel, her expression asking whether Maggie's company would be welcome.

"Yes, come back if you'd like, Maggie." She wasn't used to the company of small children under normal circumstances, and current conditions were far from normal, but she had little choice but to accept the presence of these children without resorting to rudeness.

As Juliet led her daughter out of the room, Maggie waved happily back toward the bed. "Don't worry, Rachel. I'll eat real fast."

It wasn't Maggie, however, who made the next appearance at Rachel's door. The boy, Phillip, based on Maggie's description, knocked softly and entered carrying a large steaming bowl. Cradling the bowl in a folded dishtowel, Philip sat down on the edge of the bed and handed the soup to Rachel.

Concerned, he said, "Mama says you're to try to eat it all." Rachel nodded, and was lifting her first taste with anticipation when he blurted out, "Rachel, don't you remember *any* of us? Not even *Mama*?"

"I…I'm trying to remember," she said, lowering the arm and attempting to smile.

He responded with a thoughtful frown. "I never heard of a body forgetting everything like that. Is it worrisome for you, Rachel?"

"Yes, it's very worrisome," she answered honestly.

Bert hollered from downstairs, "Phillip, I told you to let your sister rest! Leave that soup and get back down here!"

"Well, I'd best go," he said, standing and heading out the door.

Rachel sat staring at the contents of her bowl. She could hear voices speaking softly downstairs, chairs scraping, plates and utensils clinking. As she listened, the aroma of the soup reached her nose, spurring her hunger, and carefully leaning forward, she blew over the surface of her spoon and brought it to her lips. The rich flavor spread warmly, deliciously over her tongue. She swallowed and let out an appreciative sigh, then raised the spoon again. By the time the bowl was empty, Rachel's body and mind felt noticeably better. She set it aside, lay back, and sank into the covers.

Before long the noises of the dinner and cleaning up below quieted, and she was wondering which Milford would show up next, when young voices began filtering through her open window from the front porch below.

"We best watch her close tomorrow," said Kate.

"Why tomorrow?" asked Phillip.

"Remember when Eb Spiggins got kicked by that livery horse last fall? He seemed right as rain, talking to everybody and all, and folks was so surprised when he up and died the next night."

"Kate!" Phillip barked.

"Well, he did."

Phillip's voice growled, "What's the matter with you talking like that, in front of Charlie even? Rachel's going to be just fine, you hear me?" After a slight pause, Phillip added, "You're just scared is all. You won't even go see her now that you know she can't remember you."

"I ain't scared!" Kate returned. "Mama says she needs quiet and not to bother her."

As if he'd been turning all of this over in his mind, little Charlie piped up, "Rachel didn't get kicked in the head, she falled down."

"That's right, Charlie," Phillip confirmed. "It ain't nothing like what happened to poor old Eb."

"I was just saying we need to look after her, is all," Kate voiced sullenly. "Come on. We best go check the calves like Mama told us."

With a huff, Phillip asked, "When did you start being in such a hurry to mind what Mama tells us?"

"You know, Phillip, you ain't but two years older than me. You got no call to boss me like you do. And I *ain't* scared to go see Rachel."

"So you say. We'll just see how..."

Their voices trailed away toward the barn.

Well, Phillip, thought Rachel, *I certainly hope I don't end up like poor Eb.* Wondering what the next moments, the next days, might deliver, she waited for Maggie to return. This time, she intended to ask more questions. But again it was someone else who appeared.

At the sound of a buggy pulling up to the house, a great fist bombarding the front door, and a male voice greeting Juliet with the delicacy of a canon, Rachel knew there would soon be heavy footsteps climbing the staircase. Juliet managed to enter her room just in front of Doc Willis, who lumbered in carrying an air of good-natured prominence along with his medical bag.

He towered over Rachel's bedside, demanding, "Well, now, how is my patient feeling?"

"Better," Rachel said.

He checked the head wound and listened to her heart, humming a waltz throughout his examination. "Ah, you're progressing quite nicely, Rachel," he pronounced at last, "quite nicely indeed. No sign of corruption. It's too early to expect the swelling to be reduced, of course, but that will come in a day or two." In a more serious tone, he said, "Your mother says your memory hasn't returned. Have you noticed any improvement at all since you hit your head?"

"Actually, I think things are becoming clearer all the time," Rachel responded, and even managed to sweeten her voice a little.

"That's fine! Just fine!"

The volume of his reply sharpened the pounding in Rachel's head to such an extent that she almost regretted the lie.

"See what good rest can do for a body? That's exactly what you need lots more of, rest."

"No, really, Doctor Willis," Rachel said, presenting a smile, "I'd feel much better to be up and... helping the family. I'll be careful not to attempt anything too strenuous."

"You're far from recovered, young lady. Just listen to that speech of yours. It sounds like you were raised by strangers! You'll be of greater help to this family once you're back to normal. No, no, I don't want you leaving that bed for at least a day or two." Giving Juliet a dictatorial stare and receiving a nod of compliance, he allowed his features to bloom into a grin. "Fine, then."

Doc Willis packed up, wished her a good afternoon, and descended the stairs with Juliet trailing after him, leaving Rachel in a far worse humor than before he'd come. Her mind was so preoccupied that she paid little attention to the hushed conversation drifting up from the front porch. But when Juliet's voice became worried, almost urgent, Rachel found herself attending closely.

"...doesn't need to deal with him on top of everything else. Stan should leave her be. Please, Doc, tell him not to come around unless we send for him. Will you do that?"

"Of course, Juliet." He gave some parting instructions for Rachel's care before he drove the buggy away.

When Juliet reentered Rachel's room and sat down beside her, she said, "Doc knows how bad you want to get up, honey, but he told me again that you are to stay quiet 'til tomorrow, and then you're to go no farther than downstairs."

The old quack. "Well, I need to get up right now, to use the...outhouse." Rachel's slim hope that Juliet would announce the presence of indoor plumbing was quickly snuffed.

"I'll take you outside, dear."

They descended the stairs, cut through the kitchen, and walked out back. Spotting the tiny building but keeping her feet moving, she brooded, *I could never get used to this. At least this time I'm going to demand soap and water when I'm finished.* Bracing her senses for the odor and flies, she tightened her fortitude, opened the door, and entered.

7

As evening approached and every shadow beyond Rachel's window lengthened and faded, she almost hoped that someone would come to disturb her. For the past two hours she'd tried to sleep again but failed, so she'd begun watching Bert, Grandpa Ezra, and Lewis as they worked the land. The children had come and gone from her view, noisily playing or doing chores, and a young man, obviously True, had shown up half an hour earlier. He'd walked out of the forest and up to Bert with a rifle on his shoulder and held out several dead birds for the older men to admire. He'd then come into the house to present the birds to Juliet before returning to the field with a hoe in place of his rifle, and was soon helping to weed the furrowed field.

It grew chillier as the sun declined, but Rachel left her window open to catch every noise that drifted her way. She heard the sounds of the family, farm animals, and forest birds and insects, but none from an airplane, telephone, or car; not a thing to refute her surroundings.

And neither man nor beast had passed their property along the road.

The sunlight continued to weaken, and at last the men knocked dirt from their shovels and hoes and walked toward the barn. Rachel momentarily lost sight of them, but soon heard the washing of hands at the water basin that resided on a bench at the back door, the same basin Rachel had used earlier. Their voices preceded them into the kitchen and mixed with the chatter of children and clatter of plates.

Before the Milfords gathered at the table, Phillip knocked on Rachel's door and entered carrying another bowl of soup, this time accompanied by a thick slice of buttered bread. Rachel thanked him and would have said more, but he blurted, "I best get down to supper," and disappeared. Sighing, Rachel left the door ajar and turned her mind to filling her stomach.

She was finishing the last few bites when she heard the rattle of harnesses and the beat of hooves approaching. With a clack of its latch the front door opened, and Juliet's voice floated up, "Why, Esther, you shouldn't be out at this hour. Your cheeks and nose are pink as a rose. Hurry up inside, now. You too, Richard."

A young woman's voice eerily like Rachel's own, said, "Richard didn't want to bring me, but I told him if he didn't, I'd come alone."

A man's voice grunted loudly as they entered the house.

"You go on ahead with papa, Richard. We'll be right along."

"If you haven't eaten, there's plenty," Bert offered, and though Richard was led into the kitchen where the family was finishing supper, Juliet remained on the porch with Esther.

Rachel held very still and Esther's voice reached her clearly, saying, "He kept finding chores he said couldn't wait until it was almost dark, hoping I would change my mind. When I'd had enough I went to the stable and started hitching the team myself. He grumbled all the way here, but he brought me. How could he suppose I'd sit in town, not knowing if Rachel was alright?"

"He just loves you, honey," Juliet soothed. "He's worried for you and the baby."

"I know, but I had to come. And I mean to stay until I'm certain Rachel's well."

"She's… not quite herself, and she says things that are hard to follow at times."

"Aunt Faith told me she doesn't even know *you*. Oh, Mama."

"Now, honey, Doc said she seems to be a little better already."

"He did? Do you think it would do any harm if I saw her?"

"I wish I knew, Esther. If she's finished her supper, and she's resting easy, it might do her good. Just let me go up and see if she's awake."

Juliet climbed the stairs and peered quietly into the unlit room. Rachel lay on the far side of the bed with her back to her. The empty bowl was on the floor not far from Juliet's reach. She watched Rachel's deep breathing for a few moments, then retrieved the bowl, retreated into the hallway, and closed the door.

Rachel didn't move until she heard Juliet's footsteps reach the first floor. Trying to avoid jostling the bedsprings, she turned onto her back and placed her hands beneath her aching head to stare up into darkness, lost in a war of speculation. While powerful reasoning clashed with senses and emotions, the battle was brutal. Her mind kept turning back, grasping old images and creating new worries. Where was Jason right now? Were he and Tim still protecting Carlo? Were Ellen, her parents, and her brother all right? Did they believe she was dead? Why wouldn't they? What else could explain what had happened? But how could this be death when she felt so alive?

Finally, as the sun's lingering rays relinquished their dominion to the first stars, Rachel took the quilt from the bed, wrapped it around her shoulders, and returned to the window. She stood with her eyes raised to the heavens. Rather than God's guidance, however, she sought the lights of a distant city, or those of a jet or satellite. As night deepened, the only light to reach her window was cast by a sea of stars more numerous and brilliant than she'd ever known, and by a three-quarter moon that divulged even its craters and mountains.

The sound of her door easing open drew Rachel around to find Charlie standing there in the darkness, the glow from the window illuminating his white nightshirt. He bent his head to the floor. In a small voice shuddering with recent weeping, he asked, "Can I see you, Rachel? Mama said I mustn't, but..." His face lifted and his lips began to tremble. He stretched his arms wide in silent appeal.

Rachel stood erect for a heartbeat longer, then slowly crouched down and nodded. She opened her arms just before he hurled his small body against her. "I know'd you was still my Rachel," he whispered as he clung to her. "They all said you forgot me but I *know'd* you didn't." Very quietly he began to weep again, this time in relief.

Rachel's throat had closed so tightly that she couldn't speak. There was something here, in the love of this child that touched her beyond reason or explanation. Though she had embraced few children in her lifetime, holding Charlie felt so pure and honest, so real that it seemed to unlock a place deep within that had never previously been opened. With Charlie's face pressing close she gently stroked his hair, and when his tears wet her cheek she didn't brush them away.

When he grew calmer, Rachel reached for the blanket that had fallen to the floor, scooted around to face the window, and wrapped the cover around them both. Over the top of Charlie's head she gazed up again and met the gaze of the stars. Charlie wiped his tears dry against her shoulder and snuggled into her warmth. Before long his breathing smoothed to the gentle rhythm of a comforted child's sleep.

"Oh, Charlie," Rachel murmured into his hair, "if you're real, then the rest must be too."

Unseen, Juliet stood in the doorway, her right hand over her mouth and her left clutching a fold in her apron. She watched Rachel cradling Charlie for a moment longer, then very quietly turned away and crept downstairs.

Rachel remained on the floor until her legs began to cramp, and then she rose with Charlie in her arms and carried him to her bed. In the faint light she watched him slumber beside her. The lump in her throat returned as she took in the way his long lashes brushed his small cheeks, his light hair feathered across his forehead, and his tiny mouth formed a perfect oval.

Without waking, Charlie reached out, found her long hair, and wrapped his hand around and around inside its tresses. Rachel smiled drowsily, and fell asleep without trying to free herself.

Rachel was just fastening her top button when she heard the clank of a pot on the stove below, and the sound caused her head to pound deeper and her stomach to rumble louder. These reactions were more than enough to decide that it was time for Charlie to be out of her bed, and she gently shook his shoulder, saying, "Charlie, it's morning."

Still lying on his side, he let out a squeaking murmur as he stretched, arching his back and tucking his heels up to meet his bottom, then opened his eyes and smiled with absolute devotion. Sitting up, he asked, "Why do you suppose it's such a wonderful-like day today?"

Marveling that such joy could manifest itself so early, Rachel returned his smile. "I don't know. Why do you think it is?"

"I don't know neither, but it surely is." He leaned out to give her a quick hug, bounced twice on the mattress, and hopped off the bed. Skipping across the floor, he waved back at her and said in a singsong voice, "Bye, Rachel."

With his disappearance, Rachel's smile slipped from her face. She knew she'd better get moving before the resolve she'd constructed during the night weakened. After many hours of mental struggle, she'd at last accepted that she had few options but to believe in this family, to believe that they were who they appeared to be and that they truly thought she was one of them. She would live in this house for the time being; after all, the Milfords seemed to be kind people who were more than willing to help her. It was deceitful, playing the role of their daughter, but wouldn't it be more hurtful to them if she simply left? And besides, it would be her best tactic for survival in this unfamiliar, inconvenient, remote, friendless and potentially dangerous place and time. She would do her best to fit in, and since it would be ridiculous to hope that any of them would accept the truth about her identity, for now at least she'd keep it to herself. Things were going to be hard enough without the Milfords thinking she'd permanently lost her mind.

So she intended to keep busy, and as soon as she could convince the family that she was healthy enough to leave them, she'd look for some kind of job in town. Maybe she'd even try working at the store for a while, where she would certainly learn quickly about this community.

Earlier, she'd mourned the absence of a hot shower, or any water at all, since the basin on the washstand was empty, and she'd slipped into the brown dress with reluctance. Now, she walked to the dresser with lingering hope and searched its drawers, intent on finding a toothbrush and toothpaste, but her hunt revealed nothing of the kind. She shoved the last drawer shut, feeling grubby and smelly from head to foot. Yet the chill in the room hurried her along and, picking up the brush, she began to battle her mass of hair that Charlie's hand had tangled into something not far removed from an eagle's nest.

Half-way down the stairs she hesitated and muttered, "Oh, damn!" at the realization that she had to face the outhouse again, and the idea was enough to make her gag. She started her feet moving again, however, and headed straight out the front door. With a discouraging glare she sidestepped the joyfully leaping dogs and, upon reaching her destination, entered without pausing. She left the tiny structure with a solid slam of the door and a feeling of satisfaction in her own fortitude.

As she approached the house she noticed with appreciation that the washbasin had been replenished with fresh water. She quickly made use of it, the bar of soap resting on a wooden shingle, and the drying cloth hanging on a peg. She'd glanced over her shoulder more than once as she washed, feeling a little like a fugitive from justice. Guessing that Juliet wouldn't be pleased that she'd left her room, especially without an escort, she listened to the family beginning to gather around the kitchen table on the other side of the wall. Pure luck must have kept her from bumping into any of them earlier. After drying her hands and smoothing wrinkles from her skirt a little longer than necessary, she straightened her spine, took a breath, and marched into the house by way of the back door.

Although she'd fixed her best smile firmly in place, her sudden appearance in the kitchen was greeted by dead silence, which didn't last long. Ezra, Bert, True, Esther, Kate, Maggie, and Charlie all stared up at her, some in surprise and others in concern. Charlie's gaze held triumphant joy. Kate let her spoon fall to the floor with a loud clatter. True and Bert both halted the spoons raised halfway to their mouths. Phillip hurried in carrying a teacup and small plate of toast, declaring, "Mama, she's not in her...", spotted Rachel, and added, "Well, there she is." Juliet turned from the stove to Phillip, holding a huge frying pan full of eggs, followed Phillip's gaze, and nearly dropped the skillet. Charlie broke the astonishment by piping up, "I *told* you she was all better."

This released a refrain of questions and shouts from the rest of the group. "She's up!" "How do you feel, Rachel?" "Come sit down, come sit down." "Over here, Rachel!" "Are you hungry?"

Trying to set the iron pan down amid the commotion, Juliet exclaimed, "Rachel! Honey, you shouldn't be up."

A little overwhelmed, Rachel attempted to subdue her Chicago accent to match the pronunciations of the family, and responded with,

"I feel just fine, really. May...may I join you?"

Bert, Juliet, Ezra and Esther exchanged worried looks, and Juliet asked, "Are you sure you should be up so soon?"

"Absolutely sure." In truth, Rachel felt far from absolute about anything, much less facing this family, though her expression gave few of her doubts away, and as she sat down on the long bench between Charlie and Esther and picked up a fork, she felt their eyes following her every movement. She glanced at Esther, who sat back on the bench because of her very pregnant torso. The young woman smiled warmly and Rachel remembered her own rudeness of the day before, pretending to be asleep to avoid their meeting. The concern Esther was trying to conceal seemed so genuine that Rachel returned the smile.

At last Juliet settled the skillet of eggs in the center of the table and stood with her hands on her hips as she tried to decide whether to order her daughter back to bed. She turned back to the stove and took down a platter of sliced bread from the shelf above the cooking surface, placing it amid the eggs, porridge, milk, jam, and butter. Standing for another moment to consider Rachel's presence, Juliet finally sighed and took her place at the table.

Everyone bowed their heads and made the Catholic sign of the cross before Bert led them in a prayer of thanks for God's blessings, and a petition for future guidance and protection. Maggie, sitting directly across from Rachel, noticed that she was fumbling to cross herself and faultering as she mumbled the prayer, so she began praying with impressive volume to cover for her sister. After the "Amen" but before the others lifted their heads, Rachel gave her a grateful glance.

Now, in contrast to their noisy greetings, everyone spoke in quiet tones, as if concerned about saying something to trouble Rachel. Food was offered to her first, and in quantities that would have been far too large even if her stomach hadn't been tied in a knot.

Charlie pressed so tightly against Rachel's side that she couldn't use her fork without leaning away from him. The child seemed to have forgotten his own hunger, content to beam up at her in possessive adoration, so she encouraged him to eat by taking a bite of her eggs and nodding at him. With this prompting, Charlie lifted his own fork, but every now and then he rested his head against her arm and patted her on the back. Strangely, this small gesture did comfort Rachel, as the rest of the family asked subtle questions and tried not to stare.

Kate, who'd been silently appraising Rachel for some time, asked, "Mama, since Rachel ain't up to many chores yet, would it be all right if we went hunting?"

Rachel choked on her bread. *Hunting?* She'd never shot anything more animate than a target on a firing range. Her Grandpa Simon had taken her to his gun club several times so she'd know something about handling firearms, just as he'd regularly taken her to a stable to learn how to ride a horse until she excelled at this skill, but that certainly didn't mean she was about to go traipsing or riding into the forest and start shooting away at wild animals. Then she remembered what she'd read in the newspaper about Indians threatening settlers, as well as some of the miners who evidently were more than happy to get drunk and aim their guns at people. Would it be men or animals that posed the graver threat if she and Kate were caught out there alone?

"Why, Kate," Esther answered sternly, "she's not going hunting today. She's got to rest for quite a spell before she takes to those hills."

Scowling at her older sister, Kate noisily attacked her porridge, which didn't seem to ruffle Esther's calm authority in the least. Much relieved, Rachel took up her own spoon and reflected that wandering in the mountains would certainly give her the lay of the land, but Esther was right; she didn't feel up to it this morning.

As the rest of the family continued eating and their words became fewer, Rachel felt that she should say something to reassure them. "I'd really like to help out while I'm... now that I'm better. I feel strong enough to be of some use." Seeing Kate's hopeful glance at her mother, Rachel added hastily, "Around the house, I mean."

Bert asked gently, "Do you remember anything more this morning, Rachel?"

"Yes, a few things," Rachel lied while looking directly into his eyes, but when nearby faces lit up with relieved joy, a surge of guilt hit her.

"What sort of things do you recall?" asked True earnestly. It was the first time he'd spoken, and he waited for her answer with an expression of almost painful anticipation.

"Well, things about each of you, True."

He gave his mother a look that said, "See, Mama, she's going to be fine."

This new falsehood fed Rachel's self-reproach until it took away what was left of her appetite, and she resected her fried egg until there was nothing but tiny pieces to scoot around her plate.

Unconvinced, Juliet said, "Doc Willis will be here before long to check on you, honey. Let's all wait and see what he has to say. When you're done with breakfast, I'd like you to lay back down 'til he comes."

Then, eliminating any remaining hope of gaining her freedom from the bedroom, Bert added, "Yes, that would be best. Kate, you and Maggie finish up and help your sister back upstairs. Once she's settled, you two can get started in the barn."

The girls and Rachel obediently headed for the stairs while Juliet and Esther gathered plates from the table.

At the top of the stairs Kate halted, stomped one foot, and grumped loudly, "It's going to be a fine day for hunting fool hens, too."

When Doc Willis arrived less than an hour later to examine Rachel, the performance that followed would have impressed any acting critic. With only the doctor as her audience Rachel used the information Maggie had provided to convince him of her returning memory, and although her wound was badly discolored, he was pleased that it was swollen only slightly and showed no sign of infection. Based on all of this, the doctor grandly pronounced that she might be able to leave her bed in a day or two, but absolutely no sooner.

Groaning inwardly, but seasoning her diction with the rustic words and inflections that she was already picking up, she tried to convince him to reduce her sentence, and failed utterly. When Doc Willis said good-bye and patted her on the head, she felt like biting his hand.

Much of that morning she felt like biting someone. Anyone. Although she tried to appear even-tempered and patient when family members came in with food or to keep her company, her restiveness was obvious. The day dragged on unrelentingly.

Having read the newspapers until she could recite much of them, she asked with little hope for any books the family might own. To her surprise and relief she was given their entire small library, including a bible, four varying levels of *McGuffey's Reader*, *The Last of the Mohicans*, *A Tale of Two Cities*, *Uncle Tom's Cabin*, and an 1862 guidebook for families traveling from Missouri to Oregon.

The last of these she opened first, wondering what the Milfords had gone through to get here, and question after question came to mind with the turning of each page. Why had they left their prior home? When had they arrived here? Was there even a town then? Who had built their home?

Against orders, at mid-afternoon she left her bedroom and made her way quietly down to the kitchen where the aroma of stewing chicken rose with comforting richness. She stood in the doorframe and watched Juliet, cracking eggs into a giant ceramic bowl. Juliet looked over at her, but before she had a chance to speak Rachel asked, "What are you making?"

With no hint of castigation, Juliet said, "Noodles, honey, your favorite. Come sit down if you're in a mood to talk."

Peeking into the bowl and noting the large number of eggs, Rachel asked, "How many eggs go into them?"

"Well, today I'll use fourteen."

"Fourteen eggs?"

"They come dear, I know, but after you got hurt your pa bought us several dozen and a couple of hens. For noodles I always count how many folks will be eating, and add maybe two or three more, and that's how many eggs I use. Do you remember what else goes in the dough?"

Rachel sat down and offered a safe guess. "Flour."

"Yes, dear. We add enough flour to make it nice and stiff, and some salt for flavor." As Juliet spoke she stepped to a lower cabinet and tilted it open at the top, scooped out a bowlful of flour, brought it to the table, and mixed it and a small palm-full of salt into the eggs. She then kneaded firmly before liberally dusting the table with flour and rolling the dough into a thin circle at least a yard in diameter.

"If you're not too busy, will you please tell me about when we first came here. I want to remember it all."

Juliet paused to study her. "Only if you'll go on back to bed when I finish these noodles. You've been up quite a lot already and you look tired."

"Yes, I will."

"Well, then," Juliet said, dusting the surface of the dough with a little more flour and then sitting down across from Rachel. "I guess I ought to start back a ways; back when we lived in Iowa on the farm your Grandpa and Grandma Milford started up. Uncle Giles, your pa's little brother, he lived there too. It wasn't near as big as this house, but we had good land and enough water, and you kids were born there fine and strong. Then in ''61, your Uncle Giles joined up to fight for the Union. That picture by the fireplace is him in his uniform."

The *Union*, thought Rachel, trying to grasp the realities of this era.

"Giles was gone some eight months before we saw him again. He came back in the middle of a January snowstorm, I remember, and he was bad sick. He told us they had camped for days and days in the swamps of Arkansas, with bad food and worse water. A good number of his company had died, and they'd never even seen the enemy.

"We cared for him the best we could, but with both our doctors away at the war we couldn't do much, and Giles never moved his left side again. He suffered from fever one minute and chills the next, and it was almost a month before the Lord took him to a better place. Your poor grandma couldn't stand losing her youngest son, and she died just two weeks later." Juliet paused, her gaze distant as her mind looked back.

"All of us were mighty scared your grandpa would follow them to their graves. He hardly talked or ate for weeks." She looked at Rachel then. "You were the only one who could rouse him, now and again. Then one day in April he came home and told us he'd up and sold the farm. Said we were moving west and we'd best start packing up because we had to leave in *three days*.

"Land sakes, that day your pa and grandpa had quite a row, one of the few they ever had, as far as I know. Your pa was mad as a hornet, kept saying Grandpa ought to have talked it out with him first, but once he got over not being part of the deciding I think he liked the idea of coming west." Juliet tucked back a strand of hair, leaving a small blotch of flour on her left cheek.

"I'd lost my folks and my little sister, Millie, a few years before to yellow fever, but I had to leave behind two sisters and a brother that I thought the world of. It was a pure struggle saying good-bye to them. I wrote every day on the trail, telling them about what we saw, but then one day it rained so hard that water got into my letterbox and ruined them before I got the chance to send them off." She sighed and smiled gently at Rachel, "But I guess I've written enough letters since we got here to make up for the soggy ones they didn't get. Your pa spoils me the way he lets me spend good money on paper, ink, and mail charges."

Rachel's eyes followed Juliet as she stood, picked up a huge carving knife, bisected the circle of dough, and placed one half on top of the other to form a half-moon. Next, she cut this semi-circle in two lengthwise, set one of these sections atop the first, and repeated this process until she'd created two long, many-layered stacks of dough. She then began slicing one thin row of noodles at a time from a thin end of a stack.

Rachel asked, "What was it like coming out here?"

"What was it like? Well, there were only seven wagons in the train we started out in, but we joined up with a sizable train. Things went fine for a while. The first trouble we had was when our poor dog, Yip, got caught under a wheel on our seventh day out of St. Joe and Grandpa had to shoot him. He was a good dog, Old Yip. That made me even more scared that Charlie might fall out of the wagon and get run over. He was just starting to walk steady, and it was quite a chore to keep him away from the cattle and the horses and the cook fires. We carried him, mostly, you and me."

Rachel kept her face blank when Juliet glanced up to read if any of her account was triggering a memory. "Please go on," Rachel coaxed, so Juliet nodded and resumed her slicing.

"Farther down the trail we had a hard time finding grass that was close to good water, because of all the earlier trains, so we camped wherever there was grass and hiked for water. Game got scarce too, but our Lord always showed us a way."

"Did you see any Native Americans along the trail?"

"Any what, honey?"

"Any Indians, I mean?"

"Oh yes, lots of Indians." Juliet's brow furrowed. "Some that I wish we'd never seen nor heard of. At first we saw only squaws of white men, traders and trappers mostly, but then we started seeing more and more braves. Some were friendly and even real helpful to us, but trouble had been stirring between the settlers and the Indians long before we ever left Iowa. We'd heard something about it, of course, but we didn't have any notion of how bad it was.

"When we'd nearly reached the Snake River, some men from the train a few hours ahead of ours came racing up saying Indians had killed two of their party and stolen most of their livestock. I was scared, but not near as scared as when your pa lit out with several of our men to go after the stolen animals. He came back several hours later, but not all the men were so lucky. Three more from that other train got killed, five in total, and about that many Indians."

"Good lord," said Rachel.

"Yes, honey, He watched over your pa that day. But when we pulled up with the other train, it was a sad thing to watch those folks lay five men in their graves. Their families were beside themselves, grieving and not knowing what they'd do to survive. And then we found out it wasn't just Indians who struck that train, maybe no Indians at all, 'cause folks said they saw white men with that bunch, and even heard some words in clear English. Red or white, they were killers and thieves.

"We saw graves all along that road, most brought on by sickness and accidents. I remember hearing about two new mothers in that same unlucky train that lost the five men. They'd died the week before the Indian attack, one from childbirth and one in a stampede. Their little babies died within a day or so of each other. Then a few days later, we came across the bodies of three other white men. They'd been... roughly treated, by Indians it seemed." Her hands stilled and her gaze grew thankful. "That's one thing I'm *glad* you don't remember, Rachel. It was a sight nobody would want to hold on to."

She shook her head. "But, to me, even the deaths of those poor men weren't the saddest things that happened along the trail, maybe because we didn't see them die." Juliet frowned. "I shouldn't be talking about such things right now. I can tell you the rest another time."

"Oh please, I want to know what it was like," Rachel said earnestly.

Juliet considered as she separated the cut noodles with her fingers and spread their wavy lengths into an even larger circle to dry. She sat down again, and continued, "When we came to Three Island Crossing on the Snake River, there was supposed to be a ferry but it was gone. So we had to decide whether to cross the Snake without one, or take the southern route, which we'd been told had little water or feed for the animals. Late as we were, we didn't think we had much choice, and we took our chances with that river.

"Our wagon master, Captain Russell, he swam his horse back and forth until he found a good route. The first two wagons made it over without losing anything but one big kettle, and we were next in line. We'd borrowed three riding horses, so we had five in all. Your pa took one of the loaned horses while True and you rode the other two. You and your brother were given the job of holding the ropes at the back corners of the wagon to keep it from tipping. Esther and Phillip were riding our two horses, with Maggie and Kate hanging on behind them. Little Charlie was right behind my seat in the wagon, packed in snug between blankets and trunks.

"The going between the first two islands wasn't so bad, but that third stretch of river was long and deep. Captain Russell moved slow and easy off the last bit of land, and Phillip and Esther brought their horses up to follow behind him. Then your pa led the wagon in. As the water got deeper, I held my breath and prayed, and worked to keep the oxen headed straight, but when the team had to start swimming, I felt the wagon tip a little before it steadied. You and True were pulling with all your might to keep the wagon stable, but all of a sudden his line broke free of the upstream corner and the wagon came around with the current. True yelled a warning and you just barely got your horse clear. I looked back, scared senseless that you'd been swept downstream, but there you were, staring back at me with your teeth clenched tight, as if to say no river was going to take you. I'll never forget that look. You were still holding your left hand high to keep that horse's head above water, and hanging tight onto the wagon line, and that wagon didn't roll over. I prayed even harder the rest of the way across, keeping watch on your pa and the kids out ahead and my ears cocked for you and True behind, and feeling Charlie's little hands clinging tight to the back of my skirt."

Her eyes were shining as she continued to hold Rachel's gaze. "I was never more proud of you kids than I was that day. Not one of you said a word about being afraid. I was purely thankful that your pa had taught you all to be strong swimmers, but that old river had the power to take us just the same. I'll never stop thanking the Almighty we made it across."

Juliet's grateful smile faded, and she turned her eyes to the window, focused on the past. When she spoke again her voice was grave. "The next wagon got across too, and then it was the Marshall family's turn. They had three little kids in the wagon with Sarah, the littlest one even younger than Charlie. They made it through the worst of the river. But just when the team started to find its footing up the bank, that current caught the tail of the wagon and hauled it back, dragging the team and Mr. Marshall with it. Sam Saunders tried to stop it and he was pulled in too. That river washed them away in seconds. Captain Russell got downstream in time to grab a little girl before she was swept out of reach, but we never could bring her around. That whole family gone, and Mr. Saunders with them. The only one we could bury was that dear child. Ruth. Ruth was her name."

Juliet stared at the noodle-strewn tabletop for a moment before she looked up and found her voice again. "The wagons still on the other side didn't try to cross. They took the southern road. We never saw them again."

Searching Juliet's face for emotional scars and bitterness, Rachel was moved to genuine admiration when she found instead a sad yet resigned acceptance. Juliet's next words gave Rachel an even clearer view into this woman's soul. "Honey, hard and sad as that trip was, we saw good things along the way, like wild, proud creatures we had never heard of before, and a sky and mountains so big and full of beauty that they took a body's breath away. We're stronger for all we went through, too. Every mile tested us, but we made it here, and this place is our reward."

Beneath the gaze of those shining eyes, Rachel couldn't bring herself to speak, and the silence lengthened between them. Finally, Juliet reached out and patted her hand a moment before Charlie skipped into the kitchen, stopped, and tilted his head questioningly at the two women. Juliet pushed her chair away from the table and scooped up her son. "Well, that was more talking than I've done in quite a spell." When Rachel still said nothing, she added, "You best be off to bed now, young lady."

Rachel didn't protest. She stood still reflecting on all that Juliet had helped bring her family through. A strong and uncommon impulse seized Rachel, to physically express an emotion, to walk around this table and embrace Juliet in gratitude for what she'd shared, but she held back. Juliet seemed to read Rachel's halted intention, and her expression became welcoming, hopeful. Rachel only offered a small smile, saying, "Thank you, for telling me," before turning toward the stairs. Charlie claimed her hand, and she didn't protest as he came along.

9

Kate cocked an eyebrow at Rachel that conveyed a suspicion her older sister might be worse off than she'd imagined. "You remember how to eat and how to get dressed, and even how to read. How could you have forgot how to milk a cow?"

"Kate," Phillip reproached, "she can't remember lots of things. You know that."

"But not even to know how to *milk a cow*?" Kate muttered.

After three days of inactivity, each filled with far too much time to torture herself with supposition, confusion, and frustration, Rachel had insisted on being allowed to help with the work around the farmstead. Juliet had reluctantly agreed, with the strict condition that she take on only light chores. The second milking of each day was undertaken when the children, all but True and Charlie, returned home from school, and this afternoon Rachel stood in the barn holding a milk bucket while trying to hide her bemusement at the interplay between the children, who obviously considered the task at hand to be one of the elemental duties of mankind.

"I'll show you, Rachel," Maggie offered eagerly, holding out her hand to relieve Rachel of the pail.

"You?" Kate scoffed. "You're only eight years old. Why should you show her?"

"I can show her as good as anybody," Maggie maintained, sticking her lower lip in Kate's direction. "I've been milking for almost my whole life."

"Go on and let Maggie show her," said Phillip.

Rachel jumped in. "Kate, perhaps you can show me how to do something else a little later."

"Why, all right," said Kate, brightening, and Rachel remembered belatedly that Kate had proposed days earlier to take her hunting. Great.

Maggie tugged on Rachel's sleeve, drawing her to a milking stool that she'd placed near one of the three cows tied over a long hay trough. The little girl took a spare milking pail from the corner, upended it, and set it next to Rachel's stool, motioning her nearer. "Millie's our easiest cow, so we'll start with her."

Rachel approached and took up her position, silently thanking her Grandpa Simon for taking her to the farm section of the Lincoln

Park Zoo when she was a child, just to show her what farm animals actually look like. She told herself several times how reasonably comfortable she felt sitting so close to the sharp hooves of this huge beast.

"There now, Millie, there now," crooned Maggie, patting the cow. Millie glanced back at them with huge brown eyes and, finding nothing to cause alarm, resumed her munching. "Just scoot that pail right under her teats. That's right, now watch how I circle my fingers around the top of a teat and squeeze down toward the pail. See? Now you try." After a couple of Rachel's clumsy attempts, Kate exclaimed, "Rachel, you got to *squeeze* as you pull down. Millie won't mind, she *wants* to be milked. Just squeeze the teat, for heaven's sake."

"All right, Kate, that's enough," Phillip said tightly. "You got chores of your own to do and you best get to them."

"But I was just..." Kate started.

"Get moving," Phillip ordered, giving her a little shove. Kate drew her arm back and swung at him. Expecting such a reaction, Phillip dodged her fist and sprinted toward the door. "If you don't get to tending the garden right quick," he shot back, "Mama's going to hear about you bothering Rachel."

Kate glowered at the empty space Phillip had vacated, then at Maggie, then at Rachel, then at the cow. With her signature stamp of one foot, she turned and clomped out of the barn.

Rachel, who had somehow managed to keep a straight face, resumed her efforts with Millie, appreciative that the animal possessed a good deal more patience than Kate. Progress was gradually made, and when the pail was half-full, Rachel slid the bucket from beneath Millie and beamed at Maggie over the warm, rich bounty of their labor.

"Imagine how much milk she'll give after her calf is weaned," said Maggie.

It was then that Rachel noticed Lewis approaching from the far corner of the barn. He came close enough to peer down into the milk pail, and smiled, before Maggie asked proudly, "See what Rachel did, Lewis?"

"Yes, miss. I sure enough do," he said, and looked at Rachel for the first time.

Rachel stood up and started to raise a hand to shake with his but then recalled that they were supposed to be well acquainted already. She lowered her arm as inconspicuously as possible, and said, "Hello, Lewis. How are you?"

"I be just fine, Miss Rachel. It's mighty good to see you up and about. I been right worried, along with your folks. " There was a southern drawl and slow gentleness to his words, and his voice was as deep and rich as a bassoon's. Although he was not tall, his shoulders and arms were thickly muscled, making the large saw he clasped in one broad hand look undersized. His skin was darkest ebony, and his broad nose and full mouth accentuated deep-set eyes.

"Thank you for your concern." Rachel said, wondering where he'd come from, and if his life had been darkened by slavery. Glancing at the saw, she asked, "Are you building something?"

"More fixin' than buildin', Miss Rachel. I'm settin' up to work on that old sluice box, and I got to get the riffles wove and set just right."

Maggie added helpfully, "For the gold mining."

"Oh, I see," Rachel said. Then, hoping to receive a more direct answer than anyone in the family had provided, she asked, "Say, Lewis, how far away is the nearest big city?"

"Big city, Miss Rachel? Why, Idaho City's got nigh onto seven thousand folks."

"But if people wanted to see an even larger city, where would they go?"

"I do believe we got more folks than Denver or Portland, but San Francisco's some bigger. That would be a mighty hard trip though, what with bad roads, and no regular stage line, and maybe even trouble with Indians. Then there's that high, high pass, where them Donner folks had such a terrible time."

The *Donner* party? Rachel remembered with suppressed aversion the story of how those poor people had resorted to cannibalism when trapped by winter snows, and they must have been far better prepared than she was to attempt such a journey. "Of course. Thank you, Lewis."

He nodded and smiled down at Maggie. "You doin' good work, Miss Maggie." Picking up a heavy box of tools, he hefted it onto his shoulder and headed out the door.

"We'd best finish with Millie and get on to the other cows," Maggie said. "Mama will be so happy that you remember how to milk, and it'll be no time before you can do all your old chores." Rachel silently moaned, but she was careful not to spill a drop of her prize as she moved the bucket and stool over to the next cow.

After they finished the milking, Rachel was allowed to do no more than sweep the lower floor of the house before Juliet ordered her back to bed. As much as Rachel yearned for the freedom to explore her surroundings, she realized that she really did need some time in a peaceful place where her mind could relax, not to recover from her injury, as Juliet believed, but to accept all that had happened and evaluate all that might lie ahead.

She'd quickly learned that privacy was an extremely rare commodity in this noisy, bustling household, whose members seemed unaware of personal comfort ranges. The Milford children came and went between each other's rooms without a thought, and usually without so much as a knock. Two mornings earlier Kate had barged into Rachel's room just as she was lifting off her nightgown, and even with the whole family astir Kate had left the door wide open. Luckily, no one but Maggie had passed by before Rachel, clutching her nightgown to her chest, roared, "Shut that door! Haven't you ever heard of privacy?" Startled by the outburst, Maggie had paused to pull the door closed while Kate turned with wide eyes and said, "Well, sakes, Rachel! What's the matter with you this morning?"

After that episode, Rachel had made a discreet search of the house and discovered that the only locks to be found were the bolts at the front and back doors. *It's a damn good thing there's a latch on the outhouse*, she comforted herself. Things being as they were, from then on she wedged a chair up against her doorknob before changing her clothes. Every night Charlie crept into her room, and each morning she awoke to find him sleeping soundly beside her with his arm secured to her hair like an anchor. She'd tried tightly braiding her hair before going to bed but he always worked it loose, sometimes without even waking her.

Now, lying on her bed alone for a change, she again searched her memory for details about this period, but came up with little that was helpful. The hardships of war, slavery, and everyday life weighed on her mind, and she allowed herself to consider the possibility of influencing the events of this small community as well as those outside it. Could she use what she knew of the future to reduce the tragedies and injustices of this time, or even just some of the inconveniences? And if so, *should* she, when the consequences could be grave? What, for example, might happen if Lincoln's assassination could be prevented? But how, when her knowledge was so limited? She decided at last that she must learn a great deal more before taking any action. And, as she was gathering this knowledge, she might also discover how to return to her real home, where she was needed and accepted for who she truly was. This hope she would not abandon.

The next morning Rachel followed the sound of Lewis' humming toward the barn, stopping just outside the door to listen. Without recognizing the tune, its sliding tones and rhythm spoke to her of painful times and deep spirituality. She entered and found him sitting on the ground carefully weaving a pile of thin round sticks into a wicker screen. An empty breakfast plate rested on a bale of hay at his back.

He started to rise but she motioned for him to remain seated. "Mornin', Miss Rachel."

She smiled and sat down cross-legged across from him, her long skirt covering even her shoes. "I hope I'm not interrupting your work."

"No, miss. I can talk and work both when I've a mind to."

"What are you making? You said it was something for a sluice box?"

He seemed pleased to explain as he continued weaving. "Yes, the riffles. We just set them down in the sluice, pour a little quicksilver in, add lots of dirt and water, and we catch us some gold."

"You use quicksilver? Mercury?"

"I never did hear it called that before, but you got to have it so the gold dust stays put under the riffles."

"Oh, and how do you get the gold out once it's under the riffles?"

"We scoop up the amalgam, that's the gold mixed in with the quicksilver, we scoop it up and strain it through a sturdy cloth. Then we heat it over a fire to melt the quicksilver out." She watched the movements of his competent hands until they stilled, and he asked kindly, "How you feelin', Miss Rachel?"

"Well," she started, but a lie simply wouldn't form under the concerned scrutiny of his gaze, and she surprised herself by saying, "I feel lost most of the time."

Lewis nodded as if he understood. "I reckon I'd feel the same if my recollections had got turned 'round. Would it help to talk some?"

"I'd prefer to listen rather than talk. I'd like to hear all about you, even about when you were small."

"Now, Miss Rachel, I don't see how me talkin' would be of any use. I generally never talk about times before I come to be here."

"If you're willing to tell me, I truly want to know."

"Mine wasn't always a good life, and you might not like what I was to tell."

"Please, Lewis."

He watched her for a second or two, pondering what to reveal. "About my boyhood, well, the marks on my body tell a good deal, maybe better than words. You seen them marks many a time, every time your Pa and True and me work shirtless in the heat."

"I don't remember any marks."

He emptied his palms and slowly rubbed them together, and without saying more he unbuttoned the cuff of his left sleeve and rolled it up. Frowning doubtfully, he bent and lifted his forearm so that its surface was plainly visible.

Rachel's stomach constricted, and she whispered, "You were branded, Lewis."

The scar was old and its edges had stretched with maturity, but the letters BSJ stood out with ghastly clarity. "They burned this into me when I was ten years old. Massa's initials." He lowered his gaze. "I was twenty-one when I lit out, and after two long years travelin' I made my way here. I told your folks about me runnin', but it didn't seem to matter none, not to them."

Two long years traveling, Rachel silently repeated. What had happened to him during those years, and what had he resorted to in order to survive? She asked him nothing more.

"I hope you don't think less of me, Miss Rachel, now I told you."

"No, Lewis! I would have escaped too, at any cost!"

He lifted his face, relief filling his eyes before the hint of a smile appeared. "I'm right glad of that. You know, Miss Rachel, you have a mighty uncommon family. I never met white folks like your mama and pa, or you kids neither, before I come here. Good as you all was to me from the start, you scared me a little, especially your mama. She acted like I was as white as her own kids, still does, and she still gets riled at me for knowin' I ain't. It's a mystery whether we'll ever come to a meetin' of the minds about some things."

Rachel pointed at the empty plate on the hay bale. "Like eating with the family?"

His smile broadened. "Yes'm, like them kind of things." After a moment, his face grew curious. "I trust you don't mind my sayin' so, but somethin' I can't figure out is why you talk some different since you got hurt. Lots of the words don't sound just the same, and some are words I ain't never heard you say before. Why do you suppose that might be?"

"It is strange, isn't it, Lewis?" was all she said.

Studying her even more closely, a little too closely for her comfort, he said slowly, "Yes, miss."

Bert opened the barn door and approached, a rifle resting on his shoulder. Lewis asked in surprise, "You fixin' to go huntin', Mr. Bert, when we have but a few good weeks of water left for workin' the boxes?"

"Sometimes, Lewis, a man has to leave the diggings for an hour or two. Rachel, how would you like to stretch your legs? Even your mama says it might be good for you." When he noticed Rachel's glance shift to his rifle, he added, "I'm just bringing this along in case something crosses our path."

"But if it would put you behind in your work..." she stalled.

"The mining's gone better than I thought it might most of this spring, even with the snow staying so late. And this rain lately will keep the creek from drawing low any time soon."

True and Phillip suddenly burst into the barn, jostling each other and coming near to inspect what progress Lewis had made with the riffles. Rachel, much preferring to listen to Lewis than traipse off into the forest, nevertheless rose and brushed straw from her skirt. To Lewis, she said, "I appreciate your talking to me, about everything. Thank you."

"Yes'm," he said with a nod so deep it was almost a bow, then picked up another wooden strip and resumed his weaving.

As the others turned to the door, Bert halted his younger son. "Phillip, you best stay here and help look after things. Your grandpa could use some help laying out the new ditches."

"Yes, sir," he said, his disappointment obvious. As Rachel left, she heard Phillip complain to Lewis in an undertone, "How come it's always True that gets to go with Pa when..." The rest was lost as they walked farther from the barnyard and started up the hill behind the homestead.

It had rained for a portion of every day since she'd arrived, and now the fallen pine needles and muddy track made the going slippery. Her long skirt became a problem almost immediately, causing her to stumble up and down the steeper paths Bert chose. The thought of swapping the cursed skirt for a comfortable pair of jeans tormented her until she was sorely tempted to grab the hem of her skirt and jam it into her waistband. The only thing that stopped her was picturing the shock on Bert's and True's faces. So she grumbled silently, and soon added thick socks and a stout pair of hiking boots to her list of wishes.

Her sporadic attendance at aerobic classes had done little to prepare her for the pace of the two ahead, who apparently assumed she could rival a mountain goat in stamina and agility. The men climbed on and on unbothered by the mud, the incline, or the thin air. With every step she grew more determined to keep them from knowing the effort she was making, subduing her panting and slapping a contented expression on her face each time one of them glanced back to check on her. She told herself more than once that she was managing to stay up with them *fairly* well, even in this abominable skirt.

When they came to a level stretch, Rachel glanced from side to side with growing edginess. At the slightest noise she imagined hungry bears or mountain lions, murderous miners, or Indians who tortured and scalped. Her own scalp began to prickle and she looked at True, who carried the rifle, for reassurance. Kate had said he was an excellent shot, and he certainly appeared to be relaxed as he and Bert scanned the trail and surrounding area, listening with apparent pleasure to the sounds of the woods. Yet after each of these brief halts, they resumed their walk without spotting either game or predator. By the time they reached the second summit, the hem of her skirt was weighing her down with accumulated mud and she was panting heavily.

Casting a broad smile at the horizon, then tilting his face toward the sun, Bert declared, "What a fine spring day we've been given to warm us." He took in a few full breaths as he surveyed the woodlands. "You can almost feel the forest waking up," he went on cheerfully. "And listen to the birds singing their hearts out." He turned to Rachel and noticed her red cheeks. "Here, now," he said with sudden concern as he strode over to her. She tried to offer him an undaunted smile, but he stood protectively close and gave her a couple of gentle pats on the small of her back. "Let's catch our breath for a minute or two. Why, I'm clean winded."

When her lungs calmed a bit, Rachel followed Bert's example and raised her head to draw in the open vista. The mountains to the east, the range she'd first glimpsed on the drive to the Milfords' place, presented their glorious heights and wild, dominating beauty even more impressively from this promontory. Captivated anew, Rachel relaxed enough to wonder, and then to ask, "What was it like when you… when *we* first arrived?"

Bert leaned against a massive granite boulder and motioned Rachel toward a shorter rock close by. "Come sit down, honey, and we'll talk a spell."

Rachel willingly complied.

Bert started, "We got to Idaho City about a year and a half ago, only the settlement was called Bannock back then and it wasn't much of a town. You see, we hadn't planned on settling here. We were on our way to Oregon when we met up with a group of miners headed here. After your mama cooked them a meal they told us about how three men named Splawn, Grimes, and Fogus found gold a few months before. They said the basin had more gold than any place they'd ever heard of, even California, and that caught my interest. Grandpa's too. Your mother and you weren't too keen on being gold miners but we decided we ought to see if it was a chance of a lifetime. We turned our wagon out of the train and the other emigrants went on without us. There weren't any roads to speak of, so we traded our wagon, one team of oxen, and a fine horse for a pack train to bring us to Bannock.

"It was even a wilder place than it is now," he continued, and True grunted in agreement. "I had to do some talking to get your mama to stay, once she'd seen it for herself."

"Did you have much trouble?"

"Not too much. A fair number of the best claims were already taken, but your grandpa and me staked out a good stretch off Mores Creek just south of town. We threw together a cabin barely big enough for all of us, and then we set to work. There weren't many families settled here yet. Your mother, your aunt, you, and your sisters were some of the few women, and I always made sure you had a rifle close by."

"Yeah," True put in with a grin. "There were lots more hurdy gurdies than family women, and Mama sure didn't want you girls spending time with the hurdies."

Remembering Maggie's use of the term, Rachel asked, "Who were the hurdy gurdies?"

Bert frowned at True but he let the boy answer. "Dance hall girls, but not like the saloon women that, uh…go upstairs with the men. The hurdies mostly just dance."

Bert's displeasure at True mentioning such things to his sister suddenly shifted to an uneasy speculation about his son's activities in town.

"Pa," True said in a wounded voice, catching his father's look, "you know I'm only telling what I've heard, *not* what I know first-hand."

"Just the same," said Bert, mostly reassured, "I don't think that's what Rachel is wanting to know." He gave True one more perusal then turned his attention back to Rachel. "The town already had plenty of saloons in those first days, and they were lively day and night. Most of the miners lucky enough to find gold spent it as fast as they could dig it up. They were mainly single men, living in tents or shabby cabins." He chuckled softly and added, "A good number of the shacks caved in when the miners dug up the ground around them, and that still happens from time to time. Our cabin was small but a little better made than most, and the saloon noise was not quite so loud there."

Rachel asked, "Did you find gold right away?"

"Yes, we were lucky, it was a good claim and we worked mighty hard. Winter was coming on fast and even though we didn't know a hoot about mining, it didn't take long to get a rocker built and find some color."

"A rocker, like the sluice box Lewis is working on?"

True offered, "A bit. It looks something like a baby cradle. A miner scoops dirt into it, dumps in water, and rocks it back and forth to sift the gold through the riffle screen at the bottom."

"Anyhow," Bert went on, "lucky for us, Grandpa, True, and I soon found enough gold to buy our land outside of town and what building supplies we needed, and we left off digging just 'til we got the house and barn up. Those were mighty long days of tough work even with the welcome help of some men from town, which your mama repaid with her good cooking. We only had a few more weeks of digging before the snows came in earnest, but we had picked another good spot and we made more money as miners than we would have done in two or three years of farming."

The shadow of a falcon passed overhead, and they all watched, fascinated, as it soared in a wide, graceful circle.

"Tell her about all the shooting, Pa," True said, then kept right on talking before Bert had a chance. "We could hear yelling and guns firing all through those early nights. It scared Mama and Aunt Faith something terrible, thinking a stray bullet might find one of us kids. And Mama was always worried after hearing about any accident around town or at the workings, from falls and dynamite and such." He turned to Bert and asked, "You remember that time a miner got his head cut clean off when he got in too close to a belted saw, Pa?"

"True," Bert huffed with disapproval, taking up the story. "I do remember how high the cost of food and lumber was. I thought of selling our last cattle, but they were so thinned down from the trip that they weren't worth much as beef. Besides, I wanted them for breeding stock since I had no intention of mining for the rest of my life. Your mama came up with a way to bring in extra money, though, baking bread and pies to sell to the miners, and you were a big help too. You've been a good cook ever since you were a tiny thing. You two and Aunt Faith must have made thirty loaves a day, and maybe a dozen pies when you could find the filling."

Rachel smiled at him, knowing she truly did have talent as a cook, although her experience and training leaned toward French gourmet.

"With the price of our own supplies being so high," said Bert, "we had to ask shameful prices for those baked goods. Even so, the miners bought them before they ever had a chance to cool off."

True said, "The miners were always polite to Mama and you, but she saw how some of them started pining for you and Esther. She wanted to get us all out of town so bad she would have moved almost anywhere, and she was right glad that day you came home, Pa, and said you'd found our new land."

Bert's eyes lightened. "If it hadn't been so cold the day she set her eyes on it, she would have been content to sleep right out under the trees. She was that taken with the place." Addressing Rachel, he said, "It didn't take long to sell our old claim and the cabin in town, but the new owners had to agree on waiting for us to move 'til late spring, since the new house wasn't built yet."

True picked up the story again. "Our new house is at least four times the size of that cabin, and we were all mighty glad to get settled in, and then Lewis found us. Mama likes to claim that it was your baking that brought Lewis to our door, just by setting a couple of pies on the window ledge to cool. Says she came out of the house to call us in to dinner and saw Lewis standing there, breathing in the smell of those pies. When he noticed Mama, he started to head down the road, but Mama called out and brought him back to the field to meet Pa and Grandpa and me. She told us she'd found a hand who needed work as much as we needed a hand."

"And did you like him right off?" Rachel asked, grinning along with the two men.

"We all did," admitted Bert. "We talked awhile, then we all shook hands and brought Lewis inside. Your mama sat him down at the table, set a plate and fork in front of him, cut one of those pies, and pushed it almost under his nose. You were there too, and you told him he was welcome to eat the whole thing, but he stared at that pie for the longest time before he picked up the fork and set to eating. He shook his head after almost every bite, like he couldn't believe how good it was. And, you know, that is the only time your mama has ever got that man to sit at our table."

Rachel wondered aloud, "How long ago was this?"

"Let's see; September, I think," said Bert. "Yes, and I wish he'd come to us sooner. We surely could have used his strength building the house and barn. But then, the miners we hired were in bad need of the work, too, since their claims didn't pay. Lewis did come in time to help get food stored up for that first winter outside of town, which we sorely needed. He taught us how to dry and jerk the meat we hunted, and this spring he gave us a powerful hand clearing land so we could put in our small crop."

"They must have been very demanding times," said Rachel.

"We made out all right, better than most. I'll never forget the day that supply train showed up in town with caged chickens strapped to the sides of every mule. I'm not a man who's careless with his money, but it had been quite a spell since we'd tasted chicken and I was sorely tempted to pay the man's outlandish price. Your mama said wait, and she was right, so we waited. When the next chickens showed up a little later, we bought eight hens and a rooster with the last of your mama's baking money. Lord, what a treat it was to have our own fresh eggs again. Then about a month ago the danged coyotes got into our hen house, and now we are back to buying chickens and eggs until those chicks I bought last Saturday get big enough to lay."

"Will this be your home for a long time?"

"Yes, if God's willing. With the gold getting a little scarcer, some of the miners are already moving on, and when the road from Wallula gets cleared, more will go. New families are coming in all the time and civilization is taking hold. Henry Greathouse says the first stage ought to be crossing the Blues soon, and won't that be something, being able to take the stage all that way in just four days? The mail and all kinds of supplies will be coming through a heap easier, too."

Rachel had no idea where Wallula was, although she remembered seeing the name in the newspaper Juliet had given her. She presumed that the Blues were a range of mountains, but she couldn't guess their location, so she had no way of surmising where a person could go once she reached Wallula.

"Do you have a map of this area?" she asked.

"Why, no, but we might get one from the newspaper office," Bert said. "I'm sure one of the Butlers would allow us to borrow one. And you could study it all you like, Rachel."

"That would be fine."

"Fine," Bert echoed. "Now then, I'm highly unused to doing so much talking. Are you ready to head back, honey?"

"Yes, but may I ask one more question?"

"Go right on ahead."

"I've been wondering, there was a man in town who seemed to know me. Stan was his name. Who is he exactly?"

Her question hung in the air for several moments. Finally, Bert said with discomfort, "It might be best for you to ask your mother about Stan, and I'd wait until you're feeling better and your mama's sitting down before you do the asking."

Rachel looked over at True, who stared at his boots as if they'd suddenly turned a captivating shade of blue. Before she could say anything further Bert took the rifle from his son, hoisted it to his shoulder, and strode down the trail at a pace that didn't allow chatter. True followed three steps behind him, and Rachel, not about to be left behind to face whatever hid in the forest, untangled her skirt from her legs with a sharp tug, lifted the hem clear of her feet, and sprinted after them.

10

As the shade of dusk descended, Juliet's voice rose from downstairs. "Rachel, honey, will you come down and talk awhile?" Having just mended a tear in True's shirt, and surprised herself to have done an adequate job of it, Rachel was more than willing to set the remaining pile of clothes aside. At first content to be a spectator of her sewing, Charlie had been growing restless in the waning light, and he hummed as he marched down the stairs by her side. The moment Juliet sat down in her rocking chair, he curled himself into his mother's lap, and Rachel took the bench near the fire.

Savoring the quiet crackle of the logs, no one spoke right away. Juliet began to rock, smiled gently at Rachel, and turned her face to the dancing flames.

Observing the pair of them, Rachel mused that the Milford children seemed to possess a form of radar that informed them whenever Juliet was about to take to her rocking chair. Charlie, being the youngest, usually got to her first, but Maggie sometimes managed to outmaneuver her little brother. Even the older children sensed when their mother had finished cleaning the kitchen or chores in the yard, because they generally gathered around her within minutes of her appearance in the front room. Rachel wondered how long it would take this evening for the rest of them to discover that their mother was temporarily immobile.

Juliet interrupted these thoughts by gazing at her fondly with the glow of the fire reflected in her eyes, her arms wrapped around Charlie's small form, her chin touching the top of his head. Sedated by the gentle swaying of the rocker and the warmth of the fire, Charlie's eyelids were already closing. "Times like this have been my treasures, the quiet hours when I could rock you kids. I look back on how it was when I carried each of you inside me, and when I nursed you as babes. I think of how you've all grown, and I'm so grateful. You'll know many such times when you have babies of your own, Rachel, and they'll be dear to you, too."

Her countenance grew even softer. "I've heard many a man say he was glad he wasn't born a woman, especially after seeing his wife bring a child into the world, but something men don't always understand is that God made a mother's love more powerful than any pain, and that kind of love never leaves us." She tilted her head and rubbed her cheek across Charlie's soft hair.

Rachel continued to watch them, her heart aching a little, unable to remember a moment of closeness anything like this with her own mother. "You're a remarkable woman," she said softly.

Juliet chuckled, gently, so she wouldn't wake Charlie. "Foot," she said, using one of her favorite exclamations, which always brought a smile to Rachel's lips. "I ain't remarkable, honey, I've been blessed, is all. I just look at my kids and the miracles I've been given are plain to see."

Rachel's smile reached her eyes, now moist with emotion. "Alright, 'blessed', then," she uttered, meaning the term slightly differently than Juliet had, meaning more honored than fortunate, and her tone said as much.

Touched, Juliet turned again to the fire. After a moment her expression clouded, and she said, "Honey, I don't mean to upset you, but your pa told me you've been asking about Stan."

"When I saw him in town he seemed to know me, so I was curious about who he is to me, to us."

"Stan O'Brien is nothing to us," Juliet said with emphasis, her rocking coming to a halt, then continuing after a pause, "no more than anyone else in town, that is, but he simply won't accept that he's nothing to *you*. He's a gambler and part owner in a saloon. Even though he's got no claim at all, he's told at least three decent men that he'd skin them if they didn't stay clean away from you. Scared them off, that's what he did."

Rachel hid her amusement. "But I've never encouraged him?"

"Lord above, no!" Juliet voiced this as if the possibility of her daughter being attracted to such a man was unthinkable. "The man's dangerous. There's talk that he killed a fellow in the last town he rode through."

Under Juliet's intensifying scrutiny, Rachel worked harder to conceal her inclination to smile. For Juliet, she said, "You needn't worry about me. I have no intention of associating with Stan." For herself, she added, "But I'd very much like to go into town."

"Now, honey, don't you think it's too soon for that?"

"I feel fine, really, just restless." Rachel got the next less-than-truthful words out with difficulty. "Going into town might even help my memory. Pa said there was a map at the newspaper office I might look at."

"Did your pa say you could go to town, or that he'd bring the map home to you?"

Juliet was quick, Rachel had to give her that. "He didn't say I *couldn't* go into town."

With a deepening frown, Juliet gave every indication that a negative response was brewing, so Rachel forestalled her by asking, "Do you know if I have any money of my own?"

"Money? What do you want money for?"

"Oh, nothing special. I've just wondered if I'd been saving my earnings from the store to start a home of my own someday. I'd hate to think I'd left cash lying around the Pinney house." Money certainly would give her more options, but Rachel's main inclination was to investigate the town and, possibly, find a link to her real life.

"I expect you did save most of the money you made," Juliet acknowledged. "You're not much of a spender. But even though you never did show any interest in one particular man, starting your own home hasn't really come up much. Course, like I said, Stan hasn't helped matters."

"Don't you think I ought to go and find whatever money I left in town?"

Juliet said guardedly, "Now, I know that since Doc took the stitches out your cut is healing fine, and your thinking is clearing up considerable."

Rachel pressed, "Well then?"

"It's just that..." She stared at Rachel earnestly, trying to soften her next words. "Honey, some of the folks in town might want to send you away."

"Send me away?" Rachel asked, truly amazed. "What have I done?"

"Nothing, Rachel dear, nothing at all, but I've heard of people being sent to an insane asylum because...because their minds weren't quite right." She rushed on, trying to comfort, "I know you're remembering more all the time, but some folks will hear how you talk a little different now, and they'll get uneasy when you don't know who they are. Certain folks are afraid of most everything, and I don't want to take the chance that they'll stir up any trouble for you."

"But surely they couldn't have me taken to an asylum without your permission."

"I've seen it done, honey, with my own eyes," Juliet said, "back in Iowa. And there are a few people here that are cowardly enough and ornery enough to do such a thing."

Rachel stared at her, noting just how real Juliet's concern was. Then she was struck by another thought. "Do I have enemies here?"

"Not of your own making, honey. You're as good and kind a young woman as ever lived. But there are men who have wanted you to love them, and women who...didn't like the way those men wanted you."

"Am *I* so cowardly that I avoid these people because they might want to do me harm?"

Rachel expected annoyance, perhaps even anger at this challenge. Instead, Juliet's voice caught with emotion of a gentler kind, her words conveying a good deal of pride. "You said almost those same words not more than a month ago." After a pause she shifted the still slumbering Charlie to a more comfortable position, and said, "No, honey, you've got enough bravery to show up a whole troop of fighting men. I guess I knew you'd want to face folks straight on, like you face everything. All right then, dear daughter, as soon as your pa comes inside I'll talk to him about taking you into town."

It was nothing remotely like driving her car down Lake Shore Drive toward the Loop, but as she bumped along the rutted road toward town in the creaking wagon, Rachel felt her eagerness build. She wanted to return to the house she'd awakened in, not for any hidden cash, but to find any thread of explanation as to why she was here.

Breaking in on her concentration, Bert asked, "Are you tired, Rachel? You're a might quiet today."

"I'm thinking," she said, matching his subtle inflections. It had grown easier to suppress her Chicago accent and eliminate uncustomary words.

Bert nodded at her. "I expect you still have things to sort out in your mind."

"Um-hum," Rachel murmured. "Pa, what do you think about the war?"

He glanced at her in surprise before his expression settled into one of rumination. "Do you remember about your Uncle Giles?"

"Mama told me he died after he came back from the war."

"Well, I guess the loss of Giles more or less sums up the war for me. War's nothing but killing or dying, and the ones that die leave families behind with pieces of their hearts taken away." He looked out far ahead of the team. "I believe in the Union, but I don't know how many lives it's worth to try to hold this country together. And slavery's wrong, honey, terrible wrong, but my brother's life along with hundreds of thousands of others, that's a high price to pay to try to stop it, especially since folks say it might have ended soon anyway."

After a moment he said, "Now that we're in Idaho, it'd be nice to think we left the war far behind us, but that ain't entirely so. This area's got more southern sympathizers than folks who feel the way we do, and some of them hate us for not thinking the same. Not all, of course, but them that do can be deadly. Seems like every time the newspaper reports a victory, a good share of the miners get liquored up and start shooting at anyone who ain't singing "Yankee Doodle" or "Dixie" when they think he should. The strange thing is, a good lot of them never even lived in the East or the South. They came from clean across the ocean, but that doesn't keep them from taking sides."

He gave Rachel a fatherly look. "Your mama and me were real edgy about letting you stay in town on your own, even for a short time. If that house wasn't just down from the sheriff's office we'd have said no." His mouth made a half-hearted grin. "That, and the fact that Stan probably would have shot anyone who looked at you. The man's been more than his share of trouble, but he keeps the mean men as well the good ones from buzzing around you."

Rachel chose to turn the subject away from the men in town. "When I asked Lewis about his life he told me he used to be a slave, and I saw his brand. Have you talked with him about his past much?"

"Only some. He escaped from a place in southern Kentucky when the war started. Heading west, he got to Texas before he decided to turn north. I know he spent some time with a band of Indians somewhere along the way: he's talked now and again about their ways. They taught him things of value, too, like how to jerk meat and what plants are good for healing."

"He's grateful you took him in."

"You've seen how your mama treats Lewis, almost like he was a brother or one of her kids. At times I wonder if she sees Lewis' coming as something to make up for Giles being taken from our family. I mean, Giles dying in a war that was being fought partly to free the slaves, and Lewis coming to us after being a slave himself. Your mama's never said as much, but she might think that way. Maybe she's right. Maybe Lewis does give some reason for Giles losing his life in that fight."

"I think Lewis gets scared when Mama treats him like she does, afraid that she'll suffer for it."

"That's so, and his worrying about our welfare makes me think even more of him, but he'd be right to worry for himself. Some men would beat Lewis to death for acting like anything but a slave. I know it makes your mother mad that Lewis doesn't eat with us, but it might be best for him that he won't."

Rachel's stomach tightened as she recognized the truth of Bert's words. Being aware of slavery's prior existence and feeling an aversion for its historical generalities from the distance of a remote future, a future attempting to leave slavery's haunting remnants far behind, was nothing like facing its cruel fears and veracities as they occurred.

Deep in thought for a time, she eventually let her gaze settle on a long wooden trough jutting from a cascading stream and continuing on a course that paralleled the gently downward-sloping roadway they were traveling. The contrivance was elevated on wooden supports and, judging from the moisture leaking from its seams, channeled water down the hill.

"I don't remember what those are called," she said, pointing.

"That's a flume, honey."

"And it carries water to town?"

"To the mining claims. This area must have eighty miles of flumes and ditches feeding off these creeks. The men who built them charge the miners for the water they use, so those flumes make real good money."

As they traveled along, Rachel paid keen attention to the miners who began to appear at the bases of slopes and ridges. Most of them worked rockers, a few merely swirled pans over a creek, but the wagon soon approached a team of men grasping a hydraulic hose the size of a small cannon and shooting a thirty-foot gush of water at the hill before them. This high-pressure spray brought rocks crashing down the mountainsides, and the men below, some leaping sideways to avoid the larger boulders, shoveled and sluiced the runoff through a long system of troughs and boxes. Some mining operations had whole crews working a common area, others just one lonely man. Rachel could scarcely believe she'd noticed almost none of this activity when the Milfords had driven her to the farm, and realized with an inward start that she'd arrived here just a little over a week ago. Now this was her life, pioneering in a mining town, at least for now. Perhaps for a long time. Perhaps forever. No, she would not try to grapple with that possibility yet.

Forcing her focus onto the miners, she worked up enough curiosity to ask, "How many people live here?"

"Oh, I'd say seven thousand right around town, and maybe fifteen thousand in the whole basin."

Fifteen thousand people in the *entire* area. She tried to picture that number. Couldn't at least twice that many fit into Wrigley Field? "I see. How many of those are men?"

"There's likely no more than a couple thousand women and children."

Rachel continued to consider these incredibly small numbers as they rumbled into town, and studied every building and face they passed. When they pulled in front of the *Boise News* office, she jumped down and nearly beat Bert to the entrance. Smiling at her impatience, he opened the door and ushered her in.

"Good morning, gentlemen," Bert greeted the two notably similar men standing at the press; both quite slim and sporting brown mustaches and dark, slicked-back hair. A pair of boys in their late teens, wearing shoulder-to-knee leather aprons as liberally stained with ink as those of their employers, stood over racks of type letters.

Wooden storage cabinets lining two walls of the small office allowed little room for the men to maneuver around the massive press, but they edged their way toward the visitors.

"Well, Bert, how have you been?" asked one with a slightly southern inflection, setting down a metal plate and wiping his hands on a rag. "And, Rachel, it's good to see you looking so well. We heard about your fall, but here you are as hale and fresh as this fine morning."

"You remember Joseph and Thomas Butler, Rachel," Bert said, discreetly pointing out each man. Bert nodded at the shorter of the boys, a redhead, and said, "I see Stephen, there, but who's this tall blonde fellow?"

"This is Scott McPherson, Bert," said Joseph Butler. "Scotty, meet Mr. Milford and his daughter, Rachel,"

Scotty mumbled, "Please to meet you, sir, and miss," his neck and cheeks reddening as he turned back to work.

"I don't mean to take up your time, gentlemen," said Bert, "but can you let us have a look at some local maps?"

"Maps, of course," said Joseph, stepping to a cabinet, opening a glass-fronted door, and shifting through a stack of papers. Joseph asked, "Have you heard about Martin Partin getting shot? Killed, unfortunately."

Bert nodded regretfully. "Who'd have guessed the ferrying trade could be so risky? Do you know the particulars?"

Joseph pulled out a sheet from the stack, then searched for another as he said, "It started as a disagreement with T. J. Favorite, the fellow who runs the Payette River ferry. Favorite stopped a bullet, too, but he's showing no sign of allowing it to end his days."

"What was the disagreement all about?"

"Ferry contracts, I believe; who had the right to run the ferry over what stretch of the Payette, whose customers should be allowed to cross first, that sort of thing."

"Speaking of the latest shootings," Thomas put in, "a couple of Mexicans got fired up in South Boise last week, and one of them put a couple of bullets into the other. Killed him instantly." Thomas shook his head. "Before long, that area will rival our own in the high number of murders, but at least one of ours has been disproven. Do you remember when they pulled James Evan out of Grimes Creek up above Centerville? Well, Dr. McIteeny said James was dead drunk at the time he drowned, so not even the sheriff thinks that one was a murder any more. As far as I'm aware, the only other man who's died lately is that fellow from Ohio called Israel Hafer. He's the latest to have the misfortune of allowing a dirt bank to cave in on him, along Elk Creek this time."

So many deaths among so few, Rachel thought.

Closing the cabinet and turning to Bert with a short stack of papers, Joseph said, "We received word that Governor Lyons was due to arrive in Lewiston last week, but I haven't heard whether he made it. I hope he hasn't run into trouble." He handed Rachel the maps and smiled. "Will these do, Rachel?"

"Yes, thank you. May I also trouble you for some paper and a pencil, so I can copy them?"

"I'm afraid Thomas and I haven't caught on to using pencils much yet. Will a pen do?" Joseph brought her the writing instruments, a chair, and a clean metal printing plate to serve as a lap desk. Once she was settled and cautiously dipping her nib pen into the inkbottle, Bert asked Joseph, "Have you had any recent reports from the Eastern papers?"

Both Butler brothers looked up, but Thomas spoke first. "Bert, you are one of the few men in this town with whom I can have a disagreement about the war without fearing a bullet afterward. So I'll tell you, regretfully for my brother and me, that the reports indicate things may be swinging in favor of Grant. For how long, I couldn't say, but as the Confederacy runs short of men and food, your general seems to be realizing for the first time that he needs a comprehensive strategy if he hopes to win this conflict. He's ordered Meade and Burnside to advance on Richmond, and sent Butler up the James River and Sigel across the Shenandoah Valley to meet the other two. Grant's hoping to box Lee in." He held Bert's gaze. "One of the latest accounts on Sherman's movements said he and a hundred thousand men are approaching Atlanta, burning and destroying as they march. He's divided his troops into two lines, meaning to come at the city from the north and the east."

"Richmond and Atlanta both," Bert muttered in surprise.

"The news is not all in favor of the Union, however," Thomas added. "General Warren was killed, and from what we've read even with most of Lee's men entrenched at Spotsylvania he's still managing to strike at Meade and Grant. He won't be overthrown easily, not him."

Bert asked slowly, "Does it look like Sherman will take Atlanta?"

Thomas couldn't keep the sorrow from his voice. "His men outnumber Johnston's forces terribly, and he has the equipment and supplies he needs. I doubt he'll be turned back."

"Then," Bert said, still meeting Thomas's gaze, "perhaps the end of this cursed war is in sight at last."

"Yes, perhaps, but what will its ending bring?"

Rachel's pen had stilled, her furtive glances moving between Thomas and Bert. Was this the first indication these men had received that the Union would win the war? She tried again to remember the date the war would end, but could only recall uncertainly that the surrender would come in early 1865. Bert had told her that a majority of the locals were southern sympathizers. How would they react when the Union won? With luck, or a miracle, she wouldn't be around to find out.

"What the end will bring, I can't tell," Bert said after considering, "but I've wondered more than once whether the war might have ended some time ago if this basin hadn't shipped so much gold to the armies of both sides. Our miners must have sent them hundreds of thousands, maybe millions of dollars' worth of gold dust, mostly to the South."

"I've wondered the same thing," said Joseph. "How many men would have lived if that gold had stayed right here?"

Remembering the presence of the two young clerks, Joseph shot them each a glance, conveying that what they'd just heard was never to be repeated. They both nodded gravely and resumed their tasks.

Stunned by this revelation, Rachel kept her nose down, her hand scratching the splotchy outline of a map while her mind circled the fact that gold from this basin had been and still was fueling, extending the war. She'd never even heard of Idaho City, and yet it evidently had made a profound impact on the country's history.

Bert waited at her side as Thomas joined Joseph at the press, but before Rachel had completed half of her first map his restlessness became apparent.

"Do you have other business in town, Pa?"

"I do have a few things to buy," Bert acknowledged.

Joseph said kindly, "Rachel's welcome to stay, Bert. You go on ahead."

"All right then. Rachel, I'll meet you at the Pinney place after I finish at the mercantile."

Less than a half-hour later Rachel sat looking over her completed maps, accepting their extreme crudeness—she would never be a cartographer after all—and evaluating whether she'd left out anything of importance.

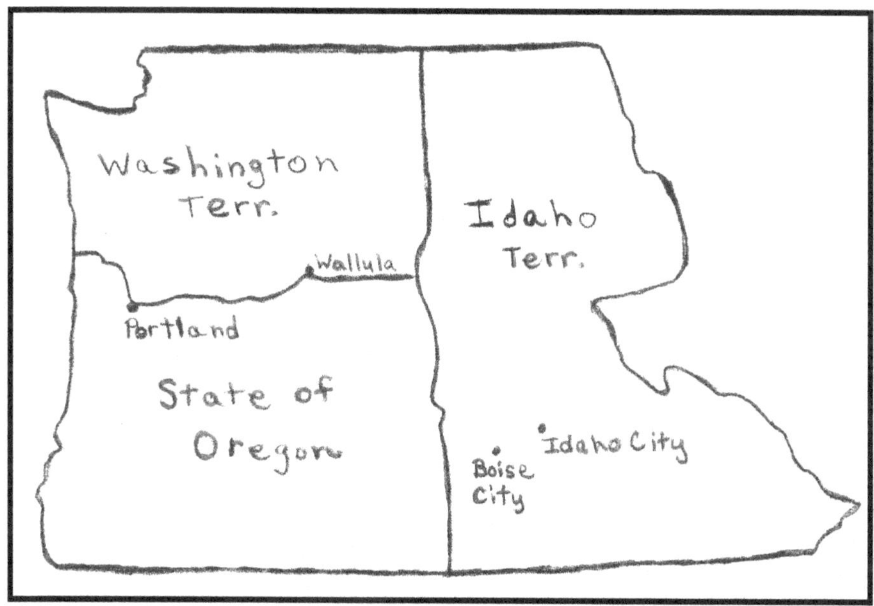

Pacific Northwest Area Map

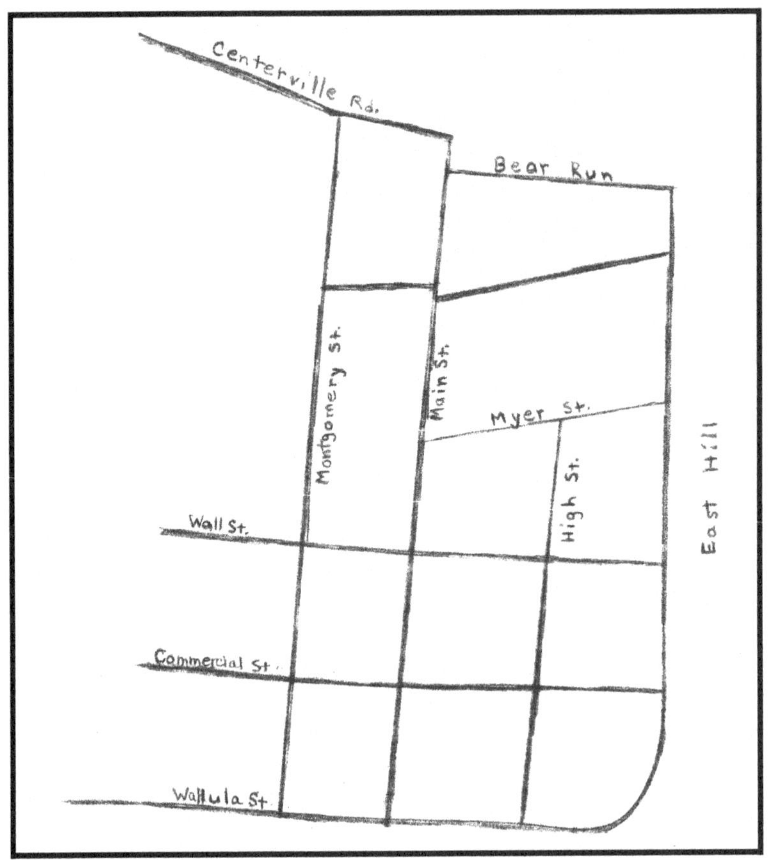

Idaho City Street Map

Ultimately she judged the sketched maps to be the best she could manage at the moment, three rough guides by which to learn the lay of the land.

Hesitant to interrupt the Butler brothers again, and guessing that Bert would need more time at the mercantile, Rachel picked an edition of the *Boise News* from a stack within reach. She unfolded the paper dated May 21, the day she'd arrived, and an article entitled "Insane" immediately caught her eye. It read, "A man by the name of A. G. Lane has at intervals during the Winter and Spring, shown signs of a distracted intellect to such a degree that he was obliged to be confined, and was sent to Portland on Tuesday by the Sheriff. He is a man of some property in this city but, having developed a disposition to shoot at his fellow citizens, it was deemed unsafe to permit him to remain at large."

Signs of a distracted intellect? They really do send people with mental problems away. She glanced at the men and boys, and shifted in her chair. To these

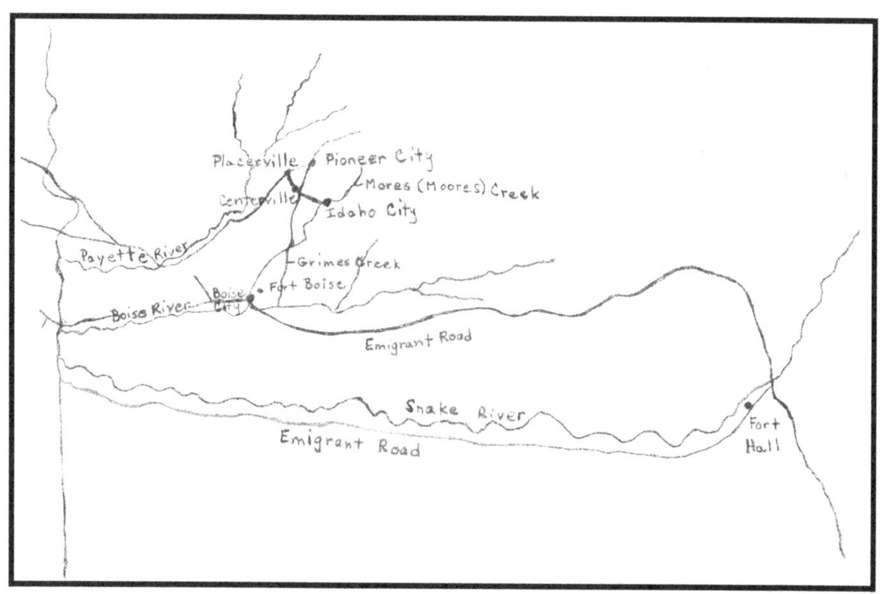

Idaho City Area Map

townspeople, she'd certainly exhibited a "distracted intellect." Could *she* be judged unsafe?

The door opened abruptly and Stan O'Brien, the man the Milfords had cautioned her to avoid, stepped into the room. In one glance she took in the black slacks, starched white shirt, and green silk vest and tie, all framed by a well-fitted black coat, and dark waves of hair beneath a black hat trimmed in beaded silver. Also noting the disapproving stares the Butlers were directing at Stan, she rose quickly and shuffled the newspapers back onto their shelf. She felt Stan step behind her, waiting for her to turn around, and when she did she was held, questioned, by eyes of the purest blue. When she didn't speak, he said, "I saw your father heading for the mercantile, but he noticed me, too, so I bided my time. Are you feeling all right?"

"Yes, just fine," said Rachel. The Butlers were still scrutinizing them, so she added coolly, "I've just been reading the news."

A grin, flashing dimples, lit his face. "The news, is it? You *are* feeling fine if you can stand there and tease me so. I should have known you were tougher than any old railing." Then, in a voice far too intimate, he asked, "When will you be letting me see more of your sweet self?"

"I don't know," Rachel said, thinking those dimples were dangerous misrepresentations. She suspected that there was no child-like innocence in this man, and that his quick humor was delivered in carefully aimed and measured doses. His self-assured worldliness was palpable, and something darker declared its momentarily restrained power through the pistol holstered at his hip. She had met men who killed in cold blood with no sign of remorse, and she believed the person before her could be one such as they. He drank Rachel in with his gaze, and as she stared back, sensing how cleverly he could disarm others, her instincts loudly cautioned her to keep her own thoughts hidden.

"Lord, it's good to see you." He took a step closer, nearly touching her, and Rachel would have shifted backward if there had been room. She glanced at the Butlers.

"Mr. O'Brien," Thomas said tightly, "Miss Milford's busy, and her father will be back any minute."

Stan ignored the warning, ignored Thomas completely. "How long will you be staying in town, Rachel?"

Catching sight of Joseph walking in their direction, Rachel said quickly, "Thank you, Mr. Butler, all of you, for letting me disturb your work." She nodded toward the door and said to Stan, "Please, let's step outside."

Stan's voice was low, suggestive, when he replied, "Now, that's better." He turned toward the printing press for the first time and, as if warmly parting from old friends, saluted the scowling men. "Gentlemen, it's been a pleasure." He winked at Rachel as he pulled the door open for her.

Casting an apologetic look toward the Butlers and their apprentices, Rachel left the office with her maps in one hand and Stan taking possession of the other. He hurried her down the boardwalk past several doors before halting between the barbershop and the feed store. "Listen, young lady, I hope you're planning—." He hushed as several men emerged from the feed store and glanced their way. The group seemed to be stoking an already heated argument that allowed only a momentary diversion, so Stan started again, "When are you moving back to town?"

As smoothly as she could, she answered, "No, no, not yet. My family wouldn't be happy if I left home so soon. They want to see that I'm completely recovered."

"What about me? You know I'd—"

Threatening shouts from the men who'd spilled into the street brought both of their heads around. A short man, his empty right sleeve tied off at the elbow, yelled over the other voices, "That ain't true! No Yank general is worth a damn at leading men! Grant ain't no better than the rest!" This drew encouraging cries from some of the growing cluster of men, and muttered defiance from others.

As the volume increased and Stan nudged Rachel closer to the barbershop, she saw a tall man come out from the feed store and ease his way behind the crowd with a large burlap bag over his shoulder. Seeming to ignore the escalating animosity, he kept his hat brim down and his feet moving, and it wasn't until he'd loaded his heavy bag into the wagon and turned that Rachel noticed his faded blue pants bore a gold stripe down each side, and he walked with a slight limp. He paused briefly to eye a stack of milled lumber against the wall of the store, then his gaze swept the street and boardwalk until it touched hers. His firmly clenched jaw and stormy eyes exposed how tightly his anger was being constrained and, tugging his hat even lower over ginger brown hair, he headed back inside.

Stan said, "Rachel, you'd best get back to the—" just as a sallow man in a grease-stained coat and a hat with an off-white feather, yelled, "You cursed Yanks don't know when you've been outfought, and until you learn, we got no choice but to keep sending gold to our troops."

Stan muttered an oath and moved Rachel back another step.

Shaking a fist, a much older man in the opposing ranks barked, "We've sent tons of our own gold to the *right* side, the Union side, and now the fighting's all but over! If your commanders had a lick of sense, they'd quit now and cut their losses."

"A Reb with a lick of sense?" someone scoffed. "There ain't no such thing."

The Confederate in the feathered hat shot back, "There's not a soldier in the whole Northern army worth his weight in horseshit!" He suddenly pointed at Stan, shouting, "And you damn Yanks had better stay clear of this town's decent women."

When Stan stiffened Rachel squeezed his arm. "Don't Stan. They're only words."

"Not to an ex-officer of the Union army." He released her hand and ordered quietly, "Go back to the Butlers, Rachel. Now." Stepping slowly forward, Stan scanned the scene like a stalking cougar. Insults were being flung with increasing challenge as he unhurriedly, almost casually, pulled the right side of his coat back and tucked it into his belt, allowing unrestricted access to his holster. It wasn't until the Confederate facing him spotted this movement that Rachel noticed the half-hidden gun beneath his soiled coat.

Her voice sharpened with fear, "Stan, come with me. Please."

"Hey, gambler!" the Confederate shouted. "Let's you and me bet on just how soon your blue boys will be running home with their tails tucked between their legs." When the crowd roared and men started shoving, the Confederate stared directly at Stan and growled, "You're all a pack of filthy, stinking cowards!"

Stan didn't move, but his adversary stepped into the street, carefully removed and tossed his coat, and widened his stance.

The crowd's din quieted as abruptly as a candle being snuffed. At that moment Bert appeared from around a corner, and heard Rachel cry, "Stop this! Stan!"

Catching sight of Bert, Stan ordered, "Take her away from here!"

Hurrying forward, Bert had not yet reached Rachel when the Confederate, his eyes still locked on Stan, crouched in undeniable challenge. There was a sudden movement from the right of the crowd as a long board swung forward and struck the side of the Confederate with such force that he was hurled to the other side of the street, landing with a heavy thump and lying unmoving, his left shoulder out of alignment by several inches. Every gaping face swung from the prone body to the man Rachel had seen loading grain moments earlier, now holding the end of the four-by-four warily as he studied the throng.

Like water from a breached dike, men suddenly surged forward, throwing themselves at one another, some attacking, some defending, fists and voices crashing in waves.

Stan ran to Rachel, grabbed her arm firmly, and yanked her away. When she tried to resist his grasp, he slowed only long enough to throw her over his shoulder before striding quickly down the boardwalk. Rachel struggled to get down only to feel his hold tighten and hear him yell, "Keep still, Rachel! Hurry along, Bert!"

Somehow Bert managed to hold his temper and his tongue as he trotted behind them toward the Pinney house, but Rachel's own anger had been strained to its limit, and she hollered, "You put me down right now or I'll kick you where it'll hurt the most!"

He did, but not until she'd squirmed and threatened for another two blocks. The moment her feet hit the boardwalk she balled up her fists, her face puffing and her cheek scarlet, and hissed into his face, "If you ever manhandle me like that again, I'll shatter whatever hold you think you have on me." Seeing the grin melt from Stan's face, Bert moved a few discreet steps away and waited.

"Rachel, I had to get you out of there, didn't I?" Stan demanded.

She could still clearly hear the rumbling mob, their shouted curses and smashing fists, the shattering of a window. "Someone should help him!"

"Help who?" There was something cool and sharp in his response.

"The man who helped *you*, Stan. He stopped that gun fight, and you might have been killed."

"Me? Not the slightest chance, and he looked like a gent who is able to take care of himself well enough. Why such concern, Rachel? Do you know the man?"

"No. Now stop wasting time. Go help him get out of that mess!"

He glanced back at the fight, blocking Rachel's searching gaze in the process. "There's no need. Listen, it's already breaking up. Anyhow, your father needs to be on his way. Come on then, and no fussing."

They walked on, Rachel reluctantly acquiescing to Bert's concern and Stan's unspoken threat to hoist her onto his shoulder again. The shouts and scuffling behind them dwindled to little more than grumbles before Stan veered off the boardwalk, offering only a bow before leaving her to explain the whole story to Bert by herself.

Rachel's search of the Pinney house produced nothing beyond seven dollars and twenty-eight cents, wrapped up in a knitted scarf that Bert identified as her own and tucked in the back corner of a drawer. The place presented no clue to solve the mystery of her arrival, and the sum found was dishearteningly inadequate for covering travel expenses, especially all the way to Chicago. With a heavy heart she stuffed the money into her pocket, packed up the rest of her limited clothing and personal items, and told Bert she was ready to leave.

They were seated in the wagon again before the thought came to her that although this money was too meager to help her leave here, she might be able to help the Milfords and herself in a few small ways. She had no idea what could be bought with seven dollars and change, but she was suddenly eager to find out.

"Pa, can you take me to the mercantile? I'd like to buy a few things."

Bert asked in surprise, "You do?"

"Yes, just personal things."

Bert gave her an even more quizzical look then, shaking his head, turned the team back toward the general store. Evidently fearing that she might buy something of a feminine nature, Bert chose to wait in the wagon.

Inside, Mr. and Mrs. Mack, for whom she'd supposedly worked for some time, greeted her warmly. She responded in kind but was immediately captivated by the goods surrounding her. The store was bustling with customers and she was able to shop without too much attention from the friendly storeowners. As she browsed and inspected she became more and more grateful for the coins she carried, and had to admit the irony of this feeling when she considered how little she had appreciated her former wealth. After studying the shelves of goods attentively, she decided that the product most closely related to deodorant was talcum powder, and she happily picked up one small tin. Although circumstances had forced her to become more accustomed to the odor of hard-working bodies, her own as well as others, she was determined not to relinquish her old habits of cleanliness without a fight. She made this and other purchases totaling less than six dollars without further delay and returned to the wagon with a small package, wrapped in brown paper and secured by a string, tucked under her arm.

Bert eyed the bundle but when Rachel made no indication of wanting to unveil its contents, he headed the team homeward without probing.

As they drove on past a saloon, Stan stepped out of its doorway, tipping his hat and sliding a teasing grin into place. Rachel stared at him for only a second before turning her head forward. Thankfully,

Bert hadn't noticed him. She had started to relax again when a loud, "Good day to you, Miss Rachel," was tossed from Stan's direction. "I'll be looking forward to seeing you again very soon, my dear!"

When Bert started to twist around Rachel caught his arm. "Please, don't even look at him." Bert hesitated, then sharply clicked his tongue to urge the horses into a brisker pace. Keeping the team at a trot all the way out of town, his body remained rigid and his voice silent. Hoping to turn his thoughts from Stan, Rachel took the folded copies of the maps from her pocket and held them out for him to see. He only muttered a few words of acknowledgment then steadily eyed the road ahead, his contemplations turning even deeper inward.

The silence stretched between them while Rachel deliberated over the details of the maps, determined to memorize them quickly. As she considered the nearby area and then the entire territory, realizing the great distances that lay between the towns and imagining the roughness of the terrain, she asked herself for the hundredth time how she was going to make her way home. But even if she could reach Chicago, she wouldn't be there during her era. It wouldn't be her home. For a moment or two, hopelessness threatened, but she gave it a mental shove. *Today, just today,* she decided firmly. *I may have nothing beyond it so I'd better make the most of what I can.*

Bert called her from this reverie. "You seem to be wrestling with your thoughts, daughter. I hope Stan didn't embarrass you too much today."

She sat a little straighter and assured him, "No, he didn't." When the worry remained on his face she gave him a soft smile. "Really."

Unconvinced, Bert hunched forward and mumbled, "That scoundrel. I'm tempted to deal with him straight out. He ought to leave you be!"

Moved by such fierce protectiveness, Rachel found nothing as worthy to say in response.

A deep rut roughly jostled the wagon, nearly causing her to drop the package in her lap, which encouraged her to refold the maps and attend to her new possessions. Reflecting anew on these purchases, she pictured the face of each Milford receiving a small gift, and she began to look forward to returning to the farm.

The wagon settled into a gentler rock and squeak as the breeze whispered through the thickening trees along the roadsides, and her mind drifted back to the fight in town. The tall man's image came to her clearly, his stance watchful, powerful yet contained, that long, heavy board in his hands, the unconscious gunman on the ground. Had his actions saved a life today, or more than one? Perhaps even her own?

Stan hadn't even told her the man's name.

For a long while speculation about the stranger took possession of her thoughts, and the maps in her lap were forgotten.

11

Charlie's expression of excited anticipation melted into one of puzzlement as he tossed the brown wrapping paper on the floor and studied the wooden instrument with stiff bristles he held in his hand. "What ever is it?"

"It's a toothbrush, Charlie, and there's one for each of you," Rachel said, circling the front room as she doled them out. She'd gathered the family and Lewis together after lunch, which she had learned to call dinner, and was finding great satisfaction in revealing her purchases. The small brushes probably wouldn't hold together very long but she intended to buy as many as they needed to keep cavities at bay, at least until her money ran out.

"Charlie," Kate admonished, "you know what a toothbrush is. Mama has had one for years."

"I never saw it," Charlie said, still mystified. "What do you do with it?"

This question was posed just as Maggie received her toothbrush, and she beamed at it, saying, "Ohhh," as if she'd received a pearl necklace. When Rachel came to Lewis in the ring of people and held his toothbrush out, he glanced uneasily from Bert to Grandpa. Rachel impatiently reached down and took his hand, deposited the gift in his palm, and curled his fingers around it before stepping on to Grandpa, and finally Bert.

Juliet had already thanked Rachel for her gift, but she asked hesitantly, "Rachel, honey, what made you spend your hard-earned money? Didn't you mean to save up for when you have a family of your own?"

Rachel caught the carefully guarded concern in Juliet's voice, and said, "Well..." Unintentionally, she glanced at Grandpa's mouth, which displayed three gaps where lower front teeth had once resided. She pulled her gaze away and said, "It's just that I...I thought we might all..."

Well aware of Rachel's bighearted intents, Grandpa put in, "I used one of these quite often when your grandma was still alive. I believe the thing got left behind when we set off from Iowa, though. Now," he said, eyeing the younger children, "if I'd thought to buy a new one of these once we got here, I'd probably have my full set of teeth today. This was right thoughtful of Rachel. It's high time all you young'uns learned how to use this fine tool, don't you think, Juliet?"

After the briefest glance of uncertainty Juliet said, "Yes, it surely is. They're plenty old enough for such things."

Wrinkling her nose, Kate said, "But I don't know a single soul that brushes their teeth."

Phillip puffed his chest a little and demanded, "You afraid of having clean teeth unless everyone else does?"

As Kate bristled, True said, "That's enough, Phillip. Kate didn't mean nothing. And Rachel, I'm right proud to have this toothbrush. I thank you." With quiet authority, he instructed, "You kids, go on and thank Rachel now."

They did, and all gathered around to taste the tooth powder that True tapped from its can into his open palm. While the children were experimenting with their brushes, Rachel pulled two simple but lovely hair combs and two red handkerchiefs from her parcel, leaving several yards of light yellow fabric.

She passed one handkerchief to Bert and the other to Grandpa, and then both combs to Juliet. The only words she could think of to explain the gifts were, "These are for you, to thank you for taking such good care of me." Nodding toward the fabric, she added, "Mama, I thought you might want to make a quilt for Esther's baby."

Juliet came to her, wrapped her arms around her, and said, "We'll make it together. You're such a dear." Loosening her embrace, her shining eyes looked into Rachel's face. "You should have kept that money for yourself, but I won't scold you for thinking of others. It's always been your way."

The men heartily admired their handkerchiefs and, watching their faces, listening to their benevolent praise, Rachel suddenly wished that these people had touched her childhood. Yet she felt the sting of guilt almost as quickly, remembering that even here, even now, she was a fraud. She didn't deserve the love of this good family: she wasn't and never could be truly one of them. Easing away from Juliet, she said, "I'll take the kids outside and show them how to brush their teeth really well. Come along, children." She left before Juliet, Bert, or Grandpa could say another word.

Not many minutes had passed before Juliet came outside to assign clothes-washing duties to some of the younger members of her family, each grinning broadly to display newly scrubbed teeth. While True and Bert hauled two washtubs down to the creek, the youngsters gathered wood and Rachel helped Juliet carry out baskets piled high with clothes and linens. The washtubs were barely in place before the three men, True, and Phillip headed for their sluice boxes around the bend of the creek.

A fire was built, a couple of lines were strung between two trees, and the torture began.

Boil the clothes, stir the clothes repeatedly in lye soap, lift the clothes from the first tub to the second, scrub the clothes up and down over the knuckle-scraping ridges of a washboard in scalding soapy water, rinse the clothes in the ice cold creek, wring the water out of the clothes, and finally hang them on the line with hands and arms growing clumsier with each load. Then start the whole hellish process over again.

More than two hours later, her hands raw and her arms heavy with fatigue, Rachel regretted being so adamant about helping. As she stirred the last huge pot of bubbling water with an old broom handle, the pungent smell of lye arose with the steam and nearly choked her. She was sore, sweaty, dirty, drained of energy, and sick to death of this smell. It only tormented her further to think of the modern washing machine and sweetly scented laundry detergent and fabric softener that she'd taken completely for granted. It seemed to her now that she'd seldom had to wash more than a couple of loads a week, and that had required almost no effort at all.

She glanced down the long lines of drying fabric. For a family who didn't seem to own many worldly goods, how could they possibly produce so much that needed washing? She shied away from the thought of doing this job in the heat of August. And how did they manage when several feet of snow covered the ground? Shaking her head, she gave the broom handle a final swirl and lifted a scalding bundle.

At last she was able to rinse and cool her arms in the clear creek, and with a sigh she straightened and scanned her surroundings. The task of keeping Charlie out of the water and away from the boiling pots and animals in the near pasture had been assigned to Maggie, and these two children were now tossing rocks into the creek not far from where Juliet was wringing out the remaining pair of socks. Kate, who had shifted between the washing and helping Maggie with Charlie, was giving her younger siblings advice on how to fling their stones farther.

Rachel arched her back in a long, deep stretch, and Juliet, having hung the socks with the last of the clothespins, smiled at her and did the same.

The weather was fine for a walk, and Rachel became curious about seeing the Milford men at work. Did they find gold often? How much might they dig up today?

"Mama," she said, "would you mind if I go take a look at how the mining is coming along?"

"You go right on ahead, honey. You've been working awful hard."

Needing no further encouragement, Rachel set off, following the creek as it bent to her left, deepened, and progressively descended.

As the stream headed south, the westward bank rose sharply to a height of over thirty feet, much higher than on Rachel's side. She spotted Lewis on the opposite embankment, his back toward her, but unwilling to relinquish her solitude quite so soon, she stepped into the shade of the trees to watch the men and boys at the water's edge.

She leaned her shoulder comfortably against a Ponderosa pine at least four feet in diameter, and a scent, sweet and enticing, drew her face closer to the tree. She glanced up and around it, sniffing, then inched her nose closer to the trunk, and breathed in. She smiled, inhaling again to pull the rich aroma of vanilla into her lungs, and marveling at the strong similarity between the scent of this pine bark and that of so different a plant. Thoroughly pleased with her discovery, Rachel continued to breathe deeply as she directed her attention to the miners.

At the base of the opposite hillside two long, wooden boxes had been judiciously placed, one of which must contain the riffle Lewis had repaired in the barn. At the moment he stood precariously balanced two-thirds of the way up the bank scooping fresh dirt down toward True and Phillip, who shoveled it along to the creek where Bert and Grandpa were adjusting the water flow and shifting the screens. They worked easily together, seldom pausing, speaking little but occasionally laughing at some subtle jest from Bert or teasing from Grandpa. Even Phillip toiled away with uncomplaining doggedness. There was little Rachel could deduce about any success they might be having, but after contentedly watching for a time she saw Grandpa bend closer to his sluice box and extract something. He let loose a loud whistle, held his find high for the others to admire, and made a comment that Rachel couldn't make out but that caused the males to guffaw loud enough to set off a spate of heated chattering from a squirrel high above. Each miner held the prize in turn, and they were all still grinning when Grandpa dropped it into a leather pouch tied to his belt. When Lewis began to climb even higher up the bank and the others resumed their prior duties, Rachel decided it was time to stroll back to Juliet.

With the clean laundry gently swaying on the line, the tubs emptied and rinsed, and the coals of the fire extinguished, Juliet allowed herself to sit with Rachel in the shade and watch the children kick a pinecone back and forth. It wasn't long before True and Phillip came into view, with Lewis, Bert, and Grandpa close behind, all treading tiredly home. Their shirts were stained with sweat, their hair hung in disheveled masses and their faces were smudged with dirt, but they were smiling in a way that showed pride in their day's work.

Phillip called out from a hundred feet away, "I'm starving, Mama! I could eat an ox. When's supper going to be ready?"

Juliet brushed the hair from her cheek and rose to her feet. "Phillip, you're always hungry enough to eat an ox." She straightened up with a soft groan and said to Rachel, "Whew, with you being hurt last Saturday the washing sure did pile up. Thank heaven there won't be quite so much next week."

Inwardly cringing at the thought of this weekly necessity, Rachel kept her expression neutral as Juliet turned and asked Bert, "How'd you all do today?"

He couldn't hide the twinkle from his eyes as he said, "Show her the nugget, Pa."

Grandpa dug the chunk from the dust and smaller pieces in his pouch and dropped it into Juliet's hand.

"Why, it's almost as big as a quail's egg!" Juliet praised as the girls gathered around. She handed it to Rachel, who inspected the lumpy ore with fascination, wondering what its discovery would mean to the Milfords; clothing for the children, a few new chickens, a plow blade?

"Pa," she inquired, "this nugget reminds me that some miners have sent gold to their armies."

"From what I hear, there have been quite a few heavy shipments. Some ships were caught by revenue cutters, some sank, but most got through. Some folks say the war might have ended a year ago if the gold from this area hadn't kept supplies flowing, especially those needed by the Confederacy."

Rachel stared, saying, "If the rumors are true, that's terribly tragic; a year longer and men dying in the hundreds of thousands."

"Not tragic if you're loyal Southerners who still believe they can win, and are willing to give a fortune to help the outcome."

As Rachel slowly shook her head, Kate appeared at her elbow asking to hold the nugget. After they'd each done so, Juliet asked True unnecessarily, "I suppose you're just as hungry as your brother?"

"Yes, ma'am, I surely am. How about I go and see if I can bring in something to stretch our supper a little."

"Foot, young man, we don't need you to go hunting every day just so we have enough to eat." Juliet's mock aggravation was easy to see through and, after eying Rachel a moment or two, she asked, "Would you like to go with him? It's still a couple of hours 'til supper time."

"*I* would! *I'd* like to go!" Kate proclaimed, hopping up and down and clasping her hands in supplication. "Oh, please, Mama, please let me go!"

Juliet peered back at True, who nodded, and announced, "All right, Kate."

Kate let out a high-pitched yip as she raced, legs skipping and arms flapping, to the house. "I'll get the rifles!"

Rachel had been weighing her chances of quietly sneaking off and collapsing in her own room but decided that Charlie and Maggie would find her there anyway. Perhaps a walk in the woods would be the better choice, although she certainly didn't intend to shoot anything.

"*Well*, Rachel?" True asked impatiently.

"Yes, I'll go," she said, trying to sound enthusiastic.

Juliet looked at Phillip. "And why aren't you asking to go along?"

"Show her your hand," True said and nudged Phillip's shoulder.

"Ah, it's nothing, Mama. Just a big blister is all."

The blister at the base of his thumb was the size of a quarter and still bleeding.

"Son," said Juliet, "it's not as bad as it might be, but you should have stopped shoveling as soon as the bleeding started."

"Yes, ma'am."

"Come on, then. Let's get it tended to." She waved for Charlie and Maggie to follow and led the way toward the house, but before they'd reached the porch, Kate threw open the door and flew by dressed in pants two sizes too big, rolled at the cuffs and cinched around her waist with a length of rope. She had a rifle in each hand and a pouch slung over her shoulder, its strap capturing her blonde braids against her back.

Rachel's surprise at seeing Kate in pants grew to astonishment when the younger girl came to a halt before her and demanded, "Rachel, why ain't you changed? True, you got a clean pair of pants other than the ones on the line?"

Rachel asked hopefully, "I can wear True's pants?"

Kate's brown eyes flashed with impatience. "Well, of course. You don't expect to go hunting in a skirt, do you? You'd trip and flounder and make a terrible clamor."

True was more than willing to lend Rachel his pants and within minutes she was standing beside him again, dressed much like Kate. The pants fit her well enough with the rope at her waist, and they allowed the old and much missed freedom in her stride as they headed up the hill behind the barn, True carrying one rifle and Rachel the other. Although she was unaccustomed to toting a long, heavy weapon over hill and dale, she wasn't about to trust Kate with it.

They'd reached the top of the second rise when a voice called out from below, "Kate! Wait for me!"

Kate spun around and hollered, "Hey, Walter!"

True groaned loudly.

Shading her eyes with a hand, Rachel saw a dark-haired boy perhaps a year or two older than Kate clambering up in their direction. His clothes were worn to the point of raggedness, and as dirty as his face and hair.

Puffing with the exertion of his speedy climb, Walter said excitedly, "Look here at my new rifle. She shoots just as far and straight as you please."

Immediately suspicious, True asked, "How'd you get a new rifle?"

"My pa bought it for me," Walter shot back defensively, and he passed the weapon to Kate for her commendation.

Something in the boy's manner made Rachel sense he was lying, and she'd had a great deal of experience reading liars in court. Just why this boy would make up a story, she had no idea, but the fact that an evidently untended child of eleven or twelve had control of a rifle, probably loaded, was enough to make her more than a little edgy.

"Well, hurry along then," said True. "We'd best get going or we won't be back before the light fades."

"True," Rachel said, "I think I need a little practice before I actually... shoot at anything."

"Why sure, you can try a few practice shots, but let's move a ways farther from our place. You know how Mama hates it when bullets land anywhere near the animals."

They hiked along the forest path until they finally came upon a level clearing that suited True. Crossing roughly a hundred feet of the open space, he examined the trunk of an enormous dead tree until he spotted his target about eight feet off the ground. "See this knot?" he asked, pointing. "Aim for that."

Without warning, Walter jerked his rifle up and fired. Bark chips burst from the tree as True threw himself sideways and Rachel let out a cry of alarm.

In an instant True had regained his feet, charged straight at Walter, yanked the rifle from his hands, and shoved him hard as he yelled, "Have you lost all the sense you ever had?"

Narrowing his eyes and not backing down an inch, Walter accused, "You ain't hurt."

With his chest still heaving, True's voice grew low and tight. "You try something like that again and someone other than me might be the one getting hurt." True took a step back and tossed a disgusted glance in Kate's direction, as if to ask how his little sister could put up with this. He growled at Walter, "You ain't going any farther with us. Get on home."

"You don't own these mountains, True Milford. You ain't but sixteen, just three years older than me, so I don't have to mind what you say. I can go wherever I like." Then, seeming to notice that True still gripped his prized gun, Walter's tone shed a share of its defiance. "Look, True, I didn't mean you no harm. I was just trying out my new rifle is all."

True cast him a look of utter disbelief.

"I'm right glad you ain't hurt."

"I said we're going on without you, Walter," True said with finality.

Withheld anger flashed across the boy's face before he controlled it and turned a look of pitiful disappointment toward Kate. "Won't *you* at least stay with me? We can sit here and jaw a bit."

Kate looked uncertainly from True to Walter.

"Please, Kate," Walter persuaded. "That was my last bullet, but you can hold my gun."

"All right, Walter," Kate gave in. "I'll sit with you."

"Oh, no...," Rachel started.

True cut her off with, "Rachel, if she wants to sit with a varmint like Walter, let her sit. Maybe spending an hour alone with him will teach her something." He shoved Walter's rifle into Kate's arms, took Rachel by the arm, and started them up the path. When Rachel began to protest True whispered, "We won't go far. We'll get out of sight then sneak back and watch them, just to make certain he's not up to something. It won't take much more for Mama and Pa to forbid Kate from ever seeing him again."

They carefully circled back to a rocky point from which they could oversee the two younger people without being spotted, noting that Walter kept glancing toward the path they'd taken. Kate gazed dejectedly from the target tree, to Walter, to the rifle in her hands, evidently wishing she'd chosen to go hunting with True and Rachel.

True shook his head and whispered gruffly, "What Kate sees in that good-for-nothing boy is a pure puzzlement."

A few quiet moments of spying passed before Rachel asked, "How long do you think we should watch them?"

"Oh, just awhile longer I guess. They're just sitting." He turned and looked at her. "How you getting along, Rachel? Are you pretty near well?"

"Pretty near."

"That's fine. It likely did you good when Pa got you walking in the woods that day. I guess it does everybody good. For a while I wondered if we'd ever go hunting together again, and I surely would have missed that."

Rachel's mind stumbled over all the things she probably should say, responses to his apparent devotion and affection, but she couldn't bring herself to be false in the face of such brotherly love.

They kept their vigil until True said, "Well, he still ain't tried nothing. I guess if he does, Kate can use his empty rifle to club him. How about you and me going off a short ways to look for game? We probably scared off everything for miles, but I'm tired of just sitting."

"I'm not sure we should leave Kate, even if she is willing to club Walter."

"We won't be gone for long, not with the sun getting so low. Anyhow, at our first shot Kate will come running."

"Not far away, then," she said, getting up and brushing off the seat of her pants.

They snuck further out of Kate's eyesight and were soon drifting along deer paths as True pointed out familiar sites and discussed signs of game in a soft, hunter's voice. Even with him so close, Rachel fought from jerking her gaze at imagined dangers, and worked to adopt True's relaxed watchfulness. When a squirrel tossed a pinecone from a tree just ahead and let loose a screeching chatter, True did no more than grin and move on. Scolding herself for nearly dropping the rifle because of a noisy squirrel, Rachel breathed deeply and hurried after him.

When the distance from Kate had lengthened uncomfortably and Rachel was about to suggest turning back, True stiffened, signed for her to stop, and eased into a crouch. She rooted herself and held absolutely still as her eyes scoured the area, the hairs on the back of her neck prickling, her grip on the rifle constricting. True listened, and after a long moment turned his head to the right. He looked back at her, his expression asking if she could hear it too, but Rachel could only shake her head. He stuck a finger in his mouth to wet it, and held it up to check the direction of the wind. Signaling her to silence, he moved with great care toward whatever he'd heard. Rachel hesitated long enough to tell herself it must be a deer, only a deer, and stepped after him.

True kept them hidden behind trees and brush as much as possible as they advanced across and slightly down the slope, and Rachel finally picked up the sound of something low and rumbling still far off. Most of the time she kept her gaze riveted to True's back, and she wondered with growing consternation why in the world he was trying to discover the source of such a feral sound. She wanted to call him away but some instinct warned her not to utter a sound. True was now peering downhill as he crept from one source of cover to another, but Rachel was too intent on watching his movements and her own footing to do the same. When he reached a thicket of almost his own height, he halted and waited for Rachel to crouch beside him. The growling and snuffling sounds were much louder here.

"Look," he mouthed without a sound, motioning down the hill with his head, then rising ever so slowly.

Even more gradually, Rachel straightened up and glanced through the dense branches. Not nearly far enough away, a grizzly bear weighing at least six hundred pounds loomed over the carcass of an elk, intently devouring its bowels. Rachel soundlessly clamped a hand over her mouth but she didn't look away. The monstrous bear, its brown coat fading to gold at the hump above its shoulders, tore the body cavity open wider, sunk it jaws into the entrails, ripped a mass free, and kept chewing as it raised its bloody muzzle, nosing the air. It abruptly stilled, and with a sudden shift it turned its head toward their hiding place and snuffled several times. Neither hunter blinked or breathed. The bear tossed its head from side to side, snorted loudly, maneuvered its massive body to find a better angle on the kill, and resumed its noisy eating without seeming to have noticed True and Rachel, or at least without any interest in challenging them.

When True pulled her down behind the bush again, she stared at him with her eyes wide, her face flushed, and her heart hammering in double-time. Unbelievably, True was grinning from ear to ear, his features radiant with excitement. She remembered the rifle in her hand, but True, undoubtedly the better marksman, hadn't raised his. He evidently had no intention of shooting this bear, so when the grunting and champing grew louder in her ears, she whispered, "Let's go."

He nodded, checked the attentiveness and position of the grizzly, and warily led her back the way they had come. Rachel, following only a couple of steps behind him, looked back only once, but a screen of pines had already hidden the bear.

They remained silent until they'd covered a good distance, but at last True turned to Rachel and asked with pent up vehemence, "Wasn't that *something*? I've only seen a grizzly once before, and he was so far off I couldn't get a good look at him. But we saw that grizzly right up close, just you and me. He must be twice as big as any black bear around these parts."

"Why didn't you shoot him, True? Isn't that bear a danger to the whole family, and the livestock? He'll definitely kill elk and other game you could be hunting."

"Shoot a grizzly? Lord above, Rachel, even if both of us had opened fire we might have done no more than make him madder than... well, plenty mad. If we had hit him, he'd have charged us for certain, and I've heard stories of grizzlies killing men even after taking twelve bullets. It's a good thing we know he's there, though. Maybe Pa can set a trap for him." Imagining this, he added, "Sakes, we'll need a trap the size of a calf to catch that one."

They stared at each other, True smiling again and Rachel astounded by his lack of fear. "Weren't you even a little afraid?"

"Not enough to miss a sight like that. A chance like that might not come along again in my whole lifetime. Yours neither." He gave her a look that said he could see right through her, that he knew she wouldn't have missed it for anything. In spite of herself she smiled back at him, and they set out at once.

They'd nearly reached the area where Kate was expected to be when they heard a shot ring out. "That lying son of a gun! Come on," True barked, and sprinted ahead. As he ran, Rachel was just able to hear him let out a curse she'd never suspected of being as old as the 1800s.

He had stilled at the edge of the clearing and as she trotted up beside him she saw Walter lifting his rifle and pointing it away from them. Across the empty space a skinny arm extended straight out from behind a rock the size of a table, its forefinger and thumb holding an inverted pinecone by its stem. Rachel opened her mouth to yell, but True grabbed her arm with a jerk. "Shhh," he hissed. "It's too late. He might shoot her hand off."

Rachel cringed as Walter aimed the rifle, and gasped when he fired. The pinecone rocketed into the air, and before it landed True burst from the trees, threw a glance at an apparently uninjured Kate, and let his rifle slip to the ground as he ran at Walter. The boy's proud smile turned ugly the moment he caught sight of Kate's brother. When the distance between them was nearly gone, Walter swung the rifle with all his strength, but True grabbed the barrel before it could complete its arc, savagely yanked the gun from Walter's grasp, and tossed it far out of reach. Gripping Walter by the shirt, True cocked an arm and smashed his fist against the boy's jaw, felling him like a tree. Still furious, he pivoted and sprinted to Kate.

Rachel reached the girl ahead of him and shook her by the shoulders. "Kate, how could you do something so dangerous? You could have been killed!" Seeing that Kate's face was fading to the shade of milk, Rachel silenced the rest of her rebuke and hugged the girl to her chest.

True stormed up and waved an angry finger. "You ever play with that Walter again, Kate Milford, and I might have to beat him to death! Is that what you want? You want me to kill Walter because you haven't got sense enough to stay away from him?"

Kate, mute with shame and fear, lowered her face.

"*Is it*?" True roared.

As tears spilled from her eyes, Kate could only shake her head.

When Rachel tried to lay a calming hand on True's arm he shook it off. He looked to where Walter had fallen but had now managed to rise to a sitting position, and grunted in disgust. All three of them walked over and stared down at him, noting that his jaw was already swelling.

Yet to be mollified, True yelled, "You could have blown Kate's arm off, you fool!"

Rachel noticed that True said nothing about the boy swinging the rifle at his head, and judging from the look in Walter's eyes, he was regretting using it as a club rather than pointing the barrel and firing. His murderous expression quickly disappeared, replaced by one of incrimination. "I never would have hurt Kate," he whined, his mouth working awkwardly. "You saw what a good shot I am."

"You're never to come near our place again, you hear me?" said True, fighting to calm himself. "My folks are going to hear all about this."

Walter dropped his gaze.

"Get up," True ordered. When the boy didn't move fast enough True again took hold of his shirt and hauled him to his feet. "Move!"

"My rifle," Walter protested.

"It ain't your rifle anymore," he growled. "I said move." True gave him a push to get him started.

Rachel retrieved all three guns, and handed one of the Milfords' rifles as well as Walter's to True. He accepted them without taking his glare from Walter's back as they started toward home. Kate, crying softly now and then, didn't try to slow their progress, and True's occasional nudge with a rifle barrel kept Walter moving.

As they approached a bend in the path not far from the Milford place, Walter suddenly leaped off the trail and raced across a meadow, sprinting toward the far trees as if demons were in pursuit.

"Don't you forget what I told you, just stay clear of her!" True hollered after him, but they all walked on without trying to hinder the departure.

At the sight of her homestead, Kate began to cry in earnest, but continued to trudge forward like a doomed prisoner. True slowed his pace and dropped back to walk beside Rachel. Speaking to Kate in a tone only slightly less harsh than the one he'd used on the hill, he commanded, "You go on in the house. We'll be right behind you."

Once Kate was beyond hearing range, True leaned toward Rachel and said with marked appreciation, "It was a crazy thing for her to do but, you've got to admit, our little sister has more than her share of guts."

Rachel stopped in her tracks and glowered at him. "Guts?"

"Sure. That little slip of a thing's braver than most men I know. Still and all, it *was* pure foolishness, so Pa's going to have to wail on her some. But that ain't bothering Kate as much as Mama's getting worried and sad. That's what'll make her think twice next time." He gave Rachel his most mischievous grin. "We wouldn't want to miss her coming clean about what happened, Rachel, so let's make certain she tells the folks everything." He hooked his arm in Rachel's and guided her forward at a lively step, easily ignoring her words of consternation.

12

Bert reined the horses to a stop near the base of East Hill and Rachel reluctantly followed Juliet's glance upward to St. Joseph's Catholic Church, dearly wishing she'd been allowed to stay behind with Grandpa and Lewis to "keep an eye on things." The temptation had arisen to claim she was unwell but Juliet's solicitude would have confined her to her room for who knew how long, so she'd chosen what she still hoped would be the lesser of two evils. Climbing down from the wagon bed with the rest of the family, she tried to ignore the nagging apprehension of being called upon to confess her sins in the middle of Mass.

Years earlier a Catholic friend had described confession, or what she called reconciliation, as a reflective and renewing rite, but Rachel hadn't asked for details and now the idea of having to admit, or at least *pretend* to admit her sins to strangers was daunting indeed. Could she come up with something, a string of convincing lies? Even as a non-Catholic the thought of perpetrating such a sacrilege made her uneasy, but she certainly couldn't confess to pretending to be one of the Milfords, or of masquerading as a Catholic when she was actually a twenty-first century holiday Lutheran. And wouldn't there be prayers of repentance she was supposed to know? If she attempted to muddle through, what would the priest say? Father Mesplie, whom Bert had spoken so highly of, would surely see through any pretense. He might even proclaim that she should be put away because of her distracted intellect.

As she hiked up the grade under a mildly benevolent sun, lifting the hem of her skirt and trying to kick up as little dust as possible, her eyes scaled the walls and steeply pitched roof of the small structure until they met an exceedingly modest belfry. Studying the bright white of the wooden siding and trim and the unmarred shine of the windows, she guessed that the church had been constructed less than a year earlier. Before the family reached the steps, greeted along the way by a few acquaintances, the bell in the tower began to ring out in beckoning tones.

Taking a breath at the door, Rachel prayed that the rituals ahead wouldn't prove to be *that* dissimilar to those of the Lutheran church she'd first attended as a child with Grandpa Simon. She remembered Bert mentioning that Idaho City was also home to a Baptist and Methodist church, either of which might conduct more familiar services, but the Milfords were Catholic; very Catholic, it seemed, since the thought of missing Mass unnecessarily was unheard of, and she intended to watch the movements of the family members closely to avoid any misstep that might betray her incongruity.

They were all dressed in their Sunday clothes. Each female, having bathed in the metal tub the night before, a strange but gloriously welcome experience for Rachel, had donned her finest dress, Juliet having thankfully removed the blood from her pink one, and arranged and pinned her hair beneath a demure bonnet. Bert, True, and Phillip had washed in the creek, dressed in starched shirts, string ties, and brushed coats, and carefully oiled and combed their hair. Charlie's once neat hair, however, sprouted tufts and spikes on the right side from leaning against Rachel's shoulder during the wagon ride, and Juliet tried with little success to tame the disarray with her fingers as she led her youngest inside.

A few paces behind the others, Rachel saw Juliet pause in the aisle, gently take Kate by the shoulders, pat them reassuringly, and position her just ahead. Rachel forced her gaze to rise until it met the simple crucifix above the altar. Offering up a quick plea for forgiveness, she walked forward, head bent, and heard the door close securely behind her. In imitation of the Milfords, she made the sign of the cross, genuflected, and knelt on a hard wooden plank before a pew. Aunt Faith found them and, casting a pleased look toward Rachel, knelt down at the end of their row next to True. Amid the soft whispers and shifting of the congregation, Rachel glanced sideways at Kate.

The journey to town had been anything but comfortable for the girl's bruised backside, but she'd quietly endured every bump and jerk. Rachel had picked up the furtive glimpses Bert had cast at Kate that morning, and believed he felt the burden of his duties, especially the requirement to paddle his children when they deserved it, more heavily than his daughter rued the punishment.

The night before, Kate had forced herself to stop crying before tersely but truthfully describing the happenings in the meadow. Juliet, Bert, and Grandpa had listened with growing dismay, but waited for the full accounting. True had then added details where he felt they were needed, all of which were reluctantly confirmed by Rachel. Once the telling had been accomplished Bert had shaken his head and marched Kate out to the barn stalls. When the two had returned several minutes later, Kate's lower lip was swollen from clamping her teeth down and Bert had grown pale. Kate was dry-eyed, though, and Rachel would have wagered that she'd remained so throughout the episode in the barn. The girl didn't start weeping again until she walked across to Juliet and looked up into her mother's troubled face.

With an obvious effort, Juliet had kept from hugging the girl. "You'd best go on up to bed, Kate."

After a subdued supper, the rest of the Milfords had drifted off to bed, leaving True and Rachel to wander into the front room and watch the fire as it faded to embers.

"Has Kate always caused so much worry?" Rachel had asked.

True had looked back at her uncertainly. "Worry?"

"Has she always been so...wild, I mean?"

"Oh, she's always pretty much said whatever she's got in her head, but Phillip's worse at times. Kate doesn't get many whippings, though. She's pushed Pa's temper many a time but he usually can't bring himself to make her pay for it. Kate's always been his favorite, after all."

Rachel's look of surprise caused him to chuckle.

"Why sure. I think it's 'cause she reminds him so much of Mama when she was a girl."

"*Juliet* was like *Kate* when she was young?" Rachel had asked, so amazed that she forgot to refer to Juliet as Mama.

"Pa's told me many a story about Mama's girlish adventures," True said, his smile lingering. "He swears she's what turned her father's hair pure white."

Rachel had allowed this rapport, born in the forest as they'd watched the grizzly, to follow them home, and she'd welcomed his company as they talked of small things late into the night.

Upon awakening at dawn, much to Rachel's surprise, Kate had shown no sign of resentment toward either True or her. On the contrary, Kate had sat beside Rachel all the way into town without a word of self-pity or accusation. Sensing Rachel's unspoken sympathy, Kate had touched her hand and said in a hushed voice, "My backside ain't so bad, Rachel. Not if I don't sit too long in one place."

And now, as they all knelt in the tiny church, Rachel remembered what True had said about Kate being so like Juliet. She surreptitiously studied the woman, and then her daughter, hunting for similarities and finding more than a few. Perhaps she was beginning to glimpse the depths of Kate's character, and True's, and those of the other Milfords.

An hour and a half later Rachel emerged from the service wishing she'd taken Latin in school, but very much relieved that things hadn't gone too badly. It had been hard to miss when to stand or kneel or sit with Maggie helpfully poking her in the side at her slightest hesitation. And, Lord, she was eternally grateful that confession had not even been mentioned.

The parishioners gathered outside the church to exchange news and pleasantries, allowing Rachel to ease to the back of the Milford clan. She hadn't been surprised when Stan failed to attend Mass, but she'd glanced over the attendees wondering if she might see the tall stranger who'd forestalled the gun battle during her last trip to town. She did so again now, thinking he could have been seated behind her pew, but he wasn't among them, and she hoped his absence wasn't the result of an injury he'd suffered during the fight.

When a few folks approached she tried to smile and murmur polite trivialities without encouraging them further, and to hide a growing impatience to leave the churchyard and explore the town below. When the first people began to disburse, Rachel caught sight of Father Toussaint Mesplie at the base of the steps, wishing his parishioners a good day. With his broad forehead, smiling eyes, and chiseled jaw, the priest emanated friendly trustworthiness. His curly brown hair had receded a bit, and she guessed him to be somewhat older than thirty years of age. An inch or two shorter, as he approached the Milfords he tilted his concerned smile up at her. Tapping his own forehead, he asked with a charming French accent, "And how is your poor head feeling today, Rachel? You are quite recovered, I hope."

"I'm feeling much better," she replied, glad that this much was true.

He glanced at Juliet for verification and received a slight nod.

Bert said, "She's nearly her old self again, Father. We feel she's even up to a stroll around town this morning."

"Ah, it is a fine day, a splendid day for a stroll," proclaimed Father Mesplie. "Enjoy your Sunday and may our Lord bless you." He shook hands with Bert, smiled fondly at the rest, and as he moved off to speak with a small group still clustering near the door of the church, Rachel, the Milfords, and Aunt Faith retraced their way down the hill.

For once the byways were dry rather than muddy, making walking a genuine pleasure. The Chinese and Caucasian vendors meandering through the streets to hawk their wares captured Rachel's interest first, their loud cries competing in a complex chorus of pitch and cadence. Balanced across the shoulders of some of the peddlers was a thick stick weighted at each end by a basket of vegetables or other fresh goods, while others vendors pushed handcarts to display their wares. Several of the Sunday walkers paused to inspect the goods, but it was the cooks emerging from restaurants and hotels that seemed to be doing most of the buying.

Hawkers and cooks were not the only ones declining to consider Sunday a day of rest, however. In all directions miners could be seen digging, sluicing, and separating, and the tilt of some of the houses attested to the zealousness of these gold hunters. Like everyone else, Rachel had to use care to avoid stepping into recently dug trenches as she made her way.

This was her first opportunity to investigate the local shops and businesses, and she explored with a curiosity and captivation that she didn't completely mask. The children and adults seemed content to let her lead their little procession, and voiced no complaints when she often paused for a closer look. In front of a Chinese laundry with a sign proclaiming Mr. Quong as the proprietor, Rachel startled this evident owner by bowing to him in greeting. Judging from Mr. Quong's quickly repeated bows and hurried shuffling away as well as the Milfords' surprised expressions, she'd made some social blunder, and she continued on in mild puzzlement as to what transgression she'd committed.

Certain that Juliet and Bert would disapprove of her poking her head into one of the many saloons, Rachel walked past most of these, but she couldn't help stopping near a door on Main Street that bore the sign, "Gem Bowling Alleys and Saloon." *Bowling?* She peeked through a window and spotted several gleaming lanes that might have been mistaken for those of modern-day Chicago, except that young men or boys were stationed at the end of each alley rather than a mechanical device to reset the pins. *Well, what do you know?*

They progressed a couple of blocks before Rachel's steps slowed again, this time before a large one-room cabin with its front door, bearing an impressive lock, thrown wide open to embrace the breeze. Drawn closer by the small sign that read "Doctors and Sick Only," Rachel peered inside to find a bed, iron stove, metal tub, rocking chair, wooden cradle, various other small pieces of furniture, and several barrels and crocks, but not a single person. She turned to True and asked, "Is this some sort of hospital? I don't remember it at all."

"It's the pest house," he said with a tone of distaste.

"Pest house?"

A little uncomfortably, he continued, "It's where they keep people who are sick with something that might be catching."

Incredulous, she probed, "Keep them? Sick people? Not against their will, surely."

"Sometimes. Most folks don't want the sick taken to the hospital since it's mostly for hurt miners, or anybody needing an operation, or if they have a disease that's not likely to spread."

Kate piped up helpfully, "They throw crazy folks in that pest house, too."

Almost before these words reached Rachel's awareness, Juliet had placed a firm arm around Kate's shoulders and strode her down the boardwalk. Without slowing her pace, Kate jerked her head back, her mortified expression relaying that she'd just realized how her words might have affected Rachel, but Juliet kept the girl moving forward, giving her no opportunity for apology.

With a shake of his head, True said to Rachel, "You see what I mean about Kate letting the wrong words out at the wrong time?"

Bert spoke up with authority, "Let's move along, True." Rachel, however, couldn't help glancing back and picturing the hardships and tragedies that such a place could impose. She hoped the risk of her being imprisoned here was small and growing ever smaller as she adapted more convincingly to this setting, but she reflected for some time on how little she'd appreciated or even deeply considered the medical practices of her time. And what if one of them were severely injured or became seriously ill? What would be the likelihood of survival? When she perceived concerned glances from the Milfords at her side, Rachel diverted these thoughts, lightened her features, and again let the town take possession of her notice.

Unexpectedly, the sheriff's office proved to be a bright spot on Rachel's tour. A modest building, just a tiny wooden rectangle with a shed roof, yet the moment Rachel spotted it she was struck by the notion that it had been plucked from an old Western. There was even a deputy slouched on the bench before it, his arms folded across his chest, and his thin, booted legs crossed at the ankles. Bert greeted the deputy politely, asked as a matter of conversation where Sheriff Pinkham might be, and was informed that the sheriff had ridden off to bring in some chicken thieves. When the deputy tipped his hat to the ladies as they passed him, Rachel inwardly chuckled at the quaintness of it all.

Quaint, indeed, but there was also grandeur in this small town on the edge of the wilderness; with an excellence and abundance that Rachel marveled at and would never have believed without seeing it. From its face and through its doorway she took her time to admire the elaborate stained-glass windows, plush velvet upholstery and drapes, etched crystal lamps and chandeliers, and polished wood of the Jenny Lind Theater. According to the large flysheet displayed in the front display case, "The Queen of Comedy and Song," Mrs. W. H. Leighton, along with the San Francisco Star Troupe, was currently being featured, and Rachel wondered what it would be like to attend a performance here. But that would take money, a thing currently unavailable to her in any significant quantity.

She proceeded to inspect the respectable hotels along their route, such as the Montana House, and was more and more impressed by the beautiful appointments the owners had paid to have packed into this remote area. The mules and their drivers must have been magical.

At the end of the street she turned around and took it all in. *Oh, how I wish I had a camera with me,* she thought. *I'd love to show all of this to Ellen, and to Mother.* It was a ridiculous notion, and yet it triggered a slight wave of regret and vulnerability, and it reminded her how deeply she missed her loved ones. She kept her face away from the Milfords until she was able to tighten her emotions enough to conceal them. Then, breathing evenly and determined to wring whatever joy she could from this day, she eased away from the hotel and walked on with her chin lifted.

A few doors down they passed an attorney's office, and Rachel, considering the practice she'd so recently left, said to Bert, "Another lawyer. Do you know how many live here?"

"Not by count, but there's a heap."

"Do they all have fairly thriving practices?"

"With so many mining companies forming or closing, and all the fighting over claims, they seem to do just fine."

From a tiny inkling an idea built itself into an insistent question. Why couldn't *she* practice law here? Almost immediately the challenges became obvious. Would a woman be accepted? Well, her mind countered, even if they wouldn't hire her as an attorney right away, perhaps she could act as an assistant working behind the scenes. But how could she explain her knowledge of the law? She gave herself a mental shake. What knowledge of the law? *These* laws, territorial laws, were entirely unknown to her. She'd have to study as if she were a first-year law student again. The possibility continued to grow, however, cluttered though it was with hurdles.

With this prospect nudging her she led the family toward the courthouse and halted long enough to steal a look inside, but there was no one there. She took a few more seconds to picture herself practicing law within this tidy wooden room, a goal that would be worth giving a damn good try.

True peered in over her head and, seeing nothing of interest, asked, "What is it you're looking for?"

Rachel pulled the door closed and gave him a conspiratorial grin, but she offered no explanation as she took his arm and turned him away. Maggie appeared at her side and claimed possession of the hand Rachel had just tucked into True's elbow, but her brother merely chuckled good-naturedly and strode on to join his father and the others.

As they headed back toward the wagon the sun shone down like a blessing, enticing Rachel to lift her face to its warmth. When she pulled off her bonnet her bun loosened and slid down her back, so she removed the remaining hairpins as she walked slowly on, freeing the golden waves completely. Pausing to deftly re-braid her hair, she heard Maggie whisper her name and looked down at the girl. Then, following Maggie's uneasy gaze, Rachel caught sight of a group of seven men leaning against the wall of the Pony Saloon not far ahead, and seven pairs of eyes turned her way, some looking as if she were the only pool of water in a very dry desert.

A quick glance showed her that Bert and the rest of the family were three blocks away, rambling on in a small cluster as they listened to one of Charlie's stories. Giving Maggie a reassuring nod, Rachel quickly re-pinned her hair while ignoring the gawking men, tied her bonnet back in place, and crossed with Maggie to the farthest edge of the street.

The crowd at the door grew larger, but Rachel and Maggie had nearly passed beyond the Pony when the girl noticed a handbill on the ground and stooped to pick it up. "Look, Rachel, there's going to be cock fights and dog fights Friday night."

Rachel got Maggie moving faster as a low voice from across the way called out, "*I'll* take you to the cock fights, Missy."

"I like mine young," a new voice slurred. "I'll take your little sister."

Defiance and outrage jerked Rachel to a halt, flooding her cheeks with color, and narrowing her eyes in challenge. She faced the saloon, daring them to say such things to her directly. One of the men guffawed, and then beckoned crassly. Another fluttered his eyelashes and clasped his hands to his heart.

Just loudly enough, she said, "Toss me one of your guns and we'll see if you're still brave enough to frighten a little girl."

For a moment that seemed to sober them, then an unshaven man with a cut lip lifted the pistol from his holster and threw it into the street. "Sweetheart, I'll let you shoot the lot of us if you can reach that before I do."

Rachel moved her glare from the man to the gun and back again, but Maggie's grasp tightened. "No, Rachel."

"Rachel!" Bert called loudly, hurrying toward them with True at his side. Some of the men near the saloon ducked back inside, but several remained, including the man who'd cast his gun into the dirt.

As Bert and True approached, Rachel let Maggie draw her toward them. She dragged her gaze from the man at the saloon door and saw that the rest of the Milfords were heading her way. They quickly circled her and Maggie, but True held back and eyed the gun on the ground.

"True," Bert barked, his step faltering as he turned toward his son.

Rachel stopped too, suddenly frightened to her bones. "No, True, please."

He hesitated only a moment longer before backing away and joining the others. Rachel grabbed onto his arm and leaned against him, trying to loosen the vice that had clamped her chest, berating herself bitterly for her rashness.

When they finally reached the wagon, Rachel found her voice. "Wait, please. Please forgive me, all of you. I'm so sorry for putting you in danger."

She'd hardly uttered the last words before Charlie cried, "I forgive you!"

Kate tried to offer comfort by saying, "We know that you can't help what you're saying quite yet. Besides, I admired the way you stared down that miner. He *needed* staring down."

Juliet pulled her close and let out one dry sob.

Bert put a hand on Rachel's shoulder and the other on his wife's. "Let's go visit Esther before we head home. It'll make us all feel better. But not a word about this to your sister. You hear me, kids?"

The next afternoon, as gentle and warm as the one before, found Rachel sitting beside Millie and admiring the contents of the metal pail. "Look at all that milk. You must be the best milk cow in the territory." It was something she hesitated to admit even to herself, but she was beginning to enjoy her time in the barn with the animals. She slid the bucket out from beneath Millie, lifting it as she stood, patted the cow and carefully pivoted toward the door.

Lewis came in carrying a long-bladed sickle over his shoulder and grinned at her. "Your pa says you all stopped off to see Miss Esther for a bit. How's she gettin' along?"

"She's the picture of pregnant health," Rachel said, setting down the pail. "She feels big and clumsy, but she's fine. Richard is nervous about the baby coming but, on the whole, they're both well and happy."

"Was there any news to be heard in town?"

"There always seems to be something wild going on around this territory, shootings mostly, and we brought a few newspapers back with us. Would you like to take a look at them?"

Lewis' smile slid into an expression of mild perplexity. "Why, no, but I thank you, Miss Rachel."

Apprehending her mistake, Rachel said, "I'd be happy to read it to you, if you'd like."

"That's mighty kind of you, but maybe after my chores is done? After supper?"

"Lewis," Juliet interrupted them from the doorway, "how many times do I have to remind you that Sunday is a day of rest?" She flung an accusatory glance at the sickle still resting on his shoulder. "You know you're not to do any heavy chores that don't truly need attention, but it's plain to see you've been mowing off that high grass south of the barn. If you don't mind Rachel reading to you, let her read. It would probably do her good, and you just might sit still for a spell."

The crafty woman, Rachel thought, hiding her amusement. "Yes, I'm sure reading would help me considerably."

Lewis couldn't keep the suspicion from his face but, after a quick study of both women, set down the sickle cheerfully enough. "All right, then. Let's commence."

"You fetch the paper, Rachel, and I'll take this milk in and get started on the butter," Juliet said, already lifting the bucket.

It took Rachel a little longer to get through the house and gain custody of a newspaper than she'd anticipated. Charlie had pricked his finger on a nail and needed Rachel to kiss it, Kate and Phillip were squabbling over who'd whittled the better bear paw and requested that she settle the matter, and Bert, who was pleased at hearing her intention, took a few minutes to point out the articles that might be of the greatest interest. When she finally reentered the barn there was no Lewis in sight, but by following his humming she found him in the tack room sitting on his cot and rubbing some sort of grease into the last yard of a leather whip.

Upon her appearance he stilled his hands and started to rise but she shook her head and motioned for him to keep his place. She eyed the whip, then stared at it and whispered, "It looks like mine."

"What's that, Miss Rachel?"

"It...may I hold it?"

Surprised, Lewis said, "Why sure you can. Just let me wipe this grease off so it don't get all over you." He pulled the whip through a clean rag several times and, rising to his feet, handed it to her.

How comforting, how familiar it was to tighten her fingers around the grip, and she faced the open door to gently flick the length of the rawhide out on the ground. She wound it up with knowing hands then softly snapped it straight again, and then a third time, testing its weight and balance. She was about to pass it back to Lewis when her thumb brushed across a rough patch in the handle, and she froze. Hesitating, almost certain of something that couldn't be, she drew it nearer to inspect the mark carved into the leather, and her eyes met a cross identical in size and shape to the one borne by her own whip. Suddenly unsteady, she found her way to the cot and with the help of his outstretched hands lowered herself to sit beside him.

Lewis scooted far over but watched her closely. "You all right, Miss Rachel?"

"I am, yes, it's just that your whip looks so much like one I used to own. It surprised me."

"You certain?" When she gave him a fairly convincing nod, he said, "Why, I ain't never seen you handle a whip before, Miss Rachel. How'd you come to use one so good?"

Her mind was still reeling. The cross on Lewis' whip, the entire whip looked too much like hers to be anything else. The only exception was that its younger age revealed itself in the lightness of the color and suppleness of the leather. But surely, her reason grappled, thousands of whips were indistinguishable from this one. What about the cross? It was a common symbol, wasn't it? And Lewis' whip simply *couldn't* be her whip. Then again, was it possible, just possible that this woven leather lash was a link to her future?

"Miss Rachel," said Lewis, studying her again, "I was askin', where'd you ever learn how to use a whip?"

Rachel looked into his puzzled face, trying to keep the disbelief and speculation from her own. "Lewis, do you know who carved that cross in the handle?"

"Yes, ma'am, I surely do. I carved it there my own self, back on May sixteenth, the day I got rightly named and baptized." He watched for a sign that she remembered that date and, seeing none, he explained, "I needed to get me a last name that could be put on the baptism paper.

It was your mama who come up with just the right one. She said, 'How about Lewis Freeman for a name?' That pleased me no end, and Father Mesplie said my new name out loud with the baptism prayers, right there in church with your mama and pa standing up for me, and all you kids close around. When we got home, I carved that cross so I'd never forget that fine day."

"Lewis Freeman is a beautiful name," Rachel said, allowing herself to accept with certainty that she'd held his whip many times before today, understanding that she'd long possessed an unknown bond with this man. Moved deeply by this knowledge, she struggled to conceal what she felt.

"Yes'm, a beautiful name. I'm grateful to your mama."

After a pause she was able to ask, "Did Pa give you this whip, on your baptism day?" She saw by his expression that this was not the case, she felt his hesitancy, but she had to know. "Will you tell me where you got it, Lewis?"

He looked at the floor for a breath or two. When at last he said, "I took it, from a man down in Texas," his voice told much more than his words.

"Did he *use* this on you?"

"He used it mostly on his animals, and his oldest boy. I took it so he never got a chance to use it again."

Rachel suspected that Lewis had committed an act of violence to protect the boy even more than himself, and she could not condemn him. She gazed at the whip again. "But why did you keep it, and carve a cross in it, if it's been used with such cruelty?"

"I put that cross there as a promise to God, a promise that I'd never let it hurt another innocent thing." It took him a minute, but he made himself confess the rest. "And I promised that there'd never come another day when I'd take somethin' that wasn't rightly mine, like I took that whip."

They were both silent, each dealing with hopes and hauntings born long ago, and then speculating about the thoughts of the other.

In the end it was Rachel who spoke first. "Did anyone else whip you, Lewis?"

"Only once." He unlocked the rest of the words. "I was eight years old. I learned that day never to question a man with a whip, not unless I grew to be big enough to take it away from him."

"Oh, Lewis, I'm so sorry."

"Why, Miss Rachel," he said, his attention brought back to the present by the intensity of her feelings, "you needn't be sorry about it. It was no fault of yours."

"He was white, wasn't he, the man who beat you?"

"Yes, he was white." His features softened as he added, "But he wasn't you."

Rachel again ran her thumb over the incised cross. "It was my grandfather who taught me how to use a whip," she said, answering his earlier question. She didn't need to explain who her real grandfather was, or why he had taught her. These words were answer enough.

"That so? What would you think about showin' me how to work it, before you commence to readin'?"

"You don't already know how to wield it?"

"I never put it to any use at all, 'cept for rememberin' my promises." Tentatively, he asked, "Did you ever have cause to use one, Miss Rachel?"

Her fingers constricted around the grip. "When I was young," she said, "someone used it for me."

He nodded slowly, apparently understanding. "You feel like readin' for a spell now?" He reached over, gently eased the whip from her grasp, and hung it on the wall. Taking down a horse collar, he said, "Now you needn't tell your mama about a little polishin', since I mean to pay close heed to your readin'," and he began to work grease into the leather.

She lifted the paper but it took a few sentences before her slightly stumbling voice smoothed. She kept her focus on the first article and soon read each paragraph with ease. Lewis seldom interrupted, but asked questions nearly every time she paused, especially about the progress of the war. His queries were very intuitive, and Rachel answered them as well as she could. He continued to listen with such intensity that she finally eyed him over the paper and said, "Have you seen anything of the war first-hand?"

"Some, in the early days, when I was travelin' west. Those were bloody, hungry times, not ones I'm pleased to recall. But I like hearin' what's goin' on now."

Rachel lowered the newspaper into her lap. "Lewis, would you like to learn how to read? I could—"

"No, ma'am," Lewis cut her off.

Frowning, she asked, "Why not?" She saw that he was donning the polite yet dogged expression he used to counter Juliet whenever the subject of eating with the family arose, but she wasn't prepared for his response.

Firmly, he said, "Niggers ain't supposed to read."

"That's absolute bullshit!"

Her language shocked the stubbornness right off his face. "Miss Rachel!"

"Don't you 'Miss Rachel' me. Surely you don't think you lack the intelligence to learn."

"I know they is things it's best I leave be."

"Because some bigot said so? You *should* learn to read."

He rose to his feet in agitation. "No, Miss Rachel. I'm a nigger.

I ain't like you, no matter what you or your mama says."

Rachel stood up too. "Will you please stop saying that word!"

Surprised anew, Lewis asked, "What word?"

She had to force it out of her mouth. "Nigger."

"But that's what I am. There ain't no white man standin' here."

"I see a *man*," she nearly shouted in his face. She was furious and sickened by what Lewis had endured, must still endure, and by everything that slavery encompassed. Before her stood its legacy; an ex-slave who'd survived untold shame and hardship at the hands of those who claimed to own him body and soul, crushing both until he felt unworthy of either knowledge or respect. With a great effort, she said levelly, "I see a fine man, Lewis, whose skin happens to be a shade or two darker than my own."

She waited, watching the play of confusion and frustration on his face, and then a shade of acknowledgement. Finally, a sad resolve replaced all other expressions, and after a drawn out moment he said, "Miss Rachel, you don't recall about it, though you have seen it many a time before, so I guess I best show you." He turned away from her, and his fingers moved slowly to the buttons of his shirt, his entire body heavily reluctant yet continuing along the course his mind had resolved to take.

Rachel didn't move or speak.

When he'd freed the top four buttons, his shirttails still tucked into his pants, he shrugged the top of the shirt from his shoulders.

She tried to swallow her gasp and failed. The raised, horizontal stripes were shinier and darker than the rest of his back, and at the end of each ugly, overlapping welt was a rough-edged knob of deformed tissue. The scars had stretched and broadened as he'd grown, further disfiguring his back from shoulder to waist. Rachel forced what composure she could manage to her face before Lewis buttoned his shirt and turned to her again.

He kept his head low as he spoke. "Like I said, it happened when I was eight. The massa's son, he was readin' his bible lessons one day and he got it in his head to teach me how to read. They caught us when we was on the second lesson. That's why they whipped me, 'cause I was learnin' to read." His eyes moved to the whip resting on the cot. "He didn't use one like that, though. It was shorter and it had three tails on it. Each of them tails had a sharp metal piece tied to the end, to cut the skin. Not too deep in the muscle, though. They was mighty careful about that."

"Lord, Lewis, I'm truly, truly sorry for stirring up so terrible a memory. I won't ask about learning to read again, not if you don't want me to."

His mouth worked itself into a resigned smile softened by guarded affection. "If I know anythin' at all about you, Miss Rachel, it's that you is a heap like your mama. If you think it's what's best for me, you'll ask." He reached down and picked up the discarded newspaper. Eyeing the words on the front page, he shook his head and grunted. "Maybe I best allow you to have your way right off. It might save us both a heap of grief."

Trying to conceal her hopefulness, Rachel asked, "Are you sure?"

"No, ma'am. I ain't sure at all. But I *am* willin'."

"Well, then," she said, shoring up her own courage a bit, "if you'll learn to read, I'll teach you how to use that whip. How's that for a deal?"

She held out her right hand and he accepted it with a look of circumspection. "Just don't you go tellin' your mama I give in to you so easy. She's likely to be gettin' more thoughts of her own about what's best for me."

"Agreed," said Rachel. "There's just one more thing, though. That word, Lewis. Nigger. Please don't use it ever again. That's not what you are, or what you ever were."

13

Two days of thunderous cloudbursts swelled the creeks to torrents and turned the barnyard into a shallow swamp, thereby significantly advancing Lewis along the path to literacy. He and Rachel spent most of those days absorbed in the words of McGuffey readers and newspapers, and she was exceedingly pleased with his steady improvement. When the showers finally calmed and the clouds disbursed enough for the waiting sun to show itself, the Milford family took full advantage of the finer weather. The adults and older children busily saw to their postponed duties from well before dawn to sunset while the little ones happily muddied themselves in the puddles. By the following noon the land had drained and dried to such an extent that their regular schedule of chores could resume.

Overseen by the watchful eyes of Phillip and the two dogs, especially since rustlers had been reported to be plaguing the area, the stock was allowed to graze for a few hours each day on the new grass in nearby meadows. The other children hauled water and wood into the house, fed and watered the chicks and dogs, and performed the morning milking before being driven to school.

To exercise her restlessness once the children had departed, Rachel threw herself into helping with almost any work to be done outdoors. On those mornings when her eldest daughter came down the stairs dressed in True's pants, Juliet seemed content with the prospect of cleaning and cooking alone, sensing Rachel's growing need for less confining spaces. More and more often, Rachel was permitted to work the sluice boxes for a few hours after sunrise, long enough for her hands to develop calluses and her muscles to adapt to such work. On most afternoons, she began the day's second milking as Juliet took up her hoe to weed the garden and the field while water flowed through the many furrows, and after the full milk pails had been set in the creek to cool, Rachel grabbed a shovel to assist her. They toiled in the dirt until their bodies were sweaty and grimy, but there were still animals to feed and water again, food to prepare, and dishes to wash. Even with so many demands on her energy, however, Rachel never failed to leave time for Lewis' reading lessons, each of which was followed by his promised instruction in the use of the bullwhip. If Juliet and the rest of the Milfords paused to wonder about the whip's snap echoing between the mountains, they withheld their curiosity from her.

Rachel looked forward to his schooling, which she usually conducted on the bench against the outer front wall of the barn. Each early evening they took up the McGuffey's Primer that Maggie had used the prior year, and went to work. From the start she had been pleased with Lewis' abilities, even when he showed signs of disgruntled impatience. Her biggest obstacle during the first days was convincing him that he was indeed making progress. Although determined, he was restive with what he feared were small successes and began to dread that he was wasting Rachel's time, so much so that on the third day he asked if she wanted to give up the attempt altogether. This suggestion she declined in no uncertain terms, and by the fifth session he could recite the alphabet, grasp each letters' phonetic symbolism, and attempt to put the sounds together with a small measure of confidence. Not until he actually read the first simple words in the primer, however, did he finally show a slight satisfaction with his own accomplishments.

Now Rachel handed him the book again and pointed to the text he was to read aloud. He raised a doubtful eyebrow, but she said, "You can read that, Lewis. I know it looks a little long but it's just a review of what you've already learned. Try it." Frowning deeply in concentration, he leaned over the pages in his thick-fingered hands and, stumbling occasionally, sounded out each word. Although she had to exert a great deal of self-control, Rachel forced herself to let him plod forward alone.

"'Tom's nag is fat; his dog is not fat. Nat is on Tom's nag. Nat's dog, Rab, can not catch the rat.'" He took a deep breath. "'See the frog on the log. A lad sees the frog. The lad can not catch it. A cat is on the mat, the cat sees a rat. Ann's fan is on the stand. The man has a lamp. A dog ran at the man. Ann sat on a log.'"

He stared at the words until a smile lit his eyes and spread to his mouth. Lifting his face to Rachel, who beamed back at him and waited for him to speak, he said quietly, "Why, look what you done, Miss Rachel. You done taught me how to read."

"I taught, but you *learned* how to read, Lewis." She reached out and gave his forearm a squeeze that conveyed her pride in him. Taking the book momentarily, she flipped the pages to the last lesson. "I read this last night, but you'll be reading it for yourself before long." She read it out loud, slowly and with feeling. "'When the stars, at set of sun, watch you from on high; when the light of morn has come, know the Lord is nigh. All you do, and all you say, he can see and hear; when you work and when you play, know the Lord is near. All your joys and griefs he knows, sees each smile and tear; when to him you tell your woes, know the Lord will hear.'"

Rachel had thought to read this passage to encourage Lewis' interest and belief in his own reading, but when she raised her head and looked upon his trembling mouth and spilling tears, she realized that she'd touched a much, much deeper faith within him.

In a strained voice, he asked, "Can you read that again, Miss Rachel?"

She did, even slower, and this time the words moved her as well.

He reached out and took the open book from her. Wiping at his eyes, he studied the poignant words for a moment, then exhaled deeply and met her gaze. "I always wondered, all these long years, why I got that whippin' after hearin' words from the good book. It troubled me for the longest time, long after my back stopped a hurtin'. Seemed like maybe the Lord meant his holy words only for white folks, like maybe I wasn't good enough to read 'em, maybe not even good enough to hear 'em." He nodded toward the McGuffey's. "Them words you was readin' just now about God, they was speakin' to me just as much as to any folks on this earth."

Rachel opened her mouth to assure him that this was so, but the intensity of his gaze silenced her.

"You teachin' me to read, Miss Rachel, for that and...more, I'm powerful grateful to you. More grateful than I can say."

"You're very welcome, Lewis." Perhaps it was the intensity and closeness of that moment, but the truth about herself, who she really was, suddenly attacked her conscience and the depth of her pretense bit sharply. What right did she have, after all, to get so deeply involved in this man's life, to gain his trust and appreciation, when she hoped to sneak away as soon as she could? It would only hurt him, perhaps acutely, when she left. His knowing how to read would remain with him, she disputed, but self-incrimination only took a stronger hold. She stood up and said as smoothly as she could, "I'd better go and see if I'm needed in the house. Good night, Lewis." She left him alone with the book and his thoughts. Yet as she crossed the barnyard with long, quick strides, it never occurred to her to discontinue Lewis' lessons.

She entered the darkening kitchen, unconsciously reached for an electric light switch that didn't exist, and knocked Bert's hat off its wall peg. "Damn it!" she muttered under her breath. When was she going to stop *doing* that? She must have knocked that hat off ten times, each time determining not to do it again. She bent and snatched it off the floor, hastily replaced it on its peg, and turned to find Juliet watching her from the other doorway. Juliet's glance went from the hat to Rachel and concern briefly crossed her face but she said nothing. Rachel could only guess how strange this habit of knocking hats around must appear.

Ignoring the small mishap and even the curse word, Juliet lit a candle and asked, "How's Lewis coming along?"

They sat down at the table before Rachel answered, "Very well. He finished the first chapter tonight."

"Well isn't that fine. You know, it seems like Maggie is applying herself more to her own lessons these days." Juliet chuckled softly, "I believe she means to keep a step ahead of him."

"She'll have to work hard, then. He's gaining speed now that he understands he really *can* read."

"Are you troubled by something, honey? You seem a little—"

Both women turned their heads at the sound of pounding on the front door. They hurried into the front room quickly crowding with children as Bert opened the door to find an excited boy of about Phillip's age.

Spotting Juliet, he panted, "Mrs. Milford, you're to come right quick. It's Aunt Esther. She's having her baby!"

The Milford youngsters burst into a chorus of questions and exclamations, and during the first moments of chaos, Rachel deduced that this visitor must be one of Richard's nephews.

Bert shouted above the clamor, "Hush, you kids! Hush so we can hear!"

Juliet came to the boy and took him by the shoulders. "Now, Mikel, who was it that sent you? Was it Esther?"

"No, ma'am, it was Uncle Richard."

"Is a doctor with Esther yet?"

"No, ma'am, she wouldn't let Uncle Richard send for one 'til I fetched you."

"Do you know how long she's been having pains?"

"Not long, at least I don't reckon so, but Uncle Richard, he's in a state fit for tying."

"And your Aunt Esther? How's she doing?"

Mikel considered. "She seemed about like always, excepting that I heard her holler at Uncle Richard that if he don't settle down he'd have to wait outside. She don't never talk to him like that. Well not regular, anyhow."

Bert asked, "Did you ride here alone?"

"Yes, sir, on Uncle Richard's gelding."

"All right then, you ride back now and let Richard know we're on our way."

Mikel nodded once, ran out the door, untied the horse from the porch post with a jerk, and leaped into the saddle. With a quick wave, he swung the horse around and galloped off.

Bert hadn't even closed the door before the children started clambering again. Juliet answered a few of their questions, then shushed them all and looked at her husband, trying to hide a spark of fear.

"I'll hitch up the team," he said, turning at once to the back door.

"I'll give you a hand, son," said Grandpa, three steps behind.

Juliet looked at Rachel and asked, "Will you help me gather up the clothing I made for the baby?" The two also collected several clean blankets and towels, and a four-foot square of canvas. As Rachel folded and packed she tried not to think about how many women and babies must die during these times, but she couldn't ignore what she understood about the inadequacy of prenatal nutrition, instrument and wound sterilization, and medical training, or the lack of antibiotics. And there would be no electronic monitoring, life-supporting equipment, or neonatal unit available. She wasn't even sure if one of the local doctors could successfully perform a caesarian section if one were needed.

She knew with brutal certainty what Esther's death would do to Juliet, to this whole family, and the unborn baby was precious to them already. The loss of its life would also be deeply mourned.

Not until everything had been packed into a large cloth bag did Juliet notice Rachel's silence. Reading the anxiety and fear on her face, she said with a little too much conviction, "Now, she'll be all right, honey. I know you always planned to be with her. Do you feel up to it tonight?"

Rachel stammered, "Well, I..."

At that moment, Bert came through the front door and asked Juliet, "You ready?"

"*I* want to come!" begged Kate. "I could be lots of help."

"Me too, me too," piped Maggie, bobbing with eagerness.

"Now, now, you two need to help out with things here," Juliet told her younger daughters. "How would Grandpa and True get along with *all* us women gone from the house? Besides, this might take days yet. A woman's first baby generally takes his own time coming."

"But I can *help* with the *baby*," Kate persisted, but to no avail.

Juliet and Bert looked at Rachel, waiting for an answer.

"Yes, I'm coming," she said, surprising herself a little. Wasting no more time, she hastily gathered up her coat and the yellow baby quilt that, under Juliet's patient guidance, she'd finished a couple of days earlier.

As they finished preparations to depart, Kate was boisterously protesting the injustice of being left behind, Phillip was lecturing Kate for her persistence, Maggie was looking broken-hearted, and True was bouncing Charlie in his arms in an attempt to quiet his wailing over being abandoned by both Juliet and Rachel.

Bert flicked a look of thanks at his father and signaled to his wife and oldest daughter with a jerk of his head toward the door. The cries and objections from the front room rose noticeably in volume, but neither Bert, Juliet, nor Rachel paused as they hurried out and climbed into the wagon.

"Don't you fret none about things here," Grandpa called from the porch, raising his voice to be heard above the noise inside. "We'll get along right fine."

By the time the Milfords arrived at Esther and Richard's three-room board and batten house, it was packed with in-laws. Young Mikel had arrived only minutes before and he, Richard's father, two brothers, and Mikel's younger sister were milling about like moths in the small front room. With Rachel in tow, Juliet gave the crowd no more than a polite mumble as she gently nudged her way through, leaving Bert behind to socialize.

Upon entering the bedroom, Juliet found Esther with her eyelids squeezed shut, her teeth gritted, her hands clenching the quilt as her swollen body fought an intense contraction. Richard's mother Arrosa moved aside for Juliet, shifting so quietly that Esther didn't immediately notice the arrival of her mother and sister. Juliet eased one of Esther's hands from the quilt and the slim fingers clamped tightly. Weak desperate noises escaped Esther's throat as she wrestled both the pain and the urge to cry out until the compressing uterus at last relented, and Esther's body gradually sagged, her breath resuming an exhausted pant. When she opened her glazed eyes to the face of her mother, tears formed and spilled down her cheeks, but she said only, "Mama." Her dry lips brought forth a tiny smile but it was unconvincing when her eyes showed so much fear and misery.

Juliet smoothed the damp blonde hair from Esther's forehead, silently measuring the skin temperature, the breathing, and the inner strength of this daughter she loved so dearly. She refused, utterly refused to consider the end of Esther's life in this bed tonight, even though she'd first seen the dangers of childbirth at the age of five when her own mother lost a child, Juliet's sister. Such tragedies had become far, far too familiar over the years that followed but she locked this dread deep inside, and said, "You're being mighty brave, Esther. You've got a big job ahead of you, but Doc and the rest of us are going to help every way we can. And then you're going to be a mama, honey, with a baby of your very own."

"Soon, I hope, Mama," Esther said, her tone wavering. Then, strengthening her voice a little, she lied, "The pain's not really so bad."

Juliet looked at Richard's mother. "How long since the pains started?"

Arrosa glanced at the clock on the dresser, and said with a heavy Basque accent, "About five hours, but things seem to be moving along faster than when any of my boys came. The birth-waters broke loose over an hour ago."

Juliet turned again to Esther. "My babies came faster than most, honey. Maybe yours will, too."

Rachel had been watching them closely, and knew that Juliet was marshaling her considerable force to appear calm and confident for her daughter's sake.

Juliet said, "I think it's time to let Richard or your pa go fetch Doc. Would that be all right?"

At Esther's nod, and a burst of nervous laughter from the men in the front room, Arrosa said, "I'll go tell them to get the doctor, and then we will all go home. Juliet, you'll send word if you need us, or when the baby comes?"

"You needn't all leave."

"Now, dear one," Arrosa said with affection, and reached out to rub Esther's blanketed foot, "I remember how it was when my times came. I wanted my mama right next to me and everyone else far away. You know we're just at the end of the road. We can be back in ten minutes if someone comes for us."

As the two women departed, Esther said, "Thank you, both," and turned her face to Rachel just as another contraction began to build. "I'm glad you came, sister. I've been thinking... how nice it would be if...if you would sing to me."

Without thinking beyond what she felt at that moment, wanting nothing but to lessen Esther's suffering if only by distraction, she said, "Of course, Esther." The words to an old song she'd learned in high school choir came to her, and in a pure tone she sang the first words to "Bridge Over Troubled Water."

Esther closed her eyes again as her pain intensified and Rachel faltered, but Juliet begged, "Keep singing, Rachel. Please."

So Rachel continued, seeing that Esther listened closely to the words and melodies she'd never heard before, and when her initial song ended she took up another. But as the contractions strengthened and lengthened, and the minutes between them dwindled away, Esther began to squirm and whimper. Rachel heard the front door close and words muttered in the front room, but Doc Willis' voice would have rattled the walls and its absence was noted at once.

"Rachel," said Juliet, "please go ask your father when Doc will get here."

She was gone only moments before returning to the bedroom and, incapable of fully camouflaging her uneasiness, she said, "Doc Willis and Doc Hogue are both spending the night in Boise City. Doc May is—he was in the—he'll be here as soon as he can." She kept the fact that the man was currently passed out on a cot in the back of a saloon to herself.

Summoning an assurance totally at odds with the trembling of her heart, Juliet declared, "Well, then, we women will manage on our own for now." She walked to the door and thrust her head out, saying, "Richard, fetch a couple of buckets of fresh water, start the water from one to boiling, and set a foot or so of twine and Esther's sewing scissors in the pot when it's good and hot. Now don't you two men worry any. Things are just fine in here." She then brought out the clean canvas they'd brought with them from home and, from Esther's bottom dresser drawer, sheets, rags, and a baby gown Juliet had helped Esther place there two weeks earlier.

When the contractions became wrenching and nearly continuous Esther cried out at last. Desperate to aid her, Rachel's memory reached back to any TV show, series, movie, or article she'd ever seen that dealt with labor. She quickly recalled the many times acquaintances had relayed their labor experiences, and hadn't her own brother Joseph detailed every stage of her nephew's birth? Everything had indicated that the prospective mother must breathe deeply and stay relaxed to keep from dwelling on the pain. Near the end of labor, when the mother wanted to push, she was to pant until her cervix had dilated to ten centimeters, but how big was ten centimeters? She concluded that Esther's rigidity was worsening her torment, and perhaps her shallow breathing was hindering her oxygen flow, making concentration and control even harder.

This sketchy knowledge was all Rachel had to offer but unable to remain at the foot of the bed any longer she moved to the side opposite Juliet and took Esther's free hand. Interrupting Juliet's gentle attempts to soothe, Rachel said in an authoritative voice, "Esther, try not to fight against the pain. You must try to make your body relax."

"I c-can't," Esther choked out.

"Yes, you can, and I'm going to help you. Open your eyes and look at me." When Esther didn't obey, Rachel repeated with more intensity, "Esther, look at me."

Esther's eyes opened wide, exposing her panic and torment.

Leaning in close, Rachel held Esther's stare with her own and said, "Take a deep breath, as deep as you can, and keep breathing evenly."

Esther made an attempt but her breath came out in choppy gasps. She closed her eyes and moaned again as her legs jerked and bent. Rachel leaned within inches of Esther's face and rubbed her hand vigorously. "Esther, *look at me*. Good, now don't take your eyes from my face. I'm going to breathe with you. Do exactly as I do."

Esther stared at Rachel's mouth and struggled to keep her mind locked on its movements. Imitating one long breath, she pulled the air into her lungs and let it out, then another, and another, each new attempt a little more determined than the one before. Gradually her twisting motions lessened. Throughout the minutes that followed, Esther was compelled to maintain this pattern of breathing and focus as she clung to Rachel's hand like a lifeline.

Juliet stood attentively by and watched them both in grateful amazement. At one point she pulled back the covers and gently moved Esther's legs apart to examine her progress. "You're doing so good, Esther. Just keep minding what Rachel tells you and it shouldn't be much longer." Juliet stepped out of the room only long enough to collect the water, twine, and scissors from Richard.

Eight or nine breaths later Esther raised her head off her pillow and strained to lift herself into a sitting position, saying tightly, "I... I think I have to push, Mama. Should I try?" As the contraction's intensity grew, and before Juliet could examine her again, Esther's body answered with a will of its own, a will that wouldn't be denied. Stealing a quick breath, she bore down, and pushed again, and then again. She had no time to lie back and rest, because the next contraction rushed to its peak almost immediately. Rachel climbed onto the bed and supported Esther's shoulders as Juliet moved back the quilt and positioned herself between her legs.

"Bend your knees, Esther," Rachel directed, "that's right, a little higher." In this more effective position Esther pushed through a third, sixth, tenth grinding contraction that dominated her entire frame, and Rachel was there coaxing, commanding, and encouraging.

As the baby crowned fully, Juliet offered up a silent, urgent prayer and pleaded aloud, "Push hard on the next one, Esther. Your baby's coming!"

Rachel cried, "You're doing great, Esther! You're almost there!"

"Again, Esther! Now!"

Sucking in a huge breath, she strained downward, and in a near shout Juliet ordered, "Keep pushing, honey!" Esther panted twice and pushed with even greater effort as she released a low guttural moan. An instant later, Juliet's tone dropped as she said, "Esther, wait, wait now." And as Esther stopped pushing Juliet's hands maneuvered in sparing yet determined motions to free the baby's shoulders. "Gently now, just one more small push."

Juliet grabbed a clean sheet, and with a weakened gasp Esther delivered the baby into her mother's arms. At the release of a very young, very robust cry Esther looked down and saw a thin fountain of yellow shooting skyward. Juliet muttered a soft, "Oh, oh," as she swiftly averted the stream, and with profound gentleness began to wipe the infant's skin clean, her eyes examining every limb and feature as she did so.

Esther murmured, "Mama?" but she'd recognized the surprise and joy in her mother's two short words and, reassured, lay back upon her pillow.

Extending a brief glance of acknowledgment toward Rachel, Juliet announced softly, "Your new son is perfect, Esther, just perfect." She lifted him for his mother to see, and then securely bound the umbilical cord in two places an inch apart and cut it between the twines. After bandaging this small wound, she lovingly swaddled the quieting baby and handed him with great care to his proud young mother. Only after taking in the unspeakably wonderful scene of her daughter and grandson lying before her safe, healthy, and happy, did the echo of the fear and uncertainty that had been subjugated during the last hours find a crack in the dam that had held them back, and tears trickled silently down Juliet's cheeks. She discreetly brushed them away and, so softly that only Rachel could make out her words, she muttered, "There never was a more beautiful sight. Thank you, thank you, Lord."

Through pooling tears of her own, Rachel witnessed the relief and happiness playing across Esther's face. Beside the bed where she'd just beheld life's most precious miracle, she felt hollow and whole and shaky and strong, and there was no need whatsoever to analyze this combination of sensations. When Juliet came around the bed and hugged her close and long it simply felt right, and the embrace was sincerely returned.

At the soft tap on the door, Juliet composed herself enough to say evenly, "All is well, gentlemen. Just give us a few more minutes."

Esther's new son had stopped crying, and he now crinkled his tiny nose and blinked and squinted his cola brown eyes up at her. While Esther and Rachel whispered endearments to the baby, Juliet moved again to the foot of the bed and checked with great relief on Esther's encouragingly slight flow of blood. Very capably she tended to the delivery of the afterbirth, and doctored and cleaned her daughter. When these things had been seen to, Juliet washed her own hands, tossed the water out the window, and prepared another basin of warm water. Exposing the gladness only a brand new grandmother could feel, she said, "That little man could use a bit more washing before he's presented to his pa. Rachel, would you like to bathe him?"

When Ester just beamed at her, and feeling abundantly privileged, if a little nervous, Rachel found a soft cloth among the other articles on the bureau and carefully accepted the babe from Esther. A little awkward at first, she soon loosened the swaddling from around his chest, settled him comfortably in the crook of her left arm and began moving the cloth with soft, slow motions over his tiny face and upper body.

Receiving the new mother's approval to do so, Juliet left the room to announce the arrival of their latest family member. At her joyous words, a burst of yells and whoops erupted from the outer room, followed immediately by robust congratulations, the slapping of shoulders, and the clinking of glasses.

As Rachel continued to bathe the baby's tiny warm body she acquainted herself with his impossibly beautiful face, his chin already showing a hint of the cleft he'd inherited from his father. His head was covered with nearly black fuzz and his delicate fingers and toes were perfectly formed. At last she picked up another clean cloth and dried him while he gazed up and spoke to her in very quiet squeaks. She moved him to the yellow quilt she'd helped Juliet make, and tenderly wrapped it around him. She was the first person, of all the people he would ever know, to bathe him. Somehow this insignificant fact was of tremendous importance to her. Smiling down at him, perceiving that he was the sweetest human ever created, she knew that her heart had been captured imprudently, unjustifiably, but completely. When the idea began to form that she might not be with him very long, she replaced it with the knowledge that she would help care for him as long as she could.

"You seem mighty taken with your new nephew," Esther said with deeply appreciative affection.

My nephew, Rachel thought as she again gazed into his face. She smiled at Esther. "You're absolutely right. I'm mighty taken with him, but I'm being awfully selfish. I'm sure you'd like to hold this handsome son of yours."

With that, she gingerly handed him over to his mother.

14

"Yes, she can stay," Juliet, amused, told Esther. "Did you think I'd say she couldn't lend a hand for another day or two? If she doesn't mind sleeping on your sofa, it's fine with me." Rachel and Esther grinned at each other like conspirators. "That way," Juliet went on, "Rachel can see that you don't overdo things, or at least she can try. You may feel like you're nearly as good as new, young lady, but it's only been three days. And you almost passed out yesterday, remember? Give yourself some time."

"But, Mama, there's so much that needs tending and I can't ask Rachel to do *everything*."

"You've got to learn to shift things around now that Conrad's here, Esther. Faith says you and Rachel don't have a thing for her to do when she stops by in the evening. I know she works hard during the day, honey, but she wants to be of use to you. Let her and Rachel do some of your chores, and let the rest go for now. They won't run off." Juliet glanced at Rachel. "I can see that your sister is more than happy to help as long as you allow her to hold that baby now and again."

Rachel, who happened to be cuddling Conrad at that moment, gently touched her nose to his, looking anything but repentant for her possessiveness.

"She was almost this bad when Charlie was born, but not quite," Juliet went on, happily shaking her head. "Do you recall how she'd hardly let you other kids hold him? It comes to mind that she was a bit stingy about sharing Maggie too. I don't know that I've ever heard of a young woman so taken with babies, unless it would be Kate. She's pining something fearful to see Conrad again."

The day before, all of the Milford children had taken a turn holding Esther's baby. Charlie and Maggie were given a little assistance, and everyone younger than True enjoyed their moments with Conrad under the watchfulness of his parents and their own. Kate had held him with utmost gentleness, declaring, "Ain't he just as fine as he can be?" She had parted with him most reluctantly and waited for a second turn with a loudly tapping foot.

Although there was still a little concern over Conrad's left foot, which had tilted slightly inward at birth, already his ankle seemed to be strengthening enough to pull his tiny foot into a normal position.

True, who had driven Juliet to town today, entered the house and announced, "The wood's all stacked, Esther." He came over to Rachel and peered at the baby, then looked over at Esther. "I'm too dirty to hold your boy right now, sister, and it appears doubtful that Rachel would give him up anyhow." They all responded with easy laughter as True headed outside to fill the wash pan at the large drum supplied by a creek channel. After chatting and sharing tea and corn bread for another half hour, Juliet kissed her daughters and her new grandson farewell, and departed for home with True.

On the night of Conrad's arrival, although she'd been invited most sincerely, Rachel had felt fairly uncomfortable to be ensconced in Esther's and Richard's small house, especially at such a cherished time, but she'd quickly busied herself with the many demands of a pioneer home with a new infant. Richard had shown appreciation for even her smallest contributions while Esther had made her feel irreplaceable. And the baby, well, with each wriggle and coo she found herself more "taken" with him, and she delighted in simply watching him sleep. By the third day, she truly wanted to remain with them at least a little longer.

During the occasions when Richard was at his barbershop, Esther and Conrad were napping, and Rachel had finished her chores, she sat in a chair on the front porch and watched the town activities. Visitors often came to the house, and were welcome to enter if Esther was feeling up to seeing them, but most passersby merely wished Rachel a good day or tipped their hats, taking only fleeting notice of her.

Stan O'Brien, however, had shown up on the first afternoon she was there, impressively dressed and endeavoring to engage her company on a stroll. She'd made it clear she had no intention of leaving her post for some time, so the following day he'd sauntered up the street and onto Esther's porch carrying his own chair, and left the chair behind when the visit had ended. He'd turned up again the next day and taken his seat as if he and Rachel had shared these afternoon talks for years. Only once during his visits had Rachel mentioned the earlier trouble in front of the feed store, asking in the most casual way about the man who'd come to their aid, and who had occupied a perceptible share of her thoughts since then. Rather than answering, Stan had pinned her with a penetrating look and deftly deflected the conversation.

It was around noon and Esther was settling the sleeping baby into his cradle, intending to sit down beside Rachel and crochet, when Stan appeared across the street. She spotted him, and her scowl of disapproval prompted Rachel to follow her gaze. Stan stood leaning against a porch post and aiming his all too knowing grin at them.

"Esther," said Rachel, "just what do you have against that man?"

"He's a gambler, for one thing, but mostly... it's the way he threatens any man that takes a shine to you, and some of them have been good men, the heathen."

Hiding her amusement at the ferocity of Esther's protectiveness, Rachel said, "You don't need to worry. I've dealt with men a lot more dangerous than Stan." At Esther's surprise and doubt, Rachel added soothingly, "We can be polite without encouraging him, can't we?"

Stan walked over and greeted them with, "What a bonny afternoon it is, ladies, is it not?"

Avoiding Stan's mischievous eyes, Esther picked Conrad up and stepped to her front door, where she paused only long enough to say, "I'll be right inside, Rachel, so you can call me if you need anything."

This drew an overly chivalrous bow from Stan, forcing a curt nod from Esther before she left them.

Stan sat close beside Rachel, ran his gaze over her face, and said, "Darlin', you fairly outshine this grand day."

"Thank you, Stan." She scooted a couple of inches away and listened with interest as he offered small bits of town news before growing quiet and looking at him thoughtfully. He let her study him for a moment or two, then said, "I'd give a ha'penney to know the thoughts inside that pretty head."

In a serious voice, she said, "Actually I was speculating about the life you lead. Does shifting from town to town appeal to you, Stan?" When he seemed unwilling to commit to an answer right away, she said, "I guess it must. I can't help wondering whether you're running from something, or someone."

"Everyone on this earth is running from something, Rachel darlin'."

She considered this remark, and how uncomfortably well it applied to her own case, running from her own truths and hiding who she really was. "You could be right about that."

"I'm right," he said with a confirming nod.

She laughed dryly. "You're awfully sure of yourself."

"Yes, ma'am." His gaze settled on her forehead. "I see your cut is healing neatly. Soon you'll be as good as new, and then... "

"And then what?"

"Then you might be reconsidering the answer you've been giving me these many months."

"Mind repeating the question?"

"Repeat it, she says. Repeat it. Now, darlin', I might not be the kind of man you dreamed of marrying when you were only a girl, but we could make a fine pair."

"Oh I see. And...you'd want to live here, I suppose?"

"I would, until the gold plays out. Then it may be that we'd move on to someplace like San Francisco."

"Move on, gambling in one saloon or another, no family, no roots. Tell me, Stan, what is it you truly believe in?"

"Outside of you, I guess that would be the Fenian Brotherhood." He leaned back in his chair, cupped his hands behind his head, and waited.

When her curiosity grew stronger than her disinclination to give in to him, she asked, "The what?"

"The name is new to you, then? Well now, a long time ago in Ireland, even before Christianity had come, as the stories go, there were legions of professional soldiers led by mighty Finn MacCumhaill. Each of his soldiers had to take a vow before entering into Finn's brotherhood." He glanced over to see if she was attending, and smiled at the concentration on her face. "The promise was four-part; first, to choose a wife for her virtues..." He paused long enough to eye her appreciatively, which she ignored, so he went on, "second, he must swear never to use violence against a woman, third, never to refuse a man in need and, lastly, never to flee from fewer than nine opposing warriors."

"You're serious?"

"And why wouldn't I be serious?" he asked, a little affronted. "Is there a part of the vow you think me unable to fulfill?"

"*Nine* warriors? That sounds suicidal."

Now he grinned. "Never in your life, darlin'. Not the way I fight."

She couldn't help laughing out loud. "You're probably right about that, too."

During his visits he was politeness itself, but Rachel didn't let herself be fooled. There was always that unspoken yet detectable desire in his eyes, which he shuttered fully only when others were with them. Still, she felt that as long as she was cautious she could handle occasions with men like Stan. If she kept him at a safe enough distance, she might even come to enjoy these short encounters on the porch.

With the passage of time, Rachel's despair and frustration at her inability to find a way home had indeed doggedly evolved into a resolution to make the best of where she was. She couldn't allow herself to believe that everyone and everything she'd known before were forever out of her reach, it was just that facing her current circumstances gave her a purpose, a usefulness that she needed as much as the air she breathed. Now, wanting to contribute to the Milfords' welfare beyond merely helping with chores, she felt the immediate obstacle to this aspiration more strongly each day; a severe lack of money. This at least she intended to change. As soon as Esther was a little stronger, Rachel would seek employment with a law firm, and once she'd saved a substantial amount of her earnings, well, she'd at least have more options. An overland trip by horse and stagecoach to Chicago or some other large city held dangers that chilled her blood, but it was the thought of leaving the Milfords rather than her fears that weakened her vague intention to move on when the time was right.

Two days later, with Esther insisting that she enjoy some time away from the house, Rachel found the opportunity to venture out and hunt for a job. Unsuspecting of Rachel's plans, Esther passed her a few small coins to buy some blue thread, and scooted her out of the house with orders not to return for a least a couple of hours. It was mid-morning on a workday and most of the men were deeply occupied with their own labors, but Rachel took the precaution of keeping her bonnet on and her gaze down to avoid inquisitive or leering faces.

Before presenting herself at any law office, Rachel wanted to make a quick circuit of the town, mentally noting which firms looked prosperous. Her walk took her down Wall Street and past the *Boise News*, and as she paused at the doorway, considering whether to ask if she might read the latest paper, her attention was drawn by the noise of hammers and saws coming from East Hill. Curious, and enjoying the thought of stretching her legs for a bit longer, she moved up the road to investigate.

She bypassed the remains of what only days before had been a cabin but what now was little more than a disorderly pile of logs, the latest casualty of overzealous digging. With the final ill-fated shovel of dirt, one support post had given way and the entire roof had fallen in, crushing everything beneath and strewing shingles and logs into the roadway and neighboring yard. A torn blanket and odd bits of furniture lay half-buried in the mess. Surveying the destruction as she slowly walked by, Rachel hoped that no one had been inside when the home had collapsed.

The hammering grew louder before slowing to silence as Rachel neared St. Joseph's Church, where a crew of men stood back to admire a newly completed water tank. Coming closer, she read the side of the wagon into which the men began loading their tools. "Hook and Ladder Co." was proclaimed in red letters neatly outlined in black. A boy who looked to be about sixteen approached the wagon toting a sledgehammer in one hand and a saw in the other, and she stepped forward and said, "Excuse me, but does hook and ladder refer to firefighting? Will the water from this tank be stored in case of a fire?"

"Mostly, ma'am," he answered, setting down the tools, snatching off his hat, and running a dirty hand through his bushy brown hair, "and maybe for when water runs short around town. We're set to start fitting pipes sometime tomorrow. There'll be pipes and hydrants all over town before we're through."

Surprised and impressed, Rachel thanked the lad and resumed her meandering while reflectively adjusting her view of the 1864 American wilderness. First a bowling alley, soon a municipal water system, and then what? Deep in thought, she didn't notice the admiring stares that followed her well down the hill.

As Rachel had planned, she ended her route through town in front of the courthouse and, hearing voices from within, drew closer to the door. She had no way of knowing whether women were considered taboo inside a courtroom, but if she intended to practice law she'd better find out. She slipped inside and quietly scooted to the center of the last row.

"What about him?" asked the black-suited, grandly mustached judge. "Let's see..." he muttered as he shuffled through the papers before him. "Here it is. John Ramsdale, that's his name. What about Ramsdale, Sheriff Pinkham? As I recall he was brought over from Placerville about a week ago. Wasn't he to have appeared in court by now?"

A tall, powerfully built man in the second row turned in his seat and spoke briefly to his young deputy, then stood to address the bench. *So this is Sheriff Pinkham,* thought Rachel. In a glimpse she took in the star-shaped badge on his lapel and the surprising combination of his long gray beard, black mustache, gloriously full head of white hair, and dark, intelligent eyes.

"He should have, yes, Judge," said the sheriff, "but I'm afraid the man has a particularly violent nature. It's my opinion that we ought not to let him loose just yet, even to appear in this courtroom. Locked in irons or not, he'd try to tear this building apart, as well as anybody standing too close. I'd like to see him settle down some before he's presented for trial."

"Very well, try to get him here within the next week or two. I'll hear the next case."

Sheriff Pinkham sat down and nodded to his deputy, who motioned a woman to join him as he made his way to the front row of chairs.

"Judge Walker, this here's Lena Herman." the deputy said. "It's her turn, I believe."

A raw-boned woman, her dishwater-blonde hair pulled tightly back into a meager bun, stood straight and proud in her drab brown dress. "I'm ready, Judge," she proclaimed.

Judge Walker demanded, "Where's her attorney, Deputy Whiting?"

"Um, she'd have nothing to do with one, your honor."

"Don't you want an attorney, Mrs. Herman?" asked the judge with concern.

"No, sir. Never had no use for 'em, myself."

Judge Walker exchanged a look of mild amusement with the sheriff. "I know what you mean, Mrs. Herman, but August Lepky is charging you with breaking his windows, and you are facing serious penalties. Are you sure you don't want to have a lawyer helping you today?"

"Sure as rain in springtime, Judge," said Mrs. Herman with a bob of her head.

"Very well," said the judge. He turned his gaze upon a scrawny man in a worn black business suit sitting farther down the same row that Mrs. Herman had vacated. "I see you are without an attorney also, Mr. Lepky. Is this by choice?"

"Yes, your honor," said the man in a loud scratchy voice as he got to his feet.

"Proceed, then," said Judge Walker to his clerk,

After both parties had sworn to tell the truth, the judge asked, "What's your side of the story, Mr. Lepky?"

With no further prompting, the man pointed a finger at the accused and spat out, "She smashed my windows with rocks, Judge, not more than two days after I got them fixed from the last time that she-devil did the same thing."

"Did you see her do it, Mr. Lepky?" the judge asked reasonably.

"No, but..."

"Did anyone else see her do it, Mr. Lepky?"

"Not that I know of, sir."

"I see from my notes that she confessed to Deputy Whiting here, then later recanted the confession. That's not very conclusive. Is there any proof that she is the one who broke your windows?"

The sheriff shook his head.

Mr. Lepky spoke up firmly, "Well, I ain't too sure what you mean by proof, but I know plain enough that she done it."

"And how do you know this, Mr. Lepky?" asked the judge.

There was a short pause during which Mrs. Herman crossed her arms over her undersized bosom and stuck out her lower lip in Mr. Lepky's direction, but he forged on despite his growing hesitation. "Well, now, Judge, she seems to think that I promised her something that I don't recall ever promising. She's been sore as a scalded cat for weeks."

The judge sighed wearily and began twisting his mustache. "If I started sentencing every woman who was angry because of a broken promise, just how many females do you think we'd have left in this town, August Lepky? Now, if no one saw her do it and you have no proof of her guilt, I have to let her go."

"Oh, I done it all right, Judge." Every pair of eyes in the courtroom, including Rachel's, locked on Mrs. Herman. "I done it and I'll gladly do it again."

"Mrs. Herman, you don't have to...," Deputy Whiting tried.

"I'll keep breaking his windows 'til he stops breaking his word," she promised, shooting a withering glare at Mr. Lepky.

With little choice to do otherwise, the judge fined Lena Herman thirty-five dollars to replace the windows, and dismissed her.

Thoroughly fascinated, Rachel watched the next case involving the assault and battery of Mr. Fell by a man named Cheeney. Without lawyer or pause, Cheeney pled guilty and was sentenced to pay ten dollars plus medical and damage costs.

The third defendant, Edward Eaton, who also declining the aid of an attorney, gave the third straight guilty plea by admitting he'd robbed the sluice boxes of Crow, Gray & Co. a few nights earlier. His fine for petty larceny and court costs amounted to one hundred dollars.

Finally a defendant in handcuffs was brought into the courthouse. His name was given as William Peabody, and the sheriff, somewhat reluctantly, stood and testified that on the prior Wednesday Mr. Peabody had threatened to whip everyone in town but only succeeded in kicking one man off the sidewalk. Watching the man as he studied his shoes before the judge, Rachel guessed that liquor had contributed to the violent streak on the evening in question, because she couldn't imagine a more placid soul. The defendant was fined fifty dollars for disturbing the peace and quietly released.

These four cases, conducted in less than two hours, seemed to prove that the judge considered petty larceny worthy of a heavier fine than assault and battery; that a small theft was more egregious than violence. She left the courtroom shaking her head at this fact, as well as the obvious lack of confidence in a legal defense, but she was no less determined to find a law firm that would hire her. Realizing how late the day had grown, she quickened her steps and turned her thoughts to Esther, Richard, and Conrad. She'd have to hurry along with her job-hunting if they were to have their supper ready on time. Perhaps she wasn't as good a country cook as she was an attorney, but she hadn't poisoned anyone yet, and she was improving steadily.

Rachel missed Juliet's excellent cooking; no, it was more than her cooking. She missed Juliet herself, and Charlie, and True. A little surprised, Rachel realized just how much she wanted to see them all. Was Charlie sleeping in her bed by himself during her absence? Was Juliet working herself to the point of exhaustion? Was Lewis continuing with his reading lessons? Was True keeping his eyes on Kate? Were Grandpa, Bert, Maggie and Phillip faring well?

Her musings were interrupted by shouts from the south end of Main Street, and she turned in that direction to see two mounted men racing toward her, their horses raising clods of dirt and clouds of dust as the men waved their hats and bellowed, "A wagon train's headin' toward town! Twenty wagons or more! A whole train of emigrants just around the bend!"

As their cries were taken up by scores of other voices, Rachel stepped behind a boardwalk railing and leaned out to keep the end of the street in sight, her eagerness and excitement rising as whooping and shouting people poured from buildings all around her. Stan appeared at her side as if he'd known exactly where to find her, put his hand over hers on the rail, and grinned broadly.

"A wagon train, Stan!" In delighted anticipation she returned his smile and began to shift from foot to foot, then leaned even farther out to gain a better view. "How far are they from town, do you think?" She heard Stan laugh at her eagerness but she paid no attention. Her breath quickened but no wagons appeared. Oh, when *would* they come? She stepped to the end of the railing and asked, "Should we head toward them?"

"Just wait, darlin'. They'll be driving to us soon enough."

And there it was! The team of the first wagon turned the far corner and lumbered on, followed immediately by another and another. "An actual wagon train," she breathed aloud. *An honest to goodness wagon train.* Spellbound by a powerful sense of awe, and abundantly grateful for this chance to witness what was drawing near, her mind clung to every detail.

Clerks, doctors, lawyers, saloonkeepers, gamblers, drunkards, hurdy-gurdy girls, laundrymen, and merchants had gathered along every boardwalk and alleyway up and down Main Street. They waved their hats or handkerchiefs or bottles and yelled greetings to the newcomers as varied as their many backgrounds. As the first team rolled slowly by Rachel took in the features of the dusty, tired people waving back in appreciation, and she saw the emanating joy and triumph at finally reaching their destination. Even the children seemed to walk with a quiet pride and shy sense of achievement. One little girl in a faded yellow dress skipped at her mother's side, waving madly back at the crowd. A man grinned at his son of about nine years, handed him his heavy revolver, and nodded his permission to fire it into the air in celebration. Other gunfire joined the boy's, and the chorus of shouts and cheers rose even higher.

They have cause to rejoice, Rachel thought, her own eyes suddenly filling with gratification on their behalf. *These men, women, and children, these pioneers have walked thousands of miles and faced death, hardship, and heartache to reach this new territory, this new home.* Rachel studied their faces even more closely, thinking of Juliet's account of the Milfords' own crossing of this vast country. She recognized the weary but unbeaten courage on every visage. And the hope, yes, hope was more vivid than anything else. *People with such strength and heart will make this place something special.*

As Rachel watched, she noticed that there seemed to be more women than men in the train, many of a marriageable age, a fact that had not been overlooked by the townsmen craning their necks for a better look. Rachel didn't doubt that by the time the train pulled into a circle outside of town, those families with attractive young females would be offered every manner of courtesy and assistance.

While the last of the cattle trailing the wagons disappeared from view, Rachel heard Stan say, "I can read that mind of yours, Rachel Milford. You'll be worrying about me being stolen away by one of those beauties. But you needn't be, darlin'. My heart's yours for ever and a day." This was said with such exaggerated seriousness that Rachel burst out laughing and Stan released the grin he'd been holding back.

"You go right ahead and let yourself be stolen away, Stan O'Brien. There's no sense in your waiting around for me." She had delivered this with the same playfulness Stan had used, but the corners of his mouth fell and his eyes grew sharp.

"I'll not have you saying such a thing, Rachel, not even in jest." He took her by the hand and hauled her along the boardwalk past several buildings in the direction of Esther's house. Feeling no serious threat and wanting to avoid a scene, Rachel didn't resist. They were still a couple of blocks away from Esther's front door when he swerved abruptly and drew her between two houses.

Before she had a chance to protest his sudden change of course, he had taken her face between his hands and was kissing her, thoroughly. She lightly pushed against his chest but he only deepened the kiss, persuasively rather than forcefully. It had been a long time since anyone had touched her like this, lovingly, coaxingly. No, never like this, she amended reluctantly. With the tilt and movement of his head, the light touch of his fingers in her hair behind her ears, and the enticing dexterity of his full lips Stan used a style that was uniquely his. Again she tried to push him back, and again his kisses became more effective. Beginning to respond despite her own intentions, Rachel decided she'd better do something before she justified Stan's confidence in his powers of seduction. She changed tactics completely by suddenly leaning into him and kissing him fully. Stan pulled back and moved his hands to her shoulders, scrutinizing her face with dazed, uncertain eyes and working hard to control his breathing.

"For more than a year I've wanted you, Rachel, more than food or drink," he said, his voice strained. "I understand both of us well enough to know we'll never marry, and I'll not ruin your chances for real happiness with a worthy man, but don't be telling me not to wait for you, to dream of having you. Far too soon someone will kill my dream, and I'll move on. Until then, let me wait."

Astounded by his words and even more by the depth of his feelings, Rachel opened her mouth to speak but he kissed her again, gently silencing her. This time his mouth claimed hers only briefly and with such absolute tenderness that she couldn't help returning a measure of his warmth. When she opened her eyes he held her gaze.

"Stan," she said, faltered, and then tried again. "You *know* I can't give you what you want?"

"I know. And I can't give you what you need; I'm not that sort of man. But by God, woman, you make me wish that I was." He held her a moment longer, and then averted the need he couldn't keep from his eyes by touching his lips to her forehead, taking her by the hand, and leading her back to the boardwalk. Within minutes and without another word he delivered her to Esther's home, merely touching her cheek and bowing before leaving her.

Rachel didn't enter the house until she'd watched Stan disappear from sight and the sound of Richard's and Esther's laughter beckoned her inside.

After a night made restless by Rachel's repeated mental review of the scene with Stan, she decided to redirect her thoughts and efforts by telling Esther about her plans to practice law. The family would find out soon enough anyway, so she might as well discover what Esther's reaction would be before announcing it to the rest of the Milford clan.

Esther had just settled Conrad into the cradle for his nap when Rachel asked delicately, "Do you think any of the lawyers in town would hire a woman?"

"A woman? Why ever would you wonder about a thing like that?"

"I'm wondering because I'm going to try to convince one to hire me. I think I could be of use to a law firm."

Seeing Rachel's determination, Esther guarded her words. "I don't doubt that you could be of use, Rachel. It's just that I never heard of a woman working in a lawyer's office. Such men don't seem to like women in their business doings."

"Even so, I'm going to try."

"You know, Rachel," Esther said reflectively, "if you want to work someplace other than at the farm or the mercantile, I have a thought. Mama and I were talking while you were doing the laundry yesterday, about how you helped me when Conrad was born. She said she never saw such an easy birthing, and she thinks you had a good deal to do with that. I think so, too. Maybe you could help other women when their times come."

"I'm glad if I helped you, Esther, but—"

"You know that lots of women won't even allow a doctor to come, because he's a man. They'd be grateful to have a woman, but we don't have many midwives around here." Esther's voice quickened as her excitement built. "If you didn't want to be there alone, maybe you could go along with a doctor when he gets called on to help with a birthing. I've heard of women working with doctors. I remember Uncle Giles telling us about doctors and nurses working together during the war. Hey now, maybe some of the doctors in town have even worked with women before."

"Esther, please listen, I have no training in medicine."

"Pshaw! Half the men that call themselves doctors aren't nearly as good as you at helping out a suffering woman."

Rachel patted Esther's arm and shook her head.

"Will you at least think it over?"

"Yes, dear Esther," Rachel smiled tolerantly. "I'll think it over, but if you don't need me for a while, I want to talk with an attorney or two."

"All right, Rachel. I can see you've set your mind to trying. You just watch out for yourself."

Picking up her bonnet with distracted eagerness, Rachel settled it over her bun, secured its ribbons under her chin, and faced Esther. "Wish me luck."

She'd chosen her destinations the day before, so she made her way through town quickly, and didn't linger beneath the sign that read "Frank Miller, Attorney at Law." Taking a breath, she took hold of the doorknob, gave it a turn, and stepped forward. There, she was inside, and being stared at by two young men, one who'd stilled his writing at a small desk and another who stood beside the more prominent desk of a slightly older, more finely dressed gentleman. Following the gazes of his younger colleagues, the senior attorney straightened, rose to his feet, and asked, "Yes, Miss? May I assist you?"

"I hope so," she said as she approached him. Just before his desk she held out her hand to shake his. "My name is Rachel Milford."

He accepted the courtesy politely but with obvious curiosity, saying, "How do you do, Miss Milford? I'm Frank Miller." Gesturing toward the other two men in turn, he added, "This is my assistant, Ronald Granger, and my clerk, Benjamin McBride." With a nod he dismissed his clerk and said to Rachel, "Please be seated. Now, what have you come to see me about today?"

"Actually, I'm hoping you might be able to use another clerk. I'd very much like to work for you, here in your office."

His eyebrows shot skyward but he surveyed her with quiet restraint before speaking. "I must admit that I'm quite surprised by such an uncommon request, miss, and I'm sorry to disappoint you, but I'm unable to offer you a position."

Rachel was prepared for such an initial rebuff. "Mr. Miller, I understand that this would create an unusual situation, one that might take the town a little while to accept, but I have a great interest in the law, have studied it, in fact, and I am a diligent worker."

"That well may be—"

Rachel broke in, "If you'll just give me a chance, I will work without pay until I've proven myself."

He lifted both hands to stop any further words. "Miss Milford, if you were to practice law in any capacity it would be more than *unusual*, it would be *illegal*."

Rachel managed to keep her face calm. "What do you mean, Mr. Miller?"

"Exactly that. Only white males of high moral character are allowed to practice law within the Idaho Territory."

As her mind rebelled Rachel stared at his apparently sincere face, then she said with exaggerated formality. "May I please see such a law?"

"I dearly wish I could show it to you in its current and enforceable version, but that isn't possible right now." Catching her look of suspicion, he went on, "As you may know if you've been reading about our political situation, when the Idaho Territory separated from Washington Territory last March, no Idaho legislative body had yet been formed. President Lincoln appointed Governor Wallace, but it took many months for the selection of our sheriff, judge, and other officers. Then Governor Wallace was sent off to Congress and that...that...," he cleared his throat, "Governor Lyon replaced him."

"I don't see how—"

"Please let me finish, Miss Milford. Governor Wallace *had* approved our new legal code, but Governor Lyon isn't in any hurry to get the laws dispersed to us attorneys. We've waited and waited, sending a flurry of requests, but he's no more efficient than any other eastern art critic would be in such a role." The title "art critic" was said in the same tone he might have used in reference to a grave robber, but then Mr. Miller reined in his opinions enough to conclude, "So, even though the legal code was adopted last December, and we've had repeated promises of their imminent delivery from the printing office in San Francisco, we've seen nothing."

Still finding this a very bitter pill to swallow, Rachel asked, "Then how do you function? How are judgments made and sentences passed? I was in court recently and the proceedings appeared to be well organized."

"For the most part we follow the old Washington code," said Mr. Miller. "It's really the only thing we have to go by."

"Won't the judgments be questioned, potentially overturned?"

"That's possible, but I doubt it, because we expect the Idaho laws to look nearly identical to those of Washington. Besides, we have little choice, other than to let offenders go free without punishment. We do the best we can, and we attorneys have our share of troubles just creating, untangling, and dissolving the multitude of corporations in Idaho City, and there seem to be as many *questionable* mining claims as there are profitable mines. There are also murders, thefts, and other crimes to be tried. It can be a very rough business, practicing law in a mining town." Seeing that she still hesitated, he walked to a bookshelf and took down a legal volume, flipped through its pages, and pointed to the law proclaiming that only moral white males were eligible to practice law in the Washington Territory.

The brutal words couldn't be denied, but Rachel was about to propose any form of assistance that might fall beyond the scope of this definition when Mr. Miller said with finality, "Miss Milford, I can offer you no position in this office, as a clerk or otherwise, and I'm afraid the answer will be the same in every law office in the territory."

Unable to hide her deep disappointment, for herself as well as for any woman or non-white male with similar ambitions, she said, "One day, Mr. Miller, such restrictive laws will not be tolerated." Knowing that the responsibility for such prejudice didn't rest solely on the shoulders of the man before her, a man who might even sympathize with her sentiments, she forced herself to add, "But I understand that you are currently bound by them." She stood and said a bit stiffly, "I mustn't take up any more of your time."

"I regret that I couldn't provide more welcome news, and I wish you well."

"Thank you, Mr. Miller."

With a sinking heart, she left, telling herself that she should have expected something like this. Still, her spirit rebelled against such a blatantly racist, sexist law, and she forced herself to enter another attorney's office to obtain corroboration. It was immediately given, with less patience than Mr. Miller had shown, and the glimmer of her hope to practice law, which somehow represented a link to her old life, to Ellen, and Jason, and even Carlo, shrank and died with a silent but acutely painful moan.

In less than an hour from the time she'd left it, she was back at Esther's house. "Well," Rachel admitted quietly as she sank into the rocking chair, "you warned me."

Saying nothing, Esther finished nursing Conrad and laid him in Rachel's arms. "Will you burp him for me?"

It was the kindest thing she could have done. Rachel held the sleepy baby to her chest, rubbing her cheek against the perfect softness of his fuzzy head as she patted and rubbed his back. When a small belch emerged from deep within him, Esther paused with a cup of flour poised over the dough on her wooden table, and smiled at them. Her gaze was filled with such tenderness that Rachel was moved, and she closed her eyes to still her own raw emotions. She continued to rock Conrad, and after a few minutes she started humming softly. As her voice steadied, her lips began to form words, and to a gentle yet beckoning melody she sang of a mystical dragon that lived on an island in a faraway sea, and of the little boy who loved him.

The metal tub resting on the kitchen table was large enough to hold several babies, but Rachel used great care to fill it just so, testing and retesting the temperature before lowering Conrad into the water, and smiling at each of his grunts and coos as the soft cloth glided gently over his skin. An hour earlier Esther had taken a long overdue walk, and Rachel was relishing this time alone with the baby. As she bathed him she felt an unwelcome pang of regret at the realization that she'd soon be seeing him much less often. Although Richard had been the epitome of polite gratitude, his growing restlessness for more privacy with his wife and new son was becoming apparent. It was well over a week since Conrad's birth, and Esther, though still sore and easily tired, was feeling much stronger. The baby was thriving and there was less and less need for Rachel's help around their modest household. Clearly, it was time for her departure, but she'd been struggling with the question of where to go.

She'd considered returning to the Pinney house, still wondering if that residence might be connected to her past, or her future. During her strolls around town she occasionally paused near it, taunted by the question of whether the place held a clue or tool that might help her find her way back. However, the gentleman who owned the residence had returned two days earlier, eliminating this choice.

Although it had been kindly offered, she'd quickly rejected the possibility of staying at Aunt Faith's house. The tiny residence was already shared with two other women, and there was no room to accommodate an additional boarder without significantly restricting their own comfort. Besides, unless she could find a way of earning money, and she'd made little progress in that regard, even her old job at the mercantile having been filled, she could afford no rent, and going back to the Milford homestead seemed her only practical option.

At times Rachel wanted nothing more than to return to the family farm, to the devoted protection and tenderness that its owners not only offered but sincerely wanted to provide. Yet at other times she was so frustrated by her dependency on others that she was almost, *almost* tempted to return some of the outlandish flirting aimed her way by the bolder miners who passed the front porch before Stan's daily arrivals. For little more than a smile, one of the more prosperous of these men might happily shell out a little gold just to hold her interest, but these random and pointless musings never included Stan as a potential victim. Stan O'Brien was intelligent and perceptive, and she tried never to underestimate him. She told herself she wouldn't be fool enough to trust him, but she'd developed a grudging admiration for his determination to live life as he chose, and she was growing fond of his company.

Ironically, the more accepting she grew of Stan or any other person or element here, the more penetrating her flashes of homesickness became, intensifying her longing for everyone who'd cared about or loved her and for everything that had provided comfort in Chicago. These moments were growing fewer, but when they struck she rebelled against her inability to escape from the people and places that were trespassing more and more upon her heart. And then again, there were moments like this, when Conrad's tiny hand wrapped tightly around her finger and his bright eyes locked on her face, that she found it very difficult to plan her departure.

As she lifted him from the tub and wrapped him in a clean towel, Esther sailed through the front room, beaming and triumphant. "Oh, Rachel!"

"What's gotten into you?"

Esther clapped her hands together and held them to her chest. "It's going to work, Rachel! It's going to work just fine!"

"What in the—? Esther, tell me this minute what you're talking about."

Still grinning, Esther hurried to Rachel, clasped her shoulder, and said, "I talked it out with Dr. Hogue and he said he'd give it a try!"

"Esther..."

"You can *work* for him; help him with mothers and *babies*!"

"What!"

"Doc Willis and Doc May both said they don't deliver near as many babies as Dr. Hogue and that I should go talk to him, so I did, and he said he'd help *train* you. He liked the idea, Rachel! He truly did!"

"Why in the world did you speak to Dr. Hogue, or any of them, before you discussed this with me?"

Still beaming, Esther continued at a gallop, "Oh, Rachel, don't be angry with me. I saw how unhappy you were about the lawyers not hiring you, and I knew you could help so many folks, and I thought you'd love the idea if you heard that a doctor really *wanted* your help." This flowed forth with such excitement and affection that Rachel's annoyance melted away.

"All right, Esther, I won't be angry with you, but I'm not at all sure I want to work for a doctor."

With absolute conviction, Esther said, "But you will want to, once you've had time to think it over. His office and treatment room are at the rear of the Union Drugstore, just a short walk, and they are both as neat as a pin." She wrapped Conrad in a baby blanket as she took him from her, and swept into the bedroom, announcing, "And Dr. Hogue said you can come see him at four o'clock!"

Rachel gaped at her receding back, threw the damp towel onto the table, and punched her hands onto her hips in utter consternation.

As the day progressed, and despite many misgivings, Rachel had to admit that the more she thought about Esther's plot, the more she warmed to it. Perhaps, just perhaps, this was a viable opportunity she'd disregarded too soon. A few minutes before four, she agreed to visit Dr. Hogue, cautioning a delighted Esther, "I'm only going to talk to him. No promises."

Leaving the house and attempting to ignore waves of both anticipation and trepidation, Rachel soon reached the drugstore and entered the doctor's office, to find him scribbling notes at a rolltop desk. As she appeared he rose to his feet and removed his glasses, studying her discreetly. Squarely built, Dr. Hogue was a few inches shorter than Rachel, and possessed pomaded dark hair parted down the middle. His round face presented scholarly brown eyes, a small nose, and a thin mouth topped by a moustache that curled up at the ends. He would have fit quite well, Rachel thought, in a barbershop quartet.

"Welcome, Miss Milford." he said cordially. "Please, take this seat." He waited for her to be seated in the wooden chair beside his desk, reclaimed his own, and the two of them commenced the task of taking the other's measure.

"I understand from Esther that you are interested in the care of women and children," Dr. Hogue began.

Rachel decided it would be best to keep quiet about any claims Esther might have made, and said only, "I would like to know more about that kind of practice, doctor."

"Fine. That interest, and any assistance along that line would be welcome in this community. We have no properly trained midwife for such a service, and the need for such a person will only grow as more families settle here. I specialize in this area of medicine, but many women are more comforted by the presence of a woman during their laying-in times. Esther told me how you helped her while she labored."

"Esther gives me far too much credit."

"Even if that's so, you seem to be a stable, strong young woman. You should know that your strength would be sorely tried during some difficult births." He scrutinized her closely yet gently before asking, "Miss Milford, do you believe you are capable of dealing with tragedy?"

Rachel had not anticipated this question, and she gave it serious thought before answering. "I think so, although the death of a child would be very difficult. I would have to rely on the possibility that my helping the mothers could reduce such outcomes. Recently I've come to believe that I'm strongest when I'm most needed."

He nodded with approval.

"Dr. Hogue, do you face a great number of tragedies?"

"Yes," he said in simple honesty, "in many forms; the death of the mother, the child, or both, or the malformation of the child. At times the abnormalities are dreadful and, far too often, the patient and her offspring do not die mercifully."

Rachel swallowed, imagining the cases he must have endured, and those that she might face if she pursued this course. At last, she said with a conviction that surprised her, "Perhaps, in a few cases, I can help prevent or lessen some of their pain."

Considering her perceptively, Dr. Hogue said, "Yes, perhaps you can." He moved on to ask more about her intentions and her background, and she detected no condescension in his words or manner, not the least hint of patronizing arrogance. He was frank about what tasks he would assign and when, his manner of instruction, the demands he would place upon her performance and her behavior, and her compensation.

After all of this had been discussed, Rachel posed questions of her own, and learned that Dr. Hogue had served in the Union army before moving to Idaho City only months ago. During his military service he'd worked with a number of women who'd proven to be quite capable of treating the sick and wounded soldiers. He was married, and he and his young wife, Jane, were expecting their first child at the end of July.

When Rachel and the doctor finally ran out of questions, Dr. Hogue said thoughtfully, "I sense a calm assurance in you, Miss Milford, which often comes only after many trials, and which might indeed provide a great deal of comfort to my patients. I also perceive, from what both you and Esther have told me, that you have a quick mind and a protective instinct, and those too will be helpful. In fact, I've decided that I'd like to see you exercise such qualities within the field of medicine." The hint of a smile appeared and the formality of his tone lessened. "The job as my assistant is yours if you want it. The pay will not be great, as I mentioned, but the gratitude will be genuine. You'll likely want to learn a great deal more before you commit yourself to such an undertaking, so I will not press you for an answer today."

"Actually, Dr. Hogue, your candor has done a great deal to solidify my intentions. Perhaps I should spend more time considering the potential hardships I'll face, but I've seen how unpredictable life can be, and I want to embrace this opportunity. I'd like to begin learning as soon as possible, so I accept your offer. As far as my earnings, until I can be of greater value to your practice, I need only enough to pay for room and board in town."

The smile broadened across his face. "That should pose no problem. Well, now, this is welcome news. I'll send you home with some material to study right away. But wait, since you've decided to embark on this new undertaking, would you like to meet my wife? In a few months she might just be one of your first patients, under my supervision, of course. I happened to mention you to her a few hours ago, and I believe she will be happy to accept your care right along with mine."

Wondering at the intensity of her own excitement, Rachel nevertheless replied without hesitation, "I'd love to meet her, as soon as possible."

"Well then, how about now?" At Rachel's nod, he stood and led the way outside and down the street.

The doctor's house adjoined a warehouse, setting itself apart from that larger structure by its freshly painted siding, a rare adornment in town. Its sunny yellow exterior and shining windows gave the dwelling an inviting approach and, upon entering, Rachel noticed how the well-crafted furnishings and small decorative touches added much to its coziness. She also appreciated the friendly handshake Jane offered without hesitation, despite the unannounced nature of her visit.

"Come in, come in, Miss Milford. Please make yourself comfortable. You two must have a great deal to talk about, and I'll be right back. I just took some cookies out of the oven, and I'll have a pot of tea ready directly." A wooden tray bearing the promised cookies and tea appeared in minutes, and once it had been set upon a marble-topped table in their small parlor, Jane glanced from Rachel to Dr. Hogue as she asked of her husband, "Now, dear, have you convinced Miss Milford to accept your offer? I've been hoping she would ever since you mentioned the possibility."

"As a matter of fact, she has," Dr. Hogue announced with pleasure, "and she wants to start learning this very day." Mrs. Hogue listened keenly to their newly forming plans, enthusiastically encouraging them both and occasionally casting subtle glances of approval at her husband.

When their conversation finally turned to some of the specifics of medical training that Rachel would encounter, she asked to borrow one or two of Dr. Hogue's reference books. Dr. Hogue turned to his wife and asked, "Would you mind if we have supper a little later than usual, Jane?"

"You know I won't mind. The sooner you provide Miss Milford with those books, the better." As they all stood, she said, "I wish you the best of luck with your studies. Please come back and visit me anytime at all." She followed them out the door and waved as they headed across the road.

Looking over his office bookshelf, Dr. Hogue found a leather-bound volume entitled *A Biennial Retrospective of Medicine & Surgery for 1862-3*, and passed it to Rachel.

Noting the publisher's name on the spine, Rachel asked, "What is the New Sydenham Society?"

"The Society? I guess you'd say it's a group that admires, and usually follows, the philosophies of Thomas Sydenham, an English physician. He's done remarkable work in the area of epidemic diseases such as smallpox and malaria. He was the first to treat malaria with cinchona bark, the source of quinine; no small discovery, that." Seating himself before his roll-top desk, he faced Rachel's chair. "During my time in the war, quinine proved to be better than anything else in treating malaria and a host of other ills, when we could get it. He would be considered a great man because of this discovery alone, but he has also done much to change how diagnoses are made."

"And how is that?"

"Before his work started to change medical thinking, many physicians diagnosed and treated patients by theory more than by examination."

"How can a patient be treated by theory?"

"He can't, in my opinion, not with any clarity or much success, unless an abundance of luck is involved. Let's say an individual is exhibiting symptoms similar to those a doctor has seen before. The physician may provide medicine that he has previously used to quell the symptoms, feeling no need to conduct a thorough examination first. Consider how dangerous this might prove to be in the case of a person who is wavering on his feet because of general dizziness, and a physician treating him with laudanum. Symptoms such as imbalance could be caused by any number of things, and such treatment *could* be fatal. Yet treatment without examination is still quite common, I'm afraid."

"Unbelievable," she said with a shake of her head, and started flipping through the first pages of the book.

"You may take that home, if you'd like. You might find some of the descriptions and diagrams fairly shocking, but allow no squeamishness or prudery, Miss Milford. This is medicine you're embarking on."

"I'm not easily shocked, Dr. Hogue."

"That would be a rarity in a new medical assistant, but I certainly hope that it's so. It will make your training much easier. I'd appreciate your bringing the book back tomorrow morning, say at eight o'clock, but you may take it or another one home every night. You will need several aprons to protect your dress, but Jane loves to sew and she'll be happy to make them for you."

"Dr. Hogue, I am so grateful for your faith in me, and for Jane's kindness. You've given me an opportunity that means more than you might guess."

"The way I see it, meeting you today will prove to be providential, Miss Milford. It's made me quite hopeful for the ladies and babies of our town."

"I'm hopeful too; a little overwhelmed by how much I need to learn, and the consequences of any mistake, but very hopeful."

Rising and shaking his hand, Rachel left the office with a resolute step and the book tucked under her arm.

Reaching home, Esther greeted her before she'd cleared the doorway by demanding excitedly, "Well?"

"You're looking at Dr. Hogue's new assistant."

Esther let out a joyful whoop and said, "Oh, I just knew he'd hire you! You'll be such a wonderful midwife, Rachel, and I'll help in any way I can with your medical lessons."

As eager as she was, Rachel found no time to read until after she'd finished the supper dishes and retired to the porch, resolute to cover as much as she could before the sunlight began to fade. At first she did no more than scan the various sections, which dealt with recent observations in a wide range of medical fields. Then her attention was captured by the *Report on Midwifery, etc.* Despite her claim to Dr. Hogue about not being easily shocked, she balked a bit at the unemotional yet detailed manner in which the medical professionals described deformities and illnesses, nearly all of which proved to be fatal, yet she read on with captivation.

When she reached the two sections entitled *Pregnancy* and *Labour*, her interest grew even keener. While many of the cases seemed downright grisly, she was relieved to read that some women had actually survived caesarian sections, though the survivors were in a slim minority. Doses of ergot, whatever that was, were given to stop hemorrhaging, and ether was the most common form of anesthesia. So, she thought, at least they have ether.

Rachel read greedily until she encountered a lengthy discussion on the use of forceps by Dr. Putegnat in Brussels. Bracing herself for what she feared could be stomach-churning, she read, "In numerous labours, the delivery has been aided in traction by one, two, and, in one case, by five assistants, all taking a point of resistance. In no case was the pelvis fractured. The pelvis is endowed with an enormous power of resistance, and pregnancy does not diminish this power. If, therefore, the symphyses are ruptured, this must be attributed to congenital or morbid weakness. As to the degree of force that the child can bear, the pressure exerted upon the head is in proportions to that of the traction upon the handles of the instrument. Delore says when he exerted a tractic force of 130 kilogrammes the head was not damaged, but when the force was increased to 140 kilogrammes...." Rachel closed her eyes, then after a moment opened them again and forced herself to read the rest of the paragraph.

Slowly lifting her face, she took a few breaths as she stared up and down the street. How many babies would be born here in the coming year? Would she be in this town for the whole year? For many years? Her whole life? If so, her mind and heart answered, she'd found a way to play a part that mattered. She would learn and work, and, aware that there would be heart-wrenching moments, she'd do what she could to make a difference.

Looking up at the soft blue sky, hearing the cry of an unseen hawk, she wondered what help she might have had in reaching the decision she'd made in Dr. Hogue's office. She felt as if she hadn't quite made it alone. Then she smiled inwardly, and after a moment bent her head to the book, deepening her concentration as her eyes traveled over the next pages.

Later, Esther came to the door and gazed at her with great fondness. "It's getting dark. When are you coming in?"

"Soon," she said, "soon."

Late the next afternoon when Rachel returned to Esther's house, her arms were loaded with medical books. After setting them down and picking up Conrad, she announced to Esther, "Dr. Hogue says I can start assisting with his cases in a week or two, or whenever I'm ready." She grinned, "He said by then I'll have read every book he owns, and he might be right."

"Oh, Rachel, I'm so happy for you, and the women you'll care for. You can get to studying right now if you want."

Rachel gave Esther a hug and the baby a kiss, laid Conrad in his cradle, and sat at the kitchen table to read. She had little awareness of Esther's quiet supper preparations or, when Conrad began to fuss, his mother's nursing him to sleep. She ate her dinner in a few hasty bites, washed the dishes quickly, and once more commandeered the porch bench.

The longer she studied that evening, the more frustrating her lack of previous medical education grew, yet she felt fairly confident in her ability to learn the written word and Dr. Hogue's practical lessons promptly. Perhaps just as important, even with her lack of professional instruction and experience, she was determined to promote methods that were not mentioned in any of these textbooks, not yet. Through her college health, biology, and anatomy (which he'd taken only on a dare from her brother) classes, educational television and media, as well as modern customs and habits, she'd obtained limited but valuable knowledge from future generations of medical professionals and scientists about nutrition and childbirth, knowledge possessed by no one else in the territory. Step by step, she would help educate mothers on better hygiene and nourishment, and a calmer way to approach the difficult process of pregnancy and birth.

The wage Dr. Hogue was paying her, in advance for the first two weeks, was modest but well above what she'd hoped for. With it, and without extravagances, she could afford to live on her own.

Despite her work and studies, she would make time to see Esther and Conrad often, but there was still a potential obstacle to her scheme, and a sizable one; getting the blessings of Juliet, Bert, and Grandpa.

She knew she'd hear the children's opinions on the matter whether she asked for them or not, and she doubted they'd be happy about it, especially Charlie. Once the Milfords' approvals were obtained, Rachel told herself, the question of where she would live in town would be no more than a minor detail.

Unexpectedly, it was Rachel rather than the Milfords who seemed to have the toughest time facing the long-term separation her work in town would necessitate. Three days after her understanding had been reached with Dr. Hogue, Rachel sat beside Richard as he drove her to the farm, saying little as her apprehension built over how the family might react. Dr. Hogue had said she could take the time she needed at the farm, as long as she kept to her studies whenever possible.

Her homecoming was loud and jubilant, with Charlie showering her with hugs and everyone eager to hear about what was happening in town. After a plentiful dinner accompanied by laughter and stories, Rachel cleared her throat and bared her intentions.

Juliet studied her for a moment, nodded, and said, "I'm not much surprised, Rachel, after seeing you with Esther. I believe this could be your calling, and I can see it's what you want. I'm happy for you, daughter, truly." Bert and True surprised her by offering only unselfish encouragement.

Grandpa, with an innocent expression but a twinkle in his eyes, said, "Maybe a likely husband will show up at the doctor's office, one who ain't too scared to take all of Stan O'Brien's devilry."

The image of Stan crossed Rachel's mind, but she merely smiled and started gathering the plates to wash.

During the early hours of the following days, she often worked in the field or beside the creek with the men, cooked, cleaned and washed with Juliet, and milked the cows with Kate and Maggie. True, who'd been filling in for her as a tutor to Lewis, good-naturedly allowed her to resume this role. Lewis had made wonderful progress, reading the newspaper now with little need of assistance and writing slowly but quite legibly, and he enjoyed the fact that Rachel was studying right along with him, saying, "You ought to start helpin' to birth them babies as soon as you can, Miss Rachel." So during the evenings she sat near the barn with him and poured over words and illustrations describing methods of suturing wounds and setting bones, along with the intricacies of obstetrics.

Later than usual on just such an evening, she and Lewis were sitting on their customary bench, both trying to ignore the mosquitoes emerging as the sun eased lower. It was a lovely twilight, comfortably warm, cloudless and windless. A huge liver-colored dog called Samson lay at their feet, only occasionally raising his head at some new sound or scent. The farm animals repeatedly lowed and nickered, adding their voices to the final calls of the day birds. True unconsciously joined their melody by quietly singing off-key at the side of the house as he split and stacked the last of the felled wood. Rachel caught the scent of fir, and pulled its freshness deep into her lungs.

While Lewis read, she closed her eyes and let her senses float. After a few delicious moments Lewis lowered his book, his gaze settling to the ground near his feet. "It's gettin' late, Miss Rachel. Our shadows is growin' awful long."

She opened her eyes and traced his gaze. "Long and slanted. They make us look like we're about to fall over." After several thoughtful moments her expression grew distant and uncertain. When she spoke again, her voice was quite soft and laced with sorrow. "Maybe that's all we are, really, just shadows. I must have stolen this one from someone else, and I'm not sure I want to give it back." She felt Lewis watching her and turned toward him. Strangely, he didn't seem startled by her words, only slightly troubled by the sadness in her voice. He slid his gaze to their images on the ground, silently considering what she'd said.

"Lewis?"

He raised his face again, but now she was staring off into the woods across the road. "Yes, Miss Rachel."

It took a second, but then she asked, "What would you do if you knew about something that was going to happen, but if you told somebody they'd think you were crazy?"

"You mean like the things that come to you when you is sound asleep?"

"Do you see things when you're dreaming?"

"Sometimes."

"What kinds of things?"

"After I lost my mama and sister, I stopped talkin' about my dreams to anybody. That is, 'til I told your mama about a few."

"Would you mind telling me?"

"Well now, do you want to tell me about yours, Miss Rachel?" he countered.

They eyed each other, and Rachel waited for True to leave the woodpile and go into the house before she spoke. "I wouldn't call them dreams exactly, but since... since I got hurt I feel like I know about things that will happen."

He nodded. "I had a dream about you the very night before you hit your head."

"About me?"

"Yes'm. I dreamed you was a lady hawk and you was bein' chased by a wolf. You had hurt your wing somehow and couldn't fly. But just when the wolf was about to catch you, your wing got strong again and you took off, flyin' way up in the sky. After your folks got you back to the farm I told your mama about that dream, 'cause she was mighty worried about you. She figured, same as me, that the dream meant you was goin' to get better. And you did."

Rachel considered the dream, and all it might mean.

"Miss Rachel, you was just sayin' you feel like you stole that shadow in front of you. Well, maybe that feelin' means the same as my dream. Maybe it all comes from you gettin' hurt and bein' some different now than you was before, but that you will be well and good right soon. You suppose?"

"Yes, that could be true."

"Now, what kind of things do *you* see, things that might come to pass?"

Quite slowly, meeting his gaze, she said, "I think someone is going to kill President Lincoln."

"Lord above!" Lewis exclaimed, his eyes huge. "Mr. Lincoln killed!" He collected his thoughts and asked, "You got any notion about when?"

"Not long after he's reelected, and after the war is over."

"He's goin' to get reelected? Then when is..." Belatedly realizing what else she'd just said, he asked carefully, "Wait now, after the war is over, you say? Miss Rachel, do you think you know what side is goin' to win this war?"

She wavered only for an instant. "I do. The North will win, but even before the end, if he hasn't done it already, Lincoln will pass a law making slavery a crime."

Lewis was so stunned that his shoulders fell back against the barn, and for a moment he could say nothing.

Locking her eyes on his astounded features, she added, "After the war, Lewis, slavery will be gone from America. Black people will have to travel a long hard road, but someday everyone will have the same rights. Someday, there will be fifty states in our country, including Idaho, and none of them will allow slavery. *Not ever again*."

His face looked back at her with a mixture of apprehension and almost painful hopefulness. "You truly believe all these things, Miss Rachel? You sound so sure in your mind."

"I'm absolutely certain, Lewis. I can't prove it to you, but I hope you believe me."

"Land sakes," he exhaled, "Miss Rachel, sometimes my own dreams don't come about, at least I don't think they do. And I ain't never had a dream like this, tellin' about so many big, far off things. What if you is plain wrong?"

"I'm not wrong, Lewis."

He shook his head and then leaned it back against the barn. "I'll pray to the good Lord that you is right about what you seen, Miss Rachel. I surely will. About everythin' except what you said about Mr. Lincoln. That would be a sad, sad loss."

They both sat quietly for a time, their minds focused inward. Lewis was the first to speak. "Do you suppose maybe you had this dream so you can do somethin' 'bout it?"

She gave him a hesitant look. "I've thought about that too," she said. "I know his killer is John Wilkes Booth, an actor. It will happen at Ford's Theater. But if I wrote a letter saying he'd be shot, do you think anyone would *believe* me?" She sighed in frustration. "They'd all think I was crazy."

"Well, we could try," Lewis said. "Leastways we can send him a letter and see."

Rachel felt her helplessness mounting. "Lewis, what if they thought I might be a threat to the president and they sent word to have the sheriff lock me up?"

"You truly think they wouldn't believe you?"

"I don't know! I wish I *did* know. How would I explain how I learned these things? If they decided I was in on some scheme, they might even wonder if my folks were in on it with me. What if the letter brought trouble for this family, not just for me? And Lewis, I'm afraid it wouldn't change anything even if they took me at my word."

"Why not, if they believe what you say?"

"Because it would mean changing what was meant to happen, and we don't know what else might be changed if we step in."

"Miss Rachel, what is the good of learnin' to write if a body can't send a letter to warn a great man about a killer?"

"But... what if, somehow, the future is worse if Abraham Lincoln lives to reach old age."

"The future worse 'cause we stopped Mr. Lincoln from bein' shot? How could that be?"

"I can't imagine, but what if it turned out that way?"

Silence took over again, lengthening until Rachel noticed that the darkness had nearly found them. "I'd better go in," she said at last, standing and turning toward him. Concerned, she said, "I certainly laid a lot at your feet tonight. I didn't intend to."

"It's a good thing, you tellin' me. You oughtn't to carry such a mighty weight all alone, knowin' what you know.

"But, Lewis..."

"You needn't ask me not to tell another soul. I won't."

She smiled feebly into his serious face, feeling ashamed for questioning his willingness to keep her confidence. "Of course you won't," she said. "And my troubles do seem lighter now that I've shared them with you."

"I'm proud that you did."

"You're a good friend, Lewis. I'm going to miss our talks when I head back to town."

"Sleep peaceful, Miss Rachel. Don't you be worryin' no more tonight."

The tiring yet fulfilling physical labor performed during the daylight hours was always rewarded with good food, warm and affectionate companionship, and blessed relaxation as the days drew to an end, and after the first week back at the farm, Rachel's resolve to take up permanent residency in town began to weaken ever so slightly as her books received a little less attention.

On Friday just before noon, a neighbor dropped by to give them an edition of the *Boise News* he'd finished reading, much to the pleasure of the adults in the Milford family. Rachel yearned for news of the war, and the paper, though its accounts were already many days old, was the best source they had. When her turn came, she read it with absorption.

Along with updates on the Civil War, reporting no definite sign of cessation, the newspaper carried an article about an attack by Indians on white traders along the stage road. Livestock rather than human lives were taken, but then, the loss of a person's stock could result in great hardship and possibly death to those barely eking out an existence. Rachel skimmed over the news on Territorial conventions and the election of new delegates to Congress. Then she found an article covering the killing of some "friendly" Indians by the cavalry; a case of mistaken identity.

Rachel's mind churned over the tragic nature of these conflicts, and the nagging question of whether she should attempt to change such events arose anew. Since her talk with Lewis she'd felt his unspoken wish that she act on what he supposed she'd foreseen. But the familiar response, that her interference could cause even greater, unforeseeable hardships, still paralyzed her. Perhaps, she concluded at last, her practicing medicine was a way to help without creating a negative backlash. Yes, perhaps.

That evening she asked Bert if he would drive her back to town the next day, and told the rest of the family and Lewis of her intended departure. Charlie was anything but pleased. He hadn't wasted a night after Rachel's return before reclaiming his sleeping place next to her, waking each morning with his arm entwined in her long hair. His reaction to her departing so soon was tearful and noisy, and she promised to keep him close by her side throughout that night. She knew that his nearness would give her comfort as well, being acutely aware of how much she would miss his sweet company.

Just before dark Rachel finished sweeping the kitchen floor and left the house to check on the chicks, cows, and horses. She loved to take in the sights of the dusky sky and the scents in the cooling air as she wandered around the homestead. Usually Charlie caught up with her before she reached the barn, but tonight he didn't come. Lewis, however, made his regular appearance at the tack room door to chat for a few moments before wishing her goodnight. She gave their stallion Choice one last pat, waved back at Lewis, and returned to the kitchen.

Juliet was sitting at the table with nothing in her hands, an unusual sight by itself, but Rachel could see by the glow of the lantern that she wore an expression of regret.

"What's wrong, Mama?"

Juliet glanced up and smiled sadly. "It's Charlie. He's mighty unhappy with me just now."

"Charlie?" Rachel appropriated the chair beside her. "Why is he unhappy?"

Juliet took one of Rachel's hands and held it in both of hers. "I believe he's gone down to the creek alone, like he knows he's not supposed to do. Will you go and talk with him? He'll most likely tell you all about it."

Rachel watched Juliet questioningly but asked nothing more. She patted her hands as she stood and, lighting the metal lantern that hung by the door, left in search of Charlie.

She found him just where Juliet had predicted he'd be, beneath a Ponderosa pine not four feet from the creek bank, a small form sitting in the gathering darkness with his knees pulled up to his chest and his arms wrapped around them. His little body was shuddering with each sob, and he was talking to himself but Rachel couldn't catch the words. She sat down beside him and held out her arms.

He crawled into her embrace and went right on crying.

"Shhh, now, Charlie," she said softly, rocking him gently while running her hand through his hair. "What's the matter?"

"Mama..." he said, but the crying took over again.

"Now, now, honey, what about Mama?"

"She-e-e, she said she won't marry me, even when I get all growed up." At the vocalization of this tragedy, his sobs gained in strength, and Rachel hugged him even tighter as she hid her smile in his hair. She rocked him until he calmed a bit.

"Charlie, Mama can't marry you, but she will always love you, always. She's feeling really low right now, just because you're sad. Don't you know how much she loves you?"

He sniffed loudly, wiped his nose on his sleeve, and lifted tear-filled eyes. "Then why won't she marry me?"

Rachel searched for an explanation that a four-year-old might comprehend. "Because you're her son, Charlie. The law says that mothers can't marry their sons."

"But, why?" Sniffs and an occasional hiccup were beginning to replace his sobs.

"She can't marry you when she's already married to Pa. You know a lady can't have more than one husband."

"But Mama said I can't marry *you* neither, and you got no husband at all."

He looked as if tears would start up again so Rachel hastened to say, "Charlie, when you're all grown up I'll be nearly an old lady."

"I don't care about that," he told her firmly.

Unable to come up with anything better, Rachel said, "Well, since it's also against the law for a sister to marry her brother, if I married you they'd throw me in jail, and you right along with me."

Wide-eyed now, he asked, "They would? For a fact?"

"For a fact."

He sniffed again and frowned deeply. "That don't hardly seem right."

"We can't go against the law, Charlie."

Letting out a slow, forlorn breath, he said, "No, I 'spect not."

He quieted by degrees as she continued to comfort him, and at last his body relaxed and his head grew heavier against her shoulder. She smiled again at the thought of such tender innocence, such pure love.

"Rachel?"

"Yes, Charlie?"

He inhaled deeply. "You smell just like nighttime."

16

After she'd sent Charlie into the house to comfort Juliet, Rachel continued to sit in the ring of lantern light and shift her gaze from the water riffling feet away to the stars dancing trillions of miles overhead. Breathing in the evening fragrances, she affectionately reconsidered Charlie's soft words and wondered how a person could smell like nighttime. With the mosquitoes thickening, she was just standing up when a movement near the barn caught her eye. She held utterly still as a shiver of apprehension ran through her, and she stared at the spot to be sure her senses weren't deceiving her. With a slight start she recognized Kate, leaning forward and frantically waving an arm in Rachel's direction, beckoning her closer. Rachel grabbed the lantern and scanned the yard as she hurried to Kate, reaching her just as the girl's legs buckled.

"Kate!" Rachel took her shoulders and helped her to a sitting position. "What is it?'

Her face and clothes were dirty and she was breathing hard. "You got to help me, Rachel."

"Are you hurt?" Rachel searched Kate's face and slid her fingers down her arms, exploring for injuries.

"Don't worry about me. It's him you got to help."

"Who?" Rachel's hands touched a soft bundle in Kate's lap.

She was holding it with her skirt pressed tight against her waist. She lowered the skirt enough to reveal a furry, brown and white puppy. "Him. He's bad hurt."

Even in the dim light of the lantern, Rachel could see that the puppy was bleeding from its mouth. After watching for any sign of life and seeing none, then placing her hand on the pup's soft chest, feeling its chilliness rather than a heartbeat, Rachel said sympathetically, "I'm sorry, but I don't think I can help him, Kate. What happened?"

"It...it was Walter."

Rachel's mind leapt back to the scene in the clearing when Walter had shot the pine cone from Kate's bare hand. "Walter! Kate, Pa told you not to see him any more!"

Kate's words rushed out in defense. "I didn't *mean* to see him. I went to check on the cows in the back pasture and he was there, waiting for me. He had two puppies with him and he said he'd brought one to give me. I told him again and again that I couldn't keep one, and then he got mad and he... he picked up a stick and hit this poor little thing.

Oh, *can't* you help him, Rachel?" she begged, petting the fur of the small lifeless body. "I'm the cause of him getting hit so hard, don't you see? I should have taken him, just to keep him safe."

Knowing there was no hope for the puppy but wanting to console Kate, Rachel took the little dog and felt along its sides and limbs. Half of its ribs and its back were broken. With an effort she fought her welling outrage at such cruelty, and she looked over at Kate's lowered head. Gently, she lifted Kate's face. "Kate, honey, the puppy's gone."

Kate's lower lip trembled and her eyes filled with tears but she didn't let them spill.

"It's not your fault, Kate. Walter's brutality has nothing to do with you." Rachel carefully laid the small furry body on the grass.

Kate's troubled gaze lingered on the puppy, but she managed to say, "I tried to stop him. It's just that he's a sight bigger than me... and he had a bigger stick. When he grabbed a branch and hit the puppy, I grabbed one too and told him to stop. But that just made him madder. When he whacked the puppy again I swung at him." Her voice was gathering strength now. "I wish I'd swung a lot harder 'cause he came after me good."

"After you!" Rachel leaned closer and took Kate by the shoulders again "Did he hit you, Kate?"

Kate wiped at her eyes with the back of her sleeve. "I won't say unless you promise not to tell Mama and Pa."

"Kate, if that boy hurt you, they have to know."

Very softly, Kate said, "Then I'll not say a word more, Rachel."

"But what if he comes after you again?"

"He won't," Kate said with such confidence that Rachel paused.

"You can't be sure of that."

"Yes, I can. He won't be back, not ever." Kate hesitated a moment, then let it out, "I told him I'd... I'd never marry him now."

"What!"

"I never said I *would* marry him, but I never said, for certain, that I wouldn't," Kate admitted. "When he saw how his stick had caught my leg, he said he was real sorry, but I wouldn't listen. I told him he'd never have me for a wife. He didn't believe me at first, but when he finally did, he looked real sad, and when I told him I'd set the law onto him if he didn't go, he got plenty scared."

"Set the law onto him?"

Kate hesitated but then let the rest out, "He told me he stole the pup, and lots more. He said his pa, who ain't good for much, has been taking Walter along to rob the shacks of some of the miners. He said his pa was leaving the territory before Sheriff Pinkham caught up with him, but Walter intended to stay here and marry me in a few years. I reckon he figured I'd never tell our folks about his part in the thieving, so they'd never tell the sheriff. When I said I would tell, he lit out. He won't be back."

"He hit your leg? Did he *hurt* you?"

"You promise not to tell?"

Rachel's mouth drew into an impatient line. "Do I have a choice?"

Kate shook her head and Rachel grudgingly nodded. Shifting her weight, grimacing, Kate lifted the side of her skirt to expose her right calf.

Bringing the lantern closer until she could make out a dark spot the size of a quarter from which blood still flowed, spreading down the length of her leg and into her shoe, Rachel said, "Oh, no." She leaned nearer to inspect the deep puncture, marveling at Kate's tolerance for pain. The girl hadn't said a word about her own injury until Rachel had examined the little dog. "Does it hurt badly?"

"No, Rachel, not much."

"I've got to get you into the house so I can wash and bandage this," Rachel said, rising.

Kate grabbed her arm and urged, "We've got to wait –til the folks are asleep."

"Mama won't go to bed without making sure we're in the house. If we don't go inside she'll just come looking for us."

Kate didn't respond.

"Kate?" When she still said nothing, Rachel sat beside her, waiting.

Kate looked at the small furry body in the grass. "That poor little pup's gone. I never thought Walter would do such a thing."

"I know. I'm sorry, Kate." For a moment she considered asking Bert to take Kate into town, but she knew such injuries were almost always dealt with at home. So with a calmness that was hard-won, Rachel said, "Well, we either have to take you to Dr. Hogue in town, or I'll try to take care of you here. I can clean and disinfect your wound, then stitch it closed. I've read all about how to do it, and I've practiced on some fabric, but you would be my very first patient."

Kate's eyes searched her face. "I want you to do it, Rachel."

"I know how brave you are, Kate. Can you hold still for my stitches?"

"I'll try."

"Everything I need is in the house. Let's go inside."

"But if Mama finds out I saw Walter again..."

"You didn't *intend* to see him, Kate. She'll understand."

Kate chewed her upper lip. "What about Pa?"

"Tell him everything. He'll understand too. They love you so, Kate, and they'll want to help take care of you."

After another moment's pause, Kate said, "All right, then, Rachel. Maybe my telling them won't hurt as bad as this leg."

Without giving her time to reconsider, Rachel helped her up, pulled the girl's arm over her shoulder, and half-carried her to the house.

As Rachel had known would be the case, the entire family poured into the kitchen when Kate's injury was discovered, everyone voicing their concern and asking questions. After Kate's story had been retold, Rachel and Juliet shooed the rest of the clan from the room, gathered up what they needed, and Rachel bent to the task of treating the injury. Just before the stitching was to begin, Phillip and Maggie peeked in and offered to go out and bury the puppy, an offer that Kate gratefully accepted.

As anyone who knew her would have predicted, Kate didn't make a whimper throughout the procedure. In no time her leg was cleansed, stitched, and bound, her face and hands washed, and her clothes replaced. And after all of this was finished and Juliet was tucking Kate into bed, Rachel sat down at the clean kitchen table and helped herself to the single but generous swallow of whiskey still remaining at the bottom of Kate's glass, toasting the patient's bravery and her own small but successful surgery.

Not long after they'd heard Kate's tale, and with no explanation, Bert, Grandpa, Lewis, and True had quietly left the house. They returned hours later, tired and grim-faced, with the report that Walter and his father had, by all the signs they could discover, left the area. They'd awakened Sheriff Pinkham and informed him about all that had happened. Wasting no time, the sheriff had ordered several deputies to join him and circled town in the hope of catching sight of the fugitives, assuring Bert that he and his men would keep a careful watch in the coming days.

17

Rolling long strips of cloth bandages at the patient's table in Dr. Hogue's office, Rachel listened tolerantly to a somewhat defensive response to the advice she'd just offered concerning the good doctor's wife.

"Jane *has* been eating the food you recommended," he said, "probably far too much of it."

"She had been eating nothing but beans, bacon, bread and butter, an entire pantry starting with the letter b. Jane also needs milk and cheese, plenty of spinach, carrots and onions, and fruit, or at least preserves."

"I don't know what books you've been reading but you apparently have been very studious."

"Yes, Doctor, I have."

As he pondered his assistant's tenacious concern for his wife's health as well as her calm assurance, Dr. Hogue ran a hand under his chin, then let it fall to his lap. "I willingly admit that I've been impressed by the commitment you've shown to your studies and your work, Miss Milford, and it's refreshing to have an assistant who is enthusiastic about discussing procedures without becoming fastidious; *however*, this tendency of yours to speak your mind so freely..."

In a reasoning voice, she asked, "Dr. Hogue, didn't you tell me that your wife was to be my first patient?"

"That doesn't necessarily mean..." He caught the earnestness in her expression, and acknowledged, "Yes, I did say that."

"Well, if you and your wife are unwilling to take my advice, how can I expect any other patient to do so?"

"Miss Milford," he said, "we're just now getting spring vegetables into town, and they come mighty dear. Besides, Mrs. Hogue is finicky about vegetables."

Easing aside this protest, Rachel offered, "I've spoken to Mr. Quong about the availability of fresh vegetables and—"

"You spoke to a Mongolian? *Alone*? Miss Milford, a young white woman simply doesn't—"

Rachel firmed her jaw and interrupted him right back. "*Mr.* Quong has managed to provide his family with quite a variety of vegetables already. Our Chinese citizens eat a much healthier diet than the rest of us. Peas, at least, can be bought fairly cheaply right now."

"Don't misunderstand my concern about Mr. Quong. He seems a decent sort, but for you to go traipsing off to talk to him alone could cause trouble for both of you."

She couldn't hide her building irritation. "At least you didn't refer to him as a Coolie like some of the people in this town."

"I don't hold anything against those folks, Miss Milford, truly, but you know there's a growing fear that a great number of Chinese will head to the basin just as soon as the California mines play out. The miners currently working for the bigger companies are afraid their wages will be cut if the Chinese agree to work for less. I've even heard talk of the legislature passing a law that would require every Chinese, male or female, to pay a tax of four dollars a month just to live in this territory."

"That's an outrageous rumor."

"Not in the least. It may very well come to pass. We have a volatile situation on our hands, and there's a number of townsfolk who don't want people, especially women, being friendly with them."

"I appreciate that you're trying to protect me, Dr. Hogue, but I won't allow bigots to choose my friends. The Chinese men I've met have never treated me with anything but courtesy. None of them is even a miner. Most seem to work in laundries or on farms, but they're entitled to work wherever they want."

"Regardless of how unjust the present circumstances may be, that doesn't change the fact that it's dangerous for you to meet with a Chinaman alone." He added in a gentler tone, "I am thinking of your reputation, which will affect our profession, as well as your safety."

"All right, but may we please change the subject? I don't want us to argue. Discuss, yes, but never argue."

"I thoroughly concur."

"Well then, concerning your wife, she's already agreed to change her diet for the good of the baby; however, she'll need a little encouragement."

Sighing in resignation, Dr. Hogue asked, "Am I allowed to know the specifics of your recommendations?"

She passed him a list she'd drafted the night before.

He surveyed the paper, and admitted, "It looks quite comprehensive. Jane never has liked the taste of milk, though."

"She can substitute cheese, and even some ice cream if she'd like, just not too much."

"Well, *that* she shouldn't object to."

Returning his half-hearted smile, Rachel picked up her scissors and began cutting more bandages from a stack of bed sheets as the doctor took up his pen to label several new bottles.

Their quiet activities allowed her to reflect on the past few days and how grateful she was for the routine demands of Dr. Hogue's practice. Since lacerations and broken bones were everyday occurrences around the diggings, most of her initial work had dealt with repairing injuries. At least as common were the knife and gunshot wounds inflicted by men who'd drunk beyond their capacities. The local saloons never closed, but business was invariably busiest after sundown, and Rachel had asked to assist at almost any hour. In just two nights, Dr. Hogue and she had treated four men, and she imagined that the other doctors in town were just as busy. She'd also assisted with the treatment of children with minor illnesses but had been spared having to face an outbreak of smallpox, cholera, or any other devastating disease. With every case, her commitment had strengthened.

Regardless of how anxious she was to gain experience in childbirth, babies weren't exactly arriving with regularity. The Turner baby was due any day, and Rachel had visited Elizabeth Turner to give her some recommendations on nutrition, but this would be the couple's fifth child and Elizabeth knew what to expect. Even so, she seemed amazed when Rachel discussed how breathing techniques could help a mother manage the worst pains of labor and prevent over-tensing muscles or pushing too early. Fascinated, and ready to try any approach that might ease her new baby's arrival, Elizabeth welcomed the aid being offered.

Although Rachel remembered that Dr. Lamaze had developed the methods she was trying to mimic, she carefully avoided using his name. She knew almost nothing about him and had been unable to find anything written about his life. It was very possible that he hadn't been born yet, which could cause nothing but trouble if Dr. Hogue or anyone else chose to investigate his work. Neither Elizabeth Turner nor Jane Hogue had questioned the source of her knowledge, and Dr. Hogue seemed to believe that instinct alone had inspired her ideas. It was Jane who first used the term "Rachel's breathing" to describe how her husband's new assistant meant to help mothers bring their babies into the world, and the phrase appeared to be spreading among the young women in town.

Upon her return from the farm Rachel had found a tiny upstairs room she could just afford at the Montana House on Main Street, not much farther than a stone's throw from Esther's house. The place was run by Mrs. Kellin and her sister, and was as fine and reputable an inn as Idaho City could offer, which was actually quite respectable. The food was hearty and the rooms were clean and comfortably furnished. Rachel was still finding the noise from the main room downstairs challenging, however, especially when she was trying to study.

Dr. Hogue's voice interrupted her musings. "Miss Milford, you'd better make up a larger supply of bandages than we usually keep on hand. I've seen posters around town promoting cock fights *and* dog fights for tonight."

She raised her eyebrows, questioning.

"Sometimes the less sober spectators jump into the middle of things. Even if that doesn't happen, there's often a spirited fist fight or two afterward."

As Rachel resumed her work, her thoughts wandered to Chicago. She smiled inwardly, wondering what Ellen would say if she could see her now, creating bandages in the back of a drugstore and waiting to treat a couple of drunken miners injured by fighting roosters. At the thought of so faithful and nurturing a friend, Rachel's hands slowed and then stilled. She'd probably never see Ellen again, or her family, or Jason. The realization was a poignant stab to her heart, and it held her in a painful grip for a moment, but she refused to let it linger. With a mental shake and renewed vigor, she snipped and rolled more of the cloth.

"Did you hear about the benefit the town's throwing for Mrs. Grimes?" Dr. Hogue asked without looking up from his bottles."

"No, doctor."

"You know who George Grimes was, surely."

"I only know there is a Grimes Creek. Was it named after him?"

"Yes, it was. He was one of the first to discover gold here, but he didn't live long enough to enjoy it. He was murdered less than a week later, killed while digging at the head of Grimes Creek. Some say it was Indians although most folks think otherwise. Anyway, his widow came to town looking for his share of the gold, now her share, only to be told that the claim had been sold. They say her share was worth around three thousand dollars. The claim manager that sold it ran off with the funds, so now local citizens are trying to raise what they can for her."

Someone knocked at the office door, entered, and met Dr. Hogue as he left the treatment room several steps ahead of Rachel.

"Doc," said a rich male voice.

"Ethan," said Dr. Hogue, in cheerful welcome, "it's been some time."

Rachel entered as the newcomer shook hands with the doctor and then removed his weathered hat. Running fingers through the flattened waves of his auburn hair, he shifted his gaze to her and held it steady.

There he stood, the man who'd beaten the Confederate gunman with a board, and something in the frankness of his expression implied that his memory of their first brief encounter was as vivid as her own. Along with wonder and curiosity, Rachel felt that she'd never seen a pair of eyes so intensely blue. Inside the confines of the small room, he looked even larger than on the street, his shoulders seeming to span the doorway behind him.

He nodded politely and said only, "Ma'am," before stepping aside and ushering two children forward. The first was an Indian boy of about Phillip's age who was cradling his left arm, the second, a young white girl, surely the man's daughter. The resemblance was unmistakable.

Dr. Hogue said, "The last time you came through that door, Ethan, you brought in the fellow with a dislocated shoulder." Doc's expression took on a look of innocence shaded with wise speculation as he added, "I was told he left for Montana. He didn't seem to take to our town much, and from what I hear I doubt he'll be missed." Turning back toward Rachel, he went on smoothly, "Here now, let me introduce my new assistant, Rachel Milford. Miss Milford, this is Ethan Stonehill and his daughter, Rose. Ethan makes the finest furniture anywhere around. And this young man," he added, indicating the Indian boy, "is Dick McConnell."

Rachel held out a hand and Ethan shook it gently, meeting her eyes. Rose shyly did the same. Unwilling to risk causing pain to the boy's injured arm, she offered him a smile, but he surprised her by reaching out with his left hand and giving her one solemn shake.

"Bill McConnell asked me to bring Dick in for you to take a look at his arm, Doc," said Ethan. "He felt awful about not being able to drive in himself, but the man is so sick with a bad cold that he could hardly stand."

"What happened, Dick?" the doctor asked as he ushered them into the treatment room.

"I got kicked by Pa's big bay, sir."

"Come over to the table, and we'll have a look."

Ethan paused and said kindly to Rose, "You had better wait in the office for now, honey."

After everyone but Rose had filed in and the door had been closed, Rachel stood a few feet from Ethan at the foot of the table while Dr. Hogue helped Dick climb up and remove his shirt. When the arm was bare she could see that two sections of the upper bone, the humerus, were slightly separated and bent at an unnatural angle, and the area was swollen and discolored. Inwardly, she winced at the pain Dick must be enduring, but she kept her expression composed. Without the doctor asking her to gather what he needed, she poured clean water into a basin and then set washcloths, a jar of ointment, splints, binding bandages, scissors, and a sling on a large tray within his reach.

After gently probing the injured arm, Dr. Hogue smiled at Dick and said, "My boy, you've got a clean break. I can set it while you're awake or give you chloroform to put you to sleep. I recommend the chloroform. What do you say?"

Dick glanced at Ethan, sat a little straighter, and said with a touch of defiance, "I will stay awake, doctor."

Ethan patted the boy's knee and said, "There's no shame in sleeping, Dick. I imagine the pain will be fierce for awhile."

The boy wavered for only a moment. "Awake," he confirmed.

After washing his hands and the boy's arm, Dr. Hogue was just preparing to set the bone when little Rose peeked into the room, her eyes large and fearful. "Maybe you should go to Rose, Ethan," said Dr. Hogue.

"Please stay, Ethan," Dick pleaded, his resolution faltering.

The doctor turned to Rachel. "Miss Milford, will you please sit with her. I won't need you for awhile."

Rachel nodded and walked to the door. "Rose," she said cheerfully, "let's go find a lollipop. I think I'll need your help." Rachel took the child's hand and glanced reassuringly at Ethan as she closed the door behind them. "Now, wherever can that candy be? Where should we look first?" Knowing full well where the sweets were stored, Rachel proceeded to rummage through drawers as if on a treasure hunt, and Rose began to enjoy the game. Just when Dick's cry of pain reached them from the other room, Rachel seemed to remember the lollipops' hiding place. "Look, Rose! Here they are at last! What color would you like?" Rose hesitated until Dick quieted, and then chose a red one. She and Rachel sat down on separate chairs, Rose eyeing her speculatively as she sucked on her treat.

"Do you think Dick is all right now, miss?"

"The hardest part is over. It will take a few weeks for his arm to heal completely, but Dr. Hogue will take very good care of him."

"My papa says he's a mighty fine doctor."

"I think so too. It was nice of your father to bring Dick to him."

"Yes, ma'am. That's because my papa is a specially nice man."

Rachel smiled. "Oh, I see."

"He's mighty strong, too.

"He is?"

"Yes'm, and he makes real pretty things out of wood."

"Well, isn't that wonderful?"

"If you need anything made of wood, like a table or a bench, he could make one. You could come to our farm and see what he made for us."

"Does your mother mind when visitors drop in?"

Dr. Hogue opened the door and announced, "All's well. You two can come on in." As they entered he said, "Ethan, please tell his father that those splints are not to be disturbed for at least a month. He's to stay in bed for a few days, and after that he's to do only light chores. I'll ride out and look in on him tomorrow and then, unless the boy is suffering and needs me sooner, I'll be back at the end of the week. Now, Dick, I know your folks will be very proud when they hear how brave you've been today."

Rose went to Dick's uninjured side and with great tenderness placed both of her hands on his good arm, saying, "You'll be strong again real soon, Dick." Almost imperceptibly Dick pressed his arm against his side, lightly capturing her small fingers.

"Say, Miss Milford," said Dr. Hogue, watching the children, "I believe we are running low on one of our important supplies. This morning I noticed that the peppermint jar was empty, and I seem to recall that Dick is partial to peppermint sticks." At this Dick perked up a little.

In a serious tone, Rachel said, "You're absolutely right, doctor. I'll just walk over to the mercantile and get some."

"I'd be happy to go, Miss Milford," Ethan offered. "A storm was heading toward town when we rode in. It could break any time and it might be powerful. Listen, you can hear the wind gathering strength already."

"No, please," she said, "you stay and visit with Dr. Hogue. I won't be long." The doctor made her pause long enough to accept a few coins that he dug from his pocket before snatching her bonnet from its wall peg and hurrying out the door.

A current of dusty wind caused her clothes to flutter before she'd left the drugstore's boardwalk, and within steps the gusting breeze was propelling her along as if by an impatient hand. With her eyes squinting and her feet planting firmly with each step, she made her way to the general store and entered with a swirl of dust. Mr. Mack, bald, short and as round as his pickle barrel, looked up in surprise. "Why, Rachel, whatever are you doing out in this weather? Can't you hear that wind starting to howl?"

While she paid closer attention, it did seem to be blowing harder as each second passed. "I just need a dozen peppermint sticks, Mr. Mack." The grocer shook his head at such recklessness, counted out the candies, told her the cost as he placed them in a small bag, accepted her coins, and then slipped a few extra sticks into the sack before handing it to her.

"Thank you, Mr. Mack," she said with a grateful smile, tucked the bag into her large apron pocket, and turned to go.

Suddenly, the shutters at the door and windows began to rattle in protest, and Mr. Mack suggested worriedly, "You'd best stay here 'til this blows itself out, young lady."

"I have a patient waiting, Mr. Mack, but thanks for your concern. I'll hurry."

Before he could advise or protest further, she opened the door aided by a whoosh of wind, and had to muscle it closed again. In front of her whirled a world of dancing dust, wildly bouncing tumbleweeds, and flying twigs. Spotting a clear space in the shifting haze, she hurried forward with one hand shielding her eyes. She'd nearly reached the middle of the street when a tide of fine sand swept down from overhead and blinded her in mid-stride. Buffeted roughly, she took several faltering steps while fighting to clear her eyes. As if taking advantage of her sudden helplessness, the next gusts seemed bent on turning her in circles as they robbed her of breath, tore at her clothes, and scoured her skin. Above the growl of the onrushing storm she heard Mr. Mack shout her name. She pivoted first one way, and then the other but could only guess at the direction from which the call had come.

As she teetered forward the sand found her throat and nostrils, encrusting them and making every breath an exertion. She jerked off her bonnet, covered most of her face, and lurched ahead. Two riderless horses raced by, one passing so close that it knocked aside her outstretched hand and caused her to stumble before both animals disappeared into the billowing dirt like phantoms. Fighting to stay calm, she flinched and ducked as the wind flung everything inadequately bound to the earth through the air. She trudged on in a jerking crouch as her surroundings fractured and crashed. A tree branch rolled from the sky and struck her right shoulder, dropping her to one knee. Kneading the bruised muscle with one hand while clutching her makeshift mask with the other, she forced herself to stand and take another few steps in what she fiercely hoped was the right direction.

A new cry of her name flew into her face, shattered, and shot past. She yanked the bonnet from her mouth to shout, "Here!" but the word was blown back down her throat with such a violent rush of sand that she doubled over, coughing and spitting. Kneeling low and using her arms to shield her head and face from the driving grit, trying to tuck her sandblasted hands beneath them, she felt panic rising, enveloping her as ruthlessly as the wind. She let out a single hacking sob.

Without warning, something heavy fell on top of her and she pushed and kicked at it in a frantic attempt to free herself of its weight. But the thing rose up and lifted her by the shoulders. "Miss Milford! It's Ethan!" Beyond caution or prudence, she grabbed him by the shirt and clung to it. He wrapped an arm around her waist and turned with her into the wind. Squeezing against his side, she gripped the hand of the arm that encircled her, lowered her head, and struggled along in the direction Ethan had chosen.

Windows on both sides of the street exploded inward as though struck by sledgehammers, and the same concussive gust nearly knocked Rachel and Ethan to the ground. He clasped her painfully tight but he kept them both on their feet. Although Rachel could see very little as they fought for each step, she could hear the sounds of more crashing glass and splintering wood, and the terrified shrieks of animals, all joining the howl of the tempest in a frenzied, brutal dissonance, and she would have covered her ears if she'd dared to release Ethan.

With a jolt they collided against the side of a wagon, its petrified ox team held fast by their twisted traces. Rachel, seeking any form of refuge, tried to draw Ethan beneath the rocking wagon bed. When he resisted, she pulled urgently and cried, "Get down!"

With desperate force Ethan yanked her clear of the wagon, and then lifted her rebelling, twisting body into his arms and pinned her there. Lowering his head and gasping for breath, he carried her around the back of the wagon and onto the boardwalk. He careened forward with Rachel still held fast, clumsily tried to open two locked doors, finally shouldered his way into a surrendering doorway, and shoved it closed with his back. As her struggles lessened he toted her to a corner at the far side of the room, where he loosened his grip slightly before leaning his back against the wall and sliding with her to the floor. Only then did he allow her to scoot away from him as they coughed and gulped for air in the darkness.

They were still gasping and fingering the grit from their eyes when the oval window in the front door shook madly, and Ethan jumped to shield Rachel an instant before the pane burst inward. He jerked and let out a bark of pain as glass shards struck his back. A scream, high and frantic, started building in Rachel's throat but Ethan staggered to his feet, grabbed her under the arms, and pulled her into a hallway toward the rear of the building. An earsplitting boom shook the sky, and she felt a shudder run through the building just before the portion of the roof that had been sheltering them seconds before collapsed.

Wavering on his feet, Ethan took her hand and they moved farther down the hallway until they found and toppled into a small windowless room. He heaved the jammed door closed with one powerful shove of his shoulder, and inside this now black chamber they sank to the floorboards like stones.

Even here the clamor of the storm was nearly deafening, the baying wind accompanied now by roar after roar of vengeful thunder. A huge, heavy object slammed against the building as if intent on dislodging it from its foundation, and the crash brought to Rachel a sudden, chest-tightening dread for the well-being of Conrad, Esther, and Richard, for all of the Milfords, and for Lewis. Her body began to tremble. In the darkness she fumbled for Ethan with outstretched arms, but before she could touch him another missile crashed against the outer wall and, turning sharply toward the sound, she smacked her mouth against an unseen shelf. Recoiling from the impact, moaning hoarsely, she brought a hand to her split lip.

When Ethan's searching fingers lightly struck her shoulder, she grasped them and released a sob of gratitude as he drew her to his chest and wrapped her in his arms. Coughing softly now and then, he murmured in comforting tones. Though she could make out few of his words over the rolling booms and harsh wails of the gale, she silently pleaded that he would keep talking. She felt that she could hold onto what little remained of her shredded courage as long as he just held on and spoke to her. She lifted her arms and drew them around him to secure his embrace, but when he flinched and sucked in a breath, she suddenly remembered the glass from the door. She forced herself to ease away, got to her knees, and moved behind him.

Rachel tried to ignore the stinging of her eyes, mouth, and skin and to quell the quaking of her body as she slid her hands blindly yet very carefully over his back. She felt the warm dampness of blood and inched her touch upward until she found its sources, one by one. Ethan sat rigidly still as she searched out and gently extracted each piece of glass that yielded to her ministrations. The largest of these was roughly triangular, the protruding sides over two inches long, the point embedded in the flesh below his left shoulder. She took only time enough to judge its smoothness and angle of entry, and to brace herself. Then, gripping it firmly, she pulled it free with one swift tug.

He jerked, stiffening against the pain, then progressively relaxed his muscles. Her fingertips continued to explore for fragments, starting at the top corner of his back and tracing a path downward, then shifting a few inches and moving down again, but she could find no more. She would need light to help him further.

When he swiveled around to face her, she welcomed his enfolding arms once more, cradling her head against his chest as he slowly stroked her tousled, sand-roughened hair.

This man, this Ethan Stonehill who had likely just saved her life, and perhaps the lives of others the day she'd first seen him in front of the feed store, was warm and solid, and possessed a quiet strength that Rachel couldn't have conceived before today. He was speaking again but she still could understand only a few words. It mattered little. What meant everything, however, was that he was here, giving her his strength and consolation. She nestled closer, absorbing the heat of his body, focusing on the gentleness of his touch, and anchoring herself to the earth with his weight. They sat closely locked together, breathing, and defying the deadliness of the sky.

Raindrops started to beat against the roof, scattered at first but quickening and strengthening to a drumming staccato until it fell in a barrage that sounded as if they were under attack. Soon the rain's pattern shifted and seemed to be competing with the violent rhythm of the gale, crashing and ebbing in waves. The battered roof held back the deluge for only a short while before drops and then trickles found their way into the tiny room.

Without fully releasing each other Rachel and Ethan shifted in an attempt to avoid the worst of the dribbles, but they were soon thoroughly splattered. Liquid dripped onto Rachel's hands, still wrapped around Ethan just above his belt, and she knew by its warmth and stickiness that the rain was washing blood down from his upper back.

She said raggedly, "Hold me tighter, Ethan. Please." She felt the circle of his arms gently constrict, and whispered her thanks.

Eternal minutes passed, perhaps ten, perhaps thirty, then, almost abruptly, she could make out more of his words.

"...quieting some. Listen," he said.

She did, barely breathing. She could hear the wind assaulting the building with weakening force and the rain dispersing, its tattoo settling into a steadier and lighter cadence. Yes, oh, yes, the storm was easing! After a few moments longer, Rachel dared to believe they would survive, and with this hope came a new onslaught of distressed worry for those dear to her. Swallowing painfully, she prayed that they were all safe, and only then did she begin to cry.

She leaned into Ethan's shoulder and quietly wept, releasing large tears that rolled down her cheeks and gradually washed away some of the sand from her face as well as horror from her mind. Soon she calmed enough to remember how this man had come to find her, had brought her to safety, and had stayed with her. And she realized with a flood of guilt that these actions had left his own young daughter out of his protective reach. She bit back her last sobs, gulped in a couple of breaths, and stilled her crying. She lifted her face as Ethan loosened his hold and eased her from his embrace.

"Ethan, our families," she said in a raw voice, her eyes searching for his features but seeing only darkness. "What if... ?"

"Doc Hogue has been watching over Rose and Dick, and your folks have sturdy homes. I believe they're safe."

Rachel found herself futilely wishing for the miracle of a cellphone with which to call her loved ones, to hear confirmation that they were all right. Yes, they *were* her loved ones, regardless of how they'd come to be, regardless of everyone who'd touched her life before, and she loved them deeply. If a phone had been within reach she would have called the Milford home and heard Charlie's sweet voice, and the voices of each of the other children, of Lewis, Grandpa, Bert, and Juliet. She'd call the Letes. She'd call Dr. Hogue and let him reassure Ethan about Rose and Dick, and she'd ask the doctor about his wife, whom he would certainly have checked on already. Thinking of Stan, she felt confident that he'd survived the tempest, that he could survive almost anything.

There was no choice but to face whatever destruction the storm had left in its wake. *But please, God,* she silently asked again, *don't let any of them be hurt.*

Ethan stood, groped his way to the door, and held still, listening. The voice of the wind had become little more than a whine that now blended moderately with a pattering of the rain. The thunder was softening too as it rolled away to the northeast. He reached for the knob and tried to open the door but it was wedged tight in its shifted frame.

"Will you move to the far wall, Rachel?" When she'd scooted away he took the doorknob in both hands and pulled harder, but it didn't budge. Lifting his booted right foot and bracing it against the doorframe, he twisted the knob, took a breath, and gave a powerful yank. The door flew open so suddenly that he fell back into the room, landing with a loud thud on his backside. The walls groaned ominously but made no movement.

The dim light seemed almost dazzling after the blackness of the storage closet that had served as their refuge. Rachel's eyes were still irritated by the grains of sand that had not been dislodged by her tears, but she could make out her surroundings. As they left the closet and entered the hall, she realized that they were inside the Brown & Co. soda factory. Cautiously, they picked their way toward the street over a wet floor strewn with splintered wood and crushed glass.

Lifting her gaze, Rachel gasped. At the end of the hallway where the front of the building had been, a gigantic hole gaped back at her. Rain was streaming into the opening and falling upon the team of oxen still hitched to the wagon Rachel had recklessly tried to use as a shelter. Now a huge pine tree lay diagonally across the flattened wagon as well as the ox closest to them. The poor creature's back had been broken, and its body driven several inches into the ground by the tree's great weight. As the tree had struck, it had split the wooden yoke that bound the team together, and spared the second animal. This ox, though miserably wet, battered, and dull-eyed from its long-sustained fear, was alive. The most severe damage it had evidently sustained was the loss of one horn. Rachel pulled her gaze from this incredible scene and squinted at Ethan, who was already moving toward the team.

"Wait," she said, "let me see to your back."

Giving her a grateful look, he said, "It'll keep for now."

Ethan untied the surviving ox and coaxed it to the next hitching post as Rachel came forward to survey the damage up and down the street. Most of the buildings, though gouged and battered by debris, stood solidly upright and tightly shuttered. Windows that had not been protected were now stripped of their glass. Muddy water swirled around downed trees and snaked along both sides of the street in search of a swollen creek. Several feet from where Rachel stood, a woman's delicate pink parasol lay crushed beneath an overturned barrel marked "Nails." A growl of thunder drew her gaze up, but its voice was low and distant, and she saw no flashes of lightning.

Soaked through and still dripping, Ethan returned to her. He searched her face, and said, "We should head back to Doc's office."

"I'll come after I've checked on my sister's family." They hesitated, their eyes confessing their reluctance to part, until Rachel asked, "Will you wait for me there, so I can take care of your back?"

"Yes, ma'am," he returned. "I'll do that."

Rachel heard voices as men began to emerge from buildings, but it took a moment to realize that Richard was shouting her name above the calls of the others. She spun around, stumbled off the boardwalk, and he was there, seizing her by her upper arms.

"Praise the Lord!" he breathed. "You're not hurt bad, are you? Esther's been sick with worry."

Her knees weakened with relief. "Oh, Richard, you're all safe?"

"Safe and sound." Giving her a faint smile, he said, "At least Esther will be once she can see you, cuts, bruises and all. Rachel, you do look a fright."

"I can't come yet, Richard. Now that I know you're all right, I need to get back to Dr. Hogue's office, but I'll come as soon as I can."

Richard seemed to notice Ethan for the first time and he thrust his hand out. "I'm Richard Lete," he said, eyeing him thoroughly. He glanced at Rachel, then back at Ethan.

"Ethan Stonehill," he said, returning the firm grip. "Pleased to know you. I apologize but I've got to go now, Mr. Lete, to check on my daughter."

Rachel took Richard by the shoulders and hugged him fiercely, and then she fell into step beside Ethan without another word.

The two of them had nearly reached the drugstore when Rachel glanced over her shoulder to scan East Hill, and stopped short. Ethan followed the direction of her stare, and saw it too. The warehouse that had once adjoined Dr. Hogue's house was now in ruins, and yet the neat yellow house stood proudly erect next to the pile of destruction. Rachel craned to see if the home had suffered major damage, and watched Jane Hogue walk onto the covered porch, her skirt and apron billowing around her large belly as she waved down at them. They paused in the rain long enough to give a quick wave in return, then sloshed hurriedly through the pooling mud toward the drugstore.

They slogged into the doctor's office with mucky shoes, wringing wet clothes, and sopping hair, much to the relief of those inside. Rose dashed across the room and clamped her arms around her father's legs, and Ethan gave the doctor and Dick a quick nod of greeting before scooping Rose up and hugging her tightly to his chest. She pulled back and took his face between her small hands to scrutinize him thoroughly while Ethan's eyes searched her features for any signs of hurt or lingering fear.

"I'm all right, Papa, but your face and eyes, they're *all red*."

"Miss Milford and I got caught in the sandstorm."

"You surely did," Rose confirmed, "but you brought her back to the doctor, just like you said you would."

Rachel cast an appreciative glance at Ethan, and then addressed the doctor. "We saw Mrs. Hogue on your porch just now. She seemed absolutely fine."

Dr. Hogue, said, "Yes, thank the Lord. I knew she'd stay safely inside at the height of the storm, and she sent word as soon as things quieted some. Now let me take a look at you two." He stepped nearer and reached toward Rachel's mouth.

She stepped away. "It's nothing serious, Dr. Hogue, but if you'll—"

"Well, at least let me examine your arms."

At this Rose piped up again. "Oh, Miss Milford, you've got blood on you."

Rachel glanced down at her reddened sleeves and back at Dr. Hogue. "It's from Ethan's back, and he needs to be treated."

"Papa!" Rose cried, wiggling to get down. "Let me see what you've done."

"Now, Rose, it's nothing but a few cuts," he said, lowering her to the floor.

She circled to his back and exclaimed, "Oh, there's so much blood!"

"Don't you worry, Rose," Dr. Hogue said, motioning Ethan forward. "Miss Milford and I will get him fixed up right quick. You just wait here with Dick for a bit." The doctor led Ethan into the treatment room and Rachel followed close behind him.

By the time she'd washed her hands and gathered up the needed supplies, Ethan had taken off his torn shirt and was standing at the side of the table.

Dr. Hogue scrutinized his bare back and said, "Would you like a shot of whiskey, Ethan? This will take a little time."

"Thank you, Doc, but not just now."

Acutely aware of Ethan's every motion, feeling his eyes following her own movements, Rachel covered the table with a clean blanket and sheet.

Ethan glanced down and considered his filthy pants, eyed the clean sheet and blanket, and raised a rueful face to her.

"The bedding is washable," she said. "A little dirt won't hurt it."

He removed his boots and hesitated only a moment longer before following her instructions to lie on his stomach.

"Miss Milford, will you please cleanse the wounds?" asked Dr. Hogue.

"Yes, Doctor," she said softly, and there was something so restrained in the way she uttered the two words that Dr. Hogue cast a curious glance in her direction.

After scrubbing her hands again, and with utmost care, Rachel washed the sand, sweat, grime, and blood from Ethan's back, removing several small fragments of glass as they appeared. Her delicate work elicited no sound from Ethan beyond a slight intake of breath at times. When she could see and feel no more shards, she stepped back.

Dr. Hogue inspected her efforts, poked and prodded here and there, and nodded approvingly. "Fine work, Miss Milford. Ethan, would you mind if she stitches up the worst of these, in four or five places? What she lacks in experience, she makes up for with a steady, gentle hand."

Ethan gingerly raised himself up on his elbows and turned enough to look directly at Rachel. "I'd be pleased if she would, Doc."

So she began steadily sewing stitch after stitch, moving from one cut to the next, noting that Ethan attempted to keep his muscles from tensing as she progressed. Undoubtedly she was slower than the doctor would have been, but she was determined to pull very little and to close each cut neatly, especially the largest one that slanted down from his left shoulder blade. His muscular back must have been beautifully smooth before he'd shielded her from that onslaught of glass, and she was using every bit of skill she possessed to make it as flawless as possible once more.

Even as the needle punctured and threaded, the only sound that came from Ethan was his breathing, which sharpened at particularly sensitive points in her stitching, but nothing more.

After she finished tying off the last stitch and cutting the thread, Dr. Hogue loomed above Ethan to examine her sutures closely, evidently noting the exceptional care with which they'd been placed. Very pleased, he said, "Pretty as a needlepoint picture," and helped Ethan up into a sitting position. "If you take things easy for a week or two, I doubt you'll have much scarring, Ethan."

In a tone that added something perceptible to his words, Ethan said, "I'm much obliged, Miss Milford."

Rachel had been gathering the salve and bandages from the cabinet, but as she turned back to the men she saw Dr. Hogue aiming raised eyebrows at Ethan, conveying surprised speculation. Ethan was returning the doctor's gaze unwaveringly, communicating no actual admission but certainly no denial, thereby intensifying whatever suspicions the doctor was fostering. Dr. Hogue then cast a glance at Rachel, who continued working while pretending not to have witnessed the silent exchange or heard anything unusual in Ethan's words of thanks. The doctor meditated on the color in her cheeks for a moment or two before clearing his throat and saying a little too smoothly, "Miss Milford, will you finish up with the bandaging? Ethan, I believe I'll step over to my house to visit with my wife, and I'll take Rose and Dick along with me. Jane will be very happy to see them. And I know she won't mind tending to your shirt." With that, he picked up Ethan's filthy, perforated garment and passed through the doorway. He was about to pull the door closed behind him but paused and, with one last glance back at Ethan, left it slightly ajar.

The silence that followed his departure heightened Rachel's awareness of the man now under her care, who was watching her with vigilant intensity as she washed her hands yet again. "Ethan, are you ready for me to bandage your back?" When he nodded and sat straighter, she walked around him. Scooping a small dollop of salve from its jar, she smoothed it lightly over one of the smaller lines of stitched skin.

At the softness of her touch, Ethan released a faint and quickly hushed moan.

She concentrated on causing him a minimum amount of pain, trying not to notice the shape, firmness, or breadth of his back or the sleekness of the skin that had not been damaged by the storm. Her attempts to attain any measure of remoteness failed, however, and as she sensed his growing attentiveness of her every move, her touch became even slower and gentler. Then, after each of his stitched cuts had been covered with salve, Rachel's fingers ventured to the areas of his back beyond the sewn skin.

She glanced around Ethan's shoulder, saw that his eyes were closed, and continued to soothe him with her touch. Neither of them said a word, but their breathing grew subtly deeper and more deliberate. Her hands betrayed an undefined significance that she didn't try to analyze or conceal. Soon it required a dogged effort to keep her body calm, an effort made greater by the sense that Ethan was wholly conscious of the effect his nearness was generating.

As she smoothed her fingers across his back for the last time, she was struck by a powerful wave of suspended yearning to know this man, in every sense. The intensity of the feeling was so unexpected, so strange, that she quickly lowered her arms, jammed the lid a little too tightly onto the salve jar, wiped her hands on a cloth, and picked up the bandages. Silently scolding herself for such volatility, she said in a carefully controlled tone, "I'm going to bandage you now, Ethan."

Again, he only nodded.

"Hold your arms out a little, please." When he'd complied, she placed a rectangular bandage over the worst cuts and held this with one hand until she had secured it by winding a single wrap of the long strip around him, then proceeded with the next wrap, and the next. Each time she encircled him, she leaned forward to shift the rolled bandage from one hand to the other at his chest, which his size barely allowed her to do without brushing her cheek against him, and the consciousness between them deepened. She avoided eye contact to keep her movements steady, but she felt him observing her from the corners of his eyes, and waiting.

Finally, behind him, she split the last yard of the cloth lengthwise, handed an end forward from each of his sides, and asked, "Will you hold these strips in front of your chest, Ethan?" She came around the table and tied them into a small knot at his sternum.

Ethan pushed himself from the table to his feet, his eyes narrowing as he slowly scanned her face.

Stepping back only inches, she took him in just as thoroughly. His was a striking face, handsome beyond its share despite the sandblasting it had received. But she'd seen many good-looking men. Outside of what had happened to them, and between them, what made Ethan compelling, Rachel decided, was the way he said so little yet conveyed so much. Right now he was using his body and expression to communicate with profound persuasion, and yet she could tell that this unspoken language was inherent rather than studied, as natural to him as breathing. When his eyes touched hers again, Rachel perceived something in his gaze that held a shadowed melancholy caused by distant tragedy, sensing this component from his past as if she'd known him since childhood. *I only met him today,* she thought in disbelief, *just a few hours ago.*

With a mental start, stunned at her own blindness, Rachel suddenly realized what must be the actual reason behind his shaded expression. It wasn't grief or regret; it was concern for another. His wife. *His wife,* she forced her mind to repeat. Of course, he must be worried about her. He had a child, after all, and a man like this *would* be married. How could she have disregarded something so obvious?

"Rachel," said Ethan, "I mean, Miss Milford..."

"No, call me Rachel, please," she said, failing to keep her disquiet concealed. When she caught his questioning look, she tightened her hold on her emotions and added, "After today, we mustn't be so formal. I'm very grateful, Ethan, for everything, but I'm sorry to have kept you so long. You'll want to go and see that your family, other than Rose, I mean, is safe."

Studying her still, he said, "It's just Rose and me now. My wife died two years ago, in Virginia. Last spring Rose and I moved to our place below Warm Springs."

Just Rose and him. Fearing he would read her reaction to these words, Rachel turned away and placed the remaining bandages in a cabinet. With her back to him, she said, "Then, if you're in no real hurry, I'd like to treat your face too. It's pretty badly burned."

"I'm in no hurry to leave, Rachel."

She dipped a cloth into a basin of clean water and, coming close, gingerly washed the dirt and sand from his chafed face. She felt his focus, even while he closed his eyes so she could wash their lids. When he opened them, she picked up the jar of salve and, keeping her touch as steady as she was able, smoothed it over his skin. "There, now, I'm all finished."

He gave her a smile of gratitude. Turning his hands over and surveying the dirt they'd collected, he said, "I'd like to wash up a little, if you don't mind."

"Of course." Rachel motioned him to the basin, gave him a cake of soap, and brought fresh water. After drying his hands, Ethan picked up another clean cloth from the stack near the storage cabinet, and dampened it. Stepping to Rachel and lifting the cloth, he said, "Fair's fair. Your face is burned too. But you'll probably be more comfortable if you sit on the table."

His suggestion was followed, and when she was seated on the treatment table it was Rachel's turn to close her eyes and feel the cloth drift over her skin, then to hold herself still as the salve was applied ever so soothingly, enticingly. His touch was feather light, especially around her bruised mouth. Rachel had to admit that he'd done a better job of appearing relaxed than she was managing. He'd also been able to meet her eyes when she'd finished touching him, which presently she could not quite bring herself to do.

Setting the salve jar aside and standing before him, the only words that came to her mind were, "If we're both finished, I guess I'd better help you with your boots."

He tried to hide his amusement at this. "I can manage, Rachel, but I thank you." After carefully sitting down in the chair, he soon had pulled both boots on. He was just looking up when something near Rachel's waist caught his eye, causing a true smile to appear and expand. It was as unhurried and warm as Stan's grin was quick and reckless, and it spread until it lit his eyes. He reached toward her, took hold of something, and pulled gently upward. Between his thumb and forefinger he held up a soggy bag of peppermint sticks.

"They've been there all this time," she sputtered in surprise and started to laugh, and the sound of her mirth was quickly joined by a robust chuckle.

Having just entered the outer office, and drawn by the laughter, Dr. Hogue, Rose and Dick looked into the treatment room. Rachel immediately motioned them closer and pointed to the peppermints, which caused the newcomers to join them in voicing their happiness and relief at having sustained no graver damage on such a day.

Rose exclaimed, "How *ever* did you manage to bring the candy back, Miss Milford, with the storm and all?"

Standing quietly to the side, Dick gazed intently at Rose's tall father, still the bearer of the treats. Noting the silent plea, Ethan raised an inquiring eye, and Rachel nodded, "if they're not too sandy," upon which the children each received one of the gooey sticks. Doc Hogue said, "You kids come along and eat those in the outer office," and ushered them out.

The smile had eased from Ethan's face, but in its place was an expression of warmth and wonder. He raised his eyes, so penetrating now, and said, "I never dreamed that peppermints had the power to bring such sweetness to a grown man."

Exceedingly pleased, Rachel felt her cheeks warm with a blush she couldn't hide.

18

Feeling somewhat at a loss as he sat in his outer office with Rose and Dick, Dr. Hogue was musing over the less than discreet glances that had passed between Rachel and Ethan when Bert Milford burst in, spotted his daughter in the next room, and muttered a quick, "Hello, Doc," as he hurried to envelope her in a suffocating hug.

"You're whole," he said with emotion, "thank heaven, thank heaven."

Squeezing him tightly right back, taking in his concern and strength as she fought to keep back tears of relief, she said, "I'm fine, Pa."

He released her only to hold her at arms' length, searching her face. "Richard said you got beat up some, but I can see you're going to be alright. Oh, honey, we all made it through that terrible storm."

"All of us?" At his assuring nod, tears threatened her again.

Seeing this, Bert eased her into a chair. "All of us, even the animals. We have a mess to clean up, but that's nothing we can't manage." He gave her a smile, saying, "Kate was so determined to come see you and Esther, I thought we'd have to tie her down."

Rachel reached over and patted his hand, returning his smile with a moist one of her own.

Dr. Hogue, closely followed by the children, walked through the inner doorway. "Mr. Milford, you can be mighty proud of this daughter of yours. She had quite a time of it, but she still tended to Ethan here with particular care."

"Pa, this is Ethan Stonehill, and the children are his daughter Rose and Dick McConnell."

"Why, yes," said Bert, pulling off his soaked hat and shaking Ethan's hand. "Mr. Stonehill, how's that calf I sold you last month?"

The men exchanged a few friendly words before Bert returned his attention to Rachel, asking about what had happened to her during the storm.

"Pa, if I know Mama she's given you strict orders to come back immediately with news of Esther's family and me. Shouldn't you be getting home?"

"You do know your mother," Bert said with affection. "You're right, she was distressed to quite a state, especially when she had to stay with the children instead of come to town, but she'll want me to know all about it."

"I can tell you everything when we get together at the farm in a day or two. For now I'll just say that the wind caught me as I was returning from the mercantile, and things got scary for awhile, but Mr. Stonehill saw me safely back here. He shielded me from the glass that cut his back."

Bert turned to Ethan and, shaking his hand even more firmly this time, said with feeling, "You did us a service beyond measure, Mr. Stonehill. I'm mighty, mighty grateful. And I do hope your back isn't hurt bad."

"No, sir. Because of your daughter's care I'll heal in no time."

"Ethan," Dr. Hogue put in, "why don't you take the children over to my place and get your shirt from Jane. She had it drying by the fire, so it should be about ready by now. I've got a big cape in the back room you can drape over your shoulders. If you're not in a hurry, stay for dinner and give these muddy roads a chance to firm up a bit."

Gratefully accepting the invitation and the cape, Ethan said his farewells and ushered the children out.

Bert had noticed that Ethan had lingered a bit over his good-byes to Rachel, and the look of admiration, and perhaps more, he'd displayed. As the door closed, Bert gave her a few moments of shrewd fatherly appraisal before saying, "This Ethan Stonehill, he strikes me as a decent sort of man."

A little too casually, Rachel said, "He strikes me that way too."

"I see," said Bert. "I heard he lost his wife a few years back." He glanced at Dr. Hogue for confirmation, which was given by a nod.

Gathering a few more impressions by the subtle encouragement on the doctor's face, Bert nodded back at him. "Well, we owe Mr. Stonehill quite a debt of gratitude. Your mama's good cooking might be just what's called for here. How about asking the gentleman and his daughter to dinner one of these first Sundays so we can give him some proper thanks?"

It hadn't really been a question. "I'll see," she said.

A thought seemed to strike Bert, and he asked Dr. Hogue as much as Rachel, "Does Mr. Stonehill happen to be Catholic? Wait now, I *have* seen him in Mass a time or two."

"Pa," Rachel said in a cautioning voice, but Dr. Hogue nodded behind her back.

"Have Esther, Richard and the baby come along too, if Esther feels up to the ride. Now I'd best be going." He gave Rachel's arm a pat and bade Dr. Hogue a good day.

Rachel walked him to the porch of the drugstore, hugged him again, and leaned against a post as she watched him plod through a few puddles and rivulets, his shoulders hunched against the now gentle but continuing rain. Mounting Choice, he tugged his hat a little tighter and waved back before turning the horse toward Juliet and home.

It took three days for the sun to reappear, and one more for Ethan to show up at Dr. Hogue's office just before their usual closing time. With the doctor standing right next to Rachel and showing no inclination to make himself busy elsewhere, Ethan said simply, "Miss Milford, I'd be honored if you'd allow me to escort you to the Montana House for supper."

At Rachel's questioning glance at Dr. Hogue, he said, "Of course, of course, Miss Milford. Things have finally quieted down after all the storm's havoc. You feel free to go on to supper if you'd like."

Out on the boardwalk, she said, "Ethan, I'd like to stop at my room and clean up a bit first." Clean up, without make-up or much in the way of clothing, that's all she could do to make herself more attractive. How she wished she had something beautiful to wear. Her thoughts momentarily shifted to the huge closet and dressers filled with clothes in Chicago that she'd seldom worn and never fully appreciated. Now she owned only two dresses, and her pink one was in serious need of mending since Kate had tried it on and fallen down the stairs. Rachel had been squirreling away her extra earnings to purchase a third, perhaps within a few weeks, but tonight she was wearing her brown dress, and she felt shabby walking beside Ethan.

He seemed to read her thoughts, and said, "You look finer than anyone who's ever graced the Montana, Rachel, and if it gets much later a rougher crowd will start filling the streets. Would you be willing to go just as we are?"

She smiled ruefully. "I guess I can't do much sprucing up anyway, not with my present wardrobe. And," she confessed, "I skipped dinner today so I'm really hungry."

"Well, we'd better hurry along, hadn't we?"

Soon they were settled at a table amid a talkative but mannerly crowd, and Ethan encouraged her to order a steak, the house specialty, which she knew would rival the size of a skillet and be accompanied by at least four hearty side dishes, all of them delicious. She didn't hesitate.

The waiter left them, and Ethan gazed across the table with an expression that told her how happy he was with her company, then he leaned closer. Will you tell me a little about your life here, and before you came?"

"I'd much rather know about you. Would you mind starting with your story?"

"Not if that's your preference. Where shall I begin?"

"When you were a boy, as far back as you can remember."

"That's a way back, but I'll try." Despite the brevity of their acquaintance, the conversation flowed smoothly, and Rachel found Ethan open, if a little succinct, about his past, his plans, his opinion of the town, and other subjects she raised. She couldn't be as frank with him, of course, but she did manage to create a somewhat believable history without too much stumbling. *What a good liar I'm becoming*, she reflected as an uncomfortable measure of guilt threatened to diminish her formidable appetite, but then the waiter finally reappeared.

When their food was spread in splendor upon the table, she dug in with relish, which seemed to please Ethan. It crossed her mind to wonder how, without a single trip to the gym or any other form of structured exercise, she could eat like a lumberjack and not gain an ounce. Then she realized that it must be because of the meals she missed altogether, probably a greater number than she heeded. As Ethan enjoyed his own meal, he continued to watch her with thoughtful appreciation.

After supper, she readily agreed to go for a walk along the creek, and as they wandered along, she said, "Tell me about Dick, Ethan. You mentioned that he was adopted by Mr. McConnell and his wife?"

"That's right. About a year and a half ago some Paiutes were raiding the lower Boise and Payette Valleys, and they brought their plunder back to the Malheur Valley. A company of volunteers caught up with them there. All the Indians were killed except three: Dick, a squaw, and a younger boy."

"They were *all* killed?"

"All but those three."

Rachel slowly shook her head at the image of such slaughter, and asked, "What happened to the woman and the other child?"

"The squaw works in a restaurant over in Centerville. It turned out that the smaller boy was a Shoshoni who'd been stolen by that band of Paiutes. John Kelly adopted the boy and named him Willie. Do you know John Kelly?" Receiving a negative shake of her head, he said, "Johnny is the finest violinist in the territory, and he's already taught Willie to play a little. He's part of John's act."

"His act? You mean he uses the boy to bring in money?" Her distaste was apparent.

Ethan looked at her with mild surprise. "He does for a fact. John's a big, kindly Irishman and he's been real good to the boy. He loves him like a son and takes him everywhere he goes."

"Like saloons?" Rachel accused.

Ethan looked a shade uncomfortable. "Well, John has a one-year lease at the Washoe Saloon."

"That doesn't sound like a proper place to bring up a child. What about Dick's adoptive family? What are they like?"

"Bill and his wife are two of the most decent people I've ever met. They have a fair-sized farm not far west of town. Bill is no more than twenty-four years old but he's a born leader, and brawny enough to defend Dick from folks who feel nothing but hate for Indians. He's rightly protective of the boy."

When they reached the creek and continued leisurely along its bank, the water providing a rippling music, Rachel reflected on the tensions between Indians and Whites smoldering throughout the West. Having only a vague knowledge about George Custer's disastrous battle at the Little Bighorn some time after the Civil War, and with an even hazier understanding of the bloodshed that followed, she wondered uneasily if any clashes had taken place near Idaho City. "Ethan, do you think the fighting will get worse?"

"Things have been getting worse ever since the first raid on the wagon trains, and there's no shortage of stories about who's to blame. I've tried to discover the truth but a good share of it seems hard to come by."

"What have you heard?"

"Many things, but they are not gentle stories, Rachel." Their feet came to rest at a stand of cottonwoods and, noting her sincere interest, he said with concern, "Dr. Hogue told me that your head might still be healing from when you fell. Maybe it would be best to leave such things for another time."

Brushing off a fallen log and sitting down, she beckoned to Ethan and he joined her. "I want to know about such things, Ethan. Please tell me."

He hesitated another moment, then began slowly, "When some of the wagon trains were hit, it was terrible, and even worse for the women and children than for the men, who were generally killed outright."

"Go on."

He looked at her closely. "Are you certain you want to hear this?"

"I do, yes."

"Well then, I've been told that the braves had their way with the women and then tortured them to death. But before that, the squaws took the emigrant children and hung them by their hair over a fire... and burned them to death in front of their mothers."

"Oh, God."

"I wish it was nothing but a false tale, Rachel, but that's just not so. In one case, an older child managed to escape after witnessing such a scene. Then too, some of the bodies were found, and ever since the burials of those poor souls a kind of hatred has spread that I fear won't be restrained any time soon."

Still meeting Ethan's eyes, Rachel tried to block out the images his words had brought to life. How could human beings be so mercilessly cruel to one another, especially to children?

"Like I said before," he went on, "I'm less than certain about who all was involved. A few who survived the attacks claimed that there were whites among the Indians. Some folks have even accused the Mormons of taking part in harassing emigrants on the trail, especially the ones passing anywhere near Salt Lake. Personally, I've always suspected that Henry Plummer's gang had a hand in hitting the northern trains."

"Who is Henry Plummer?"

Furtively studying her, as if realizing that her memory must still be recovering, he went on patiently, "He used to be the sheriff of Bannock, in the Montana Territory. Plummer was the worst sort of desperado, smart and ruthless. His gang raided and killed at will. He knew how to keep his men quiet, though. Every new man had to sign an oath of secrecy with what they called devil's ink, but it was actually blood they'd collected from their victims. The gang finally killed a German miner, and the next day the miner's friends formed the Montana Vigilantes. It's a formidable group. They hanged Plummer and twenty-three of his gang members about six months ago."

"Vigilantes hanged a sheriff?"

"If ever a man needed to be dispensed with, Plummer did. Still, his lynching caused quite a stir. Southern sympathizers claimed he was hanged because he was helping ship gold to the South, but that wasn't the chief reason. The man was just plain bad."

"Are there any vigilantes around here?"

"As a matter of fact, Bill McConnell is the leader of the vigilantes in these parts." When Rachel started to sputter, he put up a hand. "Now, now, please don't judge him to be less than he is, not by that. Bill's a good, moral man and he's as brave as they come. He's nothing like the lawman in Boise City. David Updyke is called a bandit by some, and a murdering horse thief by those who know him best. There is a general suspicion that the surviving members of the Plummer gang are working hand-in-hand with Updyke, running their stolen horses through his livery stable and sharing the loot. It's just a matter of time before Boise's sheriff gets hanged, too, and rightly so. It's plain that Bill McConnell's vigilantes have done more to discourage lawbreakers than Updyke and his deputies ever will."

"What about Sheriff Pinkham? Is he a good man?"

"He's the very best of his breed, from what I know. We're lucky to have him."

More to herself than to Ethan, Rachel mused, "So Sheriff Pinkham and our vigilantes are the real law enforcement here."

"They are."

"That's good to know, but, Ethan, will you tell me more about the Indian situation?"

"What more do you want to know?"

"Everything." When he smiled, she added, "Do you think the hostility could lead to fighting around here?"

"It's possible. The Bear Creek trouble didn't help matters."

Rachel shook her head. "I don't remember about Bear Creek."

Again his voice held gentle tolerance as he explained, "Last January a federal colonel by the name of Patrick Connor was called in to control things between the Shoshonis and the Mormon settlers near Salt

Lake. Connor might have had good intentions, but he didn't control his men."

When Rachel saw his reluctance to tell her anything further, she said, "Ethan, you can tell me. I'm tougher than I look, and I need to remember such things."

He sighed, nodded, and continued, "Connor and his troops surrounded Chief Bear Hunter's camp of around three hundred warriors and their families. It started as a battle, soldier against warrior, but after most of the braves had been killed, the federal troopers started in on the women and children. What was done to the squaws was as bad as anything ever done to white women at the hands of Indians. While some of the soldiers were abusing the women, others were taking body parts as trophies. And the children… I heard about one little girl who was shot ten times, and she was one of them who lived. Reports said four hundred Indians were killed, but there may have been many more." He paused and gave Rachel an assessing look.

She stared back at him, her eyes wide, and she nodded for him to go on.

"A few months later, some Shoshoni chiefs signed a treaty that gave most of their land to the federal government, but that didn't stop the fighting. I heard just today that more troops are being sent to the new fort outside of Boise City. They mean to protect the folks settling in that valley as well as emigrants passing through. We can only hope that with more soldiers in place, things will quiet down rather than escalate."

"You said that the Mormons might have been involved in the Indian trouble? Do you think so? Have you spent time with any Mormons?"

"Very little. One supper is all, and those folks certainly didn't seem hostile."

Her eyes brightened with new curiosity. "Were there many wives in the family?"

"I'm not sure what you'd call many." He was grinning at her now. "It seemed like too many to me."

Trying to ignore that grin, she asked with genuine interest, "What was it like?"

"To tell you the truth, it made me more than a bit nervous."

With just a touch of impatience, she said, "Ethan, please, tell me all about it."

He chuckled in surrender and began, "All right, all right. I'd gone south with a pack train to pick up some tools coming in from the East. One young fellow who was helping with the mules happened to be the cousin of a woman in the Mormon household, and when we got to town I was invited to supper." He shook his head, remembering well. "I've seldom tasted such pleasant or abundant home cooking in my life, but the feminine attention from four wives, and the sit-up-straight obedience from fifteen kids, all for just one man, well, it made me acutely uneasy. When the meal finally ended and the head of the household tried to bring me around to his way of living and praying, I thanked them all kindly but didn't linger."

Amused by the image of him extricating himself from such a predicament, she said, "I want to know so much more about your life. You said you served as a Union cavalry captain. How long were you in the army?"

He slowly lifted his gaze to the tree limbs overhead and his voice grew distant. "Three years."

A silence drew itself out until Rachel said gently, "You must have seen things that were very painful for you."

With an effort he lowered his gaze to her face, and said, "Some things were more painful than much of the killing I'd seen and done earlier. Three weeks after I took a bullet in my leg, my wife was shot. I got word that they were sending me home, and a few hours later I received the letter telling me of her death." He steadied his voice, and said with finality, "So I was released from the army to go home and care for my daughter, and when I was stronger we came out here."

Rachel watched him look up again, beyond the branches and into the deepening sky of early dusk, and she asked nothing more.

However serious his leg wound had been, it had now healed to the point that almost no limp was noticeable. But how did any man recover from the murder of his beloved wife, the mother of his child? Rachel moved very close to his side, silently offering him physical comfort. He looked down again and studied her face, possibly considering the strength of her sympathy. She returned his scrutiny with unflinching eyes, but his features slowly became unreadable.

Looking away at last, he said, "I'd best get you back to the hotel, and take Rose home before darkness catches us." Pushing himself off the log and offering his hand to help her rise, he stepped back to let her lead the way up the path.

She remained where she stood, facing him, and reached out to touch his face, but he stilled her hand with a look that was gentle but unyielding. "After you, Rachel."

19

"Miss Rachel?" a woman's voice called from a leaden distance. It drew only a muffled, monosyllabic response. "Miss Rachel, are you awake? Miss Rachel?" the voice persisted.

Neither Rachel's mind nor body was quite willing to release her from the slumber she'd been savoring, but the voice that beckoned was joined by a rapping on her door that increased in volume right along with the words, "Doc's waiting for you downstairs, and he says you're to hurry. Elizabeth Turner needs you to come right quick."

Rachel sprang upright a little too hastily and needed an instant to overcome dizziness. "I'm coming, Mrs. Kellin! Please tell him I'll be right down." Struggling to get out of bed in the darkness with a blanket twisted around her legs, she stumbled forward a few steps before freeing herself. Lighting a lamp with somewhat unsteady fingers, she then tossed off her nightgown, pulled on her dress, splashed water over her hands and face, ran her toothbrush around the inside of her mouth, and whipped her hair into submission. In four minutes she was bounding down the stairs, still fumbling with the last of her buttons. Leaping into the buggy before Dr. Hogue had a chance to help her up, she turned to him as he stood on the boardwalk, saying, "Well, let's go!"

Dr. Hogue was still chuckling at her excitement as he clicked his horse into motion toward the Turner house two miles west of town. "I'm impressed by your eagerness, Rachel, but I suppose I should warn you that we may not get there in time."

"What?" she cried.

"When Mr. Turner showed up to fetch me, he said his wife thinks the baby is coming faster than her other four did."

Rachel's dread of missing the birth was unmistakable. "Why did they wait so long to come for us?"

"Elizabeth's labor started no more than an hour ago, but sometimes there's no warning at all. Why, I've heard of a baby being delivered while the mother was still sound asleep."

"Asleep? After knowing what Esther went through, that's hard to imagine."

"Nevertheless, it's true. Now, now, we may yet arrive in time."

"Can you hurry your horse up a little?"

He coaxed the gelding to a brisker pace and they moved along the dirt road with the light from the buggy's lantern dancing into the darkness.

To Rachel's relief and great satisfaction, they did make it to the Turner home before the birth. She was able to breathe with Elizabeth during the last and most trying half-hour of labor, and to help her into a more effective position from which to push. She also comforted and praised the young mother until well after her new son had entered the world. The infant, whom his parents named William, was delightfully healthy, and his mother had endured no complications to cause exceptional concern. Dr. Hogue had been gentle and respectful throughout the course of the delivery, causing Rachel's already considerable admiration for the man to increase appreciably.

Just before they left the house, Jacob Turner stepped away from his wife's side and into the living room to join Dr. Hogue and Rachel, who held the bundled baby with a touch of possessive pride. Jacob grabbed Dr. Hogue's hand and shook it vigorously, and then took Rachel's and jerked it up and down with such enthusiasm that she was almost in danger of dropping William. "A boy!" cried Jacob. "After four girls! I would never part with any of my daughters, you understand, but to have a son! How can I thank you, Doc, and you too, Miss Milford?"

Dr. Hogue chortled as he said, "I'm afraid we can't take credit for your baby's gender, Jacob. You know my usual fee, and you can settle up next time you drop by the drugstore. Take good care of your family, now."

They headed back to town with the sunrise brightening their contented faces. "I know it's not usually this easy," Rachel said, "but when it is, it's wonderful."

"It certainly is." He glanced at her appreciatively. "Now that I've seen more of your methods and nurturing for myself, I understand fully what Esther meant when she said you have a way with mothers and babies."

Warmed by his sincerity, she said, "I've never received a finer compliment, Dr. Hogue, and I can't thank you enough for everything you're teaching me."

"You are entirely welcome, Miss Milford. I hope this is just the first of many births we encounter together, and may each of the babies prove to be as robust as little William."

By four o'clock that afternoon Rachel was feeling her lack of sleep in every part of her body, and finding it more and more difficult to keep her weariness from showing. Noting her drooping eyelids, Dr. Hogue suggested that she leave the office early for once, to which she gratefully agreed, although she gathered up a few books to take along with her. She was just leaving the drugstore when she heard a young girl's voice call, "Miss Rachel, hello!" She turned and almost bumped into Ethan, whose smile mirrored that of Rose.

"Well, hello to you," Rachel greeted them both as Ethan swept off his hat.

Before he could get out his first words, Rose exclaimed, "Pa wants to take you to the ball!"

With a fleeting look of embarrassment, Ethan's jaw tightened and he lowered his eyebrows directly at his young daughter.

Rachel managed to stifle a laugh and merely grin. "He does?" She faced Ethan and waited, making a weak attempt at assumed innocence.

Casting one more frown at Rose, who only snickered into her hand, he said, "Yes, Miss Rachel, I surely do. Will you do me the great honor of accompanying me? I promise to leave this little secret-breaker with Mrs. Hogue on that evening."

His exaggerated politeness enhanced Rachel's amusement. No one would doubt that he was a gentleman in manner or intention, but she recognized the less-than-tame side of him, a side not entirely dissimilar to one of her own.

"How kind of you to ask me, Ethan, and with so little help from your daughter," she teased. "I'm afraid..."

"Oh, Miss Rachel, you *mustn't* say no," Rose blurted, her expression suddenly crestfallen. "Pa will be dreadful unhappy."

"That's enough, young lady," Ethan said, scooping his daughter up, carrying her to the handsome gray horse tied to a nearby railing, and plopping her down in the saddle.

Rose lowered her eyes as if remorseful, but she kept peeping at them to monitor her father's progress.

When Ethan stepped back to Rachel he motioned her several strides down the boardwalk, keeping his back to Rose. "I'll just let her sit there for awhile. Knight minds her like a doting aunt." He gave a quick glance over his shoulder and noted that his horse was standing as if a crystal chandelier were balancing on his back. With an expression that offered apology as it requested forbearance, he said, "She's not quite six years old. She must have thought I needed a little help with such things."

To relieve his discomfort at having his romantic maneuverings so thoroughly thwarted, Rachel said, "I was *going* to say that I don't know much about the ball. It's on the fourth of July?"

"Yes, at Pickwick Hall," he said hopefully. "It should be quite an event."

Her soft chuckle brought him relief even before she said, "I'd love to go with you."

"*Well*, will she *go*?" hollered Rose from her perch atop Knight. Ethan nodded and Rose whooped loud and long enough to draw several curious people outside. "He's a good dancer, too, Miss Rachel! He will see to it that you have a wonderful time!"

Among those who had heard Rose's jubilance, and who now appeared at the door of the saloon just down the block, was Stan O'Brien. Rachel saw him glance their way, stand for a moment in total suspension except for the hardening of his expression, and deliberately ease out of sight.

"I wish we had more time to spend in town," Ethan was saying, "but my best mare is due to deliver any time and it's her first foal. She may need my help."

The image of Stan's face as he'd watched them still lingered, but Rachel managed to ask, "Would you like me to come?"

"I appreciate the offer, but I believe the mare will be fine, and I've dealt with such things a time or two before. Besides," he said with a glance at the books in her arms, "you'll be studying this evening."

Wanting to keep him beside her a little longer, as well as to share her experience of the night before, she said, "Ethan, I helped with the Turner baby last night, a boy. Everything went beautifully."

"That's grand, Rachel, just grand. I don't doubt that you were a great comfort to Elizabeth, and Jacob must be highly pleased."

"He certainly is."

After taking in her joy for several moments, he overpowered his strong reluctance to leave and said, "I guess I'd better head out. I wish you a fine evening, Rachel."

"Good luck with your mare. Good-bye, Rose."

"Evenin', Miss Rachel!"

As she waved good-bye to the pair, uneasiness began to creep over her, and Knight had barely disappeared from sight before Stan stepped from the saloon and walked toward her. Fleetingly, she considered ducking back into the drugstore, but silently chided herself for such cowardice and held her ground as he drew closer.

Coming very near her, he said evenly, "I gather that Stonehill has asked you to the ball." Without giving her time to respond, he reached down and took her hand, watching it intently as he gently moved his thumb across its smoothness. "I wanted to ask you, darlin', but I thought I must be tending to the saloon that night. If I'd known that man had intentions toward you, I just might have burned the saloon to the ground." He looked into her face, searching, and asked, "Did you say you would go with him?"

She started to speak but her eyes had already answered. Gently, he placed two of his fingers against her mouth, and she remained silent as he lowered them. His eyes grew darker and his breathing deeper. Although barely above a whisper, he said with clarity, "I don't know that I'll let him have you, Rachel." He turned slowly from her, and Rachel watched him stride away without glancing back.

The days that followed were busy enough to leave Rachel very little time for speculation or trepidation, but now and then Stan's words echoed hauntingly through her thoughts, raising concern for Ethan. This she tried to quell with her belief that Stan was no ruthless killer and her confidence that Ethan could defend himself, but she was thankful for each hour that passed peacefully.

The fourth evening in July found her sitting on a chair before the mirror in her hotel room, wearing a lovely satin dress of pastel green and watching Juliet arrange her hair into a work of art. She cared little about the outcome of Juliet's efforts, however, because she was far too preoccupied with the conviction that she must be completely out of her mind. Here she was, about to attend a ball with a man she was attracted to beyond all reason, a man whose life happened to have ended long before she'd been born. Even ignoring this last fact, which her mind seemed ridiculously willing to do, she was risking the possibility of Stan showing up and starting trouble. On top of that, this dear woman who refused to leave her hair alone was just one of a whole pack of family members she'd stolen for herself—yes, stolen—and Juliet and Bert would be accompanying Rachel and Ethan to the frontier ball.

Although, until earlier that day, Bert was the only Milford who'd ever met Ethan, it was quite apparent that they were all excited about her going to the dance with someone much more suitable than Stan, since they were already, none too subtly, planning her future.

Ethan. He'd come to town several times since she'd accepted his invitation, usually in the evenings, and they'd shared meals and long walks together. She felt herself drawn to him more intensely with each meeting, and the more time they spent together, the more difficult it became to suppress her mounting frustration.

She saw many signs of his attraction to her as well; in the gently searching way he looked at her, almost *into* her, and how his voice grew warmer and his movements more subtle when she was near, but if he felt any temptation to touch her, he didn't yield to it. Always kind, attentive, charming, and patient, he kept his hands and mouth exasperatingly to himself. Rachel had never desired a man physically as she did Ethan, and the strength of this unsatisfied element was unsettling to both her body and mind. It made her reflect paradoxically on the many times she'd rebuffed the advances of men who had sought her company or her body.

She hadn't held herself away from them all, however. The few lovers that had become fleeting parts of her life had been little more than casual friends, sharing the comforts of their bodies for a time while keeping their emotions detached, and soon easing away. What she truly might have meant to them, whether they'd wanted more from her than they'd felt confident to reveal, she'd seldom considered so deeply before. There had been an exception to this shielding of her heart, just one, but the pain of that parting had lessened with time. These past exceptions to her aloofness from men, by the standards of the 1860s, made her what people here would consider a harlot. Respectable, unmarried women simply didn't have lovers in their backgrounds. For Ethan, she wished she could be favorable in all ways, even in this, but it was unchangeable.

With him everything was immeasurably, sometimes annoyingly, different, often settling into a gut-deep longing. She was sure he wanted a closer tie as well, perhaps as strongly as she did, but he hadn't touched her since the day of the storm, hadn't so much as taken her hand. Though she understood that the tenets of today were genuinely distinctive from her time, she didn't believe they were dissimilar enough to explain the magnitude of Ethan's restraint, if that's what it was. If it was something else, she wanted very much to learn how to overcome it.

Yet during all of Rachel's complicated, troubled musings, she was forever chiding herself for wanting *any* kind of a relationship with a man she was deliberately deceiving about her own identity. What if he found out? What if he turned away from her? What if she hurt him terribly?

She started to shake her head but stiffened at Juliet's squeak of protest.

Lord, it had already been a long day, she thought back. Almost everyone in town had turned out to watch the Independence Day parade, with the festooned wagons filled with local dignitaries, the marching bands, and the decorated horses and riders. Everything and everyone had been brightly adorned in red, white, and blue. Watching it all had become a bit hazardous when a number of parade participants displayed their lack of sobriety by firing guns in many directions, and onlookers had to step lively to avoid stray bullets.

The noon picnic in a tree-lined clearing at the edge of town had started peacefully enough. Rachel had introduced Ethan to the family, including Aunt Faith, and he'd begun gaining their goodwill from the very first. Rose and Charlie had built the foundation of a friendship while playing tag with a pack of other small children, and it was so pleasant to laugh along with Ethan at their antics. After a hearty picnic had been spread on the ground atop a huge tablecloth, Rachel had been handing him a plate of food when every voice around them was suddenly cut short by an explosive blast that shook the air. Ethan had sprung to his feet and stood protectively near Rose and Rachel as his gaze raked the sky in the direction of the sound. The explosion had come from just outside the clearing, and it sent dirt, branches, and a two-hundred-pound anvil flying high into the air. Everyone had stared in amazement as the anvil fell to earth with a low thud forty feet from the nearest picnicker.

Folks had been counting their offspring and muttering angrily when Juliet noticed that two of her own children were missing. "Where are Kate and Phillip?" She'd looked anxiously from Bert, to Rachel, to True, whose eyes filled with suspicion.

"Come on, Pa," True had said, and raced off in the direction of the blast with Bert close behind him.

A few moments later, Kate and Phillip had been marched by their father and big brother from their hiding places behind the trees. Grandpa had met them at the edge of the clearing and silently fallen in step. Scowling with grave disappointment, Bert had ushered his two children ahead of him, into the midst of the grumbling crowd. Kate's lower lip had quivered and Phillip's face had grown paler than normal, but they'd both kept their frightened stares aimed at the ground.

"Phillip," Bert had growled, his jaw tensed.

"I'm real sorry about all this fuss," Phillip had addressed the onlookers miserably, peeking up just long enough to catch a glance at Juliet's face before lowering his head again, looking even more wretched.

"I'm sorry, too," Kate had declared hastily, lifting her face for one quick sweep of the crowd but carefully avoiding her mother's gaze. "We didn't mean for it to come flying this way. Honest we didn't." Then, as if still trying to figure out what had gone wrong with their calculations, she'd added, "We stuck rocks under one side to aim the blasted thing due west."

"Shush, Kate," Phillip had hissed with a slight jab of his elbow.

"Who else was involved in this?" Bert had demanded. "You two couldn't have moved that anvil by yourselves,"

Silence had been their only answer.

Evidently the murderous glint in Bert's eyes had been enough to convince the crowd that the two guilty parties would be summarily dealt with, because the incensed rumblings had soon diminished.

Bert had nudged Phillip in the shoulder to get him moving, and muttered to his wife as he passed, "You go on ahead and eat, Juliet. True, Grandpa, and me will be right back. These two will spend the rest of the day at Esther's place. When we get home tomorrow, we'll settle the rest of this affair." This announcement had meant that the two wrongdoers would not be allowed to attend the rest of the picnic, or the ball that would have been the first formal dance for each of them. But the part about settling up tomorrow was what had made Phillip swallow hard and Kate's lower lip start to quiver again.

After questioning the prisoners at Esther's house about where the anvil had originated, True had quietly organized a few young men to help lift it onto a low sled, hitch a team of horses, and deliver it back to the Bentley & Barton blacksmith's shop.

The joyful moods of the various Milfords had been greatly subdued by the misbehavior and punishment of Phillip and Kate. Rachel had tried to cheer Maggie, who was the most downcast of them all, but without success. Embarrassed and saddened, Juliet had said very little as the rest of them sat back down and she resumed her duties as matron and hostess. The remainder of the picnic had felt somewhat strained, although Ethan had seemed to take what had happened in easy stride.

Juliet's mood had improved greatly since she'd thoroughly scolded Kate and Phillip, following her harsh words with several hugs of reassurance that conveyed how much she loved them despite their thoughtless and dangerous behavior. As Juliet's frame of mind had continued to lift, Rachel had begun to suspect the cause to lie in the hopes she harbored concerning Ethan.

And now here Rachel was, hours later, perched in front of a mirror, her hair at last settled into a lovely display upon her head.

Juliet smiled, surveying her handiwork. "I know you've been saving every penny to buy this dress. My, you look pretty as a picture in it."

"Thank you, Mama. You look absolutely beautiful."

Juliet's dress was pale lavender with just a touch of delicate lace at the neck and cuffs, and it showed off her still appealing figure superbly. "I've had this dress for many a year, but it's held up well enough." She studied Rachel more closely, and read a great deal there. "Is something bothering you tonight, honey?" When Rachel hesitated, Juliet gently probed, "Something between you and Ethan?"

"No," Rachel said. Then, suddenly needing to confide at least some of what she'd been feeling, she blurted, "But, honestly, at times I question whether I am good for him."

"Good for him? Anyone with eyes can see that he's in love with you. Why ever would you think you might not be good for him?"

"What if I'm not what he thinks I am?"

Juliet came around to face her and lovingly held her upper arms. "Ethan will be the luckiest of men to win you, Rachel, and he knows it."

At the depth of affection in Juliet's gaze, even more than her words, Rachel felt her eyes begin to pool, and she looked down. After a calming breath or two she was able to change the subject by saying, "It's a shame Lewis had to miss all the celebrating today."

"Well, he's coming to the ball," Juliet said with satisfaction. "Your pa saw to it that he had a suit, so that took care of his last excuse. Grandpa headed back to our place over an hour ago and he'll send Lewis back with the wagon.

Gathering the nerve to reveal another source of her recent uneasiness, Rachel confessed, "Mama, I've been a little worried to tell you about something. I still can't remember how to dance."

Juliet quickly concealed her concerned surprise. "Well then, let's just go over a step or two, and maybe it will come back to you."

In the time allowed before they were to meet the men downstairs, Juliet went through the maneuverings of the various dances Rachel would likely encounter. Though they concentrated deeply at first, they were soon grinning over Rachel's smallest triumphs and laughing aloud at their mutual missteps. They left the room arm-in-arm, both in delightful anticipation.

Reviewing the dance steps in her mind as they descended the stairs to the hotel's lobby, Rachel was caught a little off guard when she heard the sound of appreciative awe rising from the small crowd gathered below. There were eight men there, but her focus was at once drawn to Ethan. Striking was the word that came to her mind as she took in his tall, formal stance. Yes, he was absolutely striking. His hair must have been barbered that afternoon because every strand was shorter now and in its proper place, and his face shone from a recent shave. The brilliantly white shirt under a fitted black coat and tie enhanced his tanned skin and powerful body splendidly. As she neared, his expression held such unguarded admiration that she was struck by the hope that he would neither constrain his emotions nor withdraw from her tonight, not tonight.

"You look like an angel," he said softly, his eyes taking her in a moment longer. Turning to stand beside her and extending his elbow, which she readily accepted, he covered her small hand with his own, and Rachel felt both happiness and relief at the warmth of his touch. Addressing Bert and Juliet but only briefly willing to take his gaze from Rachel, Ethan said, "Mr. and Mrs. Milford, you have a most enchanting daughter."

"Yes, we do," Bert agreed. Casting an appreciative glance at his wife, he added, "She's always taken after her mother."

With the other men in the lobby looking on with open envy, Ethan asked, "Shall we go?"

They reached the Pickwick Hall to find it already noisy and crowded with revelers, but Rachel didn't mind the commotion. Right now, she didn't mind anything. She spotted Aunt Faith on the other side of the room, waltzing with a thin gentleman sporting gray hair and a pointed beard. The couple moved well to the music, a waltz played with skill on brass and drums by the nine members of the smartly uniformed Paston Band. Although the music strongly enticed Rachel, she felt less than confident about trying her newly-learned dance steps, so she talked with Ethan while occasionally surveying the crowd. No one seemed to have trouble with the dances, whether they were quadrilles, reels, schottisches, waltzes, or polkas. The tunes followed one another with lively enthusiasm, and Rachel soon found it impossible to keep her feet still regardless of how minimal their training had been.

Ethan, sensing her growing eagerness, asked, "Would you like to dance now, Rachel?"

"I may need a little help."

"Forgive me if I doubt that," he said benevolently.

He led her smoothly, covering her few missteps with grace and just the right hint of humor, and before long she'd gained confidence enough to relax in his arms and smile up at him in pure enjoyment. They had shared only three tunes, however, when another man asked Rachel for a dance, which according to custom, she'd been told, she was forbidden to refuse. Accepting with hard-earned poise, she watched Ethan withdraw to the wall and join Bert and Juliet. As the evening progressed and the music played on, Rachel had no shortage of attention from other gentlemen; so much attention, in fact, that she was beginning to consider trampling the dictates of custom when Ethan broke in. After that, evidently feeling that even generosity had its limits in certain realms, he allowed other men their dances only when he could not graciously outmaneuver their approaches, and she wanted it no other way.

When the band at last took a break, and the high temperature and exertion of dancing sent Ethan in search of cool drinks, Rachel found Lewis standing at the back of the room. He looked uncomfortable and hot in his suit, but he greeted Rachel with a broad smile.

"Lewis," she said warmly, "it's so good to see you. How handsome you look tonight."

"Now, you oughtn't to flatter me like that, Miss Rachel." He looked at her keenly, saying, "I must say, you surely do look mighty happy."

"I am happy," she said, her eyes reinforcing her words. Her expression became more serious as she said, "I've wanted so badly to see you, to tell you something important." She motioned him to a quieter corner. "Remember when I told you that slavery was going to be illegal some day?"

Nodding, he gave her his complete attention.

"I went to Mr. Miller's office yesterday and did some more checking. The law that made owning a slave in the rebelling states illegal, the Emancipation Proclamation, was enacted last year, but *it* didn't cover states like Kentucky, where you came from. Even so, just a couple of weeks ago Congress voted to repeal the Fugitive Slave Act. By now, the president must have signed the bill."

"What does all that mean, Miss Rachel? Please, tell me quick what it means."

"It means that people won't be risking a thousand dollar fine and a jail sentence if they help a runaway slave, whether he came from a rebel state or not." She leaned closer and, keeping her voice low but emphasizing each word, said, "It means that a man who was once a slave in Kentucky and who has made his way to a free territory doesn't have to worry that someone will find him and *take him back*. An ex-slave can stay where he is, Lewis, and not be afraid for himself or for any of the people who gave him a home."

At first Lewis could only stare at her in painfully suspended hope. "Miss Rachel," he breathed, and started to reach for her hand but just managed to lower his arm before touching her. "Miss Rachel," he repeated. His eyes closed tightly to hold back tears, and he could say no more for several more moments. When he looked at her again, his eyes reflecting the soul-deep relief the news had created, he said, "I won't forget this night, not for one minute my whole life long. And I won't never forget it was you that brung me these good words."

"It will stay with me always, too, Lewis. And I want very much to dance with you, to celebrate." At the shocked look on his face she quickly assured him, "I know you won't, that you can't, and I understand why. But I wish so desperately that things were different now, as they will be someday."

"It takes a powerful heap of dreamin' to picture things bein' that different, but it seems like we all took a big step closer to someday, with Mr. Lincoln puttin' his pen to that paper."

"Yes, it was a huge step." They stood in silent reflection until Rachel said, "Speaking of putting pens to paper, have you been keeping up with your lessons?"

"Yes, miss, I surely have. I been workin' on my writin' just as much as my readin', and they's both comin' right along. Next time you come home, I got somethin' to show you, somethin' I wrote."

"I'm very proud of you, Lewis."

He said with a quick grin, "I'm gettin' right good at usin' that whip too,"

She laughed softly as she said, "I'll bet you are. If I don't make it home for awhile, please bring what you wrote the next time you come to town."

"I'll do just that. Now, I see Mr. Ethan lookin' for you in this crowd, so you'd best go on over to him. I thank you greatly for your news, Miss Rachel, and I thank our dear Lord that your family will be safe from here on out."

Before Lewis could drift away Ethan joined them, and Rachel introduced the two. Ethan shook Lewis' hand in sincere welcome, no differently than he'd done with members of the Milford family, a gesture that here and now showed rare acceptance and respect. Rachel knew that Ethan had fought for the Union, but he'd been born in Virginia where many people still supported slavery. Watching him, Rachel felt a pride in his character that she knew she had no right to claim. All the same, she didn't try to deny it.

The two men exchanged a few words, but shortly Lewis claimed that he had some special news to share with a few friends, and he left them. Rachel and Ethan again joined the throng on the dance floor, where their joyful faces brought smiles to many who watched them, especially the Milfords. After only a few dances, however, the heat and the closeness of the hall caused them to escape outside in search of a breeze.

The stars and a three-quarter moon shed enough light for them to see fairly well as their feet took their customary direction northward. There were groups and couples wandering the boardwalks and standing at the edge of the street, and Ethan steered Rachel through and beyond them until the sound of voices grew less and then silent. They finally stopped at a small clearing they knew well, where Rachel breathed in deeply, relishing the soft wind upon her face, neck, and arms.

"Rachel," said Ethan, capturing her full attention by the seriousness in his voice, "I hope you are enjoying this evening, as you seem to be."

"I am, thoroughly. But, is something wrong?"

"Not anything that can't wait," he said, trying to lighten his tone. "This should be a night of celebrating."

"For a while now I've felt that there is something you're holding back. I'd very much like to know what it is."

He stepped near and said with uncertainty, "It's just that... I've told you a little about myself, but there are other things that you should know."

Rachel felt the irony of his words sharply. "Things *I* should know?"

"Yes. You see, my first wife, Colette, wasn't happy, not with me or our marriage."

Rachel sensed how painful it had been for him to utter those words, so she said, "You don't have to tell me about your marriage, or anything else."

"But I do." In a voice determined to tell it all, he went on, "My wife was very delicate, and when she realized she was pregnant, she became extremely afraid of the delivery. As her pregnancy advanced she grew to resent me for her condition. The birth was difficult, perhaps as bad as she'd feared it would be and, afterward, she didn't allow me to come to her. She said she would never let it happen again. Things grew tense between us, and then the war broke out. When I joined the Northern army, she went to stay with her family. She never answered my letters, and eventually I stopped writing them. Shortly after I was wounded, while I was still in the hospital, a small band of deserters found and ransacked her father's plantation. Rose, praise God, was saved by a maid who had hidden with her in the woods, but those men killed Colette and her parents." He took a moment, staring at nothing, and then went on. "I tried to find the killers, but couldn't ever learn which side they'd deserted from."

"Ethan—."

"I need to tell you the rest, Rachel," he said, but looked away from her. "I've been with other women since the start of the war, three of them." After the words had been released, he met her gaze.

His shame was so exposed, his conscience so obviously expecting her condemnation, and here she stood with so many and such unexplainable secrets that this honorable man could never imagine or accept. "Ethan...you didn't need to tell me this. Your past is none of my business."

His gaze grew penetrating. "I'd hoped you'd begun to consider it your business."

"I mean it's not important."

Surprised, he asked sharply, "Not important that I've been with women I wasn't married to, wasn't even in love with?"

"It's not so crucial that I would condemn you for it, or change how I feel." At his evident doubt, and despite a lifetime of disguised restraint, she blurted out, "If I'd been with someone else, would you condemn me?"

He was so shocked by this that he took a step back. An instant later he took three steps toward her, and asked, "Is that true?"

On his face was pain so acute that Rachel's own confused emotions were cut deeply. She could barely speak, sensing, fearing all that she might have just lost or might still lose, but she couldn't lie to him now. "Yes."

"When?" he asked, his voice little more than a whisper.

She turned away and took several paces before he caught her arm and spun her back to him. She tried to keep her tears imprisoned but a few escaped to wet her cheeks. "It really doesn't matter when, does it?" she managed to ask. "It only matters that I'm not what you want me to be."

"No, Rachel, *you* matter."

"Not like I did a minute ago."

"I was surprised, because I never imagined that, that—"

A numbing calm, a familiar sensation of inescapable isolation took hold of her, and she suddenly stopped crying. "It's all right, Ethan," she said, her voice hollow now. "It was foolish to try to forget who I am. I wanted to forget because of you, and all I've done is hurt you, and myself. Perhaps I shouldn't have told you, but I'm so tired of pretending."

"Are you pretending right now, Rachel, pretending that you don't care about me, about us?"

She closed her eyes, knowing that they would betray her, but when he touched her face, she opened them again and he saw her answer.

She tried to draw away but he brought one of her hands to his cheek.

"Ethan, wait, I can't let you think that I've revealed everything. I have to tell you that... it wasn't just one. There have been several men."

"You needn't say anything more."

She didn't mean to tell him the rest, didn't intend for the words to tumble out, words that had been tightly locked away for so many years. It was the horrible secret only she, her Grandpa Simon, and one other man had even known, the forbidden truth that had haunted her life, and that she'd meant to take to her grave. But the words formed and broke free just the same, gut-wrenching and unstoppable once they'd begun to flow.

"The first—the very first——...It was so long ago. I've never told anyone about him, about what happened that day. I knew I had to keep it a secret, always, or terrible things might happen to someone I loved." She closed her eyes, trying to gather her strength, but she could feel herself start to tremble. "I was twelve years old when a man, a man who worked for my grandfather... smiled at me and said he wanted to show me some flowers. He led me to the boxwood bushes near the house, always smiling, but there weren't any flowers. I didn't understand, and was growing afraid of the way he was looking at me. I tried to back away but he grabbed me. He put his hand over my mouth and threw me down by the bushes." Tears welled again, but she held them back with the rushing current of her words. "I fought him but he was so much stronger, and when I tried to scream he hit me in the stomach. I couldn't breathe. He tore at my clothes, and I kept trying to push him away with my hands and my knees, I tried to scratch his face, but he hit me again. I almost blacked out, but I didn't. I didn't. I tried so hard but I couldn't stop him. He hurt me badly, and kept hurting me." As she remembered it all with brutal clarity, she tried to stifle the soft moaning sounds coming from deep within, but they escaped between her words. "He kept... hurting me... inside."

She was only dimly aware that Ethan's arms had come around her, but his voice, breathed in an agonized whisper, reached her. "Rachel, Rachel, stop now."

But she couldn't stop, neither the reliving nor the telling. "When he got off of me, I rolled away and lay very, very still. I prayed that I would die right there so I would never have to move again. I heard him laugh, and then I heard my grandfather's whip crack. I looked up and saw the man try to run, but Grandpa's whip caught him around the neck and jerked him backward, pulling him off his feet. Grandpa jumped on his back and held the whip around his throat. The man kicked and bucked, but Grandpa pulled so tight that his fingers went white. Finally, finally, the man was still, and Grandpa let the whip drop to the ground. It was over. But everything had changed." She was shaking irrepressibly now, her teeth chattering slightly, and Ethan held her tighter. Fearing that her knees would weaken, he quickly spread his coat on the ground, lowered her, and tucked her against his shoulder.

Her weeping broke loose at last, each sobbing breath linking the words that followed. "My grandfather, he was crying so hard when he came and picked me up. I'd never seen him cry. As he carried me to the house I looked back at the man on the ground. I hoped he was dead, and he was. My grandfather had made sure."

Although her words ceased at last, she continued to cry without moderation, her tears doing as much to cleanse away the shame, bitterness, and regret as fresh water to a dirty wound. All the while Ethan held her close and rocked her as he smoothed her hair, his own anguish carefully hidden.

When at last she began to calm a bit she turned swollen eyes to Ethan, accepted his handkerchief, and blew her nose. Breathing more evenly and feeling slightly less shaky, she said, "That night while I was sleeping, my grandfather hid the body somewhere. But I grew terrified that someone would find out where it was and my grandfather would be arrested. Because of my fears, I convinced him that we must tell no one. He'd lived alone since my grandmother's death, and I begged him to let me stay with him. I pleaded and cried until he finally told my parents he'd like to keep me there for another couple of weeks. He was so patient and kind. He had a doctor come check on me and give me some medicine, and then he accepted my many long periods of silence, asking no unwanted questions." The image of her beloved Grandpa Simon rose in her mind with acute clarity, strengthening her further. "Neither of us ever told anyone what happened, not a soul, not until today."

Softly, hoarsely, Ethan said, "And you've had to battle this hell, this memory, alone for all these years." He waited until she looked at him, and vowed, "I swear to you, Rachel, if anyone ever tries to harm you again, *I'll* kill him."

They held each other close until her breathing became steady. When she was able, she said, "I never meant to tell you this."

"It's better that you did." With the night growing late, Ethan asked her, "Do you feel up to getting back?"

"Yes," she responded, but she felt as if her body had suddenly doubled in weight, and it took an effort to try to stand. Ethan helped lift her to her feet and brushed dirt and pine needles from the hem of her dress. Her headache was pounding, and she knew her eyes must be red and swollen from weeping. "I must look awful," she said. A feeling of uncertainty and vulnerability threatened to surface as she considered how she'd just exposed her frightful confidence, exposed it to Ethan of all people.

But his expression and voice held only tenderness. "You look wonderful."

For a moment she was afraid she'd start crying all over again, but she managed to hold onto to her composure, and diverted her emotions by saying, "I suppose by now we've caused some sort of scandal, walking off like this for so long."

"I suppose so," he said without the least sign of concern. "Do you mind?"

Rachel caught the hint of a jest in his voice and it lightened her heart considerably. "Not for myself, but I don't want to cause a problem for the family."

"Let's walk for just a bit first," he coaxed. "I think your family presumes I'll keep a good watch over you. Perhaps I shouldn't confess this, but your mother and I already have a sort of understanding."

Rachel stopped and tried to read his face. "Ethan, after what I've told you, I would accept it if you want to change that understanding."

He considered for a moment, eyeing her just as thoroughly. "Do you want me to change it, or do you think you could find happiness with me?"

"Are you asking whether I can find physical happiness with any man? Oh, Ethan. If you're wondering if I will find pleasure in your arms, in your bed, my answer is yes. You needn't worry about that."

He hadn't realized he'd been holding his breath but he released it with relief. "Then I must tell you that I have never met a finer woman than the one standing before me now, despite what you've told me tonight, or anything else you might tell me about your past." His expression evolved from deep sincerity to shielded longing, which he tamped down by saying, "Maybe we'd better head back."

The night breeze stirred the scent of pines, and as Rachel drew it into her lungs she felt as though the fragrance was healing her battered emotions a little. She and Ethan circled the clearing and made their way back toward Pickwick Hall. Before they came within view of the circulating partiers they made one more sweep of Rachel's dress and Ethan's suit for any remaining telltale dirt, grass, or twigs. Rachel tried to tighten a few hairpins but had little success. When they judged themselves to be as presentable as possible they stepped forward, mingling steadily with people near the hall.

Rachel walked ahead of Ethan as she stepped onto the porch and, looking up, she met Stan O'Brien's steady stare. He was standing against the building with a cigarette in his mouth, which he removed slowly as he studied her. His gaze moved down her dress and back up to her face before lingering on her loosened hair. He shifted his eyes to Ethan, who stood tensely alert beside her. She made a move to pass Stan but he stepped in front of her, saying tightly, "Good evening, Rachel."

"Good evening," she said, then sidled around him.

Ethan, his mouth tightened and his eyes narrowed, paused before Stan. No words were needed as their gazes dueled, and neither man moved. "Ethan," Rachel said at the door, her eyes beseeching. Abruptly, he stepped around Stan and escorted her into the room.

20

Returning to the doctor's office the day after the ball was a relief to Rachel, since it prevented her from thinking so much about other things, about other people, about Ethan. She'd done little but that throughout the previous night, and now she was working diligently to stay alert enough to avoid making mistakes. It seemed that she was destined to spend a great deal of her new life feeling worn out, but then, she reflected, she was probably no different in that respect from any other pioneer. Filling a trio of brown medicine bottles she'd lifted from the bottom bookshelf, she paused and quickly held a hand to her mouth to muffle a yawn, and her mind drifted back again.

She and Ethan had danced to only two more tunes after encountering Stan at the hall, their preoccupied thoughts becoming more and more difficult to conceal. Progressively taking their leave of the Milfords and several acquaintances, they had made their way back to the Montana House, where Ethan had wished her goodnight surrounded by revelers in the lobby and waited at the bottom of the stairs until she'd had time to reach her room.

As she'd leaned against her locked door, she'd felt that she could sleep for a week, but no rest would come. Since her haunting childhood memories had been stirred up anew, she couldn't keep that dreadful day from rising in her mind, and she'd repeatedly asked herself *why* she'd told Ethan about what had happened. Even knowing what she felt for him, which she'd finally stopped trying to deny, how could she have let that overpower her awareness that such a revelation could only complicate the fact that she didn't belong here? She didn't even know how she'd ended up here, or when she might leave.

Yet she simply couldn't regret the telling, at least not fully. It gave her too much comfort and relief to have shared it with him, but the guilt of doing so, with its implication that he now knew the worst of her secrets, wouldn't let up. She also feared that after Ethan had had time to consider all that he now knew, he couldn't accept her. Even if he could, what if she revealed who she really was? What could he possibly think but that she was deranged? And then she'd certainly lose him.

So she'd remained awake, her head pounding and her thoughts tormenting until nearly dawn. Then she'd pulled on her clothes, cleaned up a little, and trudged to the back of the drugstore.

She'd found the scrawled note Doc Hogue had left for her the evening before, instructing her to clean the office and treatment room and check the supply cabinets this morning. That much she'd been able to handle. Thankfully, no patients had shown up requiring surgical attention. Though it was nearly noon, the good doctor had not yet arrived, evidently having fallen victim to overzealous celebrating the night before.

Now finished with the medicine bottles, Rachel was standing on a chair and cleaning the top panes of the window in the treatment room when Dr. Hogue entered almost on tiptoe and offered her a soft "Good morning." Following a little more noisily, Lewis and Maggie came through the door wearing warm smiles of greeting. As Rachel climbed down, Maggie threw her arms around her waist.

"Well, this is a nice surprise," Rachel said, bending to return the hug.

Dr. Hogue offered them what looked more like a grimace than a smile, and then sorted through the contents of the cabinet nearest his desk while massaging his forehead.

With the doctor making no attempt at conversation, Lewis said, "Miss Rachel, we jus' come to say good-bye before headin' on back to the farm. We all hope you had a good time at the ball."

Rachel could see by his expression that he hadn't missed her red eyes when she and Ethan had reentered the hall. "I did, Lewis, truly."

Maggie asked breathlessly, "So are you going to marry Mr. Ethan? Mama and Pa are wanting you to."

As Dr. Hogue quickly stifled a hoot, Rachel said, "Maggie, I don't know him very well yet." After the words had been uttered, Rachel realized that they weren't true at all. She knew Ethan as well as she'd ever known anyone, and now he knew about her most appalling ghost, even if he didn't know about the rest of her life in Chicago.

"Miss Maggie, we mustn't keep your sister from her work. We best get on back now," Lewis said.

"But aren't you going to tell her?" Maggie asked him.

"Now, Miss Maggie, we said..." he started.

Maggie asked innocently, "You didn't mean not to tell *Rachel*, did you?"

Growing more suspicious by the second, Rachel said, "Let's step outside, you two," and ushered her visitors onto the boardwalk, around the corner, and into an alley. "Now," she said, "just what weren't you going to tell me, Lewis?"

But it was Maggie who stated proudly, "He wrote a letter all by himself, only I helped a little, and I took it to the post office, and it's going to President Lincoln!"

Rachel was staring at Lewis when she asked, "Oh, he did?"

Maggie nodded and beamed up at him.

Looking guilty as charged but not overly ashamed, Lewis said, "I had to do it, Miss Rachel."

"Maggie," said Rachel evenly, "if you go back inside and sweep the floor, I think Dr. Hogue might give you a peppermint stick."

With a little hop of excitement, Maggie disappeared in the direction of the drugstore.

She'd barely gone before Lewis said hastily, "Miss Rachel, you don't need to fret none. I never used my real name."

"But you had Maggie take it in?"

He looked uncomfortable at this. "The post man would never have took it from me. She just tol' him a man give it to her."

"Oh, Lewis." She studied the unuttered request for understanding on his face. "Do you think anything good will come of it?"

"If there's a chance to save that fine man, even a small chance, I had to try. Don't you see?"

"Yes, Lewis; yes, I do see." She managed a smile, but then shook her head in wonder. "How could you have believed what I told you so completely? Didn't you doubt my dream even a little?"

"Not any more than a trace, 'cause I seen too many things come true from my very own dreams. I believe God sends us messages sometimes, and it didn't seem right to let this one slip by without takin' notice."

"Maybe you were right to send the letter. Anyway, it's done now. Chances are probably slim that it will reach Mr. Lincoln, and even slimmer that we will find out if it does, but we can hope it results in only good. And I admire your determination to try to help him."

Maggie reappeared eating her peppermint stick, and the three of them walked back to the drugstore. As Lewis opened the door for Rachel, Ethan walked out and said warmly, "Good morning to all of you."

"Good morning," said Rachel.

Maggie exclaimed happily, "Now you can get to know him better, Rachel!"

At Ethan's quizzical look and Rachel's red cheeks, Lewis said, "We truly best be off, Miss Maggie. Good day now."

"Take care, you two," Rachel said as Lewis hurried Maggie down the street.

As Ethan stood two feet in front of her, his face revealing that he was nearly as weary as she was, he was nevertheless cleanly dressed, newly shaved, and unforgivably handsome. A small groan acknowledging the inescapability of her capitulation cleared Rachel's throat before she cut it off.

He gave her a slow smile. "That didn't sound like much of a welcome. Care for some dinner? A neighbor is looking after Rose at home, and I just spoke with Dr. Hogue, who said he could do without you for an hour or two."

"I know it's awfully warm today, but I'd much rather walk for awhile, if you don't mind."

"Not in the least."

Their feet led them slowly up East Hill, past the new water tower, and onto a forest path until they finally stopped in the shade of a few conifers. He faced her beneath a huge fir, each leaning a shoulder against it, and took one of her hands. After the previous night, words didn't seem as essential as they had then, and for a few moments they were both content just to look at each other. Ethan, lifting his free hand, softly swept a strand of hair from her forehead, then let his fingers trace the softness of her cheek.

Her gaze searched his, trying to find answers.

"I'm glad you wanted to walk today," he said, "because I can talk to you here. Last night, I believe we learned what we needed to know about one another, and I hope you feel the same." He hesitated, and then the emotion behind his gaze deepened. "I want you in my life, Rachel, no matter what comes, so I am asking if you will become my wife."

She stared at him as she eased her hand free. "You *what*?"

Unperturbed, grinning a little at her stunned reaction, Ethan caught her hand again, went down on one knee, and asked, "Miss Rachel Milford, will you do me the very great honor of marrying me?"

She was still too shaken to do anything but sputter.

"Please," he added, his grin only broadening.

"I... I... you." There were so many objections that her mind worked like a roulette wheel trying to come to rest on one of them. When it finally settled on a single concern, she voiced it. "But, what about Rose?"

"She says I've already taken too long to ask you. "

"*Too long*? We've only known each other a *few weeks*... " The next words escaped before she could stop them. "You haven't so much as kissed me and you're asking me to *marry* you?"

"Well if that's what's troubling you..." His arms came around her and his mouth lowered, but when his lips were three inches from hers he paused, his eyes questioning just long enough to be sure of her response, and Rachel's expression removed all doubt. When his lips touched her mouth, warm and full, she reveled in the feel of them. Her arms wrapped around him and she pressed her body closer. The kiss deepened, explored, enticed, until her body threatened to insist on a continuance beyond the boundaries of what Ethan might deem decent.

With an effort he lifted his head slightly. "Lord, Rachel, I've dreamed day and night of kissing you, ever since that storm caught us. But my dreams didn't do justice."

She wanted him to kiss her again and to go on kissing her. She wanted to lie down amid the sparse grass and pinecones and forget everything but making love to him. But she could see that he was forcing himself to step away, and that he expected her to say something. So she tried to quiet her breathing.

He took the moment to calm his own body, and asked, "Now will you give me an answer?"

"Ethan," she said with difficulty, "I should tell you so many things, things that might change your mind."

In a grave voice he said, "The rest doesn't matter, not if we don't let it. I've come to realize that people have a choice in this world, to hold onto what keeps them from happiness or to open up room in their hearts to start again. I hope that after last night, after telling me about what has tormented you for so long, you are able to let it go. During the war, I was a part of things that have shamed and plagued me, but I'll not let them rule me, not anymore. We can make a good life together, I'm sure of that, and I want you exactly, *exactly* as you are."

Her throat had tightened at the magnificence of his words. When she spoke, she voiced more a plea than a question. "Can that really be true? Can we make it true?"

Taking both of her hands and bringing them to his chest, he drew close again. "We can and we will, if we are true to each other, and with God's help." He kissed her again, ever so gently this time. "Will you become my wife, Rachel?"

"But, we've only known each other—"

"Long enough."

"...And my work?"

"Rose and I can look after the ranch well enough if you want to keep working with Dr. Hogue."

"You're sure?"

"As sure as the sky holds a sun and a moon."

"Then, yes, Ethan," she whispered, "heaven help us both, but I will."

When he pulled her nearer still and kissed her joyfully, she clung to him, letting his lips convert every reasonable objection into a prayer that all he'd said would be so.

Before she was ready, he loosened his embrace enough to gaze at her with a touch of humor, and ask, "Does this mean as long as I kiss you first I'll always get my way?"

Smiling back at him, drinking him in, she said, "Maybe so. It's hard to resist a man with such persuasive talents."

"I might even have another talent or two."

"I wouldn't be a bit surprised." She stepped back, the smile refusing to leave her face, smoothed the front of her skirt, and said, "If I'm going to be your wife before long, I guess you'd better show me that ranch of yours."

"That ranch of ours," he corrected.

Only vaguely aware of the rest of the world, they talked of small things as they made their way to the Montana House for dinner, with Rachel's arm tucked inside Ethan's and their happiness impossible to mask. When Ethan said he intended to ask Bert for permission to marry his daughter, Rachel laughed out loud. "Permission? He'll be more than pleased, believe me. He thinks very highly of you, and he'll be relieved that I won't end up a spinster."

During their meal, they agreed that there was no need for a long engagement, and that they would be wed in the early fall. This would give Ethan the time he wanted to spruce up the ranch for her. He supported, even encouraged her continuing her medical studies and working even after they were married. "It will be so beneficial for the women in this area and," he'd added with a touch of mischief, "with the way you kiss, that sort of knowledge might come in quite handy around our house soon." At this prospect, Rachel found herself envisioning a baby of her own, a baby as sweet as Conrad who would grow up to be like Ethan, and she warmly shared these thoughts with him.

After they finished their meal, they walked to Doc Hogue's office and, after telling him of their engagement, received his enthusiastic best wishes and permission for Rachel to take the rest of the day off. They then decided to hire a livery horse for Rachel and ride to the ranch to tell Rose about their news. There were still hours of daylight remaining when they left the stables, and Rachel's excitement to see Ethan's ranch continued to build steadily along the few miles they rode southwest of town.

The time passed quickly with their contented frames of mind and soon Ethan slowed Knight and turned off the main road. Less than a quarter-mile up this new lane Ethan halted his horse, pointed ahead and said, "There it is."

"Oh, Ethan," Rachel said, her voice and expression declaring her appreciation for the homestead and its setting.

He watched her reaction with a mixture of relief and satisfaction. "I've been wanting to show you the place for some time."

They gently kneed their horses into motion and approached the farm slowly. Twelve huge Ponderosas had been spared from clearing, to stand as majestic sentinels along the front boundary of the farm, leaving a gap on both sides of the road wide enough to make the approach welcoming. Reaching this break in the trees, Ethan dismounted and opened a gate beneath the span of a twelve-foot-high crossbeam that bore in its center a large carved oval of a running horse that, with its proud head, arched neck, and high tail carriage, must have been modeled by Knight. Seeing how anxious Ethan was to reach the house, Rachel forced herself not to linger beneath the striking carving, and rode forward.

Several horses grazed in a pasture that ran from the barn to the lower slope of a hill beyond, and one of the mares, upon seeing Knight, raised a cry of recognition. On a portion of ground between the house and the barn, set back and to the left, lay a vegetable garden protected from foraging game by a seven-foot, split-rail fence.

As they drew up to the house, Rachel was received by a blanket of yellow and deep blue wild flowers that spread in a wide arc encircling the porch and bordering both sides of the path that led up to the steps. Unlike the Milford home, Ethan's house had been built from framed wood rather than logs, and it rose only one story high. Three large windows were spaced across the façade, and between two of these rested a carved front door presenting another image of Knight, now standing proudly on a tree-lined knoll.

Ethan was carefully watching her study of the front door.

"Did *you* carve the door, Ethan, and the sign over the gate?"

"Yes, ma'am. My uncle taught me to carve when I was a boy."

"They're remarkable, and so life-like! I'd heard you could make the best furniture anywhere, but no one told me you were an artist. Folks would love your carvings."

"Not many people have seen my place, and I haven't taken any carvings to town yet."

"So, you've decided to show me more than one hidden talent today?"

He laughed affectionately at this reference to his kisses, and after they'd dismounted and led their horses to the barn, Rachel insisted on helping to remove their tack and bring feed and water to their stalls. Walking back toward the house, Ethan paused and pointed out the boundaries of his land. The acreage wound between two timbered hills, with a stream at the base of the eastern slope and craggy mountains climbing skyward behind. An aspen grove threw shimmering shadows across a wide meadow at the farthest corner of his land.

"It's beyond beautiful here," she breathed. "It's magnificent." She turned and found him taking in the scene before them with an unreadable expression, his mind far away.

He must have felt her gaze because he observed quietly, "There's something powerfully healing about this place." The words and the manner in which they'd been voiced reminded Rachel of the mental and physical wounds he'd suffered, and the grief. With his eyes slowly scanning the treed slopes, he went on, "I think the mountains teach us to look up, far away from ourselves, and while we're in them it becomes easier to mend our spirits. They'll be here long after we've gone, and they remind us to take whatever joy is offered while we can." He pulled the sweet scent of pine into his lungs, let it out slowly, and at last he looked at her. "When I first came here I thought it was the prettiest spot I'd ever seen, but it's never looked half as lovely as it does today."

He reached out to draw her into his arms and hold her close. With their eyes raised, they drank in the mountains together.

Minutes later a small girl's voice called out, "Papa, Miss Rachel, we've been making soup!"

Before they'd made it back to the house, Rose leaped off the porch and came racing in their direction while a huge dog of questionable heritage bounded to Ethan well ahead of her. "Stay down, Scruff," Ethan commanded, and the dog pranced along beside him while casting curious glances at Rachel. "This mutt wouldn't win any prize for his looks, but if anyone ever threatened me or Rose, he'd have them by the throat. He'll be a good protector for you, too, Rachel."

When Rose reached them she cried, "Miss Rachel, Miss Rachel! Are you...?"

She halted both her words and her feet, and looked anxiously at her father.

He nodded, the grin on his face an additional confirmation.

"Then you finally asked her, Papa!" She glanced at Rachel. "Are you really going to marry him?"

Rachel nodded and, crouching to Rose's level as the child bounded toward her, caught her up into a hug. "Yes, I think I just might, if it's all right with you."

"Oh, hooray!" Rose squealed, raced to her father, and threw herself into his arms.

"That's exactly what I said," Ethan chuckled heartily. At the appearance of a lanky woman of perhaps sixty years on the porch, Ethan waved to her and said, "We'd better allow Mrs. Jameson to get back home, Rose, but first let's introduce Rachel to her."

Harriet Jameson greeted them all with, "Well, I can see from your faces that something pleasant has been going on here. You must be Miss Milford."

"She is indeed, but not for long," Ethan confided.

"Is that so? That's the best news I've heard in a month, although I'll miss coming over regular to visit with little Rose." To Rachel, she explained, "Willis and me, we never were blessed with children of our own, but I enjoy their company wherever I can, and I'm particularly fond of this little girl."

"You and Willis are always more than welcome here," Ethan said.

"Of course you are," Rachel said, "and please call me Rachel."

As Ethan saddled Harriet's horse, Rachel chatted companionably with this cheerful neighbor, listening to how she and her husband had started their farm only a few months before Ethan and Rose arrived, and soon Harriet was offering to share some treasured family recipes. When Ethan led her little mare up to the porch, Harriet was saying, "It'll be nice having a woman so close, only a mile up the road;

it surely will." She mounted, and smiled as she said, "Ethan, she'll do just fine. You have my best wishes, all of you."

As she trotted off, Rose asked, "*When* are you going to get married, Papa?"

"Let's head inside and we'll talk it over," said Ethan.

They spoke of this and many other details as Rachel entered the house and was shown around by the two Stonehills. The house was surprisingly tidy, although Juliet's version of a thorough scrubbing wouldn't have hurt it. Each room held pieces of furniture that were comfortable as well as pleasing to the eye, and Ethan had added much to the appeal of the dwelling by the meticulous inclusion of his carvings here and there. The mantle above the fireplace bore a scene of the mountains that backed Ethan's meadow, the one they'd just been admiring, and the likeness was remarkable. In the kitchen, upon each handle of the cupboard doors, the profile of a different wild animal had been engraved. A menagerie of wild turkeys, deer, moose, and elk encircled the outer rim of a large wooden bowl resting atop the polished table. Rachel had only moments to appreciate this room before Rose eagerly towed her to the next, her own.

The room was enchanting, and Rose was rightly proud of it as she pointed out that each handle of her dresser drawers had been shaped into a rose. A handmade quilt of varied green and pink fabric lay spread over the log bed, and Ethan had carved leafy vines that circled to the top of each of its four bedposts, generously gracing every vine with rose buds. Curtains across the window would be helpful to provide Rose some privacy, Rachel silently observed, but her gaze was drawn back to Ethan's bedposts.

"You made the bed?" Rachel asked. Ethan nodded, and she studied the bed more closely. "I don't see any nails."

"No, I shaped the length ends to fit into the proper holes."

"Isn't it a pretty bed?" asked Rose.

"It certainly is, and it's perfect for you."

"Rachel," said Ethan, "I'd like you to do whatever you want to make this your home, too."

Her home, she thought, only half believing, hers, and Ethan's, and Rose's.

The last part of the house to be explored was Ethan's bedroom, soon to be her own, as well. It was larger than Rose's room, and although the six-drawer dresser was much like the one he'd made for his daughter, the drawer handles had been whittled into the shape of pine cones. The large bed was covered with a blanket of deerskins sewn to form a sunburst pattern, and at the tops of his bedposts, each facing outward, the heads of eagles had been masterfully carved.

While Rachel ran her fingers over one of the eagles, admiring its intricacy, she caught a glimpse of Ethan's face and had to work to keep from smiling. From the effort he was making to avoid looking uncomfortable, it was evident to Rachel that he hadn't had many women in this room before. This thought was so reassuring that she chose to relieve Ethan's uneasiness by a touch of mischief, saying over Rose's head, "What an attractive bed. It looks so inviting."

His face reddened slightly before he realized she was teasing him. With a quick glance at Rose's beaming face, he countered, "Why, thank you. Would you like to lie down and see just how comfortable it is?"

With a sweet smile, she answered, "I'd love to try it out, thoroughly. Do you think we have time?"

Ethan blinked twice while Rachel appeared angelically calm, then he uttered, "Um, it's getting late and I'd better get you back before dark. Rose, honey, you'd best ride along with us."

"You and Ethan! Engaged!" cried Esther, hugging Rachel with Conrad squeezed between them. "How wonderful! I felt in my bones there was something special about that man, and you said yes to him, Rachel, you said yes. Oh, the two of you will make a fine couple, and little Rose is such a sweet child. Sit right down and tell me all about your plans."

"I'll tell you everything," Rachel laughed at Esther's joyful exuberance, "but first I need you to agree to tell only Richard, and to swear him to secrecy, until Ethan talks to Pa and I tell the rest of the family on Sunday after church?"

"Of course I agree," Esther said, still bubbling. "Now, you hold this baby boy of mine while I pour us some coffee, and tell me everything."

Rachel happily complied.

When Sunday arrived, Ethan and Rose accompanied Rachel, her family, and Aunt Faith to church, turning more than a few heads and disappointing a couple of the male members of the congregation. After the service Rachel, Ethan, and Rose drove towards the Milford farm with Esther's young family tucked in the back of the wagon. As the team drew to a stop in front of the house, Rachel was surprised to realize that she was getting nervous. She found herself wondering if she'd been wrong about Juliet and Bert being so fond of Ethan. They might object to how short Ethan's courtship had been, or may feel it would be unwise for her to marry a widower with a child. As Ethan helped her down from the wagon, and True and Bert appeared on the porch wearing smiles, however, she tried to tell herself that these speculations were nothing but foolishness. She climbed the porch steps hoping Rose would manage to withhold their secret just a little longer, and couldn't help noticing Esther's covert grin as she handed Conrad to her. The rest of the Milfords, Aunt Faith, and Lewis greeted the new arrivals wholeheartedly as they entered.

While the women busied themselves with the final meal preparations, four loaves of bread and a huge cake having been baked earlier, Kate took the young children to the creek to skip stones. Bert, Grandpa, True, and Phillip suggested Ethan come along for a short walk in the shade of the trees. Soon Rachel, spying from a window, spotted Ethan and Bert breaking away from the others to wander farther along the well-worn path alone, and she felt uncertainty rise again.

The men reappeared at the edge of the farm, but Bert and Ethan held back, beyond where their expressions could be read by Rachel as she helped carry wooden planks out to the shade and place them atop barrels to form two long tables. Several blankets were arranged nearby for some of the children just as Juliet announced that dinner was ready, and everyone was called to wash up.

When Bert and Ethan rejoined them, it would have been difficult to say which of their grins was broader. Rachel, allowing herself a quiet sigh of relief, had no need to ask how their talk had gone. Everyone took their places to offer a prayer of thanks, and it seemed to Rachel that Bert led the prayer with even more sincerity than usual. After the "Amen," everyone began chatting cheerfully as they admired the feast before them.

The food was more than plentiful and it all smelled delicious. On each table rested a beef roast large enough for twice as many as those present, red beans and bacon, the first of Juliet's cucumbers and peas, a round of yellow cheese, a bowl of tiny wild strawberries that must have taken the children days to pick, fresh bread and butter, and an enormous burnt sugar cake, a few gouges excavated from one side by small fingers and a large slice missing. Holding to their established methods of battle, Juliet had urged Lewis to join them for dinner, but he'd politely refused. So she'd dished up his plate first and delivered it to him in the barn before she'd taken her seat at the table.

Everyone began eating heartily, or so Rachel thought, until she noticed that Grandpa had hardly touched the food on his meagerly-filled plate. She looked up at his face and could see that he wasn't feeling well. He sensed her eyes on him and met her gaze, gave her a smile meant to reassure, and took a big bite of bread. Unwilling to risk embarrassing him by asking questions in front of everyone, she smiled back, but intended to check on him after dinner.

As the last bite of cake was disappearing from True's plate, Esther cleared her throat rather longer than was common. Ethan caught the signal and gave Rachel a slight but encouraging nod. She hesitated only until Juliet stood up and reached for Bert's empty plate. "Mama," she said, "can we wait a minute before we clear the table? I'd like to tell you all something."

Rachel's tone caused Juliet to lower Bert's plate and remain standing, watching her closely. All eyes were now turned Rachel's way, and she could feel concealed amusement coming from Ethan, evidently finding her slight agitation rather entertaining. Beneath the table he nudged her with his knee. She gave him a slight kick in the ankle, but he just kept looking at her as if he had no idea what she was about to say.

She strengthened her voice, and declared, "Ethan has asked me to marry him, and—"

She didn't get the rest of it out before Charlie started wailing and everyone else jumped up from their seats, congratulating her with hugs and tears, and pounding Ethan on the back with gusto. Bert beamed as if the whole thing had been his idea. Juliet, her eyes gleaming as she stepped back to give the others a chance to embrace Rachel, noticed Bert's expression and demanded, "You *knew*?"

"I only found out a few minutes ago, Juliet," he assured her with hands raised in defense. Then he came over and took her hand, their faces shining with mutual joy.

Grandpa and Rose, the only ones who remained relatively calm, sat watching everyone's reaction. Grandpa looked over at the little girl and winked at her.

She grinned back and snickered, "I knew it all the time, well, at least for a few days."

"I didn't *know* but I was hoping," Grandpa confided.

Lewis was drawn from the barn by all the commotion, and Phillip ran to tell him the news. Rachel followed, and reached Lewis just as Phillip declared, "Rachel's getting married!"

Lewis looked stunned for a moment, but recovered quickly. Looking into Rachel's face, his eyes warming, he said, "Well, now, miss, that's purely fine. It's time you was gettin' married." He glanced at Ethan and Rose, and then back at her. "I always thought you was meant to be a mama. Now you found a good man and even a little girl that needs you. Yes, Miss Rachel, it's time."

She said softly, "I may be gaining a family, Lewis, but that won't change how I feel about my friends. I want you to come and see me as often as you can, and I'll come home every week."

"Yes, Miss Rachel," he said, so quietly that she could barely hear him. He gave her a smile and walked over to Ethan to shake his hand. He said only, "That's right fine news, Mr. Stonehill." He nodded to the rest of the family, turned, and walked back to the barn.

Rachel watched him go before returning to her seat, and for the next half hour she and Ethan answered question after question about their plans. When Juliet again began gathering plates, and Grandpa got up and headed for the house, Rachel discreetly trailed after him and found him lying on the sofa in the front room. When he saw her he tried to sit up, but she eased him back down.

"It's nothing to concern you, Rachel. Them beans ain't sitting too well, is all."

Rachel felt his forehead, which wasn't very hot, but it was sweaty. "Grandpa, tell me what hurts you. I can see that it's more than indigestion."

"Oh, honey," he said kindly, "it's most likely nothing but being old. There's no sense in making a fuss. If you want me to feel better, you go on out and join your young man."

"Will you let me bring Dr. Willis or Dr. Hogue out to check on you?"

"Heavens, no. What a waste of the doctor's time that would be." His eyes softened as he looked at her. "Rachel, I'm real happy for you, honey, real happy. That Ethan is the kind of man I hoped you'd marry, and it's plain he's awful taken with you. I'm proud you had the heart to pick him. I remember back when your pa was young, he looked at your mama just the same way Ethan looks at you. Now that I ponder on it, when Bert thinks no one's around to notice, he still does look at your mama that way. I expect I looked at your grandma like that my own self."

She picked up his wrinkled, large-knuckled hand and held it to her cheek.

Lifting his free hand he rested it on the top of her head, gently smoothing her hair. "There now," he said, "you do as I say and head back outside. Let your old grandpa rest a spell."

She stood and left his side, but looked back when she reached the door. His eyes had already closed, his face relaxed, so she watched his even breathing for several moments before quietly leaving.

Despite Juliet's many helpful queries regarding Rachel's wishes for the wedding reception, as well as Charlie's need for more attention than usual, she and Ethan managed to leave Rose in Esther's care and wander along the creek path for a short time. It was a very warm, heady afternoon, sweetened by the scent of buck brush and Ethan's hand in hers. They walked unhurriedly until he came to a stop in the deep shade of some trees and pulled her to him.

"I guess there will be no backing out now, Miss Milford, now that your family knows."

"I guess not," she said, waiting for him to kiss her. He'd barely brushed her lips, however, before they heard Maggie call Rachel's name. She was not far away, with Kate and Phillip trotting close behind. Rachel groaned. "I don't suppose we can outrun them?"

"I doubt we can."

When the children reached them, they joyfully tagged along, chattering like birds about when Rachel's first baby would arrive, how many babies would follow, and what each one should be called. Listening to Ethan's good-natured responses to their animated questions and declarations, Rachel felt a new wave of tenderness for the man who walked beside her. She caught his gaze a time or two, and the warmth of his glances made her want nothing more than to begin their marriage as soon as possible.

Not for the first time, she speculated about whether she'd have to wait until the wedding night before Ethan did anything beyond kissing her. Based on his behavior so far, he intended to wait, and she was certain that this willingness to delay their intimacy was driven by his desire to protect her; to keep from harming her reputation, from beginning a pregnancy too soon, or diminishing their wedding night.

Still, she was sorely tempted to persuade him otherwise, fully noting the reversal of traditional roles she would be transgressing, and if she was *very* persuasive, and if they were extraordinarily discreet... She suddenly laughed aloud at her own folly. When her companions turned puzzled gazes her way, she only shook her head and kept walking.

21

After the initial exhilaration created by the wedding announcement began to subside, Rachel settled again into her old routine with a quiet contentment she'd never known. She was scratching notes onto a scrap of paper from one of Dr. Hogue's journals when a young, dark-haired man in merchant's clothing rushed into the office, his stricken face foretelling dreadful possibilities.

"Why, Mr. Wallace, come in," Dr. Hogue said as he ushered the distraught man to a chair.

"It's my little boy," Mr. Wallace said, struggling to hold himself together. "He's gone, Doc. Just eighteen months old and he's dead and gone. My wife's in a terrible state. It's her I've come about. You got to come and calm her or she might do something dreadful to herself." He slumped forward and buried his face in his hands, breathing deeply to fight back his emotions.

Dr. Hogue caught Rachel's eye and nodded toward a cabinet. She got up and filled a glass of whiskey while the doctor pulled a chair close to Mr. Wallace and placed a hand on his bent back. "We'll come, but take a minute to tell me what happened."

Mr. Wallace sat up very slowly, as if barely able to carry his burden. Pushing the hair from his face, he turned haunted eyes to Doc Hogue. Rachel handed the liquor to Mr. Wallace, but he took it without cognizance and didn't lift it to his lips. "We was up a good share of the night with him, my wife mostly," he said shakily. "The baby didn't seem too sick, just fractious, with sniffles and a cough. About four this morning the coughing got worse and he wasn't breathing so well. We had just decided that I would come fetch you if he wasn't doing better soon but...but...he fell asleep and never woke up, Doc. You were so close, I should have come, but he died before I ever left the house." His body began to shudder with restrained sobs, and his hand shook so badly that half the whiskey spilled.

"Here now, Alonzo," Dr. Hogue said softly, "take a swallow or two from that glass. It'll do you good. Then we'll all go out and see to your wife."

As Alonzo had said, they didn't live far, just down Wall Street, and the three of them reached the house in minutes. Walking inside, Alonzo picked up a little girl no older than three. "Good boy, Joseph," he said, looking over his daughter's shoulder at a six-year-old boy. "You watch Clara for just a spell longer now while we talk to your ma." He set the girl down near her brother and motioned Rachel and Dr. Hogue to follow him into a bedroom.

Matilda Wallace didn't glance up at their entry, but lay curled on the bed rocking and moaning softly. Dr. Hogue came near to her and offered gentle words of comfort while Rachel silently rubbed Matilda's limp hand. He continued to speak softly as he checked her heart rate and her eyes, but Matilda heard very little and responded even less. Eventually Dr. Hogue straightened and moved away from the bed. "She needs to sleep, Alonzo, and someone to stay close by her. I will leave you a bottle of medicine, and she's to take just three drops in a half-glass of water after dinnertime and that much again after suppertime. That will help her through the next few days, but grief like this will take some time to overcome. And, Alonzo," Doc said, his gaze deepening slightly, "don't let your wife know where you keep the bottle."

Matilda's husband stared at him, understood, and nodded.

After re-entering the room and watching Alonzo give Matilda the first modest dose of laudanum, Dr. Hogue and Rachel were led to the body of her son, lying in a tiny bed set in a corner of the home's second bedroom, apart from two other small beds. Alonzo pulled back the woven blanket that covered the little boy entirely, and his throat caught raggedly as he stepped back. Looking down at the child, Rachel tried to maintain a measure of professional detachment, but merely succeeded in masking her feelings. While Doc Hogue conducted his examination, she couldn't keep herself from observing what a beautiful child this was, what promise he must have held, and how profound a tragedy had befallen this family. Tormenting her heart further, the question arose as to whether antibiotics, not yet known, would have prevented all of this suffering.

The doctor at last pulled the blanket gently over the small face once more, and said quietly, "The cause of his death was congestion of the lungs, Alonzo. There is very little I could have done." Again, the young father was able to respond with no more than a nod.

As Rachel took in Doc Hogue's sympathetic yet calm demeanor, while her own heart constricted and her eyes battled back tears, she wondered if she was tough enough to witness such sorrow time and time again. But a voice within answered, "You'll have to be, if you hope to save any of them. Dr. Hogue has learned to accept death. So must you."

When Ethan came to call on her that evening, explaining that Rose was staying with friends, Rachel told him about what had happened at the Wallace home. He pulled her comfortingly into his arms and said, "May God help them." These words and his nearness helped lighten her heart somewhat and, realizing that sharing such times with him would make them less difficult to bear, she was newly thankful that they would soon be wed.

Ethan asked, "How about taking a stroll around town instead of to our meadow this evening?"

She agreed and they set out at a leisurely pace, enjoying the light breeze and the music that drifted to them from numerous locations. They ended up taking a different route than they often did through town, along the busiest part of Main Street. Halfway past the Washoe Saloon, the muffled sound of someone singing to a violin reached them through the heavy door, and Rachel came to a halt to listen. Remembering what Ethan had told her about a talented Irish violinist, she asked, "Is John Kelly performing here tonight?"

"It's likely. He plays here most nights."

She drew him closer to the door where a flyer had been posted and, confirming his assumption, it read:

NIGHTLY CONCERT

by

John Kelly

The Concert will consist of Ballads, Violin Solos,
Budgets of Wit and Comicalities, with an entire new Programme.

Also,

Willie Kelly

In his wonderful and astounding feats of posturing, with New Tricks.

Two miners edged by them, one raising his hat to Rachel as he entered the Washoe. She tried to peer in before the door closed after them but saw almost nothing.

"We ought to be moving along, Rachel," Ethan said, glancing around at the people milling in their general area.

"Let's go inside," Rachel said excitedly.

"Inside? Rachel, I don't think that would be such a good idea. Respectable women don't go into places like this."

"But respectable *men* do?" Rachel challenged.

"Rachel—"

"Have you ever been in there?"

"Yes, I have, but it's more acceptable for men to—"

"Why is it more acceptable?"

"Rachel, honey, the place is full of men, hard-drinking men, mostly. There are fights almost every night; every time a Union sympathizer raises a glass to Abe Lincoln or gives a cheer for the United States, fists start flying. Some times the fights go beyond fists and some fool pulls a knife or a gun."

When Rachel gave no sign of weakening, Ethan made one last attempt. "It *wouldn't be safe* to take you inside those doors."

"All right then, we'll stand in the far back." Ethan was about to raise a new protest, so she quickly added, "We won't stay long, and if anyone looks like they might cause trouble we'll leave immediately."

He still looked highly doubtful.

"Please, Ethan, just for a minute. I promise I won't order a drink or say a word about President Lincoln. Please."

Clearly acting against his better judgment, Ethan lifted his eyes skyward, begging forgiveness, and then stepped forward to open the door for her.

The music faded away but the noise increased considerably once the door had shut behind them. Tobacco smoke hazed the dim lights and bit at her nostrils, but the cigar smokers helped mask the smell of so many unwashed bodies. Impatient for the next song, men hollered curses and encouragement, stomped feet, and banged chairs on the floor. *Here I am*, she observed silently, *in an honest to goodness western saloon*. She flinched when two shots rang out from the far side of the room, but when she saw that the bullets had only hit the ceiling she resisted Ethan's half-heard suggestion that they head back outside. Straightening to make herself taller, she scanned in the place, trying to capture every detail within her memory.

It was very little like what she had expected, which was an image of the saloon she'd seen in classic *Gunsmoke* reruns. Here, dozens of oil lamps mounted on the colorfully papered walls cast a yellow glow over rows of men seated at tables arranged in a circular pattern that rippled outward from the middle of the room, leaving a large gap in the very center for the stage. Chairs had been provided to the members of the audience closest to the performers, but most of the onlookers stood shoulder-to-shoulder behind these fortunate few. If the musicians had been seated on the small stage, Rachel and much of the audience would have been able to see nothing of them through the mass of bodies. This, however, was not the case. Grandly and strategically suspended from the ceiling, out of the reach of the crowd below, hung a huge iron cage. Within it sat John Kelly, tuning his violin, and a very small, dark-skinned boy who could only be Willie.

Rachel could see that John was a man of considerable bulk, and even in the imperfect light she could make out his brown wavy hair and a round mustached face, which at that moment bore a playful grin. The Irishman wore a formal black suit, whereas little Willie sported a remarkable replica of a Southern gray uniform. Evidently Mr. Kelly fostered sympathies similar to those of most of his fans.

Feeling indignation at the exploitation of this child, Rachel watched the boy closely and was surprised to see how much he seemed to be enjoying his surroundings, occasionally glancing up at John with an expression of complete adulation. Ethan's story of how Willie had been adopted forced Rachel to consider where the child might be if Kelly hadn't taken him in, but she couldn't get comfortable with his dangling above the crowd.

When demands for the next song rose to a thunderous level, someone hollered above the din, "Play 'My Mother's Grave,' John!"

"Yeah, John, that's a good one!" another voice cried out.

Mr. Kelly smiled indulgently and nodded. "All right boys, although it's mighty early in the night for that one."

He lifted his violin, tucked it beneath his chin, and raised his bow with a graceful sweep. From his first note, perfectly defined, sweet, and elegant, Rachel was astounded. Scarcely believing the height of his purity and excellence, she strained to hear each note coming from a man who made his home in this raw, uncivilized place. The melody was simplicity itself, but John Kelly played it more finely than Rachel could have dreamed possible. He might have been trained for years in Vienna or Venice, and yet here he was.

Spellbound during his opening movement, the crowd hushed to utter silence, then Kelly took a deep breath, and Rachel held completely still as he began to sing, accompanied by nothing beyond his own violin. But his instrument superbly framed and enhanced the richness of his baritone voice and, like everyone else in the place, Rachel hung on every word.

"Holy precepts by thy lips were given,
Where the valley brook is slowly creeping,
And the wood bird sings its lonely song,
Where the willow boughs are sadly weeping,
Where the zephyr's murmurings pass along,
There my gentle mother's form reposes,
Dearly loved in childhood's happy day.
At the grave I kneel 'mid clustering roses,
Weeping twilight's still hour away.

Can I 'mid the toils of life forget thee,
Angel guardian of my infant years?
Every care compels me to regret thee,
Every smile is chased away by tears.
How I've kept them let my anguish own,
Dearest mother, from thy home in heaven,
Lean down and listen to my anguished moan."

As the last chord was drawn lovingly to a close, men were openly weeping, but even those with tear-stained faces cheered riotously as John Kelly rose and bowed to them.

Now Ethan was pulling on her arm, moving in the direction of the door. This time she reluctantly complied, but she continued clapping until they reached the boardwalk.

"He's absolutely wonderful!" she breathed.

Ethan shook his head, even as a grin played at the corner of his mouth. "He is indeed, but I hope nobody saw you young lady. It could smudge your good name for quite some time. And your pa would likely want my hide tacked to his barn for taking you in there."

"Oh, foot, as Juliet would say. If stepping in there for just one song has dirtied my good name, it wasn't very shining to begin with. And Pa isn't likely to find out."

Chuckling at this, Ethan hooked her arm in his and intently escorted her forward.

As the days passed, Rachel progressively learned more about Ethan's intentions and hopes, his likes and habits, and she became ever more attentive to his happiness. Ethan gave every indication that he would be a considerate, passionate husband, but she began to worry that he was spending too much time away from his beloved ranch for her sake. When asked about this, he claimed that he had time enough to make the place as worthy of her as he could, and he continued to come to town.

Always a gentleman when they were alone, behavior that Rachel found challenging to emulate at times, Ethan seemed to value their time together as much as she. Usually they met near her hotel or Dr. Hogue's office, but from time to time they spent a few free hours at the Milford farm or Stonehill ranch.

On one of these trips to Ethan's place, Rachel secretly measured the window in Rose's room. Then, happily parting with a little of her frugally saved earnings, she bought a few yards of white cotton fabric sprinkled with tiny red roses. Grateful for Juliet's sewing instruction while working on Conrad's quilt, Rachel found time to complete the curtains in just three days.

When Ethan and Rose came to call a few evenings later, Rachel was waiting for them on the hotel porch. The curtains, wrapped in brown paper and bound with string, were hidden behind her back. Rachel watched as they approached on Knight, waving her welcome without leaving her chair. Ethan dismounted, helped Rose down, and tied his horse to the rail.

"Hello, Miss Rachel," said Rose skipping up to her. Ethan smiled, saying, "Evening."

Lifting Rose onto her lap, Rachel announced, "I have something for you, young lady."

"You do?" asked Rose, shooting a glance at her father to see if he knew about the surprise, but he only shrugged.

Rachel pulled out the package and placed it on Rose's lap.

"Oh, my! But, it's not my birthday until November."

"This is just something I wanted to make for you, Rose."

Ethan crouched down and, eyeing Rachel appreciatively, said, "Go ahead and open it up, honey."

Needing no further encouragement, Rose untied the string, spread the paper wide, and drew out the fabric. "Miss Rachel! It's *so* pretty."

"They're curtains for your room. I'm so glad you like them."

Rose pressed the curtains to her chest with one hand and hugged Rachel with the other. Then she eyed the curtains again as if she'd never seen anything so grand. "They even have *roses* on them. See, Papa? Oh, thank you!"

Ethan said sincerely, "They're mighty fine, Rachel. It was kind of you to make them."

"I was very happy to."

Rachel lifted Rose down and stood, and the three of them were about to head inside for supper when they spotted a rider careening toward town at a full run.

"Why, it's True!" Rachel cried out in sudden fear. He would never push Choice like this without need.

He met them in a cloud of dust as he pulled the horse to a dancing halt. "Rachel, you got to get on home," he said breathlessly, trying to keep his face and voice calm. "It's Grandpa. Pa can't wake him and he's barely breathing. I'm going to get Doc Willis."

"Doc Willis?"

"Pa said that Grandpa hasn't ever had anyone else."

Rachel forced the dread down her throat. "All right. You go on, True. Ethan—?"

"You take Knight. I'll tell Richard and Esther, and we'll follow you in their wagon."

They turned toward the hotel, and while Rachel rushed up the stairs to gather the small store of medical supplies she kept in her room, Ethan untied Knight, checked his cinch, and held him ready. Rachel mounted, threw a quick glance at Ethan, and nudged Knight forward until she was racing toward the Milford farm at a break-neck speed.

With Knight's powerful legs drumming the road beneath her, Rachel cursed herself for not insisting that Grandpa see a doctor sooner. Now he might be dying. No, she told herself, refusing to accept this, she'd get him stabilized until the doctor came. They'd take care of him, all of them. They'd see to it that he took things easier. But despite her resolve, a surge of helplessness and anger claimed her, and she wished impossibly that there was an ambulance that could reach him faster, that could provide the proper equipment, medicines, and people. Could Dr. Willis and she save him, with so little available to them?

Knight leaped sideways to avoid a boulder in the road, almost unseating her. She hung on, and as they sped forward she told herself that she would reach Grandpa in time, that he would be fine.

Maggie was sitting with her head bowed on the top step of the front porch when Rachel drew in the sweating stud, leaped down, and looped the reins around a post. Maggie lifted her face, and Rachel saw the tears before she reached her. She took her by her shoulders, saying, "Maggie, honey?"

"Grandpa just passed on, Rachel."

Giving Maggie a distracted squeeze, hoping it wasn't so, Rachel hurried into the house. At a glance she took in Phillip and Kate standing back slightly from the others, wearing uncertain expressions, Juliet comforting Charlie while trying to hold back her own tears, and Bert lifting a blanket over Grandpa's dark red face. She went to the couch and Bert moved aside for her. She pulled the blanket down and felt his neck for a pulse. She could detect no heartbeat but his skin was still warm. "Mama, please take the children outside," she said with such calm authority that Juliet quietly obeyed.

"I have to try to save him, Pa."

"Honey, he's gone. It's too late."

"When did he stop breathing?" she demanded.

"Just now. About a minute ago."

"Then it might not be too late. You have to help me." In seconds she told Bert what she intended to do and ignored his shocked reaction. Quickly checking his mouth for any obstruction, she leaned over him, intending to begin administering mouth-to-mouth resuscitation.

"No, Rachel," said Bert.

"There's no time to argue with me!" Rachel countered urgently.

"It's not right. He's gone."

"This may *save* him!"

Bert didn't make a move to comply.

"I learned about it from the doctors in town," she lied. "I've *seen* it work."

While Bert still hesitated, Rachel took in a deep breath and began the procedure, blocking out everything but whether his body was responding to her actions. Between the first few breaths, she gave Bert swift orders to help her move Grandpa to the floor, directing him how and when to push down on his chest. Very reluctantly, Bert followed her instructions.

With each breath Rachel prayed that she was remembering how to do this right and that it was working. It had been years since her college health class, and then she'd been working on dummies rather than a person, and this man beneath her hands was one whose absence would be painfully felt by herself but immeasurably more by those she'd grown to love. She lost track of the minutes as she worked, and prayed, and watched for any sign of breath.

At last Bert ceased his efforts and said very quietly, "Rachel." She paused and looked up into his sweating face. With tenderness yet unquestioning authority, he said, "You tried, Rachel, but now we have to let him go." Not waiting for her reaction, Bert picked up his father's body and returned it to the couch.

Rachel watched him vacantly, helplessly.

Taking a last look at the face he had loved his entire life, Bert pulled the cover over Grandpa's body. Then he lowered his head with a sigh of profound weariness and loss.

Rachel hadn't moved from the floor. She didn't know if she could move. The acceptance of Grandpa's death was still fighting its way through her mind and numbing her body.

Bert sat down next to her and put his arm around her shoulders.

Rachel said weakly, "I should have convinced him to see Doc Willis before this happened. He said it was just an upset stomach, but I didn't believe him. I didn't even insist on listening to his heart."

"It wouldn't have changed things, honey. It was Grandpa's time, and he was ready. He knew his heart was giving out on him."

It took a second for these words to take shape. "*He knew*?"

"Yes, he told me about a year ago."

"A year ago! Why didn't you tell me? Why didn't you tell Doc Willis?"

"Grandpa asked me not to say a word. I didn't even tell your mother."

"But we could have helped him." Her tears began to pool, then fall.

"Rachel, he didn't want help. He wanted to go when the Good Lord decided it was his time, and this was his time. Your grandpa is with my mama and my brother now, like he wanted, and as it should be."

"I'm so sorry."

He wasn't sure what she regretted, but when she turned her face into his chest it didn't matter. While she wept, he patted her back and uttered sounds of consolation.

That was how Ethan, Juliet, Esther, and Richard found them. Bert helped Rachel to her feet and turned her toward her mother's outstretched arms, knowing that both would find comfort from the other. When Kate and Maggie came in, Rachel went to Ethan, and his arms engulfed her like a warm cocoon.

Minutes later, True and Doc Willis arrived, and the doctor ushered everyone outside, including Rachel, while he did his examination. Shortly afterward he emerged and confirmed that Grandpa had died from heart failure.

The children gathered on the porch, now releasing their grief openly, and unashamedly snuggled close to Rachel or Juliet as they cried. Bert remained dry-eyed but quietly somber, and he and Lewis soon left them to finish the day's chores that would not be denied even at such a time, while Ethan saw to Knight's care after his hard ride from town.

Holding Charlie in her lap, Rachel watched True and Kate wander down to the trees by the creek and sit on a huge stump, talking with their heads close together and Kate's shoulders slumped with the burden of her sadness.

Later, Juliet and Bert asked the other adults to step inside. Phillip and Maggie watched over Rose and Charlie, both very subdued, while those indoors discussed what was to be done next. It was soon decided that Richard would return to town with Esther and the baby, and arrange for Father Mesplie to oversee the services the next day. True was to ride to their neighbors and friends and tell them about Grandpa's funeral. Ethan would go home to see to his animals and to make the coffin, which he would bring to them in the morning, and Rachel, complying with the traditions of the times, would help Juliet prepare Grandpa's body for burial.

The group of adults lifted their heads from their conversation when Kate, who had been listening unnoticed, came up to Juliet and asked, "What about us, Mama? What can we do?"

Juliet thought for a minute. "I was almost forgetting," she said. "Since we want Grandpa to have a proper funeral we'll be needing lots of flowers. They mustn't be picked yet, mind, but you kids would be a big help if you'd go and find where all the prettiest flowers are blooming. You can pick them in the morning just before we leave."

Kate's face lightened somewhat, and she left her mother's side to organize the other children for their wildflower hunt.

Separating from the others as the light began to fade, Rachel walked with Ethan to where Knight was tied and rubbed the horse's soft gray muzzle. "Thank you for feeding and watering him, Ethan. He was a good friend today."

"Are you sure it's all right that Rose stays here with you tonight?"

"Of course," she said, hearing the hollowness of her own voice. "Rose is the only person Charlie would let sleep with him and me."

Ethan lifted her face to meet his eyes, and said with compassion, "It was his time, Rachel."

"That's just what Pa said."

Ethan nodded.

"I want you to know, Ethan, Grandpa told me that you are the kind of man he'd hoped I'd marry, and said he was proud of me for choosing you." After a pause, she said softly, "He had such a generous way of reading people. I always felt, when he talked about me or the other kids, he saw only the best in us. What a rare gift."

"I'm glad I had the chance to know him. And I'll always be grateful for his life, because it led to yours."

She wrapped her arms around him and pressed her cheek against his shoulder. "Ride safely."

He held her close for a moment longer, placed a kiss against her temple, and mounted his horse. "I'll be here early tomorrow," he said from his saddle. With a final wave to her and the Milfords on the porch, he rode Knight out of the farmyard and down the road at an easy canter.

The funeral was something of a blur to Rachel, with sorrow and lack of sleep subtly dulling her awareness whenever she paused in carrying out the day's duties. And yet, at other moments her emotions heightened to a painful sharpness.

Not long after Ethan had left the previous evening, Juliet and Rachel had washed Grandpa Milford's body, dressed him in his one suit, and combed his thin hair. They'd then covered him with a clean sheet and called for the men, who had gently placed him on several boards they'd joined together, carried him to the coolest corner of the barn, and set him atop four storage barrels.

With Lewis offering to watch over Grandpa's draped body during the night, he, Juliet, Bert, Rachel, and True had each claimed a portion of the task. Heavily weary, Rachel had lain down not long after dark with Rose and Charlie curled up beside her, but sleep eluded her for hours. Finally, she'd gone to the barn to sit with Bert, well before her assigned time. In the stillness interrupted only occasionally by the hooting of an owl, her mind had dwelled on the events of Grandpa's life, on how he'd lived so fully, what he'd meant to so many people, and in what ways he'd been similar to Grandpa Simon, and she'd realized that this pioneer version of a wake and Bert's quiet presence were providing much solace. When Bert's period of vigilance had elapsed, he'd proposed remaining with her, but she'd sent him to the house to join Juliet in bed for a few brief hours. When True had come to relieve her she'd stayed on with him, encouraging the recounting of his memories until a dim light began to frame the door and Lewis appeared.

When full morning and Ethan had returned, Rachel had felt her fatigue threatening to intensify her emotions to a less than containable level. Even so, she'd determined to be strong for the rest of them as they all went about their previously assigned tasks for the day.

Her intention to hold her tears in check had been sorely tested, however, when she'd come across True and Kate sitting on the top step of the porch as the rest of the family was preparing to leave for the funeral. The two hadn't noticed Rachel standing by the slightly open front door and, sensing their need to talk, she'd stepped back to keep her presence unknown. They'd spoken softly to one another, their tones revealing the earnestness of the subject.

"It's so strange that we're to bury him today," Kate had said in a troubled voice. "I purely wish I could let him know how much I loved him, True. I never did think to tell him, not 'til now. If only he could go walking with me along the creek just one more time... Do you suppose he knew, even without me saying so?"

"He knew, Kate, but you can still tell him if you have a mind to. Even though he ain't where you can see him or touch him anymore, he'll hear you just the same."

"How can that be?"

He'd considered for a bit. "You recall how you and Grandpa carved your names in that big cottonwood not long after we moved here? Do you suppose those letters are still there, even though Grandpa died yesterday?"

"Why, surely they are still there."

"Well, seems to me, when a person loves you, he leaves a mark on your heart, something like the letters on that tree. When that happens, even if he dies, he ain't really lost from your life, because he's grown to be a part of you. Grandpa is always going to keep watch over you, Kate, and do what he can to keep you safe. He won't ever go so far off that he can't hear you when you have a mind to talk. Why, I'm certain he'd truly appreciate hearing from you every now and again."

Kate had looked off in the direction of the cottonwood tree and sighed softly. When she turned back to True, she'd said, "It's real good to know he ain't so very far off after all."

Feeling her chest tighten, Rachel had retreated into the house in search of a chore that might need her attention.

Without being requested to do so, the brass portion of Paston's band had met the family just outside of town, and Bert had accepted their kind offer to walk before the funeral party. The musical group had led the caravan of wagons, playing tunes of appropriate solemnity and cadence as they'd proceeded slowly along. Bert, Juliet, and True had ridden in the first wagon with the casket, while Rachel had joined the rest of the family and Aunt Faith in Richard's and Esther's wagon. Ethan had held little Rose in front of him on Knight just behind the two lead wagons. Many friends in wagons, on horseback, and on foot had followed Ethan, with even more of them merging with the procession as it made its way through town.

The service at St. Joseph's Church, where Father Mesplie spoke of Grandpa's life and voiced his confidence in God to reward such a worthy soul, had been so unlike the grandeur and pomp of her Grandpa Simon's funeral. Yet it had been similar in the sincerity of its tribute to a loved one who'd left them, as well as the comfort extended to those who would miss him most.

The good women from within the church and beyond had shown their respect and affection for the Milfords in the form of numerous lovingly prepared dishes delivered to the house after the services, but Rachel had eaten very little. She'd wanted nothing more than to remain seated on the porch bench, lean her tired head against Ethan's shoulder, and hold both little Rose and Charlie on her lap. The two children had sat quietly for once, as if absorbing the comfort of Rachel's body. Before long, they'd fallen asleep in her arms in spite of the many voices and movements around them. Ethan had inched his face close enough to brush his lips against her hair and said quietly, "Are you feeling all right, Rachel?"

"As long as you're here next to me."

His arm around her had tightened. "I'm here."

22

The hours of deep summer lengthened to days and then weeks, and Rachel and the others resumed the activities that defined their lives. She was in the treatment room, rolling down her sleeves after washing her hands, when she heard Kate and Maggie enter Dr. Hogue's office before they peeked in at her.

"Rachel, we've been looking for you," Kate said softly, to which Maggie added with an uncertain glance at the doctor and the patient resting on the table, "Hello, Rachel."

"Hush, you two," Rachel said in mock severity as she came out with them. "Dr. Hogue's got a man in the next room who's not feeling well. He needs his sleep."

Dr. Hogue appeared at the door and nodded kindly at the girls before saying to Rachel, "I can handle things here. You go right along and visit with your sisters." He glanced at his pocket watch. "Good heavens! I had no idea the evening was creeping up on us. It's well past time for you to leave; besides, it's sweltering in here. Some fresh air will do you good. Off with you now. Good day, girls."

The three headed outside, where it wasn't much cooler but the wind at least seemed to lighten the weight of the heat. Rachel pulled in a breath and picked up the scent of newly-sawn logs. The hour was indeed growing late and dusk was approaching quickly.

"Pa and Lewis are at the mercantile," said Maggie, swinging Rachel's hand in hers as she skipped along.

"Pa brought in a load of vegetables," Kate informed her. "Mama stayed home to work on your wedding dress. She and Pa can't seem to think or talk about anything *but* your wedding. Mama's so pleased she's even been reckoning about when I get married. Imagine that."

Rachel smiled affectionately, and then said with a touch of self-reproach, "Oh, dear, I thought I might buy you two some licorice sticks, but I've forgotten to bring any money. Should we see if we can talk Pa into buying you some before he leaves?" Receiving emphatic nods, she steered their course in that direction.

When they entered the store Lewis spotted them first. "Miss Rachel," he said, smiling, "how you gettin' along?"

Bert turned from his discussion with Mr. Mack long enough to wave at her, then resumed his lively debate over the price of cabbages with the storeowner. Maggie and Kate approached the candy counter and weighed their options with grave reflection as Rachel and Lewis stepped slightly farther from the group.

"I'm feeling fine, Lewis. And you?"

"Right as rain, Miss Rachel. Say, did you hear about tomorrow?"

"Tomorrow? I don't think so."

"Mr. Bert tol' me about Mr. Lincoln askin' everybody to pray tomorrow. The whole country's to pray so that the rebel army will lay down their guns."

"Yes, of course. I did read about a national day of prayer. It's a wonderful idea." Rachel remembered other presidents, future presidents, calling for such action by the American people during times of war and terror. But those occasions seemed lifetimes away to her now.

Watching her acutely, Lewis asked, "You suppose the war's fixin' to end soon?"

"I wish I knew exactly when it will end, but I don't."

He lowered his voice a touch. "I keep thinkin' about what you said, about Mr. Lincoln gettin' shot after the fightin' stops. Well, I haven't heard one thing back since we sent that letter off. I guess them men in Washington thought I was just some kind of fool."

"Or, perhaps, they'll be extra watchful now. Maybe your letter will make a difference, Lewis."

"Anyhow, I been prayin' like Mr. Lincoln said we should. I like to think that everybody's prayers will keep him safe if my letter don't."

"What happens is up to God, Lewis, whether we understand it or not." Even as Rachel said these words, she marveled at how the past months had generated such a statement. No, she corrected, it was more than a statement. It was a belief now, a trust. Somehow she'd grown to embrace a good measure of the Milfords' faith, from the services she'd attended but even more from how they worked, and reached out, and loved. Without fully realizing it, she'd also applied this trust in God to her coming here. That too, she was beginning to suppose, was up to Him. Pondering this, she saw that by allowing this gradual transition, she'd gained a peace, an acceptance that she hadn't known before.

She gave Lewis a smile of assurance as Bert, having finished his business with Mr. Mack, approached them with a few small parcels under one arm. He gave Rachel a fatherly pat on the cheek with his free one. "How is my doctorly daughter today?"

"Just fine, Pa. Is everyone well at home?"

"Healthy and just a shade ornery, all of us."

Happy to see that his grief had lifted for a time, Rachel said, "My, you're in a good mood."

"Your mama's vegetables brought a dear price, and she's going to be mighty pleased. She'll fix us up quite a spread tonight."

"Pa, can we have a nickel for some licorice?" Kate asked.

"Since we've been blessed today, I think a nickel can be spared, and I'll throw in another nickel if you buy some to take home to your mama and brothers." Bert fished in his pocket and handed the coins to Kate, who grabbed Maggie's hand and hurried back to the candy jars. Then Bert enquired, "How's that young man of yours doing?"

Rachel couldn't keep from grinning, "Healthy and just a shade of ornery."

They laughed and chatted until they were rejoined by the girls, both of them chewing licorice and Kate carrying a small wrapped bundle.

"How long will you be in town?" Rachel asked once they were outside.

"It's nearly supper time but Lewis and I still need to pick up a plow blade that Richard sharpened for us, then we'll stay for a short visit with Esther. She makes her special chocolate cake almost every Thursday, as you know. It's worth our getting home a little after dark."

"Can we meet you there in awhile, Pa," Kate asked hopefully, "so we have some more time with Rachel?"

"I suppose so. Plow blades aren't the sort of thing to interest young ladies. In about a half-hour, then?"

Rachel nodded, and said, "Ethan said he was dropping Rose off with some friends for the night, so he might reach town later than usual. I'll leave word for him at the Montana House that we'll be at Esther's."

The two small groups walked away from the mercantile porch in their separate directions.

Contentedly listening to Kate and Maggie expound on the latest doings at the farm, Rachel leisurely steered the girls toward her hotel as the light began to fade. It didn't take long to write a note for Ethan and leave it with Mrs. Kellin, but a recent patient, still on crutches, stopped her in the lobby to thank her again for her care. His earnest but long-winded praise of her services threatened to make them late to Esther's house, and Rachel finally had to cut him off as politely as she could while hurrying the girls back outside, where darkness was gently gathering.

Walking more briskly now because of the delay, they were passing the entrance to one of the saloons when two burly men in worn, dusty clothes shoved the swinging doors wide and faltered onto the boardwalk, almost on top of them. The slightly thinner and younger of the two men bellowed to be heard over the banging of the piano and the voices behind them. "Why, it's the Milford girls, Clyde. Hold on there, we'd like a word with you."

Rachel's rapid glance had noted that these two might be brothers, with their similar thin brown hair and long noses. Maggie and Kate had lurched to a halt to avoid being trampled and now stood staring at the men, but Rachel tugged on their arms and got them moving again. Before they'd taken four steps, however, the younger man, and perhaps the more sober, planted himself in front of them while Clyde slipped behind. Rachel, now clenching a hand of each sister, tried to step around the man facing her, but he shifted to stop her.

"Get out of our way," Rachel demanded, and tried to shoulder around him.

At a subtle signal between the two men, Clyde suddenly pushed Kate into the arms of his brother, clamped a hand over Rachel's mouth as he twisted her left arm back and up, pressing her hand between her shoulder blades. Maggie frantically tried to tug her out of his grasp while Rachel wriggled fiercely to free her left arm and kick at his legs, but Clyde jerked her arm savagely upward. He growled at Maggie, "One sound from you, girl, and I'll break her arm." He shot a glance around for observers, lifted Rachel off her feet with Maggie still clinging to her right hand, and hastily hauled her past a few lightless windows and into an alley.

Urgently yanking her hand from Maggie's grip, Rachel cocked her elbow and jabbed her captor in the ribs with a blow greatly strengthened by her fear for the girls. His breath exploded and his hold weakened enough for Rachel to pull away, but he quickly grabbed her arm again. Rachel's desperate gaze swept the darkness as she tried to tear free. Four feet away Maggie stood frozen in place. Kate and the other man were nowhere in sight. Panic, ugly and sharp, seized Rachel, and she bent her knees and heaved her weight back against the attacker, yelling, "Run, Maggie!" The girl raced out into the street calling out for help, her voice sounding pitifully small and diminishing.

"Kate!" Rachel screamed, wrestling the man as he regained his balance, but her second cry was cut short by a blunt blow to her head that knocked her to the ground. Straining to focus her vision, she saw him standing over her, the butt of his pistol ready for another strike. "Just one more yell out of you, and I'll cave your skull in."

She had no weapon, none but the dirt beneath her. Concealing her actions behind her skirt as she slowly, clumsily rose to her feet, her head throbbing and left arm weak from its wrenching, she filled both of her hands. The man eyed her, considering, relishing what would come next. "I guess maybe I don't need my gun no more," he gloated. When he shoved it into his holster, grinned nastily, and took a step closer, Rachel pitched both fistfuls of dirt into his eyes. She ran stumbling toward the street but before she could reach it, another tall male loomed in front of her and reached out.

"Stan!" she cried, tumbling to him.

Even with his left arm wrapped protectively around her waist, Stan's right arm lifted with quick, deadly grace, his pistol pointing at her assailant. Clyde held perfectly still except for the blinking of his eyes. His expression implied that he recognized Stan and his hand remained carefully away from his holstered gun.

"Maggie found me, Rachel," Stan said in a voice of terrible calm. "She's safe. Now go."

"Stan, another man's taken Kate!" Rachel cried, and left him at a run.

In the street, Rachel glanced in one direction and then the next, but there was no sign of Kate. *Oh, God,* she thought. *Dear God, not Kate.*

When the two strange men had first approached the sisters, Kate had felt only vaguely uneasy. They'd said their family name, must have known their parents, so she'd guessed it unlikely they meant any harm. She hadn't been afraid until Clyde had shoved her and grabbed Rachel. Kate had tried to leap forward to help her, but the man behind had grasped a handful of hair and yanked her backward, then flattened her to a building where they were likely invisible in the darkness. She'd tried to yell, but he'd clapped his stinking hand over her mouth so roughly that she could scarcely breathe. Lifting and wedging her under one of his arms, he'd lugged her at a lope across the street and behind several buildings farther from the saloon before ducking to the rear of the *Boise News* office.

Now he had Kate backed against this building, pressing close, his breath rank through rotting teeth, with one hand still over her mouth and the other pinning her wrists to her chest. Struggling for breath, she suddenly squirmed and kicked so furiously that she managed to sink her teeth into his flesh all the way to the bone. He flung her down and stared at his wound in amazement, but his eyes rapidly grew mean. "You little bitch," he hissed.

He came at her as she sprang to her feet, scrambling until she again felt the wall at her back. Glancing from side to side, she found nothing to serve as a weapon. She set her legs in a slight crouch and raised her fists.

"So you're a fighter, eh?" he said, with an amused snort. "Not for long."

He grabbed for her, but Kate was quicker. She jumped to the side and swung at his face. He grunted in surprise more than pain from the impact, and, moving with agility he hadn't appeared to possess, he cut off Kate's retreat by grabbing her arm and heaving her backward yet again. Before Kate could scream he slapped her across the mouth and flung her at the wall. Stunned and breathless, she slid to the ground.

"You might just as well decide to be friendly," he sneered down at her. "It won't do no good to fight. You might just make me mad enough to hurt you."

Kate glared back at him with more defiance than fear. She didn't say a word as she got to her feet, wiped the bleeding corner of her mouth with the back of her hand, and raised her fists again.

Before she could dodge him he swung at her face, but she partially blocked the blow with her right arm. She swayed but quickly replanted her feet, locking her eyes on him and raising her fists even higher.

"Hell, I've had enough of this," he snapped. "It's time I teach you another kind of fun." He knocked her arms aside with a forceful down-sweeping stroke, then grasped both of her wrists in his right hand and yanked her arms straight up from her shoulders. He brought his face close but Kate twisted sharply to the side and his mouth landed behind her ear. He squeezed her hands painfully as he said, "You be nice and stop your fussing, and this won't be so bad at all."

When he seized the neck of her dress, Kate screamed, "Don't!" She fought him with a ferocious will, kicking her knees and wriggling to avoid his touch, but he was three times her weight. He punched her in the stomach, momentarily reducing her to the limpness of a ragdoll, and forced her hands even higher up the rough siding as he pressed his bulk against her, compressing her lungs. When she began to struggle again, he snarled, "I got a knife in my belt. You hold still or I'll start carving you up." He eased back and lowered his left arm to fumble with the bottom of her skirt.

Squirming weakly, her hope and strength ebbing, Kate caught sight of someone moving closer from the side of the next building. Pulling her astonished glance back to her attacker, she writhed with all of her remaining energy. He instantly moved his hand to his knife scabbard.

Just as he grabbed the hilt of his blade, a whip exploded, and the man pinning Kate jerked backward with a cry of pain. Kate fell to her knees, pushed clear of him, and scrambled free.

He drew his knife and rounded like a wounded bear, crouched and swaying from foot to foot, poised to strike the figure looming in the shadows only steps away. But rapidly reconsidering the weapon he held, he made the mistake of dropping the knife to grab for his pistol. With the flick of her arm Rachel lashed his face, slicing open his right eye socket and tearing his cheek. He bellowed in rage, but before he could clear his gun from its holster, the whip carved a trench across his right arm, severing tendons above the wrist. As the gun fell to the ground, he lunged forward, only to be cast back by a blow that left another long gash across his face. Blood flowed from his torn eyebrows into his eyes, blinding him, and he dropped to his knees. He groped for his gun with his left hand, but Rachel let the whip fly again, catching his left arm above his wrist and jumping backward to jerk him onto his gruesome face.

Momentarily forgotten by the combatants, Kate shouted, "Rachel, wait!" and leaped in close enough to kick the gun out of his reach and pick it up. She kept it aimed at his heart, her hands shaking as she backed away.

The man started to rise, but Rachel's well-trained arm whipped him around his neck and heaved back, twisting him as he fell again. The next stroke caught his shoulders with no less force, destroying his shirt and leaving another deep incision in his skin. The whip sang again and again, allowing no time between strikes for either defense or retreat.

Blood from the pistol-whipping Rachel had received from Clyde now mixed with sweat as it ran down her cheek. Her jaw was set like a clamp, her brows drawn down low, and her eyes chillingly formidable. She didn't take notice when Kate's attacker stopped moving, didn't recognize that he had lost consciousness. She brought the whip up high once more and slashed another slit across his back.

"Rachel," Kate called to her, but she didn't stop. Another crack of the whip sounded over the man's body, tearing more than his shredded shirt.

Someone took hold of her wrist, firmly but not threateningly. For a moment she held very still, neither releasing the whip nor taking her eyes from the bloody body on the ground.

"Rachel." She turned and looked into Stan's face to find equal shares of pain, pride, and worry in his expression. He kissed her forehead with absolute gentleness as he freed the whip from her hand.

Kate ran to her, thrust the gun to Stan, and buried her head in Rachel's shoulder, weeping at last, now that they were safe. "You found me," she cried. "You stopped him."

Stan pulled a handkerchief from his pocket and dabbed at the blood still trickling from Rachel's head wound, then handed her the cloth to press against the gash. He looked at the whip, and then, questioningly, at her.

"I took it from the livery stable," she said.

Nodding, Stan walked over to the body, still motionless except for its shallow breathing. Standing over it, he tapped the barrel of the man's pistol against his palm, considering, sighed as he let the moment pass, and tucked the gun into his belt. He then bent down and took possession of the knife that lay not far from his feet. When Stan straightened and returned to Rachel, he wrapped his arms around her and Kate, and pledged, "Heaven may forgive these two men, but I never will."

The fever born of fear and retribution that had burned so hotly in Rachel was cooling at last, and she trembled slightly as she held Kate, smoothing her hair and saying, "It's all right now, honey. It's all right." She took a calming breath or two, and looked up at Stan, his eyes lingering on her forehead. Managing to give him a weak smile, she said, "Somehow I keep hurting my head, don't I?"

Her gaze rose higher, to the stars overhead, and on another plane of awareness, Rachel felt as though old, strangling manacles that Ethan's love had loosened had somehow been pried wide open on this awful night. Her mind's eye watched as the shackles crumbled bit by bit and fell away, leaving someone less vulnerable and less broken behind.

Stan said gently, "Rachel, take Kate to Esther's place now. I'll be along shortly."

She hadn't seen them approach, hadn't noticed the lanterns, but when she turned and took a few steps, Ethan was there, gently helping Kate toward Bert and Richard, and pulling Rachel into his arms. He was breathing hard, his heart pounding beneath her cheek, from relief, or rage, or both.

All Rachel could do was cling to him, murmuring his name. He held her close for a long moment, then lifted his head, and his body tensed. As he shifted to step in front of her, Rachel turned around.

Stan stood motionless near the body, facing them. Even in the near-darkness, Rachel could see the storm of suspended anguish and the potential for vengeance on Stan's face, the gun at his belt, the knife in his half-raised hand. His features grew harder as they held Ethan's gaze, and she realized in one terrible instant that while watching her and Ethan, witnessing the scope of their attachment for the first time, Stan had been wounded more deeply than a thrust of that blade.

No one moved.

Rachel was about to speak when Lewis, whom Rachel hadn't seen until that moment, walked slowly forward and seemed to unintentionally place himself between Stan and Ethan. Facing Stan, he said, "Mr. O'Brien, all of us is mighty grateful to you for helpin' these young ladies like you done. Yes, sir, mighty grateful."

Stan's gaze moved from Lewis, to Ethan, and finally to Rachel. He stared for several breaths, searching, until her face had told him everything, and his own had revealed what strength it took to accept what he could not change. His expression became unreadable as he lowered the knife and drew his attention back to Lewis.

A knowing, mirthless smile crossed Stan's mouth, and he said in a tone that held more than a little respect, "Why, you're most welcome, Lewis." After one last glance at Rachel, Stan addressed Ethan in a much tighter voice, "Hadn't you better take the ladies home?"

Ethan nodded slowly, acknowledging what Stan had just saved, and then painfully surrendered to another.

Rachel left Ethan's side, passed by Lewis, and walked up to Stan. Letting him see her gratitude and more, she leaned close and kissed him on the cheek as gently as he had kissed her moments before. "Thank you, Stan," she whispered, "For Kate, and Maggie, and me."

He couldn't meet her eyes, but said very softly, "As long as you aren't harmed beyond what time can heal, all of you, that's thanks enough, darlin'." And then his gaze lifted and found hers, but only for an instant. Taking a step back, he turned his face to Bert and the other men, and said, "I've got the other brute tied up in the alley. I'd best be fetching him."

"Rachel," said Ethan, "please go to Esther's so I can help Stan finish up here."

"I'm staying too," Bert declared. "Richard, will you go with them? Esther will need you."

After a very reluctant pause, Richard nodded.

"I'll stay as well, Mr. Bert," said Lewis, in a more determined tone than Rachel had ever heard him use.

She was about to ask what they intended to do, but stopped herself as she scanned their faces. She'd never seen Bert look so rigid and distant. Lewis was working hard to appear stoic, but couldn't fully conceal a slow fire smoldering within. Ethan's expression was one he might have worn facing a battlefield; detached and reconciled, yet calculating. Stan looked perfectly ruthless now, and even more deadly than Ethan.

Growing fearful of the men's next actions, Rachel hesitated.

"Rachel," said Bert, "go on now, and take care of your sister." Giving her no more time to think, he and Lewis followed Stan out of the alley. But before she let Ethan leave her, Rachel had to ask, "What will you do with those two men, Ethan?" He didn't answer her right away and Rachel guessed that he was deciding what he could tell her without lying.

"What needs doing," he finally said.

She swallowed painfully, fearing, knowing. "What about Rose?"

"She's spending the night with the Humphreys."

"Ethan—."

He touched her cheek, then turned and left her, striding quickly away to catch up with the others.

With rising dread she heard Richard say beside her, "Let's get you and Kate home, Rachel." She felt Kate take her hand, and allowed herself to be led away.

When True arrived at Esther's house, sent by his concerned mother over the failure of Bert and the others to return home, he was told what had happened. It took a good deal of talking to calm his furious reaction and to keep him from leaving them in search of his father, but Kate and Maggie asked him to take them home to Juliet, and he finally agreed to leave Choice for his father's ride home, load his younger sisters into Bert's wagon, and head back to the farm.

The hours that Rachel waited with Esther and Richard seemed endless, and all talk dwindled until each of them was left to sit in silent, torturous speculation about what might be happening out there in the night.

At long last Bert, Lewis, and Ethan reappeared, unspeaking and unreadable. The weight of their unwillingness to meet the eyes of those around them kept Rachel from voicing a single question. Everyone sat or stood at the table, where they seemed held captive by the depth of their memories or conjectures. The ticking of Richard's German mantle clock sounded unnervingly loud as they stared at the lantern on the table, or at their feet, or at the floor.

It was Bert who finally spoke, saying, "I don't see the girls."

"True took them home, Pa," said Esther.

"Well, Juliet must be worried, and it's mighty late. Let's be heading home, Lewis. Rachel, would you like to come with us?" He was just rising and reaching for his hat on the table when a pounding on the door stilled the movements and thoughts of every person in the room. Glances went from face to face. Their expressions of dread and apprehension were hurriedly replaced by calmer facades as Richard rose, moved toward the knocking, and opened the door.

Sheriff Pinkham stood there alone, hat in hand. "I saw your light. I'd like to come in, Mr. Lete."

"Sure, Sheriff," Richard said quietly, gesturing him inside and offering him a chair, which he politely refused.

Although Rachel had bandaged her cut and washed her face and neck, her hair had been only hastily re-pinned and she was still wearing her dirty, blood-spotted dress. Sheriff Pinkham's glance took all of this in before saying, "I heard that a couple of fellows caused you folks some trouble today."

Bert, still standing, took a step forward and said evenly, "That's right. Some men were bothering my daughters, Sheriff."

Pinkham turned his attention back to Rachel. "I was also told that one of the men got a thorough whipping. Folks saw him being led from behind the *Boise News*."

Rachel wasn't being asked a direct question, and her instincts as well as years of training demanded that she say nothing, but a louder inner voice warned that if she didn't respond to this man immediately, things could go much worse for the men she loved.

"I borrowed the whip from the livery stable, Sheriff, and used it to defend myself and my little sister," she said, surprised at how calm she sounded.

"Do any of you know the names of those men?"

"One of them called the other Clyde." Rachel told him. "That's all we know."

The lawman listened and watched her intently, and then took his time with the next question, his eyes lowering to his hat as he turned it round and round in slow circles.

"Would you have any idea of their whereabouts now?"

As Rachel watched the sheriff continue to stare at his hat, wondering why he wasn't studying the faces of everyone in the room, she sensed that he was avoiding the possibility of learning what they might reveal.

Before the silence drew out any longer, Bert said, "Well, Sheriff, I drove them outside of town, and I told them that if they ever came back I'd see to it that they'd be facing a judge."

Fearing that Bert's lack of experience with what she suspected to be lies might betray him, Rachel broke in. "My pa scared those two off for my sake, to save me and my sisters from the humiliation of a trial."

Again taking his time before speaking, the sheriff asked, "Do you suppose those men will *stay* scared off?"

Bert answered without a pause, "We surely hope so, Sheriff."

Pinkham let his eyes sweep briefly over the people around him, lingering just long enough on Rachel for her to be certain. He knows.

Resettling his hat on his head, the sheriff said to Bert, "If not, I'll deal with them." He stepped to the door and opened it, but faced them again before leaving. "If ever you folks run into trouble again, you'd best come to me." It was not a request. There was strength behind his warning, and every one of them heard it clearly.

"Yes, sir, and we all hope there won't be any more trouble," Bert said, offering his hand.

Sheriff Pinkham accepted it. Then, as if just remembering, he said, "By the way, word's spreading through the saloons that Stan O'Brien's left town. You folks expect to see him any time soon?"

Heads shook and glances shifted around the table as if puzzled by the question, and the sheriff seemed to have expected no other reply. "If you happen to see him, send him my way, will you? We have a matter or two to discuss."

Rachel saw that this last was added for the sake of formality rather than any expected result, making her even more certain that Sumner Pinkham was a perceptive man.

He nodded again and left them.

Turning to Bert, Rachel asked, "Is that true about Stan? Has he really left town?"

Bert shifted uneasily and Ethan answered, "We tried to stop him, Rachel, but he said if anybody discovered... what took place, they'd remember it happened on the same night he disappeared. He wanted any blame, if it came, to follow him."

"He left for *good*?" she asked in painful surprise. "He left everything behind?"

"Everything." Ethan's eyes told her that he knew just how much Stan had relinquished.

After all he'd done for her tonight, for all of them, and now this. "Oh, Stan," Rachel whispered.

"We couldn't stop him, Rachel," said Ethan, "not by any means short of shooting him."

Bert said softly, "He said you would understand, honey."

Yes, all too clearly, she understood. She buried her face in her hands, feeling as if her heart were being wrung.

It had taken Rachel several moments to notice that Bert and Lewis were preparing to leave, and not long afterward she and Ethan also departed from Esther's house for the night. They made their way toward the hotel with Rachel's arm tucked tightly between Ethan's elbow and chest, his free hand covering hers. Though she was only vaguely conscious of it, the heat of the day had relented and the late breeze lightly swept them with its coolness. The noise from the saloons ebbed and flowed around them, but even this seemed uncommonly subdued.

It didn't occur to Rachel to press Ethan for answers, her thoughts being so heavy that they kept her words minimal. She was immeasurably thankful that Stan had found her in the alley, that she'd been able to reach Kate in time, and that Maggie hadn't been physically harmed, but what about the harm done to Stan? Where was he now, and would he eventually find peace somewhere? She tried not to dwell on what had happened to the two attackers, to pretend she didn't know, but her attempts were futile. These apprehensions and worries over whether Sheriff Pinkham would let the incident drop, and whether Maggie and Kate would survive the incident without horrendous emotional scars, plagued her with tenacity.

Leaning her cheek against his shoulder as they slowly walked along, she tightened her hold on his arm, giving and taking encouragement. When at last the light from the Montana House's lanterns touched them, she stopped and faced Ethan. Wrapping her fingers around the back of his neck she brought her mouth to his. She tried to intensify the kiss but Ethan gently lifted his head. "Rachel, I should leave, so you can rest."

"What I need more than anything right now is you, all of you. Please take me home, Ethan. You can bring me back before dawn, but give me tonight."

He touched his forehead to hers, considering, wanting.

Rachel knew that he didn't plan to collect Rose from his friends until midday tomorrow, so no one was likely to find out. If she became pregnant, their wedding was only weeks away, and no disgrace would arise from the delivery of a baby a few days early.

Although Ethan's mind must have been traveling along similar paths, he wavered. "It has to be right for us, Rachel, especially the first time. I don't want what has happened to lessen our happiness."

"I won't let men like that rob us of anything. Ethan, I love you almost more than I can bear. We will make it right." Reaching up again, she drew him into a kiss meant to heal, and thank, and offer.

Sighing softly, Ethan held her as if he was afraid she couldn't be real, afraid she couldn't be his, but the expression she wore as he released her said otherwise, and they turned away from the hotel.

Riding Knight toward the ranch, with Rachel in the saddle and Ethan's arms wrapped around her from behind, they made their way, needing no more light than that yielded by the stars and half-moon, speaking seldom, unwilling to waste words on things of less importance than what lay ahead.

While Ethan led the horse to the barn, Rachel went into the house, lit the lantern on the shelf by the door, and carried the light to the kitchen table. She found a clean cloth and a bucket almost full of water, which she set aside until she'd located a brush and a light blanket in Rose's room. Returning to the kitchen, a sweet scent met her and she breathed it in deeply. "Cinnamon," she murmured. She glanced around in search of its source, fleetingly wondering what Ethan had made with the spice, but she found no answer. Smiling at the thought of Ethan baking sweets, perhaps for her, she removed her shoes, took off her dirty dress, and slipped out of her undergarments.

The tepid water from the bucket was wonderfully soothing, and with each pass of the cloth she felt her spirit lighten a little. When her washing was complete she wrapped herself in the blanket, tucking it together above her breasts. The sound of the pump outside being worked vigorously, and then the splashing of water, hurried her hands as she picked up the brush, carefully avoiding her small head wound, and drew it through her long hair until it felt silky to her touch.

The front door opened and she turned in that direction, waiting. Ethan, his shirt in his hand, his hair and chest wet, lifted his head, saw her, and stood very still. Rachel's gaze held him there as she very slowly loosened the blanket and let it fall to the floor.

With the glow of the lantern behind her, every contour of her body was framed and accentuated, giving her an ethereal form. His eyes found every curve and indentation as they traveled down her length, so unhurriedly and with such admiration that Rachel almost felt the gaze as a caress. She waited until his eyes met hers once more, and opened her arms.

Continuing to savor her beauty even as he came to her, he wrapped her in his arms. "I'm thankful beyond words that you'll be my wife, Rachel, that we'll be together for all of our lives, and I promise before God to be a loving husband to you." He met her raised lips in full, lingering exploration. Lifting her and cradling her close to his chest, he carried her to his bed.

There, he made love to her with a generosity and fervor that fueled her own longing until she cried out for him, and they surrendered their bodies and hearts with a thoroughness, a harmony that was new to them both. Twice more before dawn they loved each other completely, and when their bodies could no longer keep sleep from overtaking them, they lingered in each other's embrace while they dreamed.

23

The sound of voices ghosted at the edges of Rachel's consciousness but the depth of her slumber allowed her to disregard them at first. They continued, however, growing louder and more persistent, and progressively activated a pounding in her head that gained in strength until it undeniably pulled her to wakefulness. She kept her eyes squeezed tightly closed, fighting the intensifying ache at the back of her temples that brought a hoarse moan from her lips, and the voices immediately hushed. The quiet lasted only a moment before the talking returned, low and excited.

Still unwilling to open her eyes, Rachel loosely wondered who had been so bold as to enter Ethan's room, and where Ethan was. She tried to reach for him but something pulled at her elbow. A gentle hand eased her arm back down and a female voice said, "Easy, Rachel."

The pain in her head was still increasing. She wanted to see who'd spoken, to understand why these people were here, to face whatever judgment they might pronounce because of her presence in Ethan's bed, but opening her eyes might make the pain unbearable. She became aware of the heaviness in her arms, and when she tried to move her legs, they, too, felt weighed down. Her vague embarrassment was starting to be overcome by a sense of dreadful apprehension, which she tried to swallow down, but her throat refused to work properly. As her fear evolved further toward panic, she just managed to hold it back by telling herself that Ethan couldn't be far away. She opened her mouth to call for him, but what came out was a coughing croak.

"Easy, dear," said the same woman's voice.

Rachel tried to speak again, only to cough harder and longer. Confused and anxious, she pried open one eye. The light hit her pupil like the stab of a blade and she pressed her lid closed before she could observe any of her surroundings.

"Get Dr. Greyson," the woman ordered, and a pair of feet quickly left the room.

Rachel tried to calm her thoughts so she could reason clearly, but her mind moved sluggishly, sporadically. Who was Dr. Greyson? Why not send for Dr. Hogue if she was ill? Then she remembered the wound on her head Clyde had inflicted, silently questioning whether it had developed complications.

She recalled every detail of the prior night until she'd fallen asleep in Ethan's arms. Oh, *where was Ethan*?

A new voice, a man's, said in a soothing manner as he patted her hand, "Rachel, it's all right. Try to relax."

She let her body loosen and tried to focus on what the man was saying.

"Can you hear me?" he asked.

She nodded slightly, her head very heavy, and even so small an action was torturous.

"Good. Do you know where you are?"

With extreme effort she edged her head first one way and then the other.

"I'm Dr. Ben Greyson. Are you in pain, Rachel?"

She managed to whisper, "Where is Ethan?"

Utterly unprepared to take in the next sound that reached her, Rachel's body jerked at the strident voice of an electronic beep. It startled her into rigidity, her brain groping for an explanation. The beep came again, agonizingly undeniable in its repetition, and her mind went numb.

Now Dr. Greyson was standing over her and gently rubbing her shoulder. "Miss Winston… Rachel…you were injured but you are healing now."

No response.

"We've been taking care of you. Do you understand?"

Miss *Winston.* That was *not* who she was. Her entire inner being screamed in defiance, and she mouthed, "No. No."

"Can you feel my hand, Rachel?"

Oh, please, God, please, don't let this be real. And yet, with ruthless and crushing certainty she comprehended that it was. Somehow, it was.

With cruel mercy the pain in her head made her lips incapable of functioning further. If she'd been able to vocalize the magnitude of her anguish at that moment, the effort might have consumed much of her remaining clarity.

Dr. Greyson tried again. "Rachel, can you hear me?" Her monitors continued to produce evidence of her wakeful state, and the doctor went on stroking her shoulder while the nurses moved in and out of the room, but she did not respond.

Eventually, a new female voice asked softly from a few feet away, "How is she, Ben?"

Subtly anxious, Dr. Greyson said, "She moved her head, and whispered a few words."

The woman was closer now. "Rachel, I'm Dr. Snyder. We are so happy you've spoken today. If you can hear me, please move your fingers."

There was no reaction.

"Can you feel me touching you?"

Still nothing.

"Rachel, your friends and family have come to visit you every day, and we all want you to speak to us, and to get fully well."

Rachel lay as if all life had left her, wishing it were so.

The woman went on, "Are you feeling any pain?"

As tears pooled at the corners of Rachel's closed eyes, all she could force her dry mouth to whisper was, "Ethan."

James Olson, a lanky, fair-haired nurse assigned to Rachel's care, moved from her bedside and introduced Dr. Samantha Snyder for the third time, giving the physician an almost imperceptible shake of his head.

Rachel's eyes were open slightly but she turned her head away from the doctor.

"Good morning, Rachel," Dr. Snyder said, in that calm voice of wisdom that seemed at odds with her youth, red hair, and freckles. "How did your physical therapy go today?"

Rachel did gaze at her then, but she didn't reply. It was still so hard to speak. Not physically; her speech had returned rather quickly and with no impediments. It was just difficult to communicate, even to someone as imperturbable as this young woman, whose nurturing ministrations had helped see her through the first nightmarish days. As composed as she was, Dr. Snyder was also quite persistent.

"Well, whether you're willing to admit it or not, you've made remarkable progress lately and I think it's time you had a visitor." Dr. Snyder avoided eye contact as she checked Rachel's leg reflexes.

Rachel shook her head.

Dr. Snyder tugged the sheet down over Rachel's legs and pulled up a chair. "We've had a devil of a time keeping Ellen and your family away, you know, and our poor nurses are getting worn out fielding calls. Dr. Greyson agrees that a few short visits would do you good."

"I don't agree."

"What about Detective Dorely? Talking to him might benefit you both?"

When Rachel had been told that Jason was alive, and that he'd visited her numerous times, she'd been tempted to see him, but hesitated. Seeing him, or any of the others, would somehow tie her more rigidly to this place, this life. Clinging to the memories of those she loved so fiercely, who still seemed more real than the people she could actually touch, was the only way she could possess them now.

Dr. Snyder was watching her, making it clear that she wouldn't leave until she'd received an answer.

"Not yet." It took Rachel another moment before she said, "Dr. Snyder, visitors will want me to leave what has happened behind, which I don't want to do, and they'll have questions that I'm not up to answering."

"That's understandable, but—"

"And I have questions of my own, like whether the men who attacked us were caught? No one has been willing to discuss the shooting with me at all."

"Perhaps we were wrong, but we thought it best not to let you dwell on that day. Now may be a good time. Yes, Rachel, the ones who were not killed by the police were caught, even *the* Valenti, who is still in jail awaiting his trial." Again, she sat with quiet patience.

"I'm just not ready."

Dr. Snyder went on unabashedly, "Dr. Cook says you've been anything but cooperative during your sessions. He might help if you'd let him."

"Not him."

"Why not him?"

Hospital staff had told Rachel that Dr. Cook was one of the best psychiatrists in Chicago, but how could she open up to a man whose greatest satisfaction seemed to be studying her as a clinical case? He had countless questions but few answers and little forbearance. She felt a yearning to understand all that she had gone through and why her mind had dealt with her injury as it had, and it was this longing that kept her from closing herself off completely from outside influences.

Each day, all day and into the night, Rachel still wanted Ethan; to see him, talk with him, and to hold him. Her awakening had torn their life together from her grasp, leaving no possibility of reclaiming it, and she felt utterly empty without him. She also ached to see little Rose, Charlie, Kate, Maggie, True, Phillip, Juliet, Bert, Lewis, Dr. Hogue, and Stan. At times she felt as if she'd unwillingly abandoned them all. And yet, it was easier to bear even this emotion than to dwell on the fact that they'd never existed. Her caregivers wanted her to make new plans, but she willfully avoided thoughts of a future without any of them in it.

How *could* she have gained and lost them all in so short a span of time?

Finally, she shook her head and said to Dr. Snyder, "Dr. Cook just can't understand."

The young doctor sat there, considering. "What if I brought you someone who could understand?"

Rachel's expression showed her doubt that anyone could truly empathize with what she'd experienced.

"There's a Dr. Marcos Castillo who might be the right person. If he comes, will you give him a chance?"

To appease Dr. Snyder, Rachel reluctantly nodded.

"Great. Now, I also want to arrange—."

"Dr. Snyder, please, will you clarify one more thing first? I'm a little confused about how long I was in the coma." It was the first time she'd said it aloud. Coma. It was far too simple, too inadequate a word, but then, what had happened to her was much more powerful than any single word.

"Your injury happened just over ten weeks ago, and you've been conscious for two of those weeks."

"But I came back near the end of July. It has to be the middle of August now. The month written on the whiteboard must be wrong."

"No, Rachel, it's right. Today is July 13th."

Eight weeks. She'd lived the best part of her life within so short a period, unconscious. In that other world, however, she'd been given thirty days more than had passed here. For that extra month, regardless of its absence of reality, she was grateful, and she meant to hold onto her time in that world in whatever manner she could.

Pulling the blanket over her shoulders, her gaze already far off, she rolled away from her doctor and allowed her mind to reach back, deeper into her remembrances.

Dr. Snyder watched her for a few moments before gently patting her back and leaving her alone with her thoughts.

"Hello, Rachel," he said, his accent musically Hispanic, his expression open and congenial. "My name is Marcos." His complete lack of professional pretention was Rachel's first surprise upon meeting Dr. Castillo, the next being that his large brown eyes offered kindness with a hint of humor. His face was still youthfully firm, but his dark hair and closely-trimmed beard were salted with white. He stood a little shorter than average height, was brown-skinned and strongly built, and he wore khaki shorts and a collared shirt alive with bright tropical fish. "Dr. Snyder has told me that something extraordinary has happened to you."

"Yes," she admitted cautiously, "it was extraordinary."

"I'm visiting you now, when I have no obligations for the rest of the day, because I love to discover as much as I can about such things, to learn from them." He sat down in a chair not far from her bed, and confided, "I have seen and heard of many, many marvelous things, ever since I was a child. You see, my family comes from a village in Peru where the wise women have told mysterious tales for ages. They taught me a great deal, those women. Since coming to this country I have studied to become a psychiatrist." He softened his eyes and gave her a gentle smile, seeming to ask her forgiveness for the formality of his title, and continued, "This was my choice of calling because the journeys of the mind are the most fascinating of them all. The mind," he said, giving his forehead a couple of slight taps, "has reasons for its behavior, even if we do not recognize them."

It was quite a speech, without a single word of interrogation, so she asked slowly, "Then, do you think there was a *reason* my mind went to such a different time and place?"

"I have little doubt, and it intrigues me. Will you allow me to help you search for that reason?"

He waited without any sign of restlessness until she said, "How would you do that... Marcos?"

"By learning about the world that you experienced, all about it. Will you share it with me, Rachel?"

"There is almost too much to tell, and that makes it hard even to start."

"Ah, then perhaps I will tell a little more of my story, yes? I have found that one story may often lead to another."

He began by vividly describing experiences he'd had in his native village, and the cases he'd encountered later while in Peru, Seattle, and Chicago. Sometimes smiling fondly, sometimes expressing the awe of a still unexplainable occurrence, he concentrated his discourse on the people he'd cared for and the vast nature of the brain's capabilities, rather than on himself. Occasionally he stood and walked to the window, pausing to consider the world beyond the hospital before returning to his chair and continuing.

One of Rachel's nurses, Connie Bond, came and went to check Rachel's blood pressure and temperature, and later to bring in a snack, but she never interrupted Dr. Castillo. An hour became three, and as time passed, Rachel grew more and more captivated by this man's work, by his entire life, and started to trust in the possibility that he could help her understand her own. At last, after a thoughtful pause, Dr. Castillo stood by her bedside, and said, "I think you have listened for long enough. You are still in need of much rest. May I come to see you again tomorrow?"

He did not try to persuade or dominate, which helped her to answer, "Yes, please come. And, Marcos, thank you for helping me see that my case is not quite as strange as I had thought."

He smiled sincerely, saying, "My dear Rachel, it is our strangeness that makes us so wonderfully fascinating. My wife likes to tell me that my peculiarities make it impossible for her to leave me. Rest well, now."

He did come, and remained with her much of the day, allowing her whatever intervals she needed to form the words that would reveal her next experience. He refrained from interrupting her, instead giving his full attention and answering whatever questions she posed, until at last she came to the end, to her waking without Ethan, and her tears began to fall. Dr. Castillo came to her then and wrapped an arm around her shoulders, offering the same comfort he would have given a beloved daughter. He soothed her in a soft mixture of English and Spanish, and let her cry. After Rachel grew calmer, he gathered some tissues and placed them in her hand.

She blew her nose and looked up at him, into a face that held such compassion, such acceptance of all she'd told him that she struggled not to start crying again.

He understood her journey, as he seemed to understand everything else, and she believed he could help her. He walked over to the window and stood in quiet reflection.

For a terrible moment Rachel feared that he was about to tell her that she should put all of her imaginings behind her and just pick up the well-organized pieces of her old life. But when he returned to her bedside, what he said instead was, "My colleagues would maintain, perhaps rightly so, that we have not spoken long enough for me to reveal my thoughts, but you have confided a great deal, and I want to say at least this much." His gaze intensified. "It seems to me that you have been given a rare and yet burdensome gift, Rachel. You were allowed to see another life for yourself, one in which you were able to face the brutal attack of your youth, which you've kept secret so long. You accepted and returned the love of a good man, as well as an entire family. But all of these wonderful things have come at a high price. Now, you must bear the burden of learning to live without them."

She let his words permeate the emotional barricade she'd built around herself, and painfully accepted that this was indeed the price. "What if I can't let go of that world, Marcos? In some ways those people seem more genuine than anyone here."

"That is because they *were* genuine to you, Rachel. Those things *happened* within your mind. It is possible that you identify in a special way with that time and place, and that your psyche created the existence as a kind of refuge. You mentioned earlier that you have never visited such a town, but perhaps you did when you were a child?"

"No, I don't think I ever have."

After pausing, he said, "Your brain will continue to heal along with the rest of your body, many memories may return, and we will try to connect these two worlds of yours. And, Rachel, the people who love you here are more than willing to help, if you will only let them."

"Not yet, please."

He waited.

"I need to stop hating that I'm here before I see them."

"All right, dear Rachel, for now. That next step can wait for a time, while you and I work very hard."

During one of their meetings that followed, attempting to lessen the resentment of her return that aggravated Rachel's recovery, Marcos suggested that she explore each detail of her experience from the medical point of view. He hoped that by learning the scientific explanations and intricacies of her case she would gradually gain acceptance, and the emotional knots that bound her to that other world would loosen.

Agreeing to research her own case, Rachel's questioning soon grew to an investigative intensity that delighted Dr. Snyder and Dr. Greyson as well as the nurses. She was communicating, and it mattered little that she badgered them for every aspect of her injury, their care, and her reactions to it. She became more responsive to the endless rounds of physical therapy, raising hope that she would be walking confidently on her own very soon.

Dr. Castillo continued to meet with her almost daily, always encouraging her attempts to find deeper descriptions and hypotheses, but Rachel could see that he was more watchful and cautious in his delight of her progress than the rest of her caregivers. She sensed that he knew that her outward attempts to subdue the memories of the people in Idaho City were less sincere than her unreasonable hope of somehow regaining what had slipped away. He also seemed well aware that this inability to accept the finality of her loss kept her from reaching out to those who identified with her present life.

Dr. Snyder had already told Rachel a good deal about her first days in the hospital, about the surgeries to remove the bullets from her head and leg, and that the medical staff had feared for almost a week that she would not survive before her body settled into a calmer rhythm. By the eighth day she'd regained good cough and gag reflexes and the tracheostomy tube had been withdrawn. The following day her swallow reflex had returned and the feeding tubes were removed. Catheters had eventually been replaced with absorbent briefs. All of this and more Rachel had learned, but she felt she had only scratched the surface.

Today Dr. Greyson was just checking the improved muscle tone of Rachel's legs when Dr. Snyder peeked in on them. Having both doctors present was an unusual opportunity that Rachel took advantage of at once. "If you two have a little time, I'd like to ask you a few more questions."

"Ask away," said Dr. Snyder, coming closer to her bed.

Rachel picked up the small paper tablet that Carlos had given her for taking notes, and probed, "Well, I know that after I was medically stable you tried to bring me out of the coma, but how often did you try, and what methods did you use?"

They looked at each other before Dr. Snyder responded with a short laugh, "Quite often, and just about everything, to tell you the truth."

Dr. Greyson, who was generally somewhat less candid, said, "On about day nine, we started your coma arousal therapy."

Rachel's expression showed her dubious reception to the term.

"What exactly is coma arousal therapy?"

"It's a technique that's been very effective for years, and is improving all the time. Basically, it is a form of treatment that stimulates the senses to bring a patient back to a state of awareness."

"Please go on, specifically."

"An example would be when we used bright lights to stimulate your pupil reaction, as well as your blinking reflex and head movements. For auditory responses we held various sources close to your ears."

"Like soothing music?"

Dr. Greyson's expression signaled for Dr. Snyder to take over. "Actually, after our initial attempts failed, we used anything *but* soothing sounds. The goal was to get an active reaction from your brain rather than let it be lulled into a deeper comatic state."

"Then what did you use?"

"You didn't react much to anything recorded, no matter how loud we played it, so we tried things like clapping blocks and clanging pipes." Dr. Snyder admitted, "We created such a racket that we had to clear the rooms around yours."

"Oh."

"As you know, we're still doing a lot of the same physical therapies, but earlier, our respiratory therapists would periodically, and very briefly, restrict your intake of air to get you to breathe more deeply. The last thing you needed was to develop pneumonia."

Dr. Greyson spoke up again. "Your therapies used to take at least twelve hours a day. Thankfully, we've been able to do away with some of your less pleasant touch therapies." At Rachel's raised her eyebrows, he confessed, "When nothing else worked, we, um, pricked your fingers and toes. As extreme as that may sound, this particular therapy might have been quite instrumental in your recovery. *All* of the different therapies have played a role."

"But we'll never know which ones were the most effective?"

"Not with any certainty," he said.

Rachel's gaze went to Dr. Snyder, who nodded her agreement. Checking her notes, Rachel said, "Okay, that covers sight, sound, and touch. What about smell and taste?"

Dr. Greyson said, "For smell, one of us held ammonia, or garlic, or vinegar under your nose. But as I recall you usually reacted most to the smell of cinnamon."

The pen stilled. Rachel remembered the scent of cinnamon in Ethan's kitchen, just before he'd come to her. "Did... did you use cinnamon the night before I gained consciousness?"

Dr. Snyder watched Rachel closely, concerned by her sudden change in manner.

"I honestly don't remember," said Dr. Greyson.

Dr. Snyder was still studying Rachel as she addressed Dr.

Greyson. "Yes, Ben, we did. I remember ordering it from the kitchen. I held it to your nose, Rachel, and I put some on your tongue."

Rachel stared at them both, and then slowly eased back in her bed, her pad and pen in her lap.

Dr. Snyder tried to regain Rachel's interest, to divert her from whatever had saddened her. "We tried lots of different things on your tongue: chili sauce, mustard, lemon juice, salt... Rachel, are you feeling all right?"

"I'd like to rest now, please."

"Sure. We've covered a lot of ground. We'll see you later," said Dr. Greyson, and they left the room.

Rachel closed her eyes and began to summon the memory of her last night with Ethan. She could almost feel his touch and hear his voice, and then an inner voice said with cruel indisputability, *Ethan doesn't exist.* Her chest tightened, but after a moment she silently responded, *He* does *exist. He's still alive, inside of me. All of them are.* She found herself picturing each of their faces, her mind drifting from one to the next.

Letting her thoughts float, she wondered whether Dr. Hogue's baby had been a boy or a girl. She hadn't been there to help deliver it, as she should have been.

24

"Yes, I have noticed it," said Dr. Castillo pensively. "She does seem to be withdrawing again."

"Over the last two days she's put less into her physical activities, too," said Dr. Snyder from behind her desk.

Dr. Castillo, seated before her, sighed heavily. "I'm afraid she may be slipping back into her old silence. She said very little during our last session." They were both quiet for a moment, and then he offered, "It may be time she was exposed to her friends and family, despite her reluctance."

"I've been thinking the same thing. Perhaps it should no longer be optional." She lifted an eyebrow at Marcos.

He hesitated, sighed again, and finally nodded. "But we must be very watchful of her reaction, and terminate the meeting if she becomes upset."

Ultimately, they brought Dr. Greyson and even Dr. Cook in on the decision, and it was unanimously decided that Jason would be the first person to see her. He was not only one of her closest friends, they reasoned, but also a police officer who'd asked repeatedly to speak with her. If there wasn't exactly an *immediate* need to discuss the circumstances surrounding her being wounded, there was little question that doing so would prove helpful to the Valenti case. There was also the fact, Dr. Greyson reminded them, that Jason had threatened to barge into her room before long regardless of any doctors' orders. All four physicians felt that she was well enough for the short interview, and they hoped it would do her far more good than she anticipated.

In preparation for the clandestine meeting, her physical therapy schedule was intensified. The more uncooperative Rachel was, the more relentless the therapists became, and her unwilling and aching muscles began to react notwithstanding her despondency. During one early morning session, the therapist put Rachel's walker in the closet and leaned her cane just out of reach. With an encouraging assistant on each side in case of a mishap, Rachel took her first unassisted steps, and even she seemed somewhat pleased by this success.

The meeting with Jason was secretly scheduled for a few days later.

Rachel absently wondered why she was receiving so much unwanted attention, but she didn't ask, choosing instead to assume that this was no more than the next phase of her treatment. Then again, she thought, as the heightened activity continued and the staff seemed to grow even more cheerful, perhaps they were up to something.

After she'd been browbeaten into taking an early morning shower by herself, with the nurse standing just outside her door, a clean hospital gown had been suspiciously inaccessible, giving Rachel little room for objections to wearing some clothes Ellen had left at the hospital front desk days before. Feeling a bit fragile after the shower, Rachel nevertheless managed to dress without assistance. Afterward, the nurse had helped her dry and brush her hair. At last the staff seemed satisfied with the thoroughness of her torture, and had left Rachel sitting in an upholstered chair and staring out the window.

Dr. Castillo strode casually into her room three hours earlier than his usual time, and said, his eyes smiling warmly, "You look beautiful today, Rachel. *Hermosa*. And this is a good thing because I have a surprise for you."

With no more warning than this, Jason walked in, crouched beside her, and gently placed his huge hand over hers on the arm of the chair. "Hello, counselor," he said softly.

Shaken, Rachel lifted accusing eyes to Dr. Castillo. He met her gaze evenly and said, "Talk to him, my dear."

Jason searched her pale, thin face, waiting for her to speak. When she didn't, he said, "You can't know how good it is to see you. Dr. Castillo told me you weren't feeling ready, but I didn't give him much of a choice."

Rachel stared at her lap.

"How are you doing?"

Rachel tried to look at him, but failed. She could hear the anxiety Jason was trying to conceal, but she couldn't relieve it.

Searching her downcast face, he said, "I thought you'd want to know, Tim Granger pulled through, too."

Tim Granger, the tall, shy officer who was shot in front of her apartment while trying to protect her. So, Tim had lived. She had wondered many times, hoping he had.

"The bullet went through his arm and his lung, but Tim's tough, still determined to get back to regular rounds. He keeps the slug in a box next to the medal of valor the department gave him."

She could feel how closely he was watching her, that he was growing uncertain about whether he was saying the right things. *This is Jason*, she told herself, *your friend. Look at him. Say something.*

Jason went on, "Carlo... Carlo and his guards, Jack and Lenny, they didn't make it."

Carlo was dead? And Jack and Lenny, Jason's two close friends?

Rachel lifted her head at last and looked into his careworn face. Behind his brave façade she could see the pain resulting from these losses, and the undeserved guilt and anguish for failing them all.

"Jason," she said quietly, "I'm so sorry."

He lowered his head and bit his lip.

Very slowly, Rachel lifted her hand and placed it on the top of his head. He drew in a rough breath and squeezed his eyes closed, struggling. As her fingers caressed his hair, he reached out and brought his arms around her, and when Rachel leaned forward and pulled Jason closer, Dr. Castillo stepped into the hallway and soundlessly closed the door behind him.

"There is something I have not told you, Rachel," said Dr. Castillo the next day, "but I believe you should know. Several days before you awoke, they were preparing to move you to your mother's home."

"My *mother's* home?"

"Yes, the doctors had no way of knowing when you might regain consciousness. Your mother insisted, and your father agreed, that you should not be moved to any other facility for ongoing care. She suggested, strongly, that you be brought there so she could oversee your well-being. I understand that she had hired two nurses. At that time, the hospital staff was teaching her and Ellen to carry out your mental and physical therapies. Everyone had agreed to move you soon. Then you started showing signs of higher cognizance, and the staff here, as well as your mother and Ellen, worked very hard to bring you out of the coma."

Her mother had helped with her therapy? Her mother, who had always been distant, or at least distracted, where Rachel was concerned. It was nearly impossible to picture Melanie Winston in a hospital room day after day, attempting to coax her back to life.

"I ask that you reflect on this, and to remember it when your parents and Ellen come to see you this morning."

She nodded her head, still in wonderment, and then looked at him appreciatively. "You know, Marcos, you're an exceptionally wise man. Not always easy, but always very wise. Thank you for telling me now. I'm not sure it would have meant the same earlier."

He smiled with fondness and walked out, passing Connie as she came in carrying Rachel's orange juice and yogurt.

Nervous with anticipation over the upcoming meeting, Rachel left the snack untouched. Dr. Castillo's words returned to her. "...your mother and Ellen worked very hard to bring you out of the coma."

She was sitting by the window when Dr. Castillo brought the visitors in, with Ellen hanging back as Dillon and Melanie Winston approached. Dillon came to her cautiously, put his hand on her shoulder, and gave her a watery smile. "It's so good to see you awake, Rachel, so very good." When he moved aside slightly, Melanie startled Rachel by reaching out and embracing her tightly. "You're here, you're with us again," she murmured into her daughter's hair, clutching her for a moment longer before holding her at arm's length and taking her in.

Rachel stared at the woman who had never hugged her like that before, the mother who now seemed much changed. She wore little make-up and her clothes were simple and neat rather than extravagantly fashionable, but the most startling change was the genuine affection in her eyes.

Melanie watched Rachel's expression and sensed her thoughts. "I got into the habit of wearing comfortable things around the hospital. Ellen and I," she added, waving Ellen closer, "we helped with your exercises for awhile."

Rachel still couldn't quite imagine Melanie turning and bathing her body, massaging her muscles, bending her inert limbs, and performing even less pleasant tasks, but evidently she had. Wanting to say something appreciative, Rachel shifted her eyes from her mother to her father, but thoughts of how little Melanie and Dillon, her *real* parents, were like Juliet and Bert tried to take precedence. With a small inner groan and silent condemnation, Rachel managed to say in a weak voice, "Thank you, all of you."

When Melanie smiled and stepped back, Ellen couldn't keep herself still any longer. She took Rachel's hand and pressed it to her cheek. "Thank the Lord..." Her throat threatened to tighten but she cleared it with a cough, sniffed, and said, "Now, now, we won't be staying long, but we want you to know that we're here if you need us."

Dear Ellen, thought Rachel. How many times had she wished she could share everyone and everything in Idaho City with her? Her friend stood so close, generous and helpful as always, and ready to hear it all whenever the time felt right.

Rachel looked again at Melanie. Here, incredible yet undeniable, was the mother's love that Rachel had doubted much of her life. She wanted to reach out and open up to her mother, to them all, but it was still too soon. She did manage to say, "You've all been so good to me, and I'm grateful. Dr. Castillo and the hospital staff are making sure I improve every day."

"They'd better be," Ellen said, smiling at Dr. Castillo. She handed Rachel a gift bag. "I brought you a few puzzles, which Dr. Castillo said would be helpful at this stage."

"How thoughtful, Ellen. Thank you."

"I'm sorry to have to say it," Dr. Castillo said quietly, "but Rachel should rest now."

Without delay or complaint, Melanie kissed Rachel's cheek as Dillon murmured a soft good-bye and Ellen squeezed her hand. All three cast Marcos expressions of gratitude and affection as they passed him. In a whisper Marcos said to Rachel, "I'll be right back," and he followed them out.

Rachel stared at the door as it closed, and then studied the skyline, reflecting for several minutes until Dr. Castillo returned.

He came to her chair and looked outside with her, his hands in his pockets, a small smile on his lips. "You pleased them very much, Rachel."

"I'm grateful for all they've done, and for your asking them to come today."

"Ahh, gratitude," he said with deep satisfaction. "None of us can find happiness without it, my dear. It is perhaps the most enlightening of all our emotions."

She held his words in her mind while she observed him, and then said, "As you must have known, I was more ready to see them than I'd thought."

"You were, indeed, and you will be ready to leave the hospital very soon. Now you will advance more quickly outside of these walls."

"That's a frightening thought."

"You are well enough to find new things that bring you contentment."

Almost to herself, Rachel said, "I still don't see how, not without recapturing what I had in that small town."

"You will learn, and it will come."

After standing tranquilly for quite awhile, he stepped back and motioned to the bed. "Will you rest now, Rachel? You have had quite a day." She complied, and once she had settled in, he sat on the couch, facing her. "Would you like to hear a song my mother used to sing to me when I was a small child?"

A little surprised, she then realized she shouldn't have been. It was so like him to share such a talent just to ease her mind. She nodded and lay back.

In an untutored yet naturally rich voice, Marcos began to sing an ancient Spanish lullaby, and although she understood few of the words, their essence reached her heart as they told of a land bordered by majestic mountains that reached high into the heavens. It was a lovely song, an exceptionally lovely gift.

As she listened, from the corner of her eye Rachel saw two nurses pause in the hallway outside her room, and smile at each other before continuing down the hall.

It had taken a bit of talking on Ellen's part to convince Rachel to take a stroll around the halls, but as the two of them made their way past the family lounge, their arms linked together, Rachel was glad she had agreed to the walk. Ellen had been so undemanding, so tolerant, coming every day after work to see her and to tell her about the happenings at the office. Rachel nodded politely, and asked the appropriate questions, but had no real interest in such things. Although she had not yet told Ellen, she didn't intend to return to work, not there anyway. It seemed strange to her now that she had found it fulfilling to spend so much of her life thoroughly devoted to a law firm.

Talking had become easier with practice and the passing of days, and Rachel had eventually told Ellen all about her other life, her other family, and everything that had happened between her and Ethan. Their talks had brought them close again, perhaps closer than ever.

"Dr. Castillo," said Ellen under her breath, as they toured the hallway, "now there's a man with charm. As always, the good ones are already taken." She glanced at Rachel speculatively. "He told me he's ready to release you as soon as you give the word."

"He's told me that, too."

"But you need more time?"

"Perhaps I do. I've told Jason everything I can remember about the morning of the shooting, which I can recall better than many things. I'll probably be up to serving as a witness by the time the Valenti trial rolls around, but the thought of going back to the firm just doesn't appeal to me. So I keep asking myself, what *will* I do? It's hard to choose a direction, to make any plans. So yes, Ellen, I need at least a few days more. Maybe then it will be easier."

"You'll be staying with your mother for awhile?"

"She's asked me to, and she's been wonderful, but I'd rather be on my own. Unfortunately, Dr. Castillo agrees with my mother."

Rachel and Ellen made two more rounds before stopping at her door. "Thanks, Ellen. You're so good to me."

"Is there anything else I can do to help?" Ellen's earnest expression demanded a real answer.

"Your visits help me a great deal, truly, but it still feels like my happiness is locked back in Idaho City. I can't help fantasizing about going back, or Ethan being here, making my life full and rich, and me introducing him to you. Short of that, I'm trying to work up to contentment, like Dr. Castillo keeps saying I should, but that seems just a little out of reach." She hugged her friend, and said, "Don't mind me. Things will be all right, Ellen. Good night."

Several days later, Rachel was standing before her hospital closet trying to decide what she was going to wear for her departure the next morning. She'd been expecting her mother but was surprised when Melanie came in accompanied by both Dr. Castillo and Ellen. They stood around her exchanging glances, Melanie looking especially uneasy.

"What's this?" Rachel asked. "Ellen, why aren't you at work?"

"I've taken a couple of days off."

"And why would you do that?"

"Rachel," said Dr. Castillo, "please sit down. We have something to tell you." He gave Ellen a go-ahead nod as Rachel perched on the side of her bed.

"I wanted to talk it over with Dr. Castillo and your mother before I told you," Ellen started.

"Told me what?"

"Remember what you said the other day, about your happiness being tied to Idaho City?" Ellen didn't wait for an answer. "Well, I've been doing some research. I made some calls to the Idaho Historical Library in Boise and to the state museum, and I contacted some local historians in Idaho City. I checked out some of the places and events you've described, as well as the people."

Rachel's gaze had grown more intense with each sentence. "Tell me."

"They were real, Rachel. Ethan was real, and all of the rest of them."

"Real?" whispered Rachel, her mind racing. She stared at Ellen, then at the file of papers she was holding, and finally turned to Dr. Castillo. "But I don't remember *ever* reading about Idaho City. How could I have known?"

Dr. Castillo stepped closer and said gently, "With your kind of injury it is not uncommon to lose memories, as we've discussed. It is possible that they will return, in time."

She turned anxious eyes back to her friend. "Please, Ellen, who did you find?"

"I found Dr. Hogue, and his wife, and their baby girl..."

"They had a girl?" Rachel's voice cracked. "Oh, Ellen."

"And Dr. Willis, Sheriff Pinkham, the attorney, Frank Miller..."

"And the Milfords?"

"Yes, Rachel, all of them."

Rachel's tears began to build. "And you found him, Ellen?"

Ellen came and sat beside her. "Yes, I found Ethan."

Rachel began to cry, reaching out for Ellen, and through her pain and relief, she pictured Ethan walking beside her once again and gently smiling down at her face. She felt her mother's hand softly rubbing her back, and managed to slow her tears. She eased away from Ellen, and gave her a watery, grateful smile.

Ellen smiled back, saying, "It's amazing how accurate you were, my friend. There was only one thing that was different. Ethan Stonehill had a daughter, but her name was Winnie, short for Winifred."

Rachel remembered Rose's room, and the care Ethan had taken to decorate it with rose buds. She thought of the curtains she'd made. Then she shook her head, and looked back at Ellen. After a moment, she said, "I have to know, Ellen, but I'm not sure I want to ask."

Ellen knew her question before she posed it. "What happened to them? Well, the Milfords did very well, so well, in fact, that there are still many of them in the Boise area."

Rachel steadied herself. "And... what happened to Ethan?"

"He didn't remarry. Winnie grew up and married a farmer in Boise. They had five children, and Ethan lived long enough to meet each of his grandchildren." Searching through her file and pulling out a piece of paper, Ellen's eyes softened as she passed the sheet to Rachel. "This is Ethan's funeral notice."

Slowly, Rachel eyes traveled over the words, her breathing growing ragged and more tears falling, the finality of this printed summary of his life and death stirring a new form of grief.

After she'd read it twice, and when she didn't speak or look up, Ellen asked, "Would you like to see the other things I found? There's something else I think you'll want to know."

Lowering the notice reluctantly, her voice hollow now, Rachel said, "No, Ellen, nothing more. I'm sorry, but not right now. You are all so dear to have come but, please, I'd like to be alone for a while, okay?"

Receiving a silent signal from Dr. Castillo, Ellen and Melanie hugged Rachel and quietly left her. Dr. Castillo sat with her a while longer, saying nothing and asking nothing of her, just humming very softly.

25

Leaving the hospital was proving to be even harder than Rachel had imagined. There had been at least a dozen people to thank and bid farewell, but at last the time had come to separate from those who'd given so much of themselves on her behalf. Melanie had come to pick her up a few minutes earlier but had discreetly gone in search of a cup of coffee to allow Rachel the time she wanted with the people remaining in her room.

Dr. Castillo and Dr. Snyder stood before her, wearing smiles of pride and optimism. Her two favorite nurses, James and Connie, had also come to see her off. They'd become so dear to Rachel that she was finding it difficult to say her goodbyes without breaking down, which she was determined not to do.

Efficient, big-hearted Connie kept brushing at her eyes as she fussed over little things in the room that didn't really need attention. When she could postpone this leave-taking no longer, she came over to where Rachel stood beside the bed and said, "If you change your mind and want me to come help at your mother's house, you let me know."

"I'll be fine, Connie. But please come as a friend. It would be so good to see you."

Connie nodded, hugged her briefly, her lips tightening to restrain her emotions, and stepped aside.

James bent his good-looking young face and six-foot, six-inch frame close, his mop of curly brown hair falling forward, and gave her a slow bear hug that lifted her five inches off the floor. When he set her down he said, "You've been nothing but trouble, you know."

Rachel laughed even as her eyes grew shiny. "Yes, I know. Will you come see me, too?"

"If these two ever give me any time off," he said with a quick glance in the direction of her doctors. "They usually can't manage around here without me, but I'll come."

"We can *probably* spare you for an hour or two," Dr. Snyder put in. Then there was a quiet pause. "How about you two giving us a moment alone with Rachel," said Dr. Snyder, so Connie and James gave her a final wave and left.

Rachel faced her doctors, took a huge breath, and let it out slowly. "I thought all of the other good-byes were hard, but just what can I say to the pair of you?"

Dr. Castillo, as he previously had done in countless ways, came to her rescue. "It has been a remarkable journey."

"It has been that."

"And it has only started, my dear, this journey of yours. From here you can go anywhere you wish."

"Except back to where I was."

"That's true, but you can keep the many things you have learned."

Her future. It was still a thing she would rather not face.

"I will see you in just a few days," Dr. Castillo reminded her.

Rachel nodded and turned to Dr. Snyder. "But I won't be seeing you in a few days."

"Not if you behave yourself. I'll call to check in, though. And I've got your mother's number in case you're resting."

Rachel smiled as she said, "You'll probably have all sorts of free time now that I'm leaving."

"Are you kidding? I'll be writing papers about you for weeks. You'll undoubtedly make me famous. Medical journals will be screaming for every detail about what you've taught us."

"What *I've* taught *you*?"

Dr. Snyder became serious. "You've taught this staff a great deal, Rachel. We have so much more experience now that we can offer to other patients. And since you let Marcos record your sessions and you've given all of us permission to publish our findings, many more will benefit."

"I hope so."

Melanie looked in the room and Rachel motioned her inside. Reaching into her suitcase, Rachel pulled out four white, overstuffed envelopes. Two of them, bearing the names of the nurses who had just left the room, she gave to Dr. Snyder, asking, "Will you please give these to James and Connie? *These* are for you two," Rachel added, giving an envelope to each of the doctors. "Ellen helped me with them."

Glancing at each other, the doctors accepted their gifts.

"Do you want us to open them now?" asked Dr. Snyder.

"Yes, please."

Dr. Castillo opened his, read the contents, and shook his head, smiling broadly. "Rachel. A round-trip for two to Lima," he said still shaking his head. He looked at her then, and saw how much his acceptance would mean to her. "I know you well enough not to try to refuse so generous a gift. This is very kind of you, my dear."

Dr. Snyder took one look at what was in her envelope, gave a most unprofessional whoop, and said, "A two-week stay in Kona, Hawaii! Well, I *have* to take some time off now." Hugging Rachel warmly, she said, "Thank you, Rachel. Thank you." She grinned at the envelope. "Hawaii. Can I ask where James and Connie are going?"

"They'll be heading for Hawaii too, but you'll each be on a different island. I didn't want to take the chance that you'd go over there and talk shop instead of relax."

"They'll be thrilled," said Dr. Snyder.

When things grew quiet, Rachel knew that the time had come to go and that she'd better not let it drag out, or her stiff upper lip would begin to tremble. "Well, you have things to do and we'd better be on our way." She hugged Dr. Snyder and murmured her thanks one more time.

Dr. Castillo helped Rachel into the hospital-mandated wheel chair, and insisted on accompanying them as Melanie wheeled the cart with Rachel's suitcases and flowers out of the hospital. After stowing the suitcases in Melanie's car near the entrance, Dr. Castillo gave Rachel a smile. "I'll see you on Wednesday. You know how to reach me if you want to share any thoughts before then. *Vaya con Dios*."

"You too, Marcos."

As the car pulled away from the hospital, Rachel looked back and watched him, still standing with his hands in his pockets in front of the building. When they turned a corner and he disappeared from her sight, she faced forward and stared at the windshield, feeling a painful hollowness in her stomach that refused to relent for miles.

The car slowed to a stop in front of the Winston's five-bay garage, and Melanie turned off the ignition. She was just reaching for the door handle when Rachel touched her shoulder. "Mother, please, can we talk for a minute?" Melanie turned to her, curious but a little concerned. Rachel continued, "I want you to know how much it means to me, all you've done, all you're still doing."

Melanie looked down for a moment. "I wanted to help you, Rachel. No, that's not quite accurate. I *needed* to help you." She met Rachel's eyes then. "I guess I've suspected all along that I wasn't much of a mother, but after the accident I... well, I started really caring about what kind of a mother I was." She sighed and softly rubbed her forehead, as if trying to massage away the pain of remembering. "Those first few days, when they said you only had a fifty-fifty chance to survive, I just couldn't accept it. You'd always been so strong. But I had to face the reality of your condition, and that forced me to realize what your death would mean to me. Those were terrible days, when you were in critical condition and I knew I could lose you without ever having been the mother you needed."

Rachel placed her hand over Melanie's, encouraging her to continue.

"Those long hours, sitting by your bed, they gave me plenty of time to think. Eventually, I swore that if I ever got the chance I'd do a better job." She smiled, a little embarrassed. "I even prayed, Rachel. It had been an age since I'd done that. And, now, here you are," she said.

"Here you are."

"It wasn't only you that made us... a little distant. I'm so glad, with Marco's help, I was able to tell you what happened to me when I was young. If I'd been able to tell you a long time ago about the rape and what Grandpa Simon did, it might have made a big difference between us. I kept myself aloof, from you and everyone else."

"You told me as soon as you could. I just hate what you went through, all alone, for so many years."

"Well, we've got today and lots of tomorrows to work with. How about we start by getting my things inside?"

Rachel had finished unpacking and was just sitting down to write a few thank-you notes when there was a knock at her bedroom door.

"Come on in, Mother," she said from her chair at the teak desk.

"It's me," said Ellen, stepping in.

"Well, hello." Rachel put down her pen and stood. Ellen was holding a wooden box the size of a brief case, which looked dimly familiar.

"How are you?" Ellen asked as she crossed the room.

"I'm doing well, really. My mother and I had quite a talk. She's been incredible through all of this, hasn't she?"

"Yes, she has. Almost losing you was the hardest shock of her life. The change is one *good* thing that's come from your experience."

"And I'm getting a bit better every day."

"Your doctors are so proud of you." Ellen hesitated, then said, "They believe it will be good for you to see what I've brought with me."

"That sounds a little mysterious. What did you bring?" She led Ellen to the edge of the bed and they both sat down.

Ellen said, "Did Dr. Castillo tell you what I was going to show you?"

"He said he wanted to discuss what your research uncovered, but nothing specific."

Ellen bit her lip and frowned. "I thought he'd mention this to you before I did."

"Mention what, Ellen?"

Instead of answering, Ellen hesitantly opened the lid to the box in her lap, and reached inside. Pulling out Rachel's old bullwhip, she placed it in her lap.

Rachel closed her fingers around the grip, her eyes tracing the whip from its tip to its handle. She turned it slightly until she could see the small, roughly made cross; the cross that she had imagined Lewis carving on his baptismal day. Tenderly, she ran her thumb back and forth over the scored surface.

The feel of this whip then brought back another memory as vivid as any reality, of Kate pinned against the back of a building in the darkness. Rachel could feel herself lashing Kate's attacker nearly to death, could hear his cries, and Stan vowing that he would never forgive those men. She even could feel the warmth of Ethan's arms encircling her as she stood shaken and bleeding. She took a long, steadying breath.

"Lewis' whip," she said aloud.

With wary hesitation, Ellen said, "Probably."

Rachel raised her head and eyed Ellen. "What do you mean?"

Still cautious, Ellen said, "I mean it probably belonged to Lewis Freeman a long time ago."

"Ellen..."

"That's part of what I was going to explain the other day, what I thought Dr. Castillo would mention. Rachel, is this box familiar to you at all?"

"I'm not sure. What does it have to do with the whip, and Lewis?"

"Weeks ago Jason got the key to your apartment to search for evidence. After the police went through everything, Jason gave me the key so I could water your plants."

"Ellen, I don't see how...."

"When I told Jason about my research he told me about this box, thinking it might be useful. Now I think it may hold some answers." From the box, Ellen pulled a file that looked like the one she'd brought to the hospital the day before. "I told you that Ethan and the others actually lived, but I didn't get a chance to tell you that the Milfords are your ancestors."

"My *ancestors*?"

"Yes, Rachel, they are. You must have gathered this information yourself. You must have looked into your genealogy, maybe years ago, before we ever met." Ellen opened the file and handed her a chart.

Rachel's hands were unsteady as she took the long, white sheet of paper and stared at it. There were their names; Bert Milford, Juliet Peterson Milford, and True Milford, then the names of a few other ancestors before it showed her grandfather, Simon Winston, her father, Dillon Winston, and, at last, Rachel.

"Look, Rachel," Ellen said, pointing to his name, "True was your great-great-great grandfather."

To make it factual, Rachel repeated, "True is my ancestor. *My* ancestor."

"He is indeed, and from what I can tell, he was a great deal like you've described him. Lewis must have given this whip to True, or to one of True's children, and it's been passed all the way down to you."

Still speaking with stunned softness, Rachel said, "Then all of them *are* my *family*, True and Bert and Juliet. Even Grandpa Milford."

"All of them."

It took a moment longer for Rachel to reason out the rest. "But, even so, how did I know so much about Ethan? Unless... Ellen, is he one of my ancestors too?"

"No, Rachel, he's not. I found his death notice and a few other records, but nothing that showed the two families ever coming together."

"Maybe I just ran across his name when I was researching, and my mind made up the rest."

After a pause, Ellen asked, "Do you think it's that simple?"

"Was... was there a Rachel Milford?"

"No, there wasn't, at least none that I discovered."

"Did you find any article about what happened to Kate and me, or to those two men?"

"Not a word."

"Then Ethan, and Stan, and the others were never caught for what they did that night."

"Apparently not."

Rachel scanned the family chart once more, her eyes filled with awe. "I can't tell you what this means to me, to have this tie to them. I still miss them all terribly, but somehow this makes it easier. This, at least, I can hold on to."

"Maybe there's another way to hold onto them," Ellen said. "And it might help if you had something to nudge you forward."

Rachel asked affectionately, "Have you and Dr. Castillo been cooking up something else?"

"Well, yes, in a way... Rachel, there are still Milfords living in Idaho, relatives of yours. And there are some Stonehills, too." Leaving Rachel no time to dwell on this announcement, Ellen pulled an envelope from her purse.

Rachel's expression was wary. "For me?"

"Open it, Rachel."

Casting a suspicious look at Ellen, Rachel opened the envelope and drew out its contents; a ticket to Boise, Idaho. "Ellen..."

"Before you say anything, I want you to check the dates. You won't be leaving for two more months. Dr. Castillo said you should be doing very well by then."

"What would I find in Boise?"

"People to talk to, places to explore, I don't know. And neither will you until you get there."

Rachel gazed at the ticket, but she said, "I have people to talk to here."

Ellen said slowly, intently, "Rachel, his descendants are still there."

"I wouldn't know any of them, and none of them would be Ethan."

"My dear friend, you *do* know one of them," Ellen said, and hurried on. "I think you met him years ago when you were researching. Why else would I have found his name and number in the box? I didn't have a clue who he was but, because of his name, Nathan Stonehill, I called him. He not only remembers you very fondly, he seemed truly concerned that you'd been injured."

Rachel squinted at Ellen, trying hard to recall any of this, but shook her head in surrender.

Ellen went on. "Even if you don't remember meeting him, you have, and Nathan wants to talk with you, to see you. He would have flown out for a visit but Dr. Castillo said it was too soon. He has a sister and two brothers. You could meet them, and the Milfords."

"Ellen, please, slow down, and try to understand. These people wouldn't be the ones I…I'm familiar with."

"But isn't it just conceivable that they'd be worth getting to know?"

"They're probably wonderful people, just not *my* people. I appreciate your going to all of this trouble, but what I'd really like is for you to keep the ticket. Trade it for one you can use, one to Hawaii or the Bahamas. Will you do that for me?" Very gently, Rachel gave the airline ticket back to Ellen.

She accepted it, but Ellen hadn't finished trying. "Rachel, just listen for one more minute. Maybe Nathan is worth the effort of your getting reacquainted. I asked Dr. Castillo and he agrees that it's possible, just possible…"

"What's possible?"

"That your imagination was able to create Ethan because you were already close to Nathan."

Rachel eyed her friend, and for several seconds she considered, hoping. But this hopefulness, though clear and sharp, was brief. She sighed deeply and shook her head. "If that were true, I'd remember him."

"Rachel…"

"No, please."

"But I haven't told you—"

"You've told me enough, Ellen, please." Rachel was struggling to take in so much so fast. Apprehension, then resignation and, finally, gratitude showed in her face. Reaching out, she took Ellen's hand. "Thank you for bringing me the box and all you found."

Squeezing then patting Rachel's hand, Ellen hesitated before saying, "I hope you'll think it over, about going to Idaho, I mean."

Rachel searched Ellen's earnest face, and then looked inward. At last she said, "Ethan once told me that people have to choose whether to hold onto what keeps them from happiness, or to push the old pain aside so there's room to start again. I believe he was right." Her eyes met Ellen's. "I will think about going, Ellen. Just give me a little time."

Offering a smile, Ellen said, "I can see how tired you are. I'd better let you get some rest." She stood up. "Where would you like me to put these records?"

"On the nightstand, please, where I can reach them, and my whip on the desk. Just knowing the Milfords are really a part of my family is so... consoling." She glanced over the family chart once more before returning it to Ellen.

Replacing the file in the box, Ellen moved the lamp aside and set it nearby.

As Rachel lifted the whip up to her, Ellen said as she accepted it, "To think of all the times I wondered how you happened to come by this thing. Now I think we know." She shook her head in lingering wonder as she walked to the desk and, looping the whip neatly, placed it there.

She returned to Rachel and asked, "Will you consider lying down for awhile so I can see that you're taking care of yourself?"

Smiling, Rachel said, "Yes, ma'am." She kicked off her shoes and lay back on the pillows. "There, happy?"

"Good girl. I'll see you tomorrow, unless you'd like me to stay."

"I'll just be resting, Ellen, but thanks again, for everything."

"Just let that busy mind of yours relax for a change."

"Okay," Rachel said, but glanced at the box next to her bed. "You know, having the records so close makes me almost feel that I can talk to the people in them."

"And why not? The ones we've loved are always close to us."

When Ellen remained by the bed, waiting, Rachel closed her eyes. She felt more tired than she'd realized, and the softness of the pillows and comforter was soothing. It would still be weeks before she fully regained her strength and stamina, and she must try to be patient. "A little rest will do me good."

Ellen lifted the afghan draped over the chest at the end of the bed, and gently covered Rachel, who murmured her thanks without lifting her eyelids. Ellen stood over her for another moment, and Rachel wondered if she was remembering the many hours she'd spent at her bedside in the hospital. Offering a fervent prayer of thanks for such a dear friend, she heard Ellen slowly move away.

Rachel heard footsteps reach the door, but not the turning of the knob. Opening her eyes, she saw Ellen standing there, her expression troubled. "Ellen?"

"Yes?"

Rachel propped herself up on her elbows. "Is something wrong?"

Ellen came back and sat on the edge of the bed. "I'm afraid there might be, if I don't deliver a message. Nathan asked me to tell you something, and it could be helpful. May I?"

"A message? All right. What did he say?"

"He said, exactly, 'Please tell Rachel that Rose and I send our love.'"

Rachel's lips soundlessly formed the word, "Rose." Nathan and Rose. She silently repeated the two names, and then again. Breathlessly, she asked, "Ellen, are there any photos in the box?"

"Yes, quite a few." Ellen searched briefly, drew out a small bundle of photos, and passed them to Rachel.

Hastily shuffling through each one, Rachel's whole body suddenly froze. Slowly, indistinctly, her memory began to weave itself around the image in her hands. He was wearing a cowboy hat and Levis, and standing at the base of rugged mountains with a small girl in his arms. It was Rose, and the man had Ethan's face, Ethan's body, and Ethan's smile. "*Nathan* and Rose. Ellen, Ellen, I remember them. Oh God, it's true. Nathan is Ethan." She clasped Ellen's fingers so hard that it drew a cry of surprise.

But Ellen was smiling as she said eagerly, "Dr. Castillo hoped that would be the case. He told me he wants to discuss this fully with you, and if you want to visit Nathan, he'd like you to take me along, just the first time."

"Dr. Castillo, he's been right about so many things." Still gazing with intensity at the photo, she said, "I remember meeting him, Nathan, on a ski trip with some friends. We spent as much time as we could together, for many months. I fell in love with him, deeply, but I was afraid of what I felt for him, for them both, afraid I couldn't give up what I had here, and couldn't be what they deserved."

"And now?"

She didn't answer right away. "I have to see them. I have to hold onto the hope that I haven't lost them after all."

"Good. I'm so glad you'll go."

Ellen gave the tickets back, but this time Rachel brought the envelope to her heart and pressed it close. After a moment she asked softly, "I'll call him, and if he's willing to see me, can you be ready in a few days?"

Smiling, Ellen said, "If Dr. Castillo gives you clearance, it won't take me long to pack."

Ellen hastened her steps to keep up with her friend as they walked along under the huge oak trees of Boise's Julia Davis Park. Rachel had been quiet most of the morning, but it was easy to sense her building excitement.

"I'm glad Nathan was agreeable about meeting us here rather than at the airport," said Ellen. "The garden must be just ahead. I can smell the roses."

"Yes, this is better. We've shared a hundred phone calls lately, but I'm so anxious to see him."

"Did you know he called me a few days ago to thank me for keeping him informed on how you've been feeling, and for coming here with you? It was very thoughtful."

Rachel suddenly pointed. "Oh, I see them, there, by the arbor!" Her strides quickened until she was almost trotting, and Nathan turned at the sound of footsteps. Searching his face, taking in his happiness, she came into his arms as naturally as breathing. Their embrace tightened, and lingered. At last she released her grasp, freeing every part of him but his hand, and crouched down to hug Rose.

The child squeezed her fiercely, and said, "I'm so glad you came back to us."

"Oh, Rose," Rachel said, "I had to come back." Her eyes lifted to Nathan, intense and promising. "I finally realized where my home is."

Author's Notes and Acknowledgement

Much time and care were devoted to the research that authenticates *The Far Reach of Yesterday*, research that ultimately led me on an extraordinary adventure that I could not have foreseen. After historical facts had been gathered, sorted, and analyzed, and the basic storyline molded, I had an even stronger desire to touch these yesterdays as personally as possible. I wanted to add vividness by binding myself intimately to my characters, to step back and become, if only for a short time, a pioneer myself. Then a unique opportunity arose that allowed me to cross the potentially deadly Snake River on horseback. I was given permission to join in a reenactment of the Oregon Trail's Three Island crossing. Having no horse of my own, I was loaned a steady mare that will forever deserve my gratitude.

An hour before we were to ford the river, I was told that the water was at its highest level in many years. Swept up in the event I'd anticipated with such eagerness, I discounted this warning and joined a small group of well-mounted Native Americans from the Shoshone and Paiute tribes. We entered the swift current and headed our horses toward the small islands near the far southern bank. Ten local riders followed close behind our group. The pull of the shallow water didn't prepare me for the force that hit us as my mount began to swim and I slid down her back, clinging to the saddle horn and holding the reins high. When several horses swimming just behind mine began to panic and flounder, their riders were forced to turn back toward the north shore. My little mare, owned by the family of the late Marv Wootan, the previous wagon master of the event, kept her nose up and her legs surging. A remarkable swimmer, she remained calm and capable all the way across, and then back again. We came out of the water safely, soaking wet and with hearts pumping. When the time came for the wagons to cross, only one made it over safely; the second was pulled downstream, a horse dragged under and a man injured, and the other wagons made the hard choice to turn back up the trail.

Being a part of this reenactment gave me an even greater respect for the Snake River and more vivid insight into how our forefathers might have felt as they encountered such challenges, and I hope Marv will look down from above and accept my thanks for allowing me to ride along.

Also instrumental in my being included in the Three Island crossing was Sherie Cooley, a generous, trusting woman who offered not only her help but her home, allowing me to stay with her during my visit to Glenns Ferry. Her kindness and company won't be forgotten.

Many people assisted me with their expertise while I searched for old books and records on the Boise Basin and the surrounding area. The staff members of the Idaho State Historical Library in Boise, Idaho were readily at hand as I tracked down the families of specific characters, explored time-appropriate maps, poured through old business directories, census and tax records, mining descriptions, newspapers, and biographical sketches. In Idaho City, the dedicated people who oversee the Boise Basin Library, especially Erin McCusker, then the director, and Duskie Swearingen, found records for me that I never supposed existed and that added greatly to the legitimacy and color of my story.

It was delightful as well as educational to meet individuals outside of the library network who have spent many years gathering historical documents of the 1800s, which they so kindly shared. Byron Johnson, the late retired Idaho Supreme Court Justice, a conscientious historian, a fine gentleman, and a man who happens to have been born exactly seventy-five years to the day after the first gold was discovered in the Boise Basin, made his vast knowledge and personal collection of treasured documents available to me. He was also gracious enough to read my manuscript and comment on its historical content.

Don and Pat Campbell, then owners of the Idaho City Hotel, which is still in operation today, shared information they'd found while conducting their own research. Prior curator of the Boise Basin Museum, Rhonda Mackin, was particularly helpful in providing biographical information on some of my historical characters.

Ever appreciative of my generous commentators and proofreaders, I acknowledge the efforts of my husband, Douglas Bender, my daughter, Anna Bender, my late mother, Phyllis Echeverria, my late father, Isaac Echeverria, and my sisters, Debra Geraghty and Teresa Townsend, my niece, Amanda Townsend, as well as my friends, Cheryl Gratton, Leslie Freeman, Kellie Gough, Vori Shewfelt, Rachel Nelson, and Alice Tracy.

A special word of gratitude must be offered to the late Lona Rash, an exceptional woman of great wit and even greater heart, for her help with this story. I will always remember our time spent over these pages in search of just the right words and discussing the personalities of the characters. I loved listening to the wonderful tales of her life, and the lives of her parents and grandparents who lived during the early days of Idaho.

To my dear children: Nicholas, Anna, Adam, and Gideon, I give my heartfelt thanks for their ever-supportive love and encouragement. And to Doug, my partner in life, I again offer my warmest gratitude for sharing me with the characters of my imagination that become such a part of our lives.

Historical Note

The background necessary for the creation of *The Far Reach of Yesterday* was gleaned from newspaper accounts, personal manuscripts, journals, census data, business records, anthropological studies, personal interviews, and much more. Historical characters such as the ex-gambler Sheriff Pinkham, the physicians Dr. Hogue and Dr. Willis, the musician John Kelly, the priest Father Mesplie, and the newspaper editors Thomas and Joseph Butler, actually walked the streets of long-ago Idaho City. Rachel Winston and her families, both in Chicago and in Idaho City, as well as Ethan and Rose Stonehill, Ellen Murphy, the police officers, the members of the Valenti family, and the medical team in Chicago, are characters of my heart and mind rather than reality.

For more books by Christine Bender:

CAXTON PRESS
312 Main Street
Caldwell, ID 83605-3299

Online Catalog at:
https://issuu.com/caxtonpress/docs/2025_caxton_press_publications_catalog

Or visit us at:

www.caxtonpress.com

Caxton Press is a division of The CAXTON PRINTERS, Ltd.